THE WEREWOLVES OF LONDON

'Humanity is in the thrall of fallen Angels . . . In *The Werewolves of London*, an epic of alternative history, black magic, and the warring factions of Heaven, Brian Stableford takes the cliche, breaks its neck, and re-animates it as his own . . . Truly magical.' FEAR

'Prolongued suspense . . .' LOCUS

'Fascinating . . . Searing . . . Impressive . . . Invigorating.' VECTOR

'Buy *The Werewolves of London*. Find how some things are thought . . . It is what Brian Stableford amounts to as a writer.' INTERZONE

'I wanted to ask the question that, if we take as a premise that there can be . . . enormously powerful beings, what sort of beings are they? What sort of universe do we have to have in order to accommodate entities like that? What are they actually attempting to do with *themselves*?' BRIAN STABLEFORD

ABOUT THE AUTHOR

Brian Stableford is one of Britain's strongest writers of imaginative fiction and non-fiction. His work includes the novels *The Walking Shadow* and *Journey to the Centre*, and the reference works *Future Man* and (with David Langford) *The Third Millennium: A History of the World 2000–3000 AD*.

Brian Stableford has degrees in Biology and Sociology and, until recently, lectured at Reading University. He is married and lives in Reading.

BRIAN STABLEFORD

THE WEREWOLVES OF LONDON

PAN BOOKS

LONDON, SYDNEY, AND AUCKLAND

First published 1990 Simon & Schuster Ltd
This edition first published 1992 by Pan Books Ltd
Cavaye Place, London SW10 9PG

1   3   5   7   9   8   6   4   2

© Brian Stableford 1990

ISBN 0 330 32267 2

Typeset by Hewer Text Composition Services, Edinburgh
Printed and bound in Great Britain by
Clays Ltd, St Ives plc

FOR MY DAUGHTER KATE,
in memory of the summer's day in 1984
when she shared with me the fascination and delight
which she had found in the legend of Perseus,
as displayed in *Clash of the Titans*.

CONTENTS

PART ONE

The Riddle of the Serpent and the Sphinx

They say that Sphynx was a monster of divers forms, as having the face and voice of a virgin, the wings of a bird, and the talons of a griffon . . . She kept also the highways, and used to lie in ambush for travellers, and so to surprise them; to whom, being in her power, she propounded certain dark and intricate riddles . . .

This fable contains in it no less wisdom than elegancy, and it seems to point at science . . . for science may not absurdly be termed a monster, as being by the ignorant and rude multitude always held in admiration.

It is divers in shape and figure by reason of the infinite variety of subjects wherein it is conversant. A maiden face and voice is attributed to it for its gracious countenance and volubility of tongue. Wings are added because sciences and their inventions do pass and fly from one another, as it were, in a moment, seeing that the communication of science is as the kindling of one light to another . . .

Of Sphynx her riddles there are generally two kinds: some concerning the nature of things, others touching the nature of man . . .

Francis Bacon, 'Sphynx, or Science'
in *The Wisdom of the Ancients*

1

*T*he surface of Hell is in perpetual turmoil; molten magma cools to form a jet-black crust, which is continually cracked by pressure from below, each fissure showing blinding white for an instant, then red for a while, before the emitted lava cools to become part of the crust.

Upon this surface a gargantuan Satan is stretched supinely, pinned by seven enormous nails which are driven through his ankles and knees, his navel, his left wrist, and his throat; only his right arm is free to reach up into the blazing sky, where clouds of incandescent gas are ripped and roiled by wayward tempests, and from which a rain of blood perpetually falls.

Satan's body is golden and lustrous, and quite without hair. His face, which is after all the face of an angel, would be very beautiful were it not for the rictus of suffering which distorts it. He is in pain – how could it be otherwise? – but it is no mere agony which torments him, for in eternity the ravages of mere physical pain soon fade. His anguish is the chagrin of loss and despair, of bitterness and remorse, of desolation and misery, which time can no more dull than it can heal.

Above his head, cocooned and haloed with a cool and comforting darkness which protects it from the fiery sky, hangs the earth. Despite that his outer eyes are closed against the rain of blood this world is clearly visible to his inner eye, whose sight is so sharp and so clear that not a single human sin is shielded from his knowledge. The legacy of the poison which he spilled in Eve's unwary ear has permeated every aspect of human life: every action and every thought; every dream and every desire. The world of men is saturated with a temptation against whose attraction the souls of men can build none but the feeblest of barriers.

Satan would repent, if he only could; he would redeem mankind

3

from the disease of damnation which spread from the seed of his envy, but it is not permitted. He could take back the venom which he carelessly spat into the world with but a single healing touch – which would upon the instant transform the world into an Eden once again – but every time he lifts his free right hand into the sky, intending to grip the earth, the planet is drawn away. It is always close at hand, yet always out of reach.

Satan has many names, and one of them is Tantalus – which recognizes that it was he and no other who stole the food and the wine of Heaven to give to mankind. Another of these names is Prometheus – which recognizes that it was he and no other who stole the fire of Heaven to give to mankind. Both these things he did in the hope of making amends for what he had done in Eden.

Sometimes, eagles come to rend his flesh and devour his beating heart, which grows to keep pace with their depredations. How many times the eagles have come and gone he cannot tell, but the number is greater than the number of atoms in the body of a man. Nor can he tell how many times he has reached up with his arm, desperate to touch the Earth, but the number is greater than the number of atoms in the Earth itself.

And yet, he has never capitulated, and never will, for the Earth will not always be what it is today, and when the day of its destined metamorphosis comes, he still has hope that he might be the author and the guide of its salvation.

For the love of God I am on fire, burning with poison! Cordelia! For mercy's sake, Cordelia! I am not dead, yet am in Hell . . . dear Jesus save me!

Pater noster qui es in caelis: Sanctificetur nomen tuum. . . .
I cannot pray . . . I cannot think . . . what is happening? Cordelia . . .

God cannot see His own face for there is no mirror which could reflect it, and yet He has an image of Himself. He does not walk in Heaven for there is no place where He might be – no pastures of Elysium or halls of glorious Valhalla – and yet there is a Heaven in his own substance, where the souls of men might be received.

The Riddle of the Serpent and the Sphinx

A man is confined by his body, and the universe contains him; he is tiny and the universe is infinite. God's true nature is conceivable by an imaginative inversion of this perspective; the universe is contained by Him and He is infinite, yet his macrocosmic form is an image which is human in its shape and in its character.

The universe is infinite from man's point of view; finite from God's. God is outside the universe, and yet is human in kind and feeling. The outer eyes of men, protected from the clarity of true sight, cannot perceive God; even the inner eye, which sometimes opens or is opened in defiance of the imminent pain which commands it to be closed, cannot see into His heart, for only His surface – his image – is apparent from the universe which He contains.

God can no more reach out to the world of men than a man can touch his heart with the insides of his fingers. He can no more save the Earth with a touch of his healing hand than Satan can, despite that He is omnipotent. Because of what He is, and what the universe is, God is always outside looking in, seeing everything and doing nothing. And yet, when the day of the Earth's metamorphosis comes, He will be the author and the guide of that transformation, for any change in the nature of the universe is, ipso facto, a change in the nature of God, its boundary.

This miraculous sight is so awful I wish that I might be blind!

Cordelia, I am naked and in pain, and seeing what I cannot ever contain! Cordelia!

Adveniat regnum tuum: Fiat voluntas tua, sicut in caelo et in terra. Panem nostrum quotidianum da nobis hodie: et dimitte nobis debita nostra, sicut et nos dimittimus debitoribus nostris. . . .

I think I am dying. O God, let me live!

Cordelia . . .

Wolves are running across a field of ice, beneath a sky of deepest black which is lit by countless stars. Some wolves are white, some are brown, some are silver-grey, and some are black. Their mournful howling echoes through eternity, for when they are not wolves they must wear the image of man, which is the image of God, and must

live with the awful burden of a will which is free (all save one, who
is forgiven freedom, guided by a will which is not his own). Where is
their prey and where is their home? What hope have they of deliverance
save for the metamorphosis of the world – and how might they seek and
strive to anchor the world, so that Satan's healing hand might touch
it at last?

The wolves are devouring the stars, Cordelia! Satan is reaching
his dark hand to claim me!

I am dying, I am dying.

*Et ne nos inducas in tentationem . . . Et ne nos inducas in
tentationem . . .*

Save me, Cordelia! I love . . . I love . . . please do not let
me . . .

*In an underground cave whose entrance reaches up towards the light,
men lie with their legs and necks in chains, unable to turn around.
A fire burns behind them, and between the men and the fire there is
a road, along which there marches a parade of creatures which have
the bodies of men and the heads of animals and birds.*

*The chained men are born and grow and die seeing nothing but
the shadows on the wall before them, thrown by the fire which burns
behind them. They see the shadows of those who move along the road,
and worship them as gods. They see Set headed as an enigmatic hog,
and Horus like a falcon, and Hathor like a cow, and Anubis like a
jackal, and Thoth like an ibis, and Sebek like a crocodile, and Bast like
a cat, and are made so afraid by these dark and awful shadows that
they pray for a redeemer, which they name Osiris. But no redeemer
can come, while they have not answered the riddle of the sphinx.*

*As they see only shadows, so they hear only echoes, and such is
the confusion of these echoes that they can hardly begin the work of
understanding.*

*But if one such man should contrive to break the chain set about
his neck, so that he might turn his head away from the wall to see
the road and the fire and the light beyond, what would he see and
how would he convince his companions that he had seen at all?*

That man would be dazzled and hurt by the true light, and confused

*by the voices which he heard instead of echoes, and yet he would know,
beyond any doubt, that what he saw was truer than what he had seen
before, and that his companions would be wrong to say that he must
be dreaming. And though he could not begin to guess what else he
might see, or whether he would be able to bear it, he would long to
cast aside his other chains, that he might cross the road and pass by
the fire, to come to the mouth of the cave and look out.*

*It would give him pain, but he could not be content until he had
done it . . . for until a man has seen the world, how can he hope to
change it?*

Cordelia, there is danger! One of those upon the road has
turned . . . it is the cat and she can see me! She can see that
I have turned to look at her, and she knows that I am free!

O God, protect me from my freedom! Put the chain about
my neck and let me see the shadows once again!

I cannot face the cat, which now has the head of a beast
and the body of a woman, now the face of a woman and the
body of a monstrous cat. She has talons to rend and eyes . . .
what eyes!

I cannot face her! Cordelia! *Cordelia!*

Sed libera nos a malo! Sed libera nos a malo! Sed libera . . .

2

David Lydyard had become so mad with delirium that
Tallentyre had begun to fear for the boy's life. The ceaseless
babble which spilled almost incomprehensibly from his lips
was such a strange disturbance of the young man's inner
being that Tallentyre was quite at a loss to understand it.
There was pain in it, but it seemed to be a pain more spiritual
than physical; and there was terror in it, but what inspired
that terror the watching man could by no means determine.

Two things Tallentyre recognized, however: the words of the Lord's Prayer, recited in Latin as it was in the Catholic Mass, and the oft-repeated name of Cordelia, his daughter.

The low-slung hammock rocked back and forth as its unlucky occupant writhed about, and Tallentyre wondered whether he should tie the boy down lest he hurt himself.

The snake which had bitten Lydyard had been very tiny, and the victim had been disinclined at the time to take his wound too seriously, recalling that he had been but recently stung by a far bigger reptile – a cobra – and had survived. But whatever venom the serpent had carried was obviously out of all proportion to its size, and Tallentyre regretted now that he had not taken more trouble to bleed the little wound.

Tallentyre felt himself to be partly responsible for the stricken man's predicament. It was he who had planned the tour of Egypt in the first place, and he who had impulsively agreed to the detour into the Eastern Desert when Father Mallorn had proposed it. If David's life were to be lost in this angry wilderness, it would be a loss whose penalty of guilt he would feel for ever, though no one else would blame him – not even Cordelia, who probably loved the boy as much as he loved her.

There was no one except Cordelia to whom Tallentyre would have to explain or justify himself, for David Lydyard had no family of his own. Tallentyre had taken David under his wing when his friend Philip Lydyard – David's father – had died suddenly six years before; he had seen the boy through school and university, and then had pressed him to come travelling, and see for himself the cradle of civilization. He had justified the trip – to his wife and daughter as well as to Lydyard – as a facet of the young man's education; but that had been in some measure a falsehood, and the boy's benefit no more than an excuse for his own self-indulgence. He felt now that he had deceived even himself, and that what he had sought in this tour was an opportunity to pretend to be young again, to travel without servants as a young man might, with vivid curiosity and reckless enthusiasm.

That project had failed; he felt older now than he had ever been – older, and more foolish. No doubt he would feel older still if the worst happened, and he was forced to tell his daughter how recklessly he had discharged his duty to her friend.

Why did I bring him here? Tallentyre asked of himself, bitter with helplessness. *Why did I listen to that foolish priest?*

The question was unfair. There were few, in truth, who could have resisted the seductive appeal of the scholarly Jesuit, given the circumstances in which he had made his offer.

Tallentyre and Lydyard had planned their tour in the modern fashion: a steamship had brought them from Italy to Alexandria, the railway had brought them to Cairo, another steamboat had conveyed them from Cairo to Aswan, and yet another from the first cataract to the second. To be sure, they had seen all that they had come to see: Giza and Sakkara, the pyramids and sphinx, Luxor and Thebes, the temples at Abu Simbel – but wherever they paused they had met more seasoned travellers, who had patronized them mercilessly by loudly singing the praises of the old ways of travel.

If one were to see the real Egypt, they had been told again and again, then one must travel by dahabeeyah and by camel, not by steamboat. The experience of visiting the pyramids and the temples had been quite ruined, they had been assured, by the institution of official guides and the hiring of carriages for the tour. The technology of the 1870s, the old hands declared, had become a barrier which prevented Europeans from establishing any true rapport with the ancient world, and modern commerce had helped to devalue antiquity itself by encouraging a huge trade in faked relics of the past.

Tallentyre had listened to all this, and had been convinced by such voices that his was a second-rate encounter with the mysteries of the past. Lydyard had listened too, and had been equally convinced – and so had William de Lancy, with whom they had fallen in and made common cause on the boat from Italy. When Father Francis Mallorn of the Society of Jesus had offered them the opportunity to visit a site which was remote and virtually untouched by tourism – to make them better acquainted, as he had put it, with 'the true history of the world' – all three of them had been excited by the notion. And all three had boldly brushed aside Mallorn's solemn warning that there were dangers in such an expedition from which the steamboat sightseers were entirely protected.

Now Lydyard was poisoned, and there was no help to be found within a hundred miles – and Tallentyre did not know what to do. All for the sight of a dozen rough-hewn tombs, which had been looted long ago of anything of value which they may have contained, and reduced by time to mere rubble.

Tallentyre wished, devoutly, that they had heeded the warning of Lydyard's first encounter with serpentkind, and had returned to England once the boy was recovered from *that* mishap.

Tallentyre's self-reproachful reverie was interrupted when the man who had brought them to this desolate and unfortunate place came into the tent. The yellow lantern-light shadowed the priest's dark eyes with apparent sobriety and Tallentyre noticed that his black hair had been subjected to the discipline of precise combing. Father Mallorn seemed, as he always did, orderly to the point of severity – but Tallentyre had ceased to think of that as a sign of sanity and common sense.

'Is there any improvement, Sir Edward?' asked Mallorn.

Tallentyre shook his head. 'If anything, he is worse. He is more than half asleep, though he is much disturbed.'

Mallorn seemed more intrigued than distressed by this intelligence. 'Can you make out what it is that he is saying?' he asked, moving past Tallentyre to take up a position close to the tossing head. He bent over, turning his ear to catch the faint but relentless stream of words which spilled from Lydyard's tremulous lips.

'I do not think that he has any dire secrets to reveal,' said Tallentyre, acidly. 'And have you not recently become his confessor, in any case?'

The priest, unperturbed, looked up at Tallentyre without ceasing to listen. 'There is a name,' he murmured. 'He calls to someone . . . *Cordelia*, he says – ah, but that is your daughter, is it not?' He sounded strangely disappointed.

'Perhaps he is reciting a passage from *King Lear*,' suggested the baronet, sarcastically.

The priest seemed, momentarily, to be considering the hypothesis, as though he were unable to recognize its irony. But then he shook his head, and said: 'But the poor boy is in mortal anguish! It is as though . . .'

'It is a nightmare,' said Tallentyre, roughly. 'Nothing more.'

The priest stood up straight again. 'Of course,' he said. 'What else?'

There was something about the way he said it which Tallentyre did not like. There was nothing in the words to which anyone could take exception, but there seemed to be a deceit in them, as though there was another possibility, and one which interested Mallorn acutely. And yet, the priest seemed ambivalent, as though torn between wanting to believe and fearing to believe. His dark eyes moved back and forth, as though a little of Lydyard's terror had infected him.

Superstition, thought Tallentyre.

To Sir Edward Tallentyre, superstition was the great enemy of modern man; a fecund mother of monstrous idols which must be cast down before the Age of Reason was secure. In general, he found traditionally religious men more tolerable than adherents of the fashionable cults who had become so numerous in London society of late, and while they had been on the steamboat cruising between the cataracts Mallorn had seemed sensible enough; but the journey into the desert had seemingly brought out the latent credulity in the man, and now it was as if he were ready to find ghosts lurking in every shadow.

'David is a young man,' said Tallentyre, austerely, 'and stronger than he seems. I do not think he will die. If he could only sleep, he might be well enough to travel tomorrow.'

'I would like to stay with him,' said the priest. 'I hear the

Lord's Prayer in his raving . . . he is crying out to Almighty God for succour, and I fear that he may need me.'

Tallentyre felt his mouth draw tight in response to the implications of that remark. He had been a Catholic once himself, and although he now reckoned himself an atheist he had no particular enmity for the rituals of the Church – but he did not want to be told that the delirious youth might prefer the company of a confessor to that of a friend, and he did not want to think that the need to which the priest referred might be the administration of Extreme Unction.

'I would rather you went to your own tent for now, Father,' said Tallentyre, drily. 'You may be sure that I will call you if any *need* should arise.'

Mallorn was clearly reluctant to do as he was asked, though the words had been framed as a virtual instruction. He opened his mouth to reply in one fashion, but changed his mind and took another tack. 'I beg you to reconsider, Sir Edward,' was all that he eventually said, and Tallentyre found himself suddenly curious to know what the man had first thought to say. Had he, perhaps, been about to claim some special knowledge regarding the boy's condition – and if so, what possible foundation could there be for such a claim?

'Why did you bring us here?' asked the baronet abruptly.

The dark man, clearly pleased that the request for his departure had been set aside, immediately looked Tallentyre full in the face, his eyes gleaming as they caught the lamplight. When he replied, his tone was level, but again the baronet was possessed by an uneasy feeling that there was some deceit in it.

'You know why, Sir Edward,' said the priest. 'I had heard rumours of the tombs here, and sought companions who would help me to investigate them. I did not mislead you at all; I did not promise you huge pyramids or carven sphinxes, but only shattered mastabas and rude rock-hewn burial-chambers, which is what we have found. I had thought you a true scholar, who would know the value of what we have seen. These are pre-dynastic relics, older than the great pyramid itself.

If Lepsius is correct in his interpretation of the chronology of the kings, the artefacts in this valley were made four thousand years before the birth of Christ. I do not think that we will find gold or pretty ornaments here, but these are among the oldest works of the human hand in all the known world. That is why I wanted to come here, and why I asked you to come with me.'

There is more, thought Tallentyre. *If this is true, it is far from being the whole of the truth.* But he was an Englishman, with the training of a gentleman, and Mallorn's apparent allegiance was to the same class. It was impossible for the baronet to suggest openly that the priest was a liar.

'You knew that the guides we hired would not come to this place,' he said instead. 'You knew that they would be afraid, did you not?'

Father Mallorn shrugged his shoulders. 'I know the superstitions of the heathen,' he said. 'Those we hired as guides were simple men, who preferred the tracks which were familiar to them. This place may have had a bad reputation once, but if so, that reputation was earned in distant antiquity.'

'It is difficult to believe such things,' said Tallentyre, sceptically. 'Oral tradition does not preserve reputations over centuries, no matter what the lore of legend and romance has to say about curses handed down from generation to generation. If the guides were afraid, I can only suppose that they were made afraid by something which has happened within living memory.' He paused then, and saw the other man's stare shift briefly towards Lydyard, whose voice had become a little louder. Mallorn was still listening as best he could to the babbling of the sick man, and Tallentyre was moved to say: 'And you are afraid yourself, are you not? There is something in the boy's sickness which disturbs you – something which finds a reflection in your own anxieties. Will you not tell me what it is?'

Mallorn met Tallentyre's stare again, and did not seem to be very upset by what the baronet had said to him, but with what effort his composure was maintained it was difficult to tell.

'I am a little anxious, Sir Edward,' he admitted. 'I did not know what we would find here. I only knew that certain others had been here, and would not have come had they not expected to find something of great interest to them. Like me, they have an interest in the true history of the world. It is true that I did not care to come here alone, and sought the companionship of others in whose company I could feel safer. I wish you had succeeded in persuading your guides to stay with us, and I am very sorry that the boy was unfortunate enough to be bitten by a snake, but I am not to blame for either of these things. It is possible that a greater danger stalks these tombs, but I honestly cannot say what form that danger may take, and a man like you would surely laugh at such anxieties.'

Superstition, thought Tallentyre, again. *But now he reproaches me for my lack of it. He fears ghosts and curses, but he will not say so, and he uses my unbelief as an excuse.*

The priest's manner annoyed Tallentyre, who did not like teasing hints about mysteriously unspecified dangers any better than he liked the stubborn insistence that there were more things in heaven and earth than were dreamt of in his materialistic philosophy – but the baronet could see clearly enough that whatever secrets Mallorn was guarding were not easily to be seduced from him. In any case, it was the plight of his friend which was of primary importance, and any reckoning with the priest had better be postponed.

'I am sorry,' said Tallentyre. 'David's injury has disturbed me, and I suppose that I am over-anxious to find someone who will share the blame with me. Go now – I will call you, if any need arises, but I hope with all my heart that it will not.'

Mallorn still seemed inclined to stay, and Tallentyre was sure that he was anxious to find a way to extend the conversation. In the end, the priest said: 'I read your article, in which you said that you would not care to live in such a world as mine, disturbed by miracles and inexplicable by reason. There is something I have always wanted to say to you about it.'

Tallentyre issued no invitation, answering with an adamantine stare. Nevertheless, the Jesuit went on. 'Suppose by way of hypothesis,' he said, quietly, 'that the world is what I imagine it to be, and not what you imagine it to be . . . accepting all your judgements of what that would imply. Suppose that Acts of Creation are possible, and that the world thus stands, as you allege, in danger of such interruption that it might at any moment acquire the substance and logic of a dream. What then, Sir Edward?'

It was an invitation to a long debate – an argumentative gambit, offering a rhetorical sacrifice by way of temptation. Tallentyre would not be drawn. 'If the world were truly like that,' he said, flatly, 'still we would have to live in it, and understand it as best we could. But I will not debate philosophy while my friend is in pain, and I would prefer it if you left us now.'

Mallorn nodded his head, politely accepting defeat, and retired.

Lydyard had fallen momentarily silent, and had ceased to turn in his delirium, but he was still sweating heavily. Tallentyre put a water-flask to the boy's lips, and induced him to drink.

For a second or two it seemed that the liquid might soothe him, but then his lips began to move again, and his head began to thrash from side to side.

On a sudden impulse, the baronet bent closer, as Mallorn had, and tried as hard as he could to make sense of the stream of sound. He caught a few coherent words – something about a road and a cat . . . then something about a chain about a neck, and shadows. Then, quite clearly: *I cannot face her!* Then again, Cordelia's name, and more Latin – the final words of the Lord's Prayer, which meant, *deliver us from evil*.

There were more sounds after that, but Tallentyre could not even be sure that they were meant to be words. Nor did the words which he *had* heard make any kind of sense: because there seemed to be no intelligible connection between their present situation and a cat with a chain about its neck. Perhaps, he thought, the notions were simply bubbling up at random, their sequence a mere accident.

And yet, the boy called out again and again the name Cordelia, as though imploring her to summon him back by magical means to wintry England, away from this land of tombs and snakes and fiery desert demons.

The flap of the tent was pulled back again. This time it was their other travelling companion, William de Lancy, who came in.

De Lancy was only three or four years older than David Lydyard, but was much more the man of the world. Tallentyre knew his family very slightly, and felt that he understood far better what manner of man de Lancy was than what motivated the mysterious Jesuit.

'The horses are alarmed,' said the newcomer, uneasily. 'I wish I had a nose like theirs, that I could judge what taint there is in the air.' As he spoke, he touched his fingers to the holster at his belt, where he wore a pistol.

Tallentyre's own guns were sporting pieces, precious enough to be kept near to hand, and the baronet's gaze went reflexively to the place beneath his own bunk where they were lodged.

'Perhaps some predator is near by,' said Tallentyre. 'I doubt that there are lions in these hills, but there may be wild dogs.'

'Perhaps,' said de Lancy, unenthusiastically. 'I looked up once and fancied that I saw some manlike creature silhouetted against the stars, which crouched down as soon as I looked more carefully. But this is the red land – inhospitable to all save the bedouin. I had far rather it might be wild animals, but do you not feel it yourself, man? *Something* is here, and I cannot any longer blame those faint-hearted ruffians who left us to our own devices.'

More superstition, thought Tallentyre, tiredly. De Lancy was a level-headed sort, and well educated, but when it came to fashionable occultism he belonged to the no-smoke-without-fire school which refused to deny the possibility of miracles, and he had an exaggerated respect for the sort of queer tale which men retired from India and the further regions of the East were inclined to tell during slow evenings at the club.

Tallentyre shook his head in schoolmasterly fashion. 'We have become over-civilized, de Lancy, and are too sensitive when we are away from the haunts of men. The remoteness of the region brings back to us those unformed and unspecified anxieties which we should have put away when we left the nursery. Poor David's plight has made us all uneasy, reminding us that even little snakes and scorpions can bring us to dire distress, if not to death. If there is something hidden by the darkness which threatens the horses, it can only be an animal – or Arab brigands.'

De Lancy came closer to Lydyard, and bent down as Mallorn and Tallentyre had each bent down, trying in his turn to make sense of the words which tumbled in quiet confusion from the young man's lips.

What is happening here, thought Tallentyre, *to draw us all to wonder whether there might be some strange enlightenment to be found in the wild murmurings of a man in pain?*

Unlike Mallorn, though, de Lancy quickly straightened up again, having failed to hear anything of significance, and being too discreet to call attention to the frequent mention of a maiden's name.

'I never saw a man like that before,' said de Lancy, grimly. 'And I do not know what kind of snake it was which bit him, though I thought I knew the vipers and their kin well enough. It was certainly no Cleopatra's asp.'

'I killed it,' Tallentyre told him. 'I have it in a jar, and will take it home to show the wise men of Oxford. Perhaps it is new, and they will name it after David, to give him something for his trouble.'

'Perhaps,' said de Lancy – but he seemed incapable of levity, and Tallentyre saw that the other man's anxiety had not been lessened at all by their exchange of reassurances. Whatever had disturbed the horses had disturbed de Lancy too, though he clearly did not know precisely how or why.

'I have lost my appetite for exploration,' said Tallentyre, wearily. 'I think the Jesuit would have us spend the morrow digging out debris and fixing ropes, so that one or other of us might descend into the cleared pit of one of the mastabas in order to see what might be left in the chambers down below, but we have not the power to move a sarcophagus even if we should be lucky enough to find one, and I mistrust this business of scrabbling in the dust for scarabs and amulets the like of which one can buy in every bazaar in the land. Whatever the tomb-robbers of dynastic times have left behind has certainly been recovered by other antiquaries, for there is abundant evidence of clearing and digging which has gone on within the last few decades. If David is well enough to travel, we must turn back.'

De Lancy smiled weakly. 'We have been a little silly, Sir Edward,' he said.

'Perhaps,' agreed Tallentyre. 'We have allowed the romance of Egyptology to infect us like a mild disease, eager to believe that we might be led by a curious priest to trawl new wonders from the sand. We know better than that really.' But then he hesitated, and when he spoke again, the tone of his voice had changed. 'And yet . . .' he said, 'the priest expected to find something here. I wish I knew what it is.'

'Have you asked him?' asked de Lancy.

'He says that he does not know.'

'Do you believe him?'

Tallentyre shrugged his shoulders. 'He swears that he has been honest with us, and when he says it he has a certain air of conviction. He is, after all, a man of the cloth.'

'He is afraid of something,' said de Lancy, quietly. 'And so am I. God help me, Sir Edward, so am I.' His hand was once again upon the flap of his holster.

'David is frightened too,' said the baronet, pensively. 'Even in the madness of his torment, he is afraid. And for all my fierce determination to resist superstition and see the world as it really is, I cannot help but feel that there is some kind test in this for my belief and my resolve.'

The two men looked at one another, each one wanting to laugh and put fear behind him, but neither quite able to do it. The only sounds which disturbed the silence of the night were the distant whinnying of the horses and the nearby voice of Lydyard's nightmare, which spoke of a cat and Cordelia, of shadows and the fear of God – and which might or might not hold some tenuous thread of mindfulness and meaning.

3

It was nearly midnight, but de Lancy was still sitting under the stars, beside the ashes of the fire which they had lit in order to make coffee. It had been a poor blaze, for there was not a stick of firewood to be found in the valley, and the meagre ration which they had brought with them was nearly exhausted.

De Lancy was finishing his last pipe of the day, in a carefully leisurely fashion. He did not think of himself as being on sentry duty, because no formal decision had been taken to post a watchman, but he could not put away the sense of threat which possessed him. He knew that Tallentyre would undoubtedly have called his fears superstitious – he had spent enough lazy evenings drinking and talking with the man to be certain of his views – but he believed in an instinct of unease whose warnings one ignored at one's peril.

Although he had never seen a ghost, he had the word of men he trusted that ghosts existed, and had the power to hurt men. In that special silence and darkness which was the dress of tombs, ghosts could walk if they would; he was sure of it.

He felt closer to the supernatural world in Egypt than in any other place he had been. In these desert sands the ancients had laid down their dead, clad in bandages and bitumen not to rest but to begin a greater journey than life itself – a journey into eternity. De Lancy believed that death *must* be the prelude to such a journey, rather than the final and bitter end which men like Sir Edward believed it to be. In his eyes, man was too fine a thing to be wasted in decay and putrefaction, deserving instead a better and more fitting destiny somewhere beyond the bounds of time and space. And yet, despite this conviction, he found it very difficult to believe in a paternal God and a redeemer. Though he could not begin to understand why, and would never have confessed the fact to a living soul, he found it easier to believe in the power of enigmatic pagan gods than in the efficacy of Christian prayer.

There was, de Lancy thought, a definite tragedy in the way that these tombs had been callously violated, and violated again, first by thieves who came to steal the possessions of the dead for their own enrichment, and then by others who came to steal the dead themselves. He made little distinction between those who had pandered to the whims of would-be magicians in bottling mummy for apothecaries to sell and those good Christian men who now pandered to the fetish of learning by carrying off the dead in their sarcophagi, to be exhibited in the museums of the world. They were all thieves . . . all careless of the rights and real interests of the journeying dead.

De Lancy did not begrudge the dead their spectral returns, and wished they might do better in teaching the living what unwisdom it was to disturb the dust of those who had gone before.

Ghosts have the right of it, he thought, as though by thinking it so distinctly he might banish the unease which teased him. *And those who will not believe in them deserve the terror of their revelations.*

None of his companions was yet asleep. Both of the tents were illuminated from within and de Lancy could see shadows moving within them both. Tallentyre clearly intended to watch over Lydyard all night if it should prove necessary. Meanwhile, Father Mallorn was keeping a vigil of his own, maintained in his alertness by the discipline of prayer.

For de Lancy, prayer had always been an imposition, against which he had secretly rebelled even as a child. His prayers had always been a pretence, though he had always assumed that the prayers of others were not merely honest, but reasoned and productive. In a way, he envied Mallorn his unbreakable faith in the God of the scriptures, and envied Sir Edward his equally unbreakable faith in the non-existence of that God. Either extreme of faith, he felt, must be more secure than an uncomfortable absence – an unfortunate void where God the Father ought to be – in harness with an instinct of unease.

He felt his hand straying towards his holster yet again, as though impelled by some will of its own. He had snatched it back more than once, but now his frame of mind urged him to take a different course. He took the gun out, and began to play with it, passing it from hand to hand. It was fully loaded, but the safety-catch was set.

He kept the pistol in his hand while he tapped out his pipe against a nearby rock. In the darkness he could not see the ashy stain which it left. He slipped the pipe into his pocket and stood up.

The ritual complete, there was no obvious reason now to keep him outside, unless he cared to invent the possibility that bedouin bandits might come upon the party under cover of night, intending to steal everything which they owned. But Egypt was not such a land of thieves as he had once suspected; his real fear was that the bedouin were no less inclined to shun this place than the hired men who had refused their wage rather than proceed into these hills, and that there was some horrid reason for that reluctance.

The combined light of the moon and stars was bright enough to cast shadows, and the yellow radiance which spilled from the two tents added to it. He could see the cleared mouths of two of the mastabas whose ruins were clustered in the hollows, and the shadows of natural slits and fissures which might have offered tombs to the remotest ancestors of the Egyptians of today.

On the previous day all four of them had been eager to look inside those few of the ancient edifices which had not entirely collapsed or filled with sand. Even here, amid the jagged rocks far above the flood-plain, time had all but obliterated the tombs, and the fact that there was anything at all to be seen was obviously due to work carried out by recent explorers. Such spaces as had been excavated were conspicuously bare; the newcomers had found no trace of any statuary, and the pits which led down to the deeper chambers where sarcophagi had once rested had mostly been refilled with debris.

As he looked around him, though, he could not help but feel that there was something in the glamour of the starlight which whispered of secrets still buried here. The ancient people who had brought their dead to this place had used the cracks and crannies of the rocks even before they had begun to build their first primitive tombs of brick and stonework, and some of their work might still be untouched, even after thousands of years. Although the antiquaries who had preceded them had gone after a brief investigation, that might have been because there was infinitely less glory and romance in the excavation of pre-dynastic relics than in exploration of the Valley of the Kings. It did not prove that there was nothing here to be discovered.

Perhaps, thought de Lancy, one or two of these cruder tombs still sheltered the relics of a past more remote than that recorded in the kinglists. It was not so difficult to believe it on a night such as this, when the valley was so elaborately dressed in moon-shadows.

He was abruptly seized by a tremor of unease. *Those shadows were moving*.

For a brief moment, de Lancy could not quite grasp the significance of it. But then he remembered, with the absurd startlement of one recalling the obvious, that the movement of the moon and the stars was imperceptible, and that the rocks were immovable – how then could the shadows in the mouths of the tombs be moving?

The thought burst upon his consciousness with a dreadful giddiness, and he took no comfort at all from the fact that his gun was in his hand – for what use could bullets be against a host of shadows?

He told himself quickly that he could not be seeing it, that the shadows could not move, and that he must be deluded – but it was not true, and he could not convince himself of it. The shadows *were* moving, and he was not mad, but only terrified.

He wanted to call upon God for succour and protection, but he knew that a false prayer could not serve him now. Nor could he cry out for help to Sir Edward or the priest, for there was nothing before him but a legion of shadows, and he was not a coward. He had been brave enough to confess his fear to the baronet when the conversation permitted it, but he was not brave enough now to let Sir Edward Tallentyre see his naked terror in the face of creeping shapes of darkness.

But the shadows *were* moving, and though they moved in their own space, at their own pace, he knew that his presence was not irrelevant to their movement. He was in danger.

He stumbled towards the tent which he shared with the priest. He knew even as he moved that he would not reach it. The air around him seemed somehow tangible, as though it were taking on substance and rigidity to confine and oppose his movement. He assured himself that it must be delusion, and yet he felt the resistance as he tried to walk . . . tried to run . . .

He was held back, and diverted from his course. He was shoved sideways in an unexpectedly brutal and awkward fashion, and he was taken by an ungainly stumble towards the hillside where the mouths of the tombs were waiting – where the swarming shadows crowded together like great black beetles, as if they were kin to the scarabs which thrived on excrement and rottenness.

I will not go living into the tomb! he cried in silence. *I will not be divided into my several souls, to face the hazards of death's journey before my time! I am no slave of conqueror kings, for I belong to a conqueror race, and you shall not have me!* But he was deeply fearful that in the empire of these dark uncanny forms, Victoria's realm was a thing of shabby substance whose power none need fear and to which no shadow-thing need owe the least obeisance.

He tried to run, but felt himself turned away from the direction of the tents. He lifted his feet from the ground as if to deny the vile air the means to impel him, but it was as if he were lost in a dream in which he could float; he was dragged over the sand-strewn rock, borne against his will towards one of the mastabas, whose mouth was a jagged slit where long-dead robbers had hewn an entrance in the brickwork.

Confronted by this apparent destination, he knew which direction he must take if he were to resist the pull of the shadows; that knowledge gave him, belatedly, some power to resist what was being done to him. He felt his boots in contact with the solid rock again, felt that he was standing up – and standing *still*, no longer helpless.

The movement of the shadows seemed more frenzied now and less coherent, as though they were dancing madly, like the helpless images whirled about by a guttering candle-flame. Were they nothing, after all, but slaves of some turbulent energy, their apparent identity and hostility mere momentary illusions?

As he stood rigidly, trying to become immovable in the face of whatever force had tried to drag him into the tomb, de Lancy felt the air exploring him, testing with its substance the contours of his face, the manner of his dress. He tried not to breathe, lest he take that prying substance into his inner being, where it might clutch his heart and rejoice in the rhythm of the blood which flowed in his veins.

Is this the seat of judgement? he wondered. *Am I arraigned before the throne of God, while the scroll of my soul must be unwound to show the record of my sins?*

There was a sound in the air: a self-satisfied purring sound, such as might be made by a pampered pet luxuriating in a calm caress.

If I can only contrive to discharge the gun, he thought, *might all these phantoms vanish in a trice, dispatched to their deserved oblivion by the power of man-made fire?*

It seemed a sane and reasoned thought, and he could not believe it; but reason had not entirely deserted him, for there was a certain curiosity mingled with his fear. Where was the face of this catlike presence in the air? Where were its claws? What greater substance might it yet attain? The sound of its purring was somehow loving as well as dangerous, and he felt strangely lost in a nest of paradoxes.

Where were the shadows now? He had been unsighted for a moment, but he did not know how. The light of the moon and stars was somehow gone, and he had no sense of being near to the tents or the horses. Had he been plucked clean out of time and brought into a dreamworld?

He knew, abruptly, that he had breathed in, without quite meaning to, and that whatever held him was now within him as well as without. He was losing touch not merely with the physical world which had contained him, but with his own fear . . . perhaps with his own soul.

He felt catlike himself, able to glide like a shadow, free from the burden of thought and word, inwardly calm and possessed by mystery.

Within his body there should have been a kind of warmth, produced by the fervent fire of life itself, but there was nothing: an absence, a void, a hurtful non-existence.

He felt himself walking . . . gliding . . . moving like a shadow among shadows, a creature of pure will . . . animal. . . .

Then he fell, and the sensation of falling awakened in him some primordial fear which was so close to the very essence of his being as to be undeniable by whatever soothing presence had caught and held him. That fear burst from him in a great and terrible scream, which expanded to fill all of time.

His finger closed reflexively upon the trigger of his revolver, but the shot was as futile as he had feared, and its sound was lost in that awful scream which, when it had lasted until the edge of forever, ended in an interminable silence.

This, he said to himself, well enough aware of the paradox of his being able to say it, *can only be the silence of death*.

4

When he heard the scream and the shot Tallentyre was quick to snatch up one of his shot-guns. He paused to break and load the double-barrelled weapon before hurrying from the tent.

The night was bright enough, but his eyes were accustomed to the lamplight of the tent, and he was momentarily struck by an impression of overwhelming darkness. Though he knew approximately from which direction the scream had come he could find no immediate target for his gun nor any sign of de Lancy.

As he struggled to see through the curtain of the dark he caught a glimpse of a shadow hurrying away from him up the hill, and had brought his weapon up to take aim before he realized that it was Father Mallorn. The dark head became suddenly paler as the priest turned round to look at him.

'Quickly, man!' cried Mallorn. 'He has gone into the tomb!'

The baronet ran forward. The priest waited until he had drawn abreast. No other sound had followed the cry of anguish, and all was now as still and quiet as the grave. As Tallentyre came to stand beside the other man he could hear nothing but the ragged panting of his own anxious breath.

Tallentyre scanned the hillside, which was hummocked with boulders and broken mastabas, pock-marked with crevices and deep shadows. He did not know where to go.

'Which one?' he demanded of the priest, but Mallorn was uncertain.

'I saw him walk into a fissure,' said the Jesuit. 'I took it for an entrance cut into one of the mastabas, but I am no longer sure which one it was. He must have fallen into one of the empty pits!'

Such an accident did not seem probable to Tallentyre; nor could he imagine that it would warrant such a horror-stricken scream. Although they had not taken the trouble to determine the depths of the few pits which previous explorers had excavated for them, Tallentyre knew that they ought not to be very deep – thirty or forty feet at the most. Such a fall might possibly kill a man, but it was not altogether likely. He could not believe that de Lancy, even if he had stumbled, would not have been able to catch the rim of the pit or slow his fall by grappling with the walls. And why should he have fired his pistol?

'Think, man!' said Tallentyre, impatiently. 'If you saw him, you must have seen where he went!' But he knew as he said it that it was not as simple as that. The whole ragged hillside was a confusion of shadows which shifted awkwardly as a man moved. It had been all too easy for the agitated priest, running up the hill, to lose sight of the place he had aimed for.

Behind them, the horses had begun again to move restlessly about, their hooves striking the rocks with small clicking sounds. Tallentyre did not bother to look back at them; he moved forward instead, trying to see where a walking man might have gone, and wondering why de Lancy had walked up here at all.

'Look out!' cried the priest – but Tallentyre had no chance to react to the warning.

Something huge and massive launched itself from the shadows, cannoning into him and bowling him over. The shot-gun went off, discharging harmlessly into the air, but the baronet kept his hold on it in spite of the impact of his fall, which jarred him terribly. A ridge of rock struck his shoulder and his hip, tipping him over on to his back.

The thing moved lithely over him. It was darkly coloured, and he could not judge what shape it had at all. He felt the slightest wind of warm breath upon his face, and then a musty animal odour which he could not identify.

Mallorn gasped, as though strangling a scream.

Tallentyre raised his head, but could not rise to his feet. The creature had seized the priest, and its weight was forcing him down the slope again, its forepaws grappling at his shoulders.

Father Mallorn was not an old man – he was younger by five years than the baronet – but he had not the strength to withstand such an attack as this, for the furious creature was far larger than he. He had no weapon, nor even a crucifix to ward off the dark enemy while he called to the Lord for aid, and though he was trying to say something the only sounds which he could contrive to utter were neither English nor Latin, but the empty syllables of panic.

Tallentyre heard the priest fall, as he himself had fallen seconds before, knocked down by the black beast which had hurled itself upon them from the bowels of the mountain.

The baronet scrambled up into a sitting position, and tried to bring his gun to bear. He had one shot remaining, and was sure that it would be enough if only the beast would stand clear of its victim and give him a sight of its eyes. But the beast would *not* stand clear, and seemed instead to be locked into a wrestling-match with the hapless priest.

He still could not make out what kind of animal it was. It had the bulk of a horse but not the shape; its head and feet were extraordinary in their largeness, and there was something upon its back which was certainly no camel's hump, but rather resembled a pair of vestigial wings.

Tallentyre struggled to his feet, ignoring the dull pain which flooded his right arm and the lower part of his back. He knew that no bones were broken, and that he was capable of firing with a steady hand if he dared to do it.

Without hesitation he moved towards the place where Mallorn had been brought down, intending to use the gun as a prod to separate friend from enemy, but as he came close the beast reared up above its fallen prey, turning to face him as no four-legged beast should have been able to turn. The wing-like appendages beat the air as though they were wings in truth, though they could never have lifted such a massive beast into flight.

It rose upon its legs almost as a man might rise, to stand massively two-footed, fully ten feet tall. The moon was behind the baronet's shoulder now, and its pale light shone directly into the creature's face, illuminating also the tawnier fur of its abdomen and the great clawed paws held wide in preparation for a strike.

Tallentyre could not believe his eyes, which beheld a thing more astonishing than he had ever seen before. Its fur was sleek instead of shaggy, far more cat-like than bear-like. There was no doubt that it was furred from neck to tail – and a tail it most certainly had, long and thrashing. And yet, the face which looked down on him from its terrifying height was hardly cat-like at all, but was instead a nearly *human* face: wrathful, snarling, demonic, but contoured like the face of a handsome woman.

Despite the face's human configuration, Tallentyre could not bring himself to believe that there was intelligence in the baleful glare, or in the horrid grimace of the bared white teeth. It was the head, and not the body, which seemed to him to be out of place in the creature's chimerical form – and the monster seemed not to know what kind of head and jaws it had, for it opened its mouth with a foolish arrogance which suggested that it hoped to take *his* whole head into its gape and bite it off entire.

There was perhaps a second when he might have fired again, but he was holding the gun quite wrongly, and could only thrust as he had planned to do. The jab, inevitably, was more provocation than opposition, stabbing at the creature's belly without any real chance of doing harm. The gesture seemed direly feeble as the yellow eyes flared – but it seemed strangely to the baronet as though that flaring was no mere animal rage, but had in it something of puzzlement and confusion.

For a second or two, he wondered if it really meant to hurt him, but he knew that he did not have time to wonder or to gamble. He struck out again as boldly as he could, and when the cuff of a great clawed hand struck him sideways he was not unready, and rolled with the blow. Alas for his readiness, the power of the thrust was altogether greater than he could cope with, and he was sent sprawling instead of rolling, his poor hip finding sharp rock yet again, as though determined to be stubborn in its awkwardness.

Again, though, Tallentyre retained his grip on the gun. He clung to it for dear life, fearing that if he let it go he would surely die, for he could not think that the monster would show him mercy now that he had moved it to irritation. He tried to scramble further away, to gain time enough to take aim, but found it strangely difficult to move, as though the shadow into which he had fallen had taken on a life of its own and was holding him back, clinging to him like some magical cloak of darkness.

His head struck stone, and the blow made him dizzy. The moon, which had been clear in his sight like a great silver shilling, was abruptly eclipsed, and the animal odour which had afflicted him before was now so strong as to be sickening.

A great weight pressed upon him, but he could not feel the claws or the silly human teeth, and he was greatly surprised that he could not judge which part of the beast it was that was smothering him, or what would happen next. Death, it seemed, would not specify the manner in which it had come to him; there was only darkness, and helplessness.

Then the weight was gone again, as if for a second time the beast had passed right over his fallen body – and *still* he held hard to the stock of his gun.

He could hear Father Mallorn's voice, which was once again able to form true words, and he heard the name *Satanas* called – which implied that the priest thought their enemy a demon indeed. But there was no time for any elaborate exorcism, whether or not it could possibly prove efficacious, for the words had drawn the monster's attention back to the other man.

As the beast moved away from him again Tallentyre managed to bring the shot-gun to his shoulder, ready to fire. When he came to a kneeling position he saw the creature crouching like a cat, no more than five feet away. It seemed somehow to have lost substance, and now appeared to be no greater in size than himself, though he could not understand how that might be. Its face was turned towards the Jesuit, its eyes all agleam with the moonlight. They had the shape of human eyes, though he had never seen that yellow colour in a human eye. Tallentyre could not read the expression in the eyes, but he could only assume that the creature was tensing its body before pouncing on its victim.

He fired, gasping as the pain of the recoil ran along his arm.

The monster leapt sideways – or perhaps was hurled aside, as indeed it should have been by such a charge. Tallentyre was certain that the shot had gone home, and sure that by any normal reckoning such a shot should have killed the beast, but he knew immediately that the writhing of the paradoxical thing was no mere posthumous reflex.

Hurt it was, but dead it was not, and as it gathered itself before coming to its feet again it seemed to be knitting its own substance from the shadows, growing again to its former hugeness.

Tallentyre could not see the priest, who had fallen to the ground again. He broke the gun, desperate to reload it, but he knew that the gesture was futile, for the creature was already looming over him again, and only needed to reach out with one of its clawed feet – which seemed, now that he had seen them raised aloft, more like talons than paws – to snatch the weapon from him.

His eyes, accustomed now to the gentle light of the moonlit

night, showed him that strange and awesome face in remark-able detail. It was dark, but in no way negroid; the golden eyes and fine-lined lips made it too exotic to be identified with any racial type which he knew.

It is the sphinx! he thought, knowing how absurd it was that he of all people should think it. *It is the face of the sphinx!*

It opened its mouth again – and this time, he half-expected to hear words spill out, intoning some legendary riddle for him to solve; but all that emerged was a thin keening sound. It was, he knew, a cry of pain . . . and yet there was more in it than pain, for it sounded curiously plaintive. Meanwhile, that great clawed *hand* was raised above him, as though to strike down at him and tear him apart.

Tallentyre froze, waiting for the blow to fall.

Then something pale caught Tallentyre's eye as it hurtled down from above, coming as fortunately and as precipitately as if the priest had indeed contrived to summon miraculous lightning from Heaven for the destruction of their foe.

As the sphinx prepared to spring it was caught by something smaller, yet fiercer, which leapt at its head as a white polecat might leap at a startled dog. But this attacker was itself a dog of sorts, and when Tallentyre saw that, he realized also that its smallness was only an illusion caused by the greatness of its adversary, for it was in fact a big creature by the standards of the canine kind, larger by a handsome measure than any hound or shepherd dog he had ever seen. In its fierceness – its deadly fearless anger, its urgent purpose – it was in his eyes a creature no less strange and paradoxical than the object of its attack.

It was a wolf, but some kind of phantom wolf, which had no right to actual existence in the world of his belief.

Tallentyre felt that an awesome battle was about to be joined, but he could not believe that the grey wolf could defeat the chimerical monster. He tried to stand up, but found his senses reeling.

The blow which the sphinx had aimed at him – if it had, after all, been a blow – was altered into a sideways swipe at the leaping wolf. The sharp claws did not strike the animal with any real force, but they ripped bloody furrows along its side, and the blood showed darkly against the unusually pale fur.

The wolf was hurled aside, but when it landed it scrambled quickly around, intent on returning immediately to the fray. Tallentyre felt an absurd desire to cry out, to instruct it to run and save itself. The sphinx retreated half a step, and the expression on its face was now unmistakably one of puzzlement and uncertainty – but then its little wings began to beat again, and it rose up on to its hind legs, splaying its wicked claws ready for use.

Tallentyre tried once again to reach into his pocket for spare cartridges, but something prevented him. It was as though the shadows all about him were in league with the sphinx, intent on raking him with talons of darkness which did not need to tear his flesh because they could reach into his very soul.

He dropped his empty gun. He could feel a dreadful roaring in his head, as though the darkness all around was not only pressing in upon him but was howling at him in anger and in glee. He felt that he could not draw breath at all, that there was no air for his gasping lungs. There was a pain in his chest, as though an iron band were being tightened about him, and what he was trying so hard to see – the impending fight between the little grey beast and the vast black monster – became, all of a sudden, no more than a crazy pattern of black and white, swirling and shifting, devoid of any sensible meaning.

Why, he thought, with a thrill of relief which was almost exultant, *this is not real! I have been poisoned, and these are the phantoms of my delirium! It was I, and not David, who was bitten by the snake! It is I, and not he, who lies abed calling out the names of things which haunt me!*

It seemed entirely right that this should be so, for he felt unreasonably certain that it was he and not David at all who *should* have been bitten by the snake. Gladly he took up the proffered burden on behalf of his friend; gladly he took the younger man's place.

Infused by righteousness he fought and fought against the darkness, but it would not let him breathe, and he could do nothing to assert himself.

In the end he fell, as though he were falling through the mountain, and through the crust of the earth itself, into an unbearably bleak and desolate hell where no sensation at all was possible.

Still he felt, perversely, greatly pleased and relieved – for he *knew* now that it must all be a dream, inspired by a combination of diseased food and the pressure of strife and stress. There was no doubt in his mind that he would wake when the moment came to find that the world was still what it had always been: real, solid, comprehensible.

The last sound which he heard was the voice of the Jesuit, howling out a scream of abandonment like the one which William de Lancy had let loose to summon them all to their meeting with unreason.

Fear not, my superstitious friend, cried Tallentyre, with the tone of a generous saviour, *for there is nothing truly to be feared in such a hell as this, from which we must in time be redeemed by the return of wakefulness and reason.*

5

By the time Sir Edward finally awoke from his unnatural sleep the sun was high in the sky, and David Lydyard had been labouring beneath it for longer than was comfortable. Even at this altitude the noonday temperature was difficult to bear.

Lydyard had made no attempt at all to bury the priest, nor had he tried in any methodical fashion to search for de Lancy.

He was still weakened by the after-effects of the snakebite which he had suffered, though he was surprised that he had been so badly affected by a mere graze, less serious even than the mild sting he had sustained near Cairo, when a cobra's fang had penetrated the leather of his shoe.

He had woken up full of memories of terrible dreams, which had refused to evaporate as dream-memories usually did, but he had thought himself quite well, and had been pleased with his feeling of well-being – until he had emerged into the morning light to discover the catastrophe which had overcome his friends while he slept.

His fever was now quite gone, but it had strained his resources to the limit to bring Sir Edward's body from the rocks to the tent, and to lodge the older man safely in a hammock.

At first, he had feared that the baronet would die of whatever mysterious cause had killed the Jesuit, but he had eventually reassured himself that Tallentyre's heart was beating strongly enough. It had been a short enough step from there to the opinion that the man would ultimately wake from his curious sleep, and that until he did there was little point in trying to deduce an explanation of what had happened.

While he waited for Tallentyre to wake Lydyard had tried to make himself useful within the limits of his strength.

He had gone to the other tent to look at Father Mallorn's belongings. It was, he supposed, his and Tallentyre's duty to find the priest's family in England and inform them of his death – or, if it should transpire that he had no family, to inform the relevant officers of the Church. Lydyard, though he was notionally of the same faith as the dead man, had not much idea who those relevant authorities might be, but in further pursuance of this assumed obligation he had also gone to the body and emptied the dead man's pockets. He had felt some shame at what he was doing, despite that it was necessary, and so he had brought the things immediately to his own tent, placing them on the hammock where he had lain in delirium.

Later, he had added the baronet's gun to the pile, having brought it down from the hillside where it lay broken open, with two spent cartridges in the breach.

Lydyard had not opened the priest's pocket-book to make a detailed investigation of his papers, but he had looked curiously at some of the other objects which he had removed. There was an odd silver ring, which Mallorn had never worn on his finger so far as he could recall, whose face was inscribed with a gnomic design which seemed to be three letters intertwined: probably O, A, and S. There was also an amulet, of the kind which was hawked in all the Egyptian markets, in imitation of ones which had been found in excavated tombs. It was of a type which Lydyard had heard identified as an *utchat*, representing a symbolic eye.

He remembered speaking to the priest about such relics; Mallorn had told him that in the beginning, the Egyptians must have worn as amulets actual parts of their ancestors' bodies, dried up by the sun or preserved in bitumen like mummies, but had in time substituted representations made from wood or clay. Lydyard could not tell what this particular charm was made of.

When he could no longer bear the ominous touch of the dead man's possessions, Lydyard had spent a little time in prayer. It was something which he still found possible to do, though the example of the man over whom he was praying – who had taken the place of his father, and was a man he much admired – had by no means left his inherited faith unshaken. Sir Edward held very firmly to the opinion that all religion was a symptom of a dying age of superstition, and that science alone was to be trusted as a source of wisdom and inspiration, and he was much more eloquent in arguing his case than Lydyard could be in testing it. Lydyard's confessor in England had offered stern warnings against the influence of Antichrists, and it was a source of mild puzzlement to Lydyard that a man as devout as Father Mallorn should have been so eager to seek Sir Edward's company on the boat to Wadi Halfa, and to make him a partner in his enterprise.

Lydyard had not only prayed for Sir Edward's safe awakening; he had prayed for the Jesuit's soul too, and for de Lancy's safe deliverance, if he needed any. For himself he had only offered thanks, that he had been spared a second time from death at a serpent's touch. But he had offered those thanks uneasily, not certain that he was yet entirely released from the effects of the serpent's bite.

When Tallentyre finally did come round Lydyard was ready beside him with a flask, from which the older man drank thirstily. He was very surprised to find Lydyard so well, and himself so weak, and was quick to demand the explanations which Lydyard could by no means provide.

When the younger man told him where and how he had been found, that Father Mallorn was dead, and that there was no sign at all of William de Lancy, he was at first astonished and then deeply distressed.

'Dear God!' said Tallentyre, with a fervour which was surely unseemly in a declared unbeliever. 'I had thought it all a dream! Perhaps it was – but suddenly I do not know what is real and what is not. Last evening I feared for your life, and now it seems that you alone have come through the night unscathed. I have suffered an evil hallucination, David, but now I find that events have conspired to reproduce the effects which it would have had if it were true in every last respect. We must find de Lancy, if we can – and then, for the sake of our sanity, we must leave this place.'

'I am not sure that either of us is well enough to ride,' said Lydyard, patiently. 'Nor am I sure that it will be easy to find de Lancy, for I have shouted out to him as loudly as I could and had no reply at all. In any case, we must bury the priest – and if we cannot make a proper Christian grave for him in this stony place, we must lay him to rest in one of these ancient tombs, and make such apology as we can to the receiver of his soul.'

'If my dream were trustworthy,' said the baronet, 'I fear that de Lancy may already be at rest in one of them. But we must search for him, for dreams never are to be trusted.' He tried to haul himself to his feet, but found the effort so painful that he accepted the restraint of Lydyard's hand.

'You must tell me what happened,' said Lydyard. 'I fear that my feverish sickness and my own dreams had me in their grip until the morning, and I know only what I woke to find.'

The older man shook his head. He ran his left hand up and down the right side of his body, testing the hip and the shoulder for injuries. 'I cannot tell what *really* happened,' he said, angrily. 'It appeared that de Lancy had wandered into one of the tombs, where he met something which made him scream in abject terror and fire his pistol. When the priest and I ran after him, we were soon brought to a halt by our confusion.

'Perhaps it was then that the dream began, and not before . . . how can I know? In my delusion, it seemed that we were buffeted about by a giant creature like a living sphinx. It seemed to swell and shrink, and then to swell again. I fired one shot by accident into the air, but fired the other barrel into its body at close range, without hurting it overmuch. This monster was pounced upon in its turn by a great grey wolf – but then the shadows choked me, so that I saw and heard no more. Did you find the body of a great cat, perhaps? Or the corpse of a grey wolf?'

'I did not,' Lydyard told him. 'But there are splashes of blood upon the rocks where I found you. I thought that they were yours, or perhaps the priest's – though neither of you seems to have been mauled or badly cut.' These words were spoken more faintly than he intended, for what the baronet had told him brought about a sudden resurgence in the memory of his own delirious dreams. 'A sphinx, you say?' he added, pensively.

Tallentyre looked up at him, and Lydyard saw the older man's eyes narrow as he too remembered something.

'*The cat – I cannot face her*,' quoted Tallentyre, softly. 'Do you remember that you said something like that, at the height of your delirium? What kind of cat was it which frightened you, David? How did it feature in your dream?'

Lydyard did not need to struggle for recall, but had to hesitate instead at the sheer profusion of the images which flooded back into his mind when Tallentyre told him what he had said.

'I saw Satan,' he whispered, 'suffering in Hell. I saw God, helpless outside the universe. I saw . . . wolves . . . which were not merely wolves. And the cat . . . no, it was not a cat . . . to begin with it had only the head of a cat, like the goddess Bast, but then – for a moment or two – it had the face of a woman and the *body* of a cat . . . it had turned aside from a stately parade of all the gods of Egypt, which took place in Plato's cave . . .'

'Plato's cave!' Tallentyre interjected, in a complaining tone.

'The cave in the *Republic*,' said Lydyard, slowly, though he knew that Tallentyre must understand what cave he meant, 'where the chained men see only the shadows cast upon the wall by firelight. In my dream, those shadows were the silhouettes of the animal-headed gods – and I was the man who turned, when the chain about my neck chanced to be broken. I was the man who saw the gods, and not their shadows . . . and it was Bast, with the head of a cat, who reacted to the fact that I could see them . . . Bast, who was also the Sphinx!' Lydyard was uncomfortably aware that his heart had quickened, and he added: 'I was terrified; even now, the nightmare is with me. The fear . . . and the blasphemy. . . .'

'There is no blasphemy in a nightmare,' said Tallentyre, dismissively. The baronet seemed preoccupied with his own memory. 'Nor as much coincidence as I had feared . . . for the brief similarity of imagery must surely be an accident.'

'That was not the blasphemy,' murmured Lydyard, reflectively. 'The blasphemy was in my vision of a helpless God, and a Satan who would redeem the world from its suffering, did not some cruel fate prevent him. I pitied that Satan, Edward . . . I raged at his imprisonment . . . before the fear. . . .'

Tallentyre seemed hardly to be paying attention. 'Perhaps,'

he said, gruffly, 'you are of the devil's party without knowing it. You have lived in my house long enough, after all. But we both dreamed of *wolves* too, did we not? You say that you saw wolves?'

'I saw wolves,' admitted Lydyard, 'but I knew, somehow, that they were really werewolves.'

'The hungry werewolves of London Town?' countered Tallentyre, feeling free to be amused by the line from the familiar nursery rhyme.

Lydyard shook his head. 'They were running across a vast glacier,' he said. 'An infinite sheet of ice.'

Tallentyre managed at last to tumble from the hammock, and it proved that he was able to stand. Lydyard did not try to restrain or help him; he was lost in his own thoughts, trying to remember what curious ideas had possessed him while he had watched those sinister wolves with the eye of his dream.

Tallentyre picked up the *utchat* which Lydyard had set down with the rest of Mallorn's possessions, but quickly put it down and took up the ring instead.

'What is this?' he asked.

'I don't know,' Lydyard replied. 'It is Mallorn's. How was it, do you suppose, that we both had such nightmares, though only one of us was bitten by the snake? And how did it come to pass that *our* nightmare slew the priest, and carried de Lancy off to God knows where?'

'I wish I knew,' said Tallentyre, bitterly. 'But what really happened will be known to God alone, unless I can shift myself to discover the truth from the relics which events have left behind. Show me!'

Lydyard nodded, and put on the straw hat which he used to keep the sun from his face. Tallentyre found his own, and frowned to see his two guns laid out beside one another – one of them scratched.

'I found it where I found you, among the rocks,' said Lydyard, to answer the unspoken question. 'I brought it down. There were spent cartridges in each barrel.'

Tallentyre said nothing, but merely preceded the younger man into the sunlight. He paused to look around at the parched valley and the lumpish wreckage of the partly dug-out tombs.

'No shadows now,' he said, in a murmurous tone. 'The high sun has banished them all.'

Lydyard followed him up the slope to the place where Father Mallorn's body lay. There were flies upon it already, and the baronet could not shoo them away. Lydyard waited while the older man confirmed what he already knew – that there was no obvious cause of death. The cuts and contusions on the man's body were nowhere near severe enough to have killed him, and for all Lydyard could tell, Mallorn's heart might simply have tired of the tedious business of beating, and stopped.

'Well,' said Tallentyre, eventually, 'he will never tell us now what really moved him to bring us here, and if that part of the truth which he hid from us has aught to do with what befell us in the night, we will have to find it out by other means.' Then, without wasting time, he stood up and looked at the upper part of the hillside.

'If de Lancy did go into one of the tombs from hereabouts,' he said, 'it could only have been one of three.' He pointed with his finger, to show Lydyard the alternatives.

They moved to investigate. One of the mastabas was half-collapsed, and it took only a few minutes to make certain that de Lancy could not have lost himself within it. The cavity of the second was little deeper, but if the pit had been recently dug out, it had also been filled in again. Only in the third was there a yawning hole into which a man might have fallen – or which might have served some lurking beast as a lair.

Tallentyre took up a small pebble, and tossed it into the pit. They should have heard it hit the bottom within two seconds, but Lydyard counted four before there came the sound of an impact, and then it was a grazing sound, which went on as the stone continued to descend.

'There must be a natural fissure in the rock,' said Lydyard.

'If it is wide enough to take the body of a man, and de Lancy fell into it . . .'

'*If,*' repeated Tallentyre, angrily. 'I am not yet ready to believe it.'

Lydyard went to the other side of the chamber, where a certain amount of litter had accumulated along the base of the wall. When he tested a discoloration with his fingers, he felt candle grease, and when he rifled through the debris he found a piece of paper, burned at one end, which must have been used as a taper.

'Sir Edward!' he said, and quickly handed the paper to the other man. It cracked and split as Tallentyre unrolled it, but he was able to place the pieces together and examine the print upon them.

'It is a page from a book!' exclaimed the young man.

'But not of any great antiquity,' said Tallentyre with a sigh. 'It is from an almanac – and see, here is a date: 1861. A relic of the former explorers, I fear. I hope that they fared better here than our own luckless expedition. The Jesuit knew that others had been here, and it made him curious to come himself, but there is no way now to discover what information he had as to who those others were, or what they may have found. Is there anything else?'

Lydyard pointed to a stain upon the stone. 'Blood?' he asked.

Tallentyre knelt to touch the stain, but could only shrug his shoulders. 'If it is,' he said, 'it too is a relic of those former seekers after wisdom. There is no trace of de Lancy here that I can see.' He put the broken piece of paper away in his own pocket-book, handling it with habitual caution.

'Show me the other bloodstains,' he commanded.

Lydyard preceded him out into the sunlight and led him to a spot some little distance away from Mallorn's body. There he pointed to another stain, already darkened by the heat to the point where it no longer seemed recent.

'I do not think it is mine,' said Tallentyre. 'And see – there is more over here, where I certainly did not go, so far as I can remember. Perhaps it is the beginning of a trail, which leads yonder up the slope. Perhaps *that* is the way de Lancy went.'

As he spoke, Tallentyre moved on, searching with his eyes for some further sign. He found it all too quickly, and Lydyard realized that a man who had been shedding so much blood as he walked or ran could not be expected to have survived for long.

While they moved up the rock-strewn slope Lydyard expected to find another body at any moment. Instead, they found that the stains grew sparser and the trail more difficult to follow. By the time they had come almost to the crest of the ridge there were no more signs to be seen, but Tallentyre did not pause, hurrying to the ridge so that he might look over and across the further slope.

When he was at the top he stopped, and Lydyard heard the impatient expulsion of his breath as he caught sight of something. The younger man hurried to catch up with him, and when he drew abreast Tallentyre grabbed his arm and pointed.

Two hundred yards away, half-hidden by an outcrop of rock, was the pale body of a man, apparently naked.

'De Lancy!' exclaimed Lydyard. 'Is he still alive?' He knew as he spoke that the heat of the sun could have done nothing but harm to a man who had lain unclothed beneath it for several hours, and he feared the worst. He cursed himself for not having made a more thorough search, instead of wasting his time in prayer.

Tallentyre was already going on, moving in an impatiently laboured fashion which testified both to the soreness of his body and to the sternness of his resolve. Lydyard, imagining that he could feel once again within his veins the venom which the tiny snake had injected into his hand, stumbled after him.

The man was indeed quite naked, and the pale and slender back which was exposed to the sun as he lay face down was already beginning to burn an unpleasant shade of red.

It was not de Lancy. This man had blond hair, and strikingly handsome features. He seemed to be about the same age as de Lancy – in his mid- or late twenties – but he was slimmer and sleeker. His torso had been lacerated fore and aft, as though by the raking claws of a great cat.

Tallentyre turned the man over so that his face and chest were fully exposed, and put a finger to his neck, searching for a pulse. Lydyard was certain that he had never seen the man before, and yet there was something odd about his appearance – something which demanded a recognition he could not quite discover.

'Who can it be?' he whispered, as Tallentyre met his stare with tired and bloodshot eyes.

'Why,' said the baronet, his voice rattling with bitter and angry sarcasm, 'who else can it possibly be but the wolf which I saw in my dream, which was no doubt a werewolf strayed from your own delirium, come to test its strength against the living Sphinx! And since that is so, what have I learned of the true history of the world in this dire and desolate place but that all that I have foolishly chosen to believe throughout my life is a lie? What has happened to us here has been done by your jealous God, to instruct me that the human mind is after all a very feeble thing, which cannot ever hope to win its struggle for a proper understanding of the world.'

Lydyard recoiled before the savagery of the complaint, and its deliberate suggestion of blasphemy. He said: 'You cannot think it.'

When Sir Edward had railed inwardly against his misfortune for a few moments more, he consented to reply: 'Indeed I cannot. Of what *we* have been the victims I do not know, but this poor man has surely been stripped by brigands and left for dead, and though he is not de Lancy he is certainly no native. We must help him as best we can, and must go as swiftly as we can to Wadi Halfa, so that we may bring others to search for de Lancy. Let us hope that they can discover how this welter of trouble was brought upon us, and by whom.'

To this, Lydyard could only add a silent amen. Then he bent to take the legs of the stricken man, while Tallentyre took his shoulders, intending that between the two of them they would carry him back to their camp as quickly as they could.

But as soon as Lydyard's fingers touched the skin of the wounded man, that recognition which had been struggling to surface within him was abruptly released. It was as though a new eye opened within him, which saw the world in a fashion very different from the two which he commonly used.

What he saw – and he was convinced that he *saw* it, no matter how paradoxical the conviction might be – was that the man he had touched had only the appearance of a man, and had beneath it the true nature of a wolfish kind of beast.

'What is it?' asked Tallentyre, sharply, as their first attempt to lift the unconscious body came to nothing.

For an instant it was on the tip of Lydyard's tongue to tell his friend and mentor what he saw, but then he remembered what kind of man the baronet was, and how intolerant of foolishness. He did not want to annoy him with a further product of his poisoned sensations.

'Sorry,' he replied. 'It was only a moment's dizziness and confusion. I can lift him now.'

But as they began to carry the wounded man to their tent in the valley below, Lydyard felt himself possessed by a dreadful anxiety that his was a dizziness and confusion which might last far longer than a moment, and that the symbolic eye which had opened inside him might not be so easy to close again.

The Compass of Reason

Or have we eaten of the insane root,
Which takes the reason prisoner?

William Shakespeare, *Macbeth*

1

Medieval English folklore is singularly barren of werewolf stories, the reason being that wolves had been extirpated from England under the Anglo-Saxon kings, and therefore ceased to be objects of dread to the people. This poverty of tradition is, however, amply compensated by the later development of the rich mythology of the werewolves of London.

Most Englishmen meet this particular superstition in the relatively innocuous guise of an admonitory nursery rhyme whose three verses enjoin children to beware of wandering alone at night, especially when the moon is full, lest they should fall prey to the 'werewolves of London Town'. The earliest references to the London werewolves which I have been able to locate are in a broadside ballad issued *c.* 1672 and a pamphlet whose probable date of publication was ten or twelve years later; a much greater profusion of references can be found in broadsides and chap-books of the late eighteenth century, when most of the better-known tales first appeared . . .

Numerous stories are told even today of the depredations of the London werewolves. Most of these nursery horror stories credit the werewolves of London with a penchant for carrying off lost and naughty children; there are, however, several notable tales of a more bizarre nature.

Two such items of folklore fit into the common pattern of stories in which human beings entertain magical lovers, but they contain an interesting difference from others of their kind. Those stories which tell of an ordinary man married to a supernaturally beautiful woman who is ultimately revealed to be one of the werewolves of London are the more orthodox, usually featuring a promise made by the husband to his bride, the eventual breaking of which leads to the discovery of her true nature – and, of course, to her loss – but they also feature the notion that the female werewolves continually seek husbands among the upper classes of the city, whose homes may then become places of refuge for entire packs (which range, it appears, from a mere handful of werewolves to a full dozen).

Stories which feature affairs of the heart involving a human female and a male werewolf are more distinctive. These rumoured liaisons do not usually involve marriage, and tend to be formed as romantic tales of a true but tragic love which cannot be consummated, on the grounds that the males among the werewolves of London – unlike their female kin – are incapable of sexual intercourse while in human form because the excitement of passion always induces metamorphosis.

The persistence of this mythology in modern times is further attested by a report in *The Times* of 27 March 1833, which describes how a mob hunted a man along Fleet Street and into Gough Square, justifying their action on the grounds that the fellow had given succour to the werewolves of London and had kidnapped children to feed them. The report insists that had they caught the man murder must have been done, but that he escaped them after doubling back towards Ludgate Circus, whereupon the pursuers became entangled with another crowd which had gathered about a barrel-organ.

In his account of *London Labour and the London Poor*, first published in 1851, Henry Mayhew offers further evidence that belief in the actuality of the London werewolves is not entirely a thing of the past. He records sincerely fearful statements by no less than four of his witnesses, including a girl crossing-sweeper, a rat-catcher, a garret master, and a potato seller.

The rat-catcher claimed to have seen the werewolves on

more than one occasion, and confessed that despite his fear of them he felt disposed to owe them a debt of gratitude, on the grounds that rats had become their customary prey 'because human flesh nowadays proves too difficult and too dangerous to be regularly obtained'. The garret master was even more voluble upon the subject, offering the opinion that the police know full well that the werewolves exist, by virtue of having the duty of disposing of their victims, but that they dare not give publicity to the scourge for fear of increasing public alarm.

The Metropolitan Police themselves, needless to say, have a different account to give. A detective to whom I recently spoke said to me that common murderers will sometimes mutilate their victims in order to create the appearance that the werewolves of London were the perpetrators of the deed, and that thieves and other felons will often collude with this primitive terrorism in order to intimidate the superstitious populations upon which they themselves are inclined to prey. This man opined that in much the same way that country poachers will manufacture and spread tales of ghostly black dogs in order to intimidate those who might try to trap them at their nocturnal work, so the vicious creatures of London's Underworld have taken the trouble to invent – or at least to sustain – the legend of the urban werewolves.

It is notable, though, that not all the tales of the London werewolves cast them as evil devourers of children. Here and there amid the welter of horror stories can be heard a more sympathetic voice, which says that after all, the werewolves are prisoners of their own perverse nature, and cannot entirely be blamed for what they do. There is a little of the wolf in all of us, these voices say, and those who will not hear the words of Jesus Christ our redeemer are to be reckoned little better than wolves, damned to spend eternity in the Inferno of their own rapacity.

Sabine Baring-Gould, *The Book of Werewolves*, 1865

2

Much of the argument for and against the Darwinian theory of evolution has been confused by misunderstandings about the fundamental nature of the theory, which is to say, what it actually attempts to argue. Many assaults upon Dr Darwin's assertions do not aim at the thesis itself, but instead attack a more fundamental notion which must be taken for granted before the theoretician actually gets to work.

It is necessary to distinguish two rather different meanings which are attached in common parlance to the phrase 'theory of evolution'. When churchmen attack such notions what they tend to be attacking is the theory that any evolution of species has happened at all, but what Dr Darwin is really offering us in his excellent book *On the Origin of Species by Means of Natural Selection* is a theory of *how* that evolution happened, which must of necessity accept the more fundamental theory as already proven.

Men of science are excited by Dr Darwin's book because it offers a sensible insight into the mechanisms of the evolution of species, and sets us on the road to an understanding of the true history of life on earth; the opposing men of religion, by and large, are endeavouring to remove the dispute to a different battleground, espousing a cause which the men of science rightly consider to be long lost.

Whether Dr Darwin is correct or not in his deductions regarding the mechanism of evolution it may be too soon to say; the hypothesis is certainly brilliant, but a verdict of 'not proven' may have to stand until the chemical mechanism of inheritance is itself revealed – until then, talk of 'variations' which are selected by the attritions of nature will remain necessarily and annoyingly vague. On the matter of the more fundamental issue of whether evolution has happened at all, however, the verdict is surely beyond all reasonable doubt. There has certainly been an evolution which has produced more complex species from simpler ones, and no intellectually honest man can reasonably doubt that all the life forms which now exist are descended from a few common ancestors.

In order to establish this fact, we need only refer to two phenomena. First, it is obvious that the diversity of living species shows distinct patterns of relatedness. This is in itself strongly suggestive of an unfolding pattern of the gradual and progressive emergence of new types. Second, we have in the fossil record an astonishing story of failed species which once existed but which became extinct; this clearly demonstrates to us that the diversity of surviving species is but a tiny fraction of the diversity of species which have existed.

Intelligent men confronting this evidence could never have doubted that the evolution of species was perfectly obvious, had it not been for an unfortunate blindfold placed upon the exercise of intelligence by the conviction that the world was not old enough for such a gradual evolution to have occurred. The written history which has been handed down to us from classical times (filtered, alas, in Western Europe by the barbarous destructions of the Dark Ages) speaks to us only of a few hundred generations, and – further aided by the conviction that certain written items were sacred, and hence indubitable – our unfortunate forefathers were seduced into an acceptance of the notion that written history encompassed the entire history of the earth and of the universe, from Creation to the present day.

We now know that this is false. The discoveries of geologists like Hutton and Lyell have proved beyond the shadow of a doubt that the earth is older by far than written history claims, and that it is older by far than mankind. The deciphering of the inscriptions left behind by the ancient Egyptians, and various excavations in Europe, have allowed men like Lubbock to demonstrate that there was a long *prehistory* of mankind, when men lived without writing, entirely dependent upon the myths of oral tradition for an understanding of their origins and existence.

Our written records, whether we call them sacred or not, are guilty of a treacherous and utterly vain ambition when they boldly compress the time which elapsedd before writing was discovered into a few dozen generations. Man is older by far than writing, and the earth is older by far than man; recognition of these two facts removes the barrier which stands between the intelligent man and the obviousness of the evolution of natural species. Once that idol has been cast down, honest men cannot help but see clearly what the relatedness of species, both extant and extinct, really implies.

There are, of course, men who cling determinedly to the apparent security of the written word, and who would far rather argue from that authority than from empirical evidence of what the world is like. For them, the God of the written word is – as He declares Himself to be – the most jealous of conceivable gods, who can tolerate no challenge to His supremacy. That God and his followers cannot allow empirical evidence to speak for itself, but must overwhelm it with the weight of written authority; it is this way of arguing which asserts, *via* the pious Mr Gosse, that the fossils and all other evidence of the antiquity of the earth must have been made by God at the same time that He made everything else, in much the same spirit that inspired Him to equip Adam and Eve with unnecessary navels.

This way of proceeding is not merely mistaken; it is ridiculous. It is one which no rational man could advance, because it flatly denies the power of reason. If the view that evidence must be subservient to authority is difficult to argue against, that is because it is a view which rejects argument itself, and this must certainly be reckoned a fatal weakness rather than a cunning rhetorical advantage.

The men of science and the men of religion who have lately crossed swords over Dr Darwin's book are not simply offering us different accounts of man. They are offering us very different accounts of how the world might be understood, and thus of what kind of world it is. Science asserts that the world is – at least to some worthwhile degree – comprehensible in terms of an ordered pattern of causes and effects operating across time; religion asserts that it is comprehensible only in terms of the intentions and commandments of a God who moves in mysterious ways, and that the pattern of cause and effect is always in principle interruptable by miraculous ordinance.

The latter belief is endorsed (frequently unthinkingly) by large numbers of our contemporaries hungry for new 'philosophical' fads whose apparatus is borrowed from ancient alchemists, mystics, and magicians. If these faddists are to be believed, the Age of Miracles, once pronounced mercifully dead, has been ingloriously restored to Victoria's England by virtue of the petty machinations of countless spiritist mediums and similar dishonest conjurers. Those who are tempted by this modern mysticism ought, however, to realize what kind of a world it is to which they are committing their faith: a world of desperate uncertainty, whose chain of causation is forever victim to whims of fate unknown and unknowable, whose every appearance may be a lie from which no true inference is possible.

It is, I believe, vitally important that we do recognize and always remember how differently grounded the beliefs of the evolutionists and the beliefs of the Creationists really are. The Creationist does not simply deny that the evidence for evolution is adequate; he denies the very meaning of the word 'evidence'. The scientist, on the other hand, must accept that whatever there is in the world, and whatever happens in the world, *must* be accounted for in terms of a logic of cause and effect, for only if this assumption is true can the world be understandable at all. It is the scientist who is right because he alone *can* be right; we must account for diversity and change as an unfolding pattern of causation, because it is otherwise unaccountable.

When a churchman refers to God as the 'First Cause' he may seem to be observing things from the same perspective as the scientist, but in fact he is denying it. 'Creation' cannot qualify as a cause because it is a denial of causation. It is an assertion that the chain of causation can be and has been casually interrupted from without, and some arbitrary insertion made for which we cannot – and need not – account. This cannot be wisdom, because it is a refusal to admit the possibility of wisdom.

According to the opponents of Dr Darwin, the fossil record and all the discoveries of geology and archaeology are arbitrary insertions into the scheme of things for which we cannot and need not account; anything else which does not accord with their own views will be similarly rejected – thus the idea of Creation avidly consumes and disposes of all attempts to make sense of anything.

Men of science cannoot and do not claim that everythiing is discoverable, but they do claim that discoveries can be made. Their opponents, by contrast, are content to claim on the one hand that everything can be known, through the medium of divine revelation or magical intuition, while on the other hand denying that there can be any such thing as true evidence or rational inference. The man of science, therefore, lives in an imperfect world where progress is possible; the man of superstition must live in a world where fantasy is free to make whatever declarations it cares to, about past and future alike.

I cannot speak for other men, but I would be very bitter and disappointed to find myself in a world of the latter kind, whose past might be very different from what every evidence implies, and which might at any time be brought to a rude and final conclusion by an intrusive and careless Act of Creation. If this is so, then the world which seems so solid and so orderly might at any moment acquire the substance and logic of a mere dream, and dissolve as easily. If that is, in fact, the kind of world in which we exist, then we must indeed cry 'God help us!' for there would be no other possibility of comfort. For myself, I am content with the presumption that evidence can be trusted, that inferences can be drawn, and that all superstition, all magic, and all miracles are delusions of the cowardly mind.

> Sir Edward Tallentyre, 'Thoughts on the Controversy Surrounding the Darwinian Theory', *The Quarterly Review*, June 1867

3

Alexandria, 11 March 1871

My dear Gilbert

It appears that we may soon be able to leave Egypt and return home; we hope to sail, or rather steam, for Gibraltar aboard the *Excelsior* early next week. The authorities here have been determined to turn our tragedy into farce, and their decision to let us go is a mere matter of washing their hands of the whole affair, inspired by despair at their inability to cope with the complexities of it. Officialdom, as you are well aware, does not like mysteries, and Egyptian Officialdom is very enthusiastic in its dislike of ours. What manifests itself to us as a single mystery appears to the clerical mind as no less than three distinct problems, each one vexatious in a different way.

The problem of poor de Lancy remains utterly intransigent. We have all of his papers and belongings but his actual person, alive or dead, has proved quite impossible to find. I remain in some doubt as to whether a sufficiently thorough search has actually been mounted in the desert south of Qina, but the Egyptians claim to have scoured the area to no avail. I have had a reply to my letter to his family, in which his father is studiously courteous – but also, as might be expected, rather cold in his manner. He assures me that no blame could possibly attach to me, but when I read between his well-penned lines I see the opinion that because I was the older man, and a baronet to boot, divine right gave me the authority to command the ill-fated excursion and the corresponding responsibility to see that all ended happily. Alas, though I have no sense of divine right at all, my conscience is in sympathy with his notion of where the responsibility lies.

The problem of Father Francis Mallorn, which seemed at first to be trivial, has also thrown up unaccountable difficulties. Whatever advantage was given to the careful accountants of men's fates by the indubitability of his death has unfortunately been cancelled out by the inadequacy of his papers. We have his belongings, and Officialdom's agents have been able to discover some of the places where he stayed on his journey up the Nile, but attempts to trace his existence further back in time have met with nothing but confusion. All enquiries, whether directed to the secular authorities of England or the records of the Society of Jesus, have been confounded. Of his family, his schooling, and his work no one can discover anything, and the investigators have reluctantly concluded that if he existed at all before we met him then he bore a different name – and why he should have changed it for our benefit (or, as it has turned out, our irritation) no one can tell. It is difficult to believe that priests travel with faked papers, but I must admit that he seemed every inch the priest to me, and am reluctant to admit that I was so easily fooled – and for what possible purpose or motive?

Thankfully, the third element of our mystery – the young man we discovered in the desert – has become slightly less mysterious. A search has revealed certain possessions, including papers, discarded in the desert not far from where we found him. These papers identify one Paul Shepherd, an Englishman, and descriptions of him obtained from those who met him as he travelled (alone) up the Nile confirm that he is indeed the person we found. It seems obvious that these belongings were stolen by thieves, and discarded when all that was valuable had been removed; we can only conclude that it was the thieves who stripped and wounded the youth and left him for dead. Alas, the limited evidence left to us by the brigands has not enabled us to trace his relatives; Shepherd is an inconveniently common name, and his only distinctive characteristic is a pair of remarkably clear blue eyes.

Mr Shepherd has now recovered fully from his wounds, which healed very quickly and cleanly. Despite being very bloody, his cuts were not deep, and though we do not know quite how they were inflicted they seem to have done no lasting damage. Nevertheless, he is far from well, and has lost his mind so completely that he cannot respond to his name or to any questions which we put to him. He wakes only for short periods of time, usually at night; sometimes he will wake three or four times between dusk and dawn, initially seeming energetic, but within the hour he becomes torpid again. He does not speak, and though I am sure that he can hear he appears unable to understand English or any other language with which I have been able to try him. He can feed himself, after a fashion, and though he will not use a fork or a spoon in his own hand he will consent to be spoon-fed by another.

I dare not ask you for an opinion about the state of this young man when you have not had a chance to examine him, but if there is any advice which you can give me which might help to break through the wall of silence which surrounds him, I would be infinitely grateful. You have mentioned to me in the past your acquaintance with James Austen, who assists in the treatment of patients at the County Asylum at Hanwell, and I would dearly like to know whether he has seen similar cases, and whether he has had any success in treating them.

I wish I could give you a more elaborate description of his state, but the unfortunate Mr Shepherd exhibits a remarkable paucity of behaviour. He seems not to play or to fidget. His curiosity seems muted, especially when he is indoors. He pays little heed to any objects which I bring to his attention. Sometimes, he stands by the window looking out into the darkness, and I have taken him out on more than one occasion to see what he would do, but while he is quick to turn towards a sound, he does not appear to have any urge to act or explore. He is in some way cut off from the world, insulated from all its stimuli. And yet he seems to have been a gentleman, for his hands and feet are remarkably free of scars and calluses.

The Egyptian authorities are obviously in two minds about poor Shepherd – reluctant to accept him as their own problem, but equally reluctant to surrender him entirely to my care so that I might bring him to England. Their prevarications in this matter have been the main stumbling-block preventing our early departure, but now they have decided that if someone must pay for his further upkeep they would rather it was not themselves.

If there is no improvement in the youth's condition, then I would like you to examine him when we return to England. Perhaps, if you think it desirable, he might be placed under Austen's care. I certainly would not want him committed to Hanwell as a pauper, but I would be glad to have Austen visit him at my own house in London or, if he prefers it, to bring the patient to Charnley. In the meantime, I would be interested to hear an opinion as to what kind of shock could have caused him to revert, as it seems that he has, to an infantile stage of mental development.

In particular, I would like to know whether there is any known drug or poison which could have induced the youth's condition. Having considered the matter very carefully in the cool light of reason I can come to no other conclusion than that some powerful narcotic must have been responsible for this alarming sequence of events. The dream in which I saw the sphinx-like creature assaulted by a wolf seemed so vividly real at the time that it cannot have been natural. I did discharge my shot-gun twice, as I remembered having done when I awoke, but what I fired at can only have been a phantom of my imagination. I do not know how this theory can account for the apparent fact that the wounds suffered by the man we later found naked were sustained close to the spot where Lydyard discovered me, but it is my earnest hope that once the man is returned to mental health he can tell us.

How a drug might have been given to me, I cannot tell. If it was administered deliberately it is conceivable that Mallorn might have done it, or even de Lancy, but I could find nothing in either man's belongings to suggest that he was possessed of such a potion. Whether David's delirium was really caused by the snake which bit him, or by the administration of a similar drug, I do not know for sure – but I suspect the latter. It may be that we can account for de Lancy's wandering away as he did by hypothesizing that he too was under the influence of a drug-induced hallucination and it is possible that Mallorn, too, could be counted as a victim. It is conceivable that the priest's sudden heart failure was induced by a vivid delusion not unlike the one which I suffered. How the young man fits into this scheme of things, I cannot tell – but I am sure that he does. He was a victim of *some* misfortune, and you will understand why I have asked for your professional opinion about possible causes of his condition.

I have given much thought to the possible motives which Mallorn might have had for asking us to accompany him to that desolate place. Sheer malice seems unlikely, and I lean to the opinion that he was afraid – justifiably so, it seems – and sought reliable companions who might stand fast with him against danger. I cannot believe that he knew exactly what would happen, but he had reason to fear something. Our protection, alas, proved woefully inadequate.

I think that David secretly disagrees with me on almost all of these points, but the boy has become distressingly wary of argument. He knows me too well to submit a frankly supernatural explanation to my examination, but I am sure that he is covertly inclined to accept that we were assaulted by evil shape-shifting spirits. He is still reluctant to shed his belief in the reality of God and the Devil (the latter has seemingly come to preoccupy his mind) and though he refuses to say so I am certain that he believes that we fell victim to some diabolically inspired haunter of the tombs.

In truth, I cannot altogether blame him, for I was very nearly convinced at the time of the reality of what was happening to me, but I am anxious on his behalf, and am uncertain as to how best to proceed in the matter of reclaiming him for the cause of reason. Whatever reason may tell us, and no matter how satisfied we are by its arguments, there is something within us all which is a prolific source of superstitious fears. Such fears flourish with every sunset, for there is not one of us in which the empire of reason is absolutely secure. David will realize in due course that our haunters are within us and not without, but for the time being I am inclined to allow him the comfort of believing that whatever tried to hurt us has been left far behind in the desert, and can no longer reach us. Physically, he is quite recovered from his ordeal, but he has not entirely shaken off the legacy of his poisoning, and his nerves are fragile, especially at night. I am determined to treat him as kindly as I can, lest he too should soon require the services of an alienist.

Although we have now been granted leave to return to England, so that I will soon be able to take matters into my own hands, there are some preliminary enquiries which you might make on my behalf, if you would consent to do it. If you can find any clue to Mallorn's history or true identity I would be glad to hear of it, but while that line of enquiry is being pursued by others it may be more useful for you to concentrate on certain other matters, in which the authorities have shown no conspicuous interest.

First, I would be very grateful if you could place an advertisement in *The Times* asking for relatives of the Paul Shepherd who was recently travelling in Egypt to come forward; they are entitled to know what has become of him. If you wish, you may report what happened to us to the editor of the paper so that he may publish it – rumours have spread so widely here that I fear the possibility of a garbled and sensationalized account appearing in one of the scurrilous Sunday rags.

Second, I am curious to know who visited our hidden valley approximately ten years ago – probably in 1861 or

1862 – and what they found there. Mallorn told us, when he volunteered to take us to a place where we could learn something of 'the true history of the world', that he had heard reports of what others had discovered; these reports must have excited his curiosity, and perhaps his anxiety too, and I would be interested to know their contents. It occurs to me that the curators of the British Museum's collection of Egyptian antiquities might know of this earlier expedition, and of any reports which have been published by its members. Samuel Birch is the man to see, if you can; his knowledge of such matters is encyclopaedic.

Third, I wonder whether you can discover anything about an odd ring which David found among Mallorn's possessions, along with his rosary and the other familiar apparatus of his faith. The authorities here have dismissed it as a mere trinket, and a Jesuit priest has said that it has no significance connected with the Society, so I am led to wonder why Mallorn had it. It is silver, and has a rectangular face on which is engraved a complex monogram, which seems to consist of the letters A, O, and S. Might these be the initials of his real name? Or are they the initials of some society to which he belonged?

Please do not put yourself out unduly in conducting these enquiries for me; if the pressure of your work would make them burdensome, let the second and the third await my return. Because we have chosen a leisurely way home you should be able to get a reply to us while we are still *en route*; perhaps you could send a letter to await us in Gibraltar. In the mean time I remain, as always,

Your devoted friend
Edward

4

London, 21 March 1872

My dear Edward

I have news of some small progress in the enquiries which you have asked me to undertake, and thought it best to write immediately lest you should have left Gibraltar before my news can reach you there.

I wish I could say that what I have so far discovered has made the affair clearer, but I cannot; indeed, I fear that such additional information as I have come across can only increase that web of mystery and confusion which surrounds it. I hope that I will know more in two days' time, when I have had the opportunity to visit the man whose name has most strikingly emerged from my investigations – but I am getting ahead of myself, and must put things in order.

After placing the requested advertisement in *The Times* I made haste to show your letter to James Austen at Charnley Hall, in case he had any advice to offer about your unfortunate young man. To my astonishment, he was able to say immediately that the name Paul Shepherd was known to him – but when he had read the remainder of the text he confessed himself to be both intrigued and thoroughly perplexed by what you have set out there.

To dispose of merely clinical matters first, Austen says that he has never encountered a case very like the one which you have described, though certain of its features are not entirely unfamiliar to him. He knows of no drug which could have induced such a state, and thinks it unlikely that any one narcotic could have had such a wide range of effects as were suffered by your companions and yourself. He is, however, well enough aware of the rapid progress which is being made in the development and deployment of new substances in medicine to be wary of saying that there is no opiate or hallucinogenic substance capable of such effects.

As to the name Paul Shepherd, Austen says that he several times met a young man of that name in the early 1860s. The man in question fitted the physical description which you give in your letter exactly – rather too exactly, as Austen points out. The man Austen encountered seemed to be in his mid-twenties then, and if your Paul Shepherd is really the same person one would have expected him to look older by a decade. But there is more than a mere coincidence of names involved here; Austen's attention was also caught by the passage in your letter in which you refer to the mysterious Father Mallorn's offer to show you something of 'the true history of the world'. Austen admitted that the phrase is reasonably commonplace, and might readily be assumed to refer to the marvellous discoveries made by Lepsius and others regarding the true antiquity of Egyptian civilization, but said that for him those words could not help but carry a very different connotation, especially in connection with the name of Paul Shepherd.

Austen sometimes admits patients to Charnley Hall as his 'guests'; usually, but not always, they are gentlefolk whose relatives are anxious to have them cared for in an expert manner but could not bear to have them committed to a public asylum. Some ten years ago Austen took into his home a man who suffered from a most remarkable delusion, who gave his name as 'Adam Clay', though Austen came eventually to believe that this was a pseudonym chosen for effect. The patient also claimed to have owned another pseudonym, which he had once attached to a book; this name was 'Lucian de Terre', and the title of the book which he had supposedly written was *The True History of the World*.

This Adam Clay claimed to have lived in France during the Revolution of 1789 and for many years before – though the fact that he was obviously no more than middle-aged made the claim seem preposterous. Austen at first considered that the book which his patient claimed to have written was merely part of his fantasy of having lived in pre-Revolutionary France, but he was eventually able to confirm that such a book did exist, and he took the trouble to scan through the first of its four volumes in the British Museum. He discovered it to be a tale of an extraordinarily wild kind, but not without a certain fascination.

The fact that *The True History of the World* had been published in 1789 seemed to make it impossible that the man at Charnley Hall really was its author. When Clay died in 1863 he appeared to be no more than fifty years of age, and was certainly not in his nineties. Nevertheless, says Austen, he gave every indication of believing that he was the author of the book, and that he was very much older than he seemed – in fact he claimed on more than one occasion to be immortal, though his eventual death gave the lie to that particular delusion. Austen could only conclude that a copy of the book had come into his patient's possession when the man's mind initially became disturbed, and that Clay had erected an elaborate fantasy around the story which he read there, assuming the personality of the notional teller of the story.

This remarkable man seems to have been by no means unreasonable in matters unconnected with this delusion, and the fact that he consented to surrender himself to Austen's care implies that he may have been secretly cognisant of the fact that he was deluded, but Austen never could persuade him of the falseness of his identification. Austen told me that he became quite fond of the long discussions which he had with his patient, which took the form of amiable contests whereby he would try to persuade Adam Clay to abandon his preposterous claims while Clay would try – not without a certain ingenuity – to persuade *him* that the fantastical tale recorded in *The True History of the World* really was the true history of the world, and that he knew it by virtue of the fact that he had lived it from beginning to end.

The reason why I have taken the trouble to record all this

is that during his time at Charnley Hall, Adam Clay had only one visitor: a young man with blond hair and very striking blue eyes, named Paul Shepherd. Austen reports that the young man was pleasant and courteous, but that he resisted all the attempts which Austen made to obtain information from him about Adam Clay. He would neither confirm nor deny that he believed Clay to be mad, and said that he had no right to give any information to the doctor which Clay would not give himself. In exactly the same fashion, Clay refused to give Austen any information about Shepherd – although Austen did say, in a somewhat cryptic manner, that he had been able to reach by deduction certain conclusions as to where and how Shepherd was accommodated in Clay's delusory account of the world. I asked Austen whether he would consent to meet you after your return to England to discuss these matters further, and he said that he would be glad to assist.

In pursuit of the other information which you requested I went the following day to the British Museum. There I asked for Mr Birch, as you had suggested, and asked what he knew of expeditions to the area where your hidden valley was located. Birch was very surprised by the question, but when I explained to him that I was acting on your behalf, and told him something of what had befallen you, he agreed to tell me what little he knew.

Birch claimed that the region which you visited was not known as an area of great interest, but that he did know of one expedition into the desert east of Wadi Halfa, which had been conducted some ten years before. Alas, he said, it was not mounted by reputable Egyptologists, but had been led by a man whose ideas he could only class with those of the 'pyramidiots' and 'Egyptomaniacs' (his descriptions) who are determined to preserve the addled interpretations of the antiquites of Egypt which make artefacts into mystical symbols and hieroglyphic writings into treatises in Hermetic magic. It was obvious to me that Birch had such a low opinion of the person in question that he was ashamed to talk about him; when he named the man I was not altogether surprised by this attitude, for it was Jacob Harkender.

I suppose you have heard of Harkender, but in case you have not I will give you a brief explanation of his character. He is a scholar of sorts, and would probably describe himself as an occultist. Bulwer-Lytton knows him, I believe. He is not what one might call a Society Occultist, whose stock-in-trade is to startle dinner parties and 'séances' with esoteric flim-flam, but he is nevertheless a great pretender to esoteric knowledge and magical power. Whether or not there really are secret societies in Britain devoted to the preservation and exploitation of supposed arcane knowledge I cannot tell, but if there are, I am sure that Harkender fancies himself an heir to the most potent of their secrets. He lives not far from Medmenham, and I have more than once heard his name coupled in speech with Dashwood's – the Dashwood, that is, who was once the self-proclaimed president of the so-called Hell-Fire Club.

I know that in your view the Hell-Fire Club and its modern imitations are no more than silly conceits of young dandies, whose supposed Satanic affiliations merely add a touch of spice to ordinary drunkenness and debauchery. I know too your utter contempt for the spirit-rappers, mediums, and assorted mystics who have beguiled London Society during these last ten years. You are well enough aware that I share your views, but I must say that if Harkender is a poseur, he is at least a very determined poseur. He has travelled widely in India and Egypt, and although a man like Samuel Birch does not hesitate to call him a charlatan there are some reputable scholars who will concede that he has devoted considerable resources to his researches in far lands, and that he has visited places where few other white men have ever been.

I would not labour this point, save for a most curious coincidence which I happened upon almost by chance. As I was leaving the Museum, it occurred to me on a whim to visit the Reading Room, and to ask for the book which Austen had mentioned to me, one volume of which he had seen there some years before. I spoke to young Gosse, whose father has tangled with you over the matter of your stout defence of the Darwinian theory and consequent attacks on men of religion (I must say that the son is not much like his father). Gosse undertook to find the book for me, but was quickly forced to report back that it was missing from its place. This, as you will imagine, caused some distress among his seniors, for there is nothing the Keeper likes less than to lose a book (and in this case, all four volumes had disappeared). The Keeper commanded Gosse to consult the records, to see when the book had last been asked for; he found that its presence had last been recorded five years before, when it had been summoned from the vaults by – Jacob Harkender!

What all this might signify, I am at a loss to suggest. I am strongly minded to pay a call on Mr Harkender, in order to ask him whether he can cast any light on your strange experience, but I have my doubts as to whether the man will be willing or able to give me a sensible answer. It is possible, I suppose, that he will seize upon your story as an opportunity to make mysteries – and the fact of your involvement may give him far more cause for amusement than you would like. Unfortunately, rumours of your adventure have already begun to circulate – presumably in consequence of the enquiries made by the Egyptian authorities – so there is no point in my trying to keep the matter secret. It will be best, I think, to approach Harkender quite straightforwardly, hoping that he will be equally honest and open and that he will consent to tell me frankly why he mounted his expedition into the desert, and what he found there.

I fear that I have nothing more to add at this stage. I have asked several people about the inscription on the ring, including Birch, but no one has yet recognized it. I suspect that it may have been a purely personal item, in which case there is nothing to be learned from it. I will mention to Harkender when I see him that you were taken to the site of his investigations by a Jesuit priest, but it remains to be seen whether that news will be of any significance to him.

I look forward to your eventual return to these shores, when we must all put our heads together – I include Austen in this – and make a concerted attempt to get to the bottom of this disconcerting matter. It is a very peculiar puzzle, but I have every confidence that it will ultimately yield up an explanation to our combined powers of reasoning.

I will write again when I have seen Harkender, in the hope that the miraculous power of steam might enable the letter to reach you before you sail for home.

Please give my best regards to David, and my hopes for his swift and total recovery from his illness.

Yours very sincerely
Gilbert

PART TWO

Revelations of the Inner Eye

Beware the days of the year, little man,
When the moon hath a face like a silver crown;
Cleave if thou may'st to the home of thy clan,
And hide from the werewolves of London Town.

Beware the coverts and courts, little maid;
Where walks the man with the coat of brown;
Though thou art abandoned, be not waylaid,
By the hungry werewolves of London Town.

Beware the starlit nights, my child,
And the pretty lady in the sleek white gown;
Though thou art forsaken, be not beguiled,
By the charming werewolves of London Town.

Traditional rhyme

1

When he was safely astride the top of the wall, with his thin legs dangling, Gabriel Gill breathed a sigh of relief. He had time now to look about in a lordly and leisurely fashion, and he did so in a suitably proud manner.

It was a survey which took in far more than the road and the fields outside the wall, or the grounds within. Once, these nearer regions had been the object of his intensest curiosity, but his curiosity had expanded most remarkably in recent weeks, and now it was the further distances which excited him. He was no longer the boy that he had formerly been.

He saw a harvest-spider moving ponderously along the wall towards him, and he silently commanded it to turn around and go the other way. He was not in the least surprised when it obeyed him. It was a very small kind of power, but it was revealing. In due course, no doubt, he would improve it, extending his dominion to bees and bats, mice and rats, birds and cats . . . and in the end, to merely human beings.

He had been merely human himself once, but no longer.

He was possessed by the Devil now.

He had not reached this conclusion easily, but once it had occurred to him, he could not doubt it. Perhaps, of course, it was only a lesser demon which inhabited him rather than Satan himself; Gabriel did not know exactly what possession usually involved, and Sister Clare – despite her evident fascination for the subject, which figured large in her homilies about the dangers of temptation – tended to be unclear in matters of fine detail. Thus, it might easily be a minion selected from the horde of those angels which fell with Satan, rather than the Devil himself, which had come to inhabit him. He could not tell.

He looked at his hand, and found that it was bleeding. There was a certain amount of pain, but the pain of such small injuries no longer seemed quite as unpleasant as it once had. In fact, the pain was allied with a curiously pleasant feeling of lightness – which made him wonder whether, if he only hurt himself badly enough, he would discover how to fly. He often dreamed of flying, and longed to master the art of it; he knew that it could be done because he had seen Sister Teresa floating in mid-air. She, of course, was assisted by a better kind of angel, but he felt very strongly that whatever her angels could do for her, his demon might one day do for him.

He had grazed and gashed his hand while he hauled himself up the inner face of the high brick wall which surrounded Hudlestone Manor and its grounds. He had clung fast to the ivy which cloaked the ancient surface, gasping with fright every time a portion of stem was pulled away by his weight. The cement between the bricks was crumbling, and the ivy's purchase was insecure, but still he had climbed, determined to reach the top.

His demon liked him to climb, just as it liked him to prowl the grounds by night, because both activities were forbidden. Gabriel thought that it was probably his fondness for forbidden things which had allowed the demon to take possession of his soul – the Sisters had given him fair warning of it, and he had not listened. Now, it was too late.

At first, he had been very frightened when he realized what had happened, but he had learned to accept it. He liked to keep secrets, and this was the greatest secret imaginable. And after all, a demon who could add pleasure to pain might be a valuable friend in a world which was so very full of hurts.

The first time Gabriel had climbed the wall – sternly urged on by his friend Jesse Peat – had been some six weeks earlier, shortly before his ninth birthday. It had seemed to him then to be the greatest achievement of his life, not so much because climbing the wall was one of the many small rites of passage celebrated by the foundlings who lived in Hudlestone Lodge, but because it had allowed him to look out for the first time upon the vast world which lay beyond the wall.

Now, only forty days later, he felt very different in himself, though he could not pin down the moment when the change had come over him. When he tried, he could remember only a more distant moment of revelation, which might or might not have something to do with his present state.

That first bright moment of enlightenment had come upon him last autumn, when he had emerged from the Lodge to go with his fellows to the Manor for morning prayers to find that there was an exceptionally heavy dew, which had been precipitated on thousands upon thousands of spiders' webs. He had looked at those webs, festooning the bushes and the grass, and had suddenly realized that they must have been there all the time, made invisible by their thinness and delicacy. That was when it had first become clear to him, in some inarticulate fashion, that the appearances which the world presented to the human eye were essentially deceptive. He had realized then that spiders – which had previously seemed uncommon and unimportant – formed an invisible legion all about him.

Perhaps, he now thought, the demon *had* been within him even then, lurking silently like a hidden spider, sending him insights which he had innocently taken for his own. Perhaps the more recent manifestations of the demon's presence and intelligence were not a beginning at all, but simply the latest phase of a possession which had begun before he was conscious of his own existence, before he had ever discovered himself as a foundling child within the precincts of Hudlestone Manor.

Such unanswerable questions did not seem to matter much. What mattered far more was a very different question: could he escape from the Manor before the nuns found out what he really was?

Escape was a favourite topic of conversation among the children at the Lodge – among the boys, at any rate. Jesse Peat talked about it all the time. Sometimes boys actually did run away, usually after they had been beaten a little more severely than custom warranted; they were always brought back, because they had nowhere to run to. Gabriel, however, had every reason to think that he might be an exception to that rule. He had a demon to guide him, and friends who had already offered to help him. Morwenna had told him that she knew what he truly was, and that she would gladly take him away to be with others of his kind. He did not know exactly what she meant by that, because he did not know what his kind was – unless she meant others who had demons inside them – but she clearly knew that he was not like the other children, and on that account alone he was disposed to trust her.

Morwenna, moreover, always spoke to him kindly, and often smiled at him, which made her different on two counts from Mrs Capthorn and her son Luke, and from the tight-lipped Sisters of St Syncletica.

Gabriel licked away the beads of blood which oozed from the cuts on his right hand and wrist. He was glad that he was no longer so troubled by the pain, for that could be turned to his advantage as a sign of status. Such signs were important in the community of his peers. Boys were not supposed to care about blood, or pain, or injury. Before the demon had possessed him, Gabriel had found some difficulty in maintaining that appearance, but now it was easy. He no longer lived in fear of the day when he must face the severest test of fortitude which his friends had to bear – for he had never yet been beaten, either by Luke Capthorn or by one of the Sisters. He had seen the dreadful effort which Jesse and others had to exert if they were to refrain from tears in such a situation, and had once been sure that he would be unable to copy them, but now he knew that he had little enough to fear, as long as the demon was inside him.

Gabriel did not know why he had never been beaten. The fact that he had never deserved it was an insufficient explanation, for he had certainly seen others beaten who had not deserved it either. It was something of a puzzle, because he was quite well aware of the fact that he was not liked. Mrs

Capthorn and Luke seemed to detest him, and the Sisters, though they posed as saintly persons incapable of hatred, did not care for him at all. The other children were immune to his best attempts to make them as fond of him as they sometimes were of one another, and he knew that the friendship and tolerance which Jesse Peat had sometimes shown him were not based in any honest affection. He had always been at a loss to account for his unpopularity, for he knew that he was not an ugly or ill-tempered child, but he had learned to mask his resentment.

Now, though, he asked himself whether the others had somehow known all along, without quite knowing what it was that they knew, that he was not one of their kind at all, but something else: demon-haunted, demon-possessed.

The taste of blood upon his tongue was not at all unpleasant – indeed, it was rather intoxicating. Perhaps, he thought, the demon was determined to teach him a love of evil, to counteract the love of virtue which the Sisters had struggled so hard to impart to him. Perhaps the demon's first and most frequent lesson would be devoted to teaching him to love cuts and blows, just as the Sisters' first and most frequent lesson was devoted to teaching their charges to fear them.

He looked up from his licking, and tried to put the demon out of his mind by looking hard at the world beyond the wall.

When he had first been granted a sight of the greater world Gabriel had been sorely disappointed not to find it more wonderful than it was. He had looked at it, and there it had been; all its anticipated marvels were present. He felt a sense of limitation because the actual world did not in any way surpass his dreams. Every time he had returned to the top of the wall he had felt the tug of that longing to find something new and exciting, but there was never anything there. Only his inner, demonic eye could show him miracles.

This particular part of the wall was one which he had not previously climbed, but there was nothing to be seen now which he had not seen before. Far away to his right were the houses on the outskirts of Greenford. In the other direction, the rooftops of Perivale were just visible.

The canal, which Jesse had pointed out to him from another vantage-point, was not visible from here. He did not care about that, though Jesse would have. Jesse had been brought to the foundling home by a boatman, and he believed that his true home must be a barge. Jesse's fantasies of escape never entertained the notion of flight by road or railway; it was by water that he intended to make his way to London, and on the water that he expected to find his destiny. Jesse had boasted that he frequently climbed over the wall in order to go to the canal and make friends with the bargemen, and Gabriel believed that he had done so once or twice at least, for he had twice seen Jesse beaten by Luke Capthorn for being caught out of bounds.

On the slope facing him there was a house set in high-walled grounds, the only other dwelling close enough to be seen in any detail. Jesse had told him that it was Charnley Hall Asylum. 'Place for loonies,' his informant had laconically observed. 'Baker's boy told me he can hear 'em scream betimes – mostly when the moon be full. Says they 'owl like wolves an' rattle their chains, but I never heard 'em. There's a bigger loony-bin in Hanwell, where they've 'undreds chained up. Baker's boy says some of *us* were born there, but 'e don't know which. Reckon he's a liar.'

Gabriel had heard Sister Clare's account of Jesus casting out devils from those afflicted with madness, and he could not help but wonder now whether *he* might have been one of those born in the loony-bin, there inheriting the seeds of his recent possession.

This was not a thought he liked, so he put it out of his mind and let his gaze roam back and forth across the panorama which was spread before him. He could see the roof of the Manor and the roof of the Lodge, but there were few windows from which he might himself be seen – most were screened by foliage. That was just as well, because climbing the wall was presumably against the rules. No one had ever told him so in so many words, but he knew from long experience that whatever was not demanded of him was likely to be proscribed.

This was not such a difficult regime to live under as it might have been. In the Lodge, where the foundlings were housed, the rules were easily reducible to a few principles of procedure. All that the Capthorns really required of the children in their care was silence and unobtrusiveness. The skill of living in the Lodge was all contained in the meek art of going unnoticed; to be noticed was to be guilty of 'bothering', and the Capthorns did not like to be 'bothered'.

Despite the fact that the Capthorns disliked him, Gabriel had become a 'good boy' who troubled them little. It was not so easy to deal with the Sisters who lived at the Manor, because they had a much keener sense of the letter of the law. The Sisters were concerned mainly with the schooling of the foundlings – with their education in the catechism and as much additional indoctrination as their brains could accommodate – and their requirements were more demanding. But in the Convent, too, Gabriel was regarded as a good boy, and an unusually clever one.

Gabriel's cultivation of the art of goodness had, of course, been motivated far more by terror of possible consequences than by any genuine desire to please, but the Sisters did not seem to mind that. They liked to school the children in what they considered to be an altogether healthy fear of the sternness of the Lord. Alas, the Lord seemed to Gabriel distant from the realm of the everyday; it was the Sisters themselves who terrified him with their ferocious expectations, their unbending demands, and their urgent concern for his soul.

Gabriel could see nothing from his present coign of vantage of those parts of the grounds where vegetables were grown, where the older foundlings must occasionally labour under the supervision of the Sisters, weeding or plucking as the season required. Hereabouts, wilderness held sway; blackberry and hawthorn bushes competed vigorously with nettles and other weeds.

He became suddenly stiff when he caught sight of a person moving among the thorny bushes, thinking that because the person wore a habit she might be Sister Clare or the Reverend Mother, and he relaxed only slightly when he realized that it was in fact Sister Teresa.

Sister Teresa did no teaching; the other foundlings were probably unaware of her existence. Lately, though, her existence had become something of which Gabriel could not help but be aware. Since the demonic sight had grown within him, showing him things which children – perhaps all men – were not supposed to see, the soul of Sister Teresa had become a perverse beacon set upon a sea of confusion. Gabriel *knew* Sister Teresa, not outwardly but inwardly. He knew what she was, and what she hoped and intended to become.

Gabriel even knew what Sister Teresa was doing now, though her back was towards him and he could not see her busy hands.

She was collecting thorns, which she intended to shape into a crown.

The work would prick her fingers, and she would bleed as Gabriel had. Like him, she was no longer distressed by pain, and was prepared to welcome its intoxications.

Gabriel was fascinated by Sister Teresa; he was also afraid of her, because he harboured a terrible suspicion that if she ever saw him, and looked into his eyes, then she would immediately see what he was – for she too had a kind of inner sight, which was not at all demonic.

Sister Teresa was determined to become a saint, and saints, like Jesus himself, had the power to find and punish demons. Gabriel did not want his possessive demon to be found, and was mortally afraid of what it might do to him were he to expose it to punishment. He knew only too well that he had collaborated with his possessor, and had casually allowed it to corrupt him. He liked the power which the demon gave him, and would not easily surrender the privilege of inner sight no matter what nightmarish things it allowed him to see. He knew only too well what life unpossessed and unseeing was

like, at least for those who had no homes or families, and no
matter how good a boy he was in his outward observance of
rules and requirements, he had no love of virtue adequate to
make him repent of what he knew he had become.

If he had to put his trust in anyone, he would far rather trust
Morwenna and his demon than God or any of *His* servants.

Carefully, holding very tightly to the precarious ivy, Gabriel
lowered himself to the ground again. When he was safely
down he ran into the bushes, heading away from the place
where he had seen the girl who was gathering thorns. When
he was safely away he reverted to his play, cocksure with the
spirit of adventure – until the twilight began to fade and Luke
Capthorn came after him, cursing and hullooing by turns, in
an obvious state of botheration.

2

Gabriel followed Luke Capthorn back to the Lodge at a
trot, hurrying to keep up with him. Luke muttered as he
strode, his complaints mingled with soft curses, alleging
that Gabriel was a dratted nuisance who was always making
trouble for him, and a little bastard who ought to know
his place.

Luke was fond of reminding the children that few of them
knew who their fathers had been; one of the few advantages
he had in life was having been born in wedlock. This advantage
had proved meagre enough; Mr Capthorn had deserted his
wife and son long ago, and was as much the stuff of legend
in the foundling home as King Herod or the werewolves of
London.

It was not until they reached the Lodge that Gabriel realized
that it had not been a random whim which had sent Luke forth
to search for him. He was taken into Mrs Capthorn's parlour,

where a metal tub was already placed upon the table and extra kettles had been set about the fire.

Mrs Capthorn moved to help Gabriel to undress – a process which he made as difficult as possible, not because he hated being scrubbed but because he did not like Mrs Capthorn's plump and energetic fingers. Mercifully, she had to leave him in order to attend to the delicate business of mixing hot water and cold to precisely that temperature which nature and her own sense of exactitude ruled proper for the bathing of young boys. This left him to complete the embarrassing business by himself. When he had clambered up on to the table-top and into the tub Mrs Capthorn hurled his winter clothes away into a corner. The time had arrived for a new suit.

Gabriel had always felt very keenly the indignity of such encounters as this. He hated all the times at which his person became a mere instrument of one of Mrs Capthorn's projects. Now that his body had become a mere mask sheltering the power and intelligence of his possessor his dislike was vastly increased, and yet he submitted. Outwardly he remained a nine-year-old boy, and in that fashion the world was still disposed to treat him. Although he had a power within him to defy such treatment, he was loath to release it, for he had as yet no plan which could guide him through the aftermath of any violent expression of resentment.

Once he was accustomed to the sting of the water its heat became a luxury, but any hope of languid enjoyment was lost when Mrs Capthorn took up her brush. To her bathing was the equivalent of confession, scrubbing of absolution. When Gabriel was sufficiently absolved of his mundane filthiness Mrs Capthorn promptly hauled him out of the tub, and called for Luke to bring in whichever child was fortunate enough to inherit his dirty water, for it could not be wasted.

Not until his new clothes had been tied and pinned about him – feeling very loose and baggy after the set which he had outgrown – did Mrs Capthorn consent to inform him of the reason for all the fuss.

'Got a visitor,' she informed him, glumly. 'Sends round to

say he'm coming, an' we all jump to it. But don't go gettin' ideas, young scamp, 'cause you've a gemmun comin' t'see ye. It don't make ye better than any'un else.'

Gabriel had been similarly admonished before, and had been given more pointed reminders by Luke, whose opinion was that even if Gabriel was a landowner's bastard – which was by no means proven – he was still a bastard, and hence worth less than any man who had his father's name. But Gabriel had noticed that the Sisters seemed to have a different attitude. Despite their hatred of sin in all its manifestations they were subtly different in their treatment of him by virtue of the fact that he had a benefactor of some quality. They were far more careful to correct his manner of speech, and exercised restraint in their treatment of him.

'D'ye know the name o' the man ye have t'see?' asked Mrs Capthorn sternly, when she had fitted him out to her satisfaction.

'Mr Harkender,' replied Gabriel, mechanically.

'That's right,' she confirmed. 'An' be sure to tell 'im 'ow well looked arfter y'all are . . . by the Sisters 'n' all.'

Gabriel looked up at her then, straight into her rheumy eyes. She started back a little, before her reflexes brought a frown to her ruddy features. Perhaps she had said such things before, but if and when she had Gabriel had considered it just one more command in an endless litany. Now, for the first time, it occurred to him that he had a favour to dispose – that it might have consequences for her if he uttered a complaint. He knew, of course, that worse consequences would surely fall upon him if he did anything to annoy her – but still, he had it in him to cause her distress, and Luke too, even without invoking the power of his inner demon.

Mrs Capthorn seemed to be awaiting a reply, and he struggled to find one. 'Has he . . .?' he began, but then stopped.

''As 'e what?' demanded Mrs Capthorn, impatiently.

'Has he come to take me away?'

'Ha!' said Mrs Capthorn, discovering the aspirant with a

flourish of self-congratulation. 'Wants ter leave, hey? Can't wait t'get away from them as raised ye. Ungrateful rag!' Mrs Capthorn handed him over to Luke again, to be taken up to the Manor.

As they came through the gardens they saw Sister Clare waiting for them by the door of the Annexe, which was the name the Sisters gave to the part of the Manor which was used as a school. Sister Clare, as usual, was fervent with righteous petulance, and Luke had no more immunity than anyone else to the effects of her moods.

'Where have you been?' she demanded of Luke. 'Mr Harkender is *waiting*.'

Luke knew better than to offer an excuse, but muttered his apology as ungraciously as he dared. The Sister took Gabriel by the hand, and dragged him away. The pressure of her fingers on his abrasions made them smart; he was briefly surprised by the pain. His slight wince only made the nun pull harder, because she took it as a symptom of recalcitrance.

Sister Clare delivered him into a sitting-room, where three people awaited him. One was the Reverend Mother and one was Jacob Harkender, but he had never previously seen the woman who sat beside Harkender – an angular, grey-haired woman, seemingly older than Sister Clare but by no means as ancient as the Reverend Mother. Gabriel took up a position facing the two visitors, while the Reverend Mother looked on from his right-hand side.

'How are you, Gabriel?' asked Harkender. He spoke softly, but he had never seemed to Gabriel to be a kindly man and he did not seem so now. In fact, as Gabriel felt the alien eye within him focusing with interest on Jacob Harkender's face, he was struck by the certainty that this was a man who had never known kindness at all, and was bitter through and through.

Harkender was by no means unhandsome, and his features were soft and rounded, but there was a hawkishness about his dark eyes which implied some kind of predatory inclination. His lips were full and he wore his hair in curious waves, and could seem womanish when he was relaxed, but when he smiled he seemed subtly menacing and delicately cruel.

Gabriel had never liked Jacob Harkender, despite the fact that he had been told often and anon what a debt of gratitude he owed to the man. Nor had he ever been convinced that Harkender liked *him* any better than anyone else did. Nevertheless, he was surprised how sharp his inner vision seemed as he stared at Harkender now. The demon within him was more excited by this visitation than Gabriel alone could ever have been.

'Very well, sir, thank you,' answered Gabriel, belatedly. He enunciated the words carefully, well aware that the propriety of his speech was on trial, in every respect.

'You have grown handsomely,' said Harkender, pleasantly, adding: 'Has he not, Mrs Murrell?'

Mrs Murrell had never seen him before, and was in no position to make comparisons, but she nevertheless replied: 'Quite handsomely.'

'But you have hurt your hands,' the man went on. 'Show them to me.'

Gabriel had been holding his arms straight at his sides, but now he put them out in front of him, palms upwards. Harkender took them in his own, and turned them over, then back again. 'How did you do that?' he asked, sharply.

Gabriel shrugged his shoulders, though he knew it would not be reckoned an acceptable reply. The Reverend Mother leaned forward, and he glanced sideways at her, meeting the stare of her dark eyes.

'He has been climbing,' she said, confidently. 'That is what you did, Gabriel, is it not?' Her voice was accented; though her English was perfect, it was not her native tongue.

Gabriel bowed his head, not liking to admit to the transgression, but Harkender seemed relieved to hear the explanation.

'It is in the nature of boys to climb walls,' said Harkender, silkily.

'The girls never do,' observed the Reverend Mother. 'They know better how to obey.'

'It is not a matter of obedience,' said Harkender, 'but a matter of will. The will which a girl has takes her by a different path, but a boy's will makes him climb. Yet boys and girls alike have it in them to be sinners . . . or saints.'

The Reverend Mother did not seem convinced.

'Did it hurt?' asked Harkender of Gabriel.

'No, sir,' Gabriel replied, automatically.

'Oh, but it did,' Harkender contradicted him. 'I know it did. But perhaps the hurt did not matter. Perhaps you had such a passion to climb that it mattered not at all, if only you could reach new heights. Was that it, Gabriel?' Harkender's tone was light, but not bantering. Indeed, Gabriel felt that he was under very close scrutiny – closer than the scrutiny which he came under when he was interrogated by the Sisters as to the sinfulness of his heart, or by the priest who came to the Manor every Sunday to hear confessions. *They* could be bluffed; Gabriel was not so sure that his enigmatic benefactor was as vulnerable to deceit as that. Something in the way that Harkender stared at him made him wonder whether the man was somehow aware of the change that had come over him, and of the fact of his possession.

Still, when he said yes – which was clearly what Harkender wanted to hear – the gentleman gave no sign of understanding that Gabriel neither knew nor cared whether it was the literal truth.

'Reverend Mother,' said Harkender, evenly, 'I wonder if you would leave us alone for a little while.' He offered no excuse or explanation, but plainly expected to be obeyed, and the Reverend Mother showed no sign of resentment. She rose and left the room, after one last ominous glance to remind Gabriel to mind his diction.

'Now,' said Harkender, 'we can talk as man to man. I was schooled by the Jesuits, and I remember how terrifying a presence they were. I felt that I could only talk freely when they were not there.'

Gabriel had never heard of the Jesuits, but he knew well enough the feeling to which Harkender alluded. Alas, he found the presence of his benefactor and the mysterious Mrs Murrell not one whit less inhibiting.

'You are well grown now,' said Harkender, with apparent satisfaction. 'I feel that I can address you now as a thinking being, and I want to talk to you about your future.'

Gabriel could think of no reply to make. On the matter of possible futures his mind was blank.

'Have you learned all your letters?' asked Harkender, twitching his hands again with a certain impatience.

'No, sir,' said Gabriel.

That was not the answer that Harkender wanted, but Gabriel knew only too well that any claim which he made would be put to the proof. Luckily, Harkender's annoyance – in so far as it showed at all – seemed not to be directed at him.

'What did you expect?' asked Mrs Murrell. 'The Sisters' first concern is for the welfare of his soul.'

'No matter,' said Harkender, to Gabriel. 'There is time, and it is not so very important. What is vital is that you must be healthy and strong. I have long intended to find a better home for you than this, but there have been reasons why I could not bring you to my own house. I have been away too often, and when at home have been involved in experiments which have absorbed my attention very fully. The Sisters have so far served your needs better than my house-servants could have, and have hidden you away from undesirable curiosity, but now your needs are becoming such that the Sisters are no longer adequate to them. I have brought Mrs Murrell to see you because I may put you in her charge – not immediately, but very soon.'

Gabriel was glad to be able to look away from Harkender, whose stare had begun to disconcert him terribly, to study Mrs Murrell. She made no attempt to meet his enquiring eye with a smile or any other gesture of tenderness, but neither did she seem so icily disapproving of him as the Sisters did. He could not tell from such a brief appraisal how she might compare with Mrs Capthorn.

'What have you to say?' asked Harkender.

'Thank you, sir,' replied Gabriel, reflexively. It was what people usually wanted when they asked him what he had to say, but in this case it would not serve.

Harkender sighed.

'You cannot blame the boy,' said Mrs Murrell. 'He does not know who we are. He has seen you before, but he does not know you.' She turned her gaze upon Gabriel, and went on: 'It was Mr Harkender who first brought you here, to the Sisters. He placed you in their care, and gave them money to pay for your keep – and one or two others besides, for not every orphan has someone to provide for him. He has taken responsibility for you, and must prepare you to take on responsibilities of your own. Are you ready to repay the generosity which he has shown to you?'

Gabriel, not knowing how to answer honestly, said: 'Yes, thank you, ma'am.'

With this, Mrs Murrell seemed satisfied – but Harkender knew the reply for the mechanical response that it was.

'Mrs Murrell is right,' said Harkender. 'You do not know me at all. It is my own fault. I should have come to see you more often, though there were reasons why I did not. You are old enough now to be curious, and perhaps old enough to understand the fruits of curiosity. You must ask me the questions which are in your mind, and I will try to answer them. By that means, we will come to know one another better, and you will learn to trust the plans which I make for you. Ask me, Gabriel, whatever you want to know.'

Gabriel hesitated, quite out of his depth. It was an unprecedented situation, and he had no stock response, nor any which seemed as if it might suitably be borrowed. He had no idea where the limits of safety lay, but cast about for a question which might be acceptable. Had his demon prompted him, he would have been pleased to listen, but the alien presence was mute and fascinated, present but not active.

In the end, he said: 'Was I born in the loony-bin?'

He saw the surprise on Mrs Murrell's face from the corner of his eye, but the expression on Harkender's face was quite unfathomable. Harkender did not reply immediately, but first collected his thoughts.

'I presume that you mean the asylum at Hanwell,' he said, gravely. 'I dare say that some of your companions come from there. You do not.'

'Who is my mother?' asked Gabriel, deciding suddenly that the opportunity must be taken. 'And who is my father?'

Again Harkender paused before replying, but then said: 'Your mother was called Jenny Gill. She died soon after you were born. She was a friend of Mrs Murrell's, and I knew her too. You bear her name and not your father's, but there is no need for you to feel an atom of shame about that, for you are better born than anyone else within these grounds – though you had better not say so to anyone, least of all the Sisters.' Harkender smiled when he had said that, and Gabriel knew that the smile was intended to be conspiratorial, and comforting. In fact, it seemed harsh and humourless, a threat rather than a promise.

'I promise that you will like living with Mrs Murrell,' continued Harkender, whose voice had dropped almost to a whisper. 'You will have better food than you have so far known, and a better bed in which to sleep. And as for climbing – why, I will show you heights to scale which few men have ever dared, and I will teach you to find in their achievement a joy which few men know.'

Harkender's eyes seemed almost to glow as he spoke thus, though Gabriel could not understand why.

'Thank you, sir,' replied Gabriel, in a similar whisper, and this time, it seemed, Harkender read a sincerity in the reply which was not there, proving himself as vulnerable as anyone else. But then, as if guided by some impulsive afterthought, Harkender reached up to touch Gabriel's forehead with the tips of the fingers of his right hand. It seemed a careless, almost unthinking gesture, but when Gabriel felt the touch he knew immediately that it was nothing of the kind.

There was a kind of power in the touch; a thrill of magic. The thought instantly sprang into Gabriel's mind that Harkender too was possessed: that he had a demon lurking inside him which looked out upon the world through the window of his corrupted soul, with a kind of sight more powerful by far than the feeble outer eyes of men.

He was afraid, because he feared that what he had seen in Harkender, Harkender might now be able to see in him: that his secret was secret no longer. His heart seemed to skip a beat as he waited with horror to see how Harkender would react to the revelation.

There was a fleeting expression of puzzlement upon the man's face, which was quickly replaced by another smile: a smile which was as ungenerous as all the others, yet oddly full of satisfaction.

'Why, Gabriel,' said Jacob Harkender. 'You must not be afraid of me. Of all the men you will ever meet, I alone can understand what you are and what you might become. I alone can guide you. You must remember that, Gabriel. Always remember that I am your friend.'

This speech was delivered in an even tone, and yet it seemed to Gabriel very intimidating. Harkender was not trying to threaten him – perhaps he was, indeed, honestly trying to reassure him – but the mere fact of what Harkender seemed to be, and what Harkender might now know, was sufficient to fill Gabriel with an awful trepidation.

But all he said, mustering the skills which a lifetime of deceit had cultivated within him, was: 'Yes, sir.'

Jacob Harkender smiled again, having received the answer which he wanted – but behind the smile, there was something else, which Gabriel could not name and did not like at all.

3

It was dark outside, and the wind carried a biting chill. The moon was nearly full but its face was first veiled by racing clouds, then revealed again for a few teasing moments. Gabriel was supposed to return forthwith to the Lodge, but no one was now on hand to guide him so he slipped away from the path to skirt the walls of the Manor. He felt the presence of the demon within him, hot and excited, and he knew how the demon loved his nocturnal expeditions.

In the dark of the night Gabriel sometimes felt that he was *all* demon, and that the ordinary consciousness which thrived on daylight, routine, and the company of others was veiled and hidden, just as the face of the moon was veiled by the clouds which passed before it.

He was very conscious of the power of his will, but he had no interest now in such delicate tricks as summoning bats and moths to flutter about his head in a madcap dance. His inner eye was in search of more interesting sights than that.

He made his way, carefully, to the further side of the Manor, which was strictly out of bounds. There the sisters had their 'cells', which were mostly not cells at all, but merely sparsely furnished and undecorated rooms. There were many more sisters there than were ever called upon to assist in the Annexe; most chose to be secluded, devoting their lives to ritual and introspection. The teaching of the foundlings was a duty shouldered by a few, in a spirit of self-sacrifice; lately, he had come to understand that they regarded it as a price to be paid for their tenancy of the Manor, and that they paid it grudgingly.

This was one of the many things which he had come to know and understand by means of his demon, which was a creature of prodigious intelligence. Despite that intelligence, though, it was plainly a stranger in the world of men, and it found much of what went on there curious and inexplicable.

Gabriel made his way to a place which he had recently found, from which he could see into the cell which most deserved that title: the cellar where Sister Teresa lived and prayed, with only stone to kneel upon, while the deathly cold shivered and mortified her fragile flesh.

The room had only a single window, set just beneath its

ceiling, which opened up into a culvert below ground level. The window-glass was so grimy that it let in little light by day, and let out only the merest flicker of candle-light by night; all that a peeping Tom could see of what went on within was blurred and inexact, and it was barely possible for ordinary eyes to judge whether the person within was standing or kneeling. Nevertheless, the window drew Gabriel like a magnet, for he did not need his outer eyes to be sensitive to what went on within that cell. With his inner, demonic eye, he could see quite clearly what Sister Teresa did to her wasted, tormented flesh – and why.

By the time he took up his position the active part of her ritual was already over, and she was lying prone upon her cold floor, as though the entire weight of the earth were pressing upon her, coldly and implacably. All sensible thought was already banished from her mind, and Gabriel braced himself to share her dream, her vision, and her illuminating pain.

Jesus is on the cross. The world's pain is not so sharp now; feeling has retreated from the surface, which is exposed to the erosions of wind and water, cracked by eruptions of volcanic fire. But in the mantle of the world there is a perpetual serenity; a cool solidity remote from that central soul which is fire and liquid iron.

The world still thinks, but its thoughts, like its feelings, have become dulled by overload. The world-mind is dizzy and slow, as though remote from itself, and there is darkness by day and cold at noon – but this mind will soon suffer a delirium from which it will never entirely recover.

Jesus is bearing the weight of the sins of the world.

The nails driven through the palms of her hands are all the evil actions which men have ever done: all the slayings and the beatings; all the carving of vile idols; all the writing of impious thoughts; all the caresses and gestures which spoke falsely of affection and amity.

The great nail driven through her overlapping feet is all the evil intentions which men have had which moved them hither and yon about the world: all flights from just retribution; all invasions and conquests; all denials of kinship and strayings from the true path of faith and hope and duty.

The crown of thorns upon her head is all the treacherous thoughts which men have ever admitted through the manifold failures of the wayward will: all careful doubts and faithless deceptions; all calculated enmities and selfish envies; all bleak despair and treasons of the intellect.

The bleeding wound in her side is all the errors of the heart: all spiteful malices and burning hatreds; all brave delusions of grandeur and luxurious desires of lust; all hungry avarice and aching bitterness; all cravings of the cowardly flesh.

She bears it all, and clothes it with her ecstasy.

Ecce homo.

The sheer force of the vision made Gabriel recoil, breathlessly. He felt a sharp sensation of sin, neither dreadful nor delicious, which was born of his knowledge that through his agency a demon from Hell was spying on the business of Heaven. While Sister Teresa advanced along the painful road to sainthood he was the instrument by means of which she was patiently observed, through which the frustration of her best and finest works was plotted.

He smiled, but knew that it was only the demon which possessed him, trying to laugh at his feebleness.

Through the filthy window, he saw Teresa's blurred form begin to move, slowly and smoothly. She had not stood, but merely risen. Her arms outstretched like angel's wings, she floated. She drifted like a languid hawk on an invisible cushion of air, moved by the faintest of draughts.

Whether it was the advantage which good had over evil, or whether it was simply the outcome of discipline and practice, Gabriel could not tell, but this was as yet one art which Teresa had mastered and he had not, and it filled him with jealousy. If there was anything in him which might be called an ambition, it was that the force of evil should one day do as much for him as the force which moved in Teresa did for her. Again he wondered whether he could do it, if only he dared to submit himself to the extremes of pain which Teresa gladly accepted.

He came away from the window then, driven to extend his spying to other parts of the Manor. He returned to the Annexe, to the window of a room very close to the one where he had been confronted by Jacob Harkender, where Harkender was now in conference with the Reverend Mother, with Mrs Murrell again looking on. He did not need his inner vision to overhear what was being said.

'Is it now your intention to take the boy into your own care within the month?' asked the Superior.

'I am still uncertain,' Harkender replied. 'You have looked after him well and you have my gratitude for that, but I wonder whether he is old enough now to embark upon the next stage of his education. I am sorry if I have not given you fair warning, but it was not until I saw him just now that I realized how much he has grown.'

'And what, precisely, do you intend to make of him?'

At this question Harkender paused for an instant, but he answered freely enough: 'He will enter my service, Reverend Mother.'

Gabriel saw that the Reverend Mother had seated herself, but stiffly, as if making a virtue of her disciplined discomfort.

'No doubt you are of the opinion, Mr Harkender,' she said, coldly, 'that you are free to make of the child whatever you wish, and that having brought him here you are free to take him away as you please. You will understand, though, that my own point of view shows the matter in a different light. You have placed Gabriel in our care, and made it our duty to see that he is properly civilized and prepared for a Christian life. We have an interest in him which cannot simply be wiped out, and my duty compels me to investigate his prospects.'

'Certainly,' said Harkender, whose voice had become equally frosty. 'Perhaps you will tell me what it is that troubles your conscience.'

'If I may speak frankly, sir,' said the Reverend Mother, 'it is your reputation. Rumour calls you a magician, an alchemist, and a necromancer.'

At this, Mrs Murrell drew in her breath very sharply; but so far as Gabriel could see, Jacob Harkender gave not the slightest indication of being perturbed by the challenge.

'You need have no fear for the boy's safety,' he said, calmly. 'I am a scholar, it is true, but there is nothing diabolical in my enquiries. Our Church has not been ashamed in the past to play host to alchemy, and if I am a magician, I am of the same breed as Albertus Magnus and Marcello Ficino, not a tawdry witch or a pact-making sorcerer. I will not argue matters of heresy with you, but if you know of any evidence which proves me guilty of material vice, feel free to present it to me.'

'I wish only to be assured that Gabriel's soul, which we have cared for most carefully, will not be endangered,' said the Reverend Mother, quite blandly. The statement seemed to Gabriel to conceal a terrible irony, and he suspected that Harkender must have the same attitude, but still the man gave no outward sign of annoyance or amusement.

'You may be sure,' said Harkender, 'that I care for his soul no less than you do, and that I am by no means poorly equipped to look after it. I was schooled by the Jesuits, as you know, and am well versed in the ways of the Church. My house can bear investigation, Reverend Mother, by the Bishop or any other inquisitor, as well as your own establishment can, and you have my leave to put me to the proof.'

Gabriel understood almost nothing of this, and there was for once no flood of mysterious intuition of the kind which he had learned to credit to the insights of his demonic guest.

The Reverend Mother seemed content with the statement, after her unsmiling fashion. 'I sought only to reassure myself,' she said, softly. 'Our interest in Gabriel will not cease when he leaves these grounds – of that you may be assured.'

'I welcome your interest,' said Harkender, smoothly. 'And I look forward to your pursuit of it, though I fear that your propensity for seclusion will make it difficult.'

The Reverend Mother stood up then, and gave them leave to do likewise. Before they emerged into the night Gabriel had ample time to conceal himself in a dark nest of shadows, so that no one would see him. When the Reverend Mother left them, Sister Clare went in search of Luke Capthorn, who had been given charge of Harkender's carriage. Once they were alone, Mrs Murrell turned immediately to her companion.

'What is it that she knows about us?' she said. 'It was a mistake to bring the boy here, as I told you at the time.'

'She probably knows no more than the rumours which she cited,' said Harkender evenly. 'The degree of the Sisters' enclosure is evidently not sufficient to insulate them from the gossip of the county. It may be that they have sensed something odd and abnormal in the boy, but that is of little consequence. Gabriel has been more effectively hidden here than he could have been at my own house. My servants certainly know more than is good for them, and there are others who take too keen an interest in my work and my movements; I dared not take any risks when poor Jenny died, else the plan entire might have gone awry. I trust the Sisters far better than I could ever trust my friends.'

'Will she interfere?' asked Mrs Murrell.

'I doubt it. I gave her fair warning just now that she has more to fear from enquiries than I have. Her nuns' constitution has never been confirmed by Rome. Though the Rule which they observe claims descent from St Syncletica it is doubtful whether its authority could stand investigation. Their inheritance of Hudlestone Manor was conditional upon the Sisters accepting certain educational duties, and though such an acceptance may seem to many to be moving with the fashion of the times I think it has been uncomfortable for the Sisters themselves.'

'Do you mean that they cannot go against you for fear of losing the Manor?'

'I doubt that it would ever come to that. But the raising of any question would be an embarrassment which the Sisters would far rather do without – and I too have heard rumours, about the Reverend Mother's encouragement of girls recruited from the foundling home. She is, it is said, very enthusiastic to find saints and visionaries within her company. It is only twenty years since the last conspicuous outbreak of anti-Catholic fervour in this country, and English Protestants are only a little less avid than French socialists for tales of the iniquitous treatment of novices by the houses into which they are seduced. If the Reverend Mother wishes to discover a new St Teresa, she will wish to pursue that end very privately.'

Far from reassuring Mrs Murrell, this seemed to distress her even more. 'But surely that is proof that she knows *something*!' she said.

'Hardly,' said Harkender. 'If everyone who starved or whipped another were questing for enlightenment, the world would long ago have enjoyed an illumination most marvellous. I do not doubt that the Church has had its visionaries, but the likes of that lady and her company have not the slightest inkling of what those visionaries really were. I do not believe that there is any threat to our project from the Sisters of St Syncletica.'

'Let us hope that you are right,' said Mrs Murrell, dubiously.

The carriage arrived then, and Gabriel watched as Harkender helped his companion to climb into it. Then Harkender turned to exchange a few furtive words with Luke Capthorn, who seemed to be on curiously intimate terms with him.

Gabriel stayed where he was until the carriage drove away and Luke strode off in the direction of the Lodge. Only then did he consider it safe to emerge from hiding – but as he did so he heard the sound of a knuckle rapping upon the window at which he had been eavesdropping, and his heart sank as he turned to see the Reverend Mother looking sternly down at him where he stood, having carelessly made himself visible in the pool of light which spilled from the gas-lit room.

Gabriel went back into the building, shivering with all the pent-up anguish of a long-time transgressor who has finally been caught and knows what a reckoning there is to be faced. He felt sure that he would be whipped, and his confidence in the power of his demon to protect him from the pain of a flogging was waning rapidly.

Astonishingly, though, it was in a very different vein that the Reverend Mother addressed him.

'You have been a good boy, Gabriel,' she assured him. 'We have taught you to be a good boy, and you have learned the lesson well. I hope that whatever may happen to you now, you will always be the child which we have made of you.'

'Yes, Reverend Mother,' said Gabriel, with very anxious politeness. 'Thank you, Reverend Mother.'

'The world is a place of trial and tribulation,' the Reverend Mother continued, in such a strangely abstracted fashion that he began to wonder if she had even noticed that he had been prying into her affairs. 'Its perils are many, and you must be strong to withstand them. I do not speak of bodily strength alone, but of spiritual strength. Flesh cannot help but be weak, but the soul can be strong – and *must* be strong, if it is to withstand temptation. Do you understand me, Gabriel?'

'Yes, Reverend Mother,' said Gabriel, striving with all his might to seem honest and dutiful. 'Thank you.'

It was not entirely a lie. He thought, at least, that he understood what the Reverend Mother was trying to tell him. She and Sister Clare and Sister Bernard had all, in their various ways, tried to make the message clear: life was hard, but suffering had to be borne; the world was full of pain, but one must bear pain willingly, and keep the Faith.

'You will be led into temptation when you leave here,' the Reverend Mother promised him, 'and you will see much wickedness. But you have learned to pray, and when you pray to the Lord, he will arm you against temptation and protect you from evil. Even if you fall among wicked men, the Lord will be with you.'

Gabriel was tempted, for the briefest of moments, to ask her forthrightly whether Jacob Harkender was one of the wicked men of whom she spoke – but the moment when he might have voiced such an notion was quickly gone, and all that there remained to be said was, 'Yes, Reverend Mother, I will remember.'

Finally, he was allowed to go, over-fully fed with warnings against the sad state of the world, which seemed hardly relevant to his present situation. Luke Capthorn had long since returned to the Lodge, but the Reverend Mother saw no necessity to assign Gabriel a guide in order to make sure that he went where he was supposed to go. As it happened, he had had enough of spying for one night, and was content to go straight to the Lodge.

He was taken by surprise when, as he reached the darkest point of the path, mid-way between the two buildings, Morwenna moved silently from the trees to stand before him.

Morwenna was not at all like the Sisters, much less the rotund Mrs Capthorn or the angular Mrs Murrell. She seemed younger by far than any of them, and had long pale hair. She wore a white dress, not unlike ones which he had seen in certain pictures of angels; it was lightweight enough to seem ethereal.

'Gabriel,' she said to him, in a soft tone, 'what did Mr Harkender say to you? Has he told you that he will take you away?'

'Perhaps he will,' he said – not without difficulty, for the words caught in his throat. 'I don't know.'

'Don't be afraid,' she said. 'He means you no good, but we will not let him take you. Please don't be afraid.'

There was nothing malicious in what she said, and yet he guessed that she knew perfectly well that telling him not to be afraid was just as likely to frighten him as anything else she said.

'Who are you, Morwenna?' he asked, in a whisper. 'Are you a ghost?' He did not believe it, despite that he thought it necessary to ask. Nor could he believe that she was an angel; no matter how hard the Sisters had striven to indoctrinate him with a proper appreciation of the true scheme of things, he could not believe that angels commonly walked the earth. But he did not know what she was, or why she had come to promise him escape.

'I am Morwenna,' she told him, as patiently as though it were an answer to his question. 'Please don't be afraid. I'll come to you again, before Mr Harkender can take you away. We are your friends, and we will keep you safe. Be ready, Gabriel – we will come for you very soon now, I promise you.'

There was such enchantment in the way she spoke, such magical charm. He longed to believe her, and he *did* believe her, but he knew that in what she would not tell him, in what she would not trust him to be told, there was a vast confusion of mysteries. He wanted to go with her, because she was so beautiful, but there was a small and doubtful voice within him – *not* his demon – which wondered whether she had been sent as a messenger precisely because she was so beautiful, and could not be refused.

'I'll be ready,' he promised, though there was still a lump in his throat which made the promise awkward.

And then, quite suddenly, she was gone. It was as though she had turned around and vanished into a hidden door into the darkness. But when he looked in another direction, where there was a patch of bare ground brightly lit for a moment by the uncertain moon, he saw something large and very pale glide away in a more natural fashion.

It could only have been a stray hound, because even Gabriel Gill knew that there were no wolves in England – with the possible exception of the werewolves of London.

4

That night, while he slept in his hard bed – to whose lumpiness he had long since become accustomed – Gabriel dreamed very strangely and very vividly.

This kind of dreaming had lately come to be a common experience, and he knew that it was one of the ways in which his inner eye exercised itself while its sight grew gradually sharper.

He had quickly come to realize that some of the things which were seen by inner eyes were not true. Bizarre visions like the one which he had earlier shared with Sister Teresa were born of hope, ambition, terror, or anxiety. He was by no means certain, though, that all the visions of the inner eye were of that kind. Sometimes, he seemed to see actual things, which might have happened, or might actually *be* happening while he watched. It was one of the ironies of this remarkable sixth sense that the brief visions he experienced while waking seemed far less likely to be actual happenings than those which he dreamed while he was fast asleep.

Tonight, the central character in his dream was Jacob Harkender – which did not surprise him in the least, for he was still acutely conscious of the bond which had been forged between himself and his benefactor in the moment when it had been revealed to him that Harkender too was one of the possessed.

Gabriel was not physically present within the dream; it was as though the demon had briefly quit his body to go roaming in the night as an unfettered spirit, but had dragged Gabriel's own soul along with it in order to maintain whatever spell had made it captive.

His disembodied spirit found itself in a most curious room

at the top of a house – Harkender's house, he presumed – which was crowned by a huge hemispherical dome of many-coloured glass. Whether the house could really have such a dome, Gabriel did not know, and there was certainly something very odd about the appearance of the room, but still he felt that he was seeing something actual.

Beneath the dome, at the centre of the extrapolated sphere, was a peculiar contraption of wrought iron, to which Gabriel could not put a name. For some reason which he could not quite fathom it made him think of a spider's web – and if it were, then Jacob Harkender had been caught by it, for he was bound to its rim by tightly wound cords which secured his wrists. Harkender was quite naked; his eyes were closed, and he was speaking to himself in a quiet and rhythmic fashion, as though he were intoning to himself some oft-repeated penance.

Harkender was watched by two other people, one of whom was Mrs Murrell. Gabriel's dream-self was in more intimate touch with Mrs Murrell's thoughts than with Harkender's; he could sense her complex feelings, and was astonished to discover that what was presently most evident within that roil of mental confusion was a kind of contempt.

The floor beneath Harkender's feet was patterned by many thousands of small tiles, which formed a vast and intricate diagram whose core was a great array of concentric circles, from whose common centre the iron web was raised. The outermost circle was rimmed by a blood-red halo whose elements were shaped like the petals of a rose; outside this rim four limbs extended, each one resembling the trunk of a tree whose elaborate crowns of multitudinous leaves were also coloured tiles.

The outermost concentric circles were divided into sections, each inscribed with a word or symbol; the innermost circles were decorated in more elaborate fashion.

To Gabriel this intricate design was fascinating, but he could glean no information as to its meaning from the whirlpool of impressions that was Mrs Murrell's consciousness. It was not that Harkender had never explained the meaning of the symbols to her, but that she had not properly taken the information in, nor even tried hard to do so. As an apprentice in magic she knew full well that she had shown not the slightest promise.

The pattern of the dome above Harkender's head was by no means as intricate as the pattern on the floor, but it was complicated enough. Gabriel judged that on a bright day, as the sun described its path across the heavens, the coloured light which shone through the multifaceted dome would illuminate the tiles which decked the floor in a marvellous and constantly changing fashion, but it was dark now, and the light of the moon was impotent by comparison with the four bright lanterns which Harkender had placed in the corners of the room, on the four arms of the cross.

The lighting cast curious shadows about the room. Mrs Murrell had positioned her chair so that she was shrouded by the darkest of them. She was not in hiding, but she was glad to be unobtrusive; it was her pleasure to observe while not drawing attention to herself. Gabriel heard, echoing plaintively in her memory, the words which Harkender had used when he told her, sadly, that her inner eye was quite blind – walled up, he alleged, by the insistent comfort which she took from the ordinariness of the world.

Gabriel knew, as he eavesdropped on the woman's thoughts, that although she had never said so to Harkender, she disagreed with his opinion; she had never thought herself comfortable in the world, nor had she ever considered that she inhabited the ordinary part of it. In her own view, she was a purveyor and inhabitant of a dreamworld made by men's idiosyncrasies. Whether her inner eye was truly blind or not, she could not tell, but her outer eyes had a cynical interest in the bizarre performances which she arranged for her clients.

This was not the first time that Gabriel's demon had allowed him to look at the world through the filter of another's thoughts and another's beliefs, but Mrs Murrell was a more puzzling individual by far than Luke Capthorn or Sister Clare; he found it difficult to understand exactly what she was, and why she thought of herself so strangely. If the demon understood, no enlightenment flowed from it; perhaps the demon did *not* understand, for it had a kind of innocence which did not quite fit in with its awesome powers of insight.

Gabriel's dream-self heard Mrs Murrell address an ironic thought to herself, as clearly as if she had spoken the words aloud: *What more magical and insightful life could a woman lead than to be a mistress and commander of rich men's whores?*

The other person in the room was a young girl. Mrs Murrell looked upon her in a fashion which had something of the maternal in it, though it was by no means loving. Almost as though he were seeing exclusively with Mrs Murrell's eyes and Mrs Murrell's feelings, Gabriel watched the girl approach the naked man who was crouched on the floor. She moved tentatively, as though uncertain of her role, but he knew that Mrs Murrell had told her clearly enough what it was that she must do.

The girl was naked save for the instrument strapped to her loins: an overlong but not unduly girthed caricature of an erect penis. The dildo was made of wood but covered in soft leather, and it had a heel which fitted inside the girl's vagina. It had been so contrived by its maker with the intention that it should stimulate its wearer while it was put to use, but Mrs Murrell knew that it was far from perfect in that regard; that did not matter in this instance, because pleasure was irrelevant.

All of this was very difficult for Gabriel to comprehend. His only experience of sexual desire and fascination was second-hand. He knew what sexual intercourse was, and even what buggery was, because he had been a passenger in Luke Capthorn's mind in earlier dreams, and he had had some vague notion of what was involved even before he had been possessed, because of the tales and warnings about Luke's habits which circulated among the older children

at the Lodge. But the understanding which Gabriel had by
virtue of his knowledge of Luke Capthorn was inadequate
to deal with what was happening here.

Gabriel and Mrs Murrell watched while the girl crouched
behind the bound man, and clumsily tried to guide the dildo
into his anus. Mrs Murrell watched without amusement; the
girl did not look at her for guidance, or to offer any apology
for her clumsiness.

At last, at some expense to her own comfort, penetration
was achieved. The girl eventually succeeded in establishing
an approximate rhythm although the effort caused her some
distress – that was written plainly enough on her face, which
was ruddy with embarrassment.

Mrs Murrell permitted herself a little smile, and studied
the girl's face very carefully as the farce proceeded. Mrs
Murrell saw the slow emergence of signs that the girl was
becoming pleased with herself – not because of the grinding
of the instrument's heel within her, but by virtue of a much
more cerebal awareness of the fact that what was being done
was a kind of humiliation . . . and that she had been cast by
unusual circumstance in the role of humiliator.

That, Mrs Murrell knew, was what Harkender sought.
Pain was only a part of it, and perhaps not the greater part;
what he required was a more subtle chagrin compounded
out of bitterness and misery, which custom somehow could
not stale. He never used male whores, this way or the
other way about, for there was something in the release
of an ejaculation which spoiled his intention. He sought
no natural end or pause, but something potentially infinite;
more than that, he sought the involvement of some artifice,
which would change the usual order of things and turn the
design of nature upside-down, multiplying perversity in as
complex a fashion as ingenuity might permit.

Gabriel saw in the exotic welter of Mrs Murrell's thoughts
and feelings her memories of past occasions when Harkender
had tried to explain the thinking behind his private rituals,
but he could not read them. Mrs Murrell had not taken such

explanations seriously; she was well used to the sophistries which men constructed in order to explain and justify their aberrations, and thought them unnecessary lies. In the days of her own apprenticeship in whoredom she had quickly become indifferent to the business of penetration, whatever was being penetrated and by whom.

The soft flow of words from Harkender's lips had decayed into silence. He swayed, now, with the rhythm which the girl had contrived to attain, and which she still maintained with painstaking, if hardly effortless, determination.

Mrs Murrell rose from her chair, cane in hand, and approached the ludicrous couple. She was fully dressed, proud in her conspicuous neatness and composure. She began to beat Harkender across the shoulders and the back, not hurriedly but not too slowly. She made no attempt to match the rhythm of the couple's simulated copulation, but was meticulous in her own fashion, distributing the cuts with scrupulous attention to strength and direction.

Gabriel could see that she took no great pleasure in what she did – not even that pleasureful contempt of which the girl was still capable. He could see that Mrs Murrell had beaten many men in her time, though rarely in this fashion, which was the fashion of genuine punishment, the flogging of servants and prisoners rather than the titillating teasing which addicts of the English vice usually preferred. But it was not simply the craving for simultaneous buggery which necessitated Harkender's taking the cane upon his back instead of his bum, for it was obviously raw hurt that he wanted, not imaginatively negotiable stimulation. The legacy of a million cruel cuts was written upon him from shoulder to waist in sullen scar-tissue.

Gabriel understood this a little better; he had seen Teresa flog herself, and had seen the record of her suffering which was written across her back.

He wondered in an oddly detached fashion whether Harkender could fly. Perhaps his wrists were tied in order to bind him to the earth, lest he float away into the multi-coloured realm of light.

Harkender was quite silent now, though Gabriel knew via Mrs Murrell that he had not yet attained the state of mental being which he sought. He called the condition ecstasy; she called it trance. A medical man, she suspected, would have a Latin name for it.

The outward signs of Harkender's progress towards this mystical communion were few and slight. There was a moment when he turned his head slightly, as if to catch a faint whisper, and another when his eyes moved flittingly from side to side beneath the closed lids, but eventually there settled upon his face an expression of calm.

Mrs Murrell signalled to the girl to withdraw, which she did most gratefully, wincing with discomfort. Despite the chill in the air she was sweating with the effort of her exertions. Mrs Murrell led her away to the chair in the shadows. The stinking thing between her legs bobbed about, stubbornly erect, and now the girl looked down at it with evident distaste. Mrs Murrell helped her to remove it.

Although Harkender's measured incantation had died away, so that his lips had ceased to move and his larynx no longer stirred, Mrs Murrell believed – and Gabriel, with the demon's powers of divination at his disposal, knew – that the spoken song went on somewhere inside him. Gabriel knew that the magician was experiencing visions of some kind, attaining mysterious association with entities whose independent existence he had no reason to doubt, and he wished for a moment or two that it was Harkender's mind, and not the whoremistress's, which was open to his inspection. But Harkender had a demon of his own, which was presumably capable of keeping Gabriel's at bay.

Mrs Murrell's opinion was that Harkender's so-called magic consisted mainly of a talent for petty tricks of hypnotism. She believed that whatever was happening to the kneeling man was happening entirely within his own head, and that whatever he saw or heard was a mere delusion, which he produced unwittingly for his own satisfaction. She did not believe that some great army of supernatural beings lived above and beyond the material world of men, and certainly not that Jacob Harkender could enter their realm as an apprentice angel and pretender to godly power.

Gabriel believed that he knew better. Gabriel hesitated to doubt that the power within Harkender was real, and that the invisible beings with whom he was communing were equally real. Gabriel already knew that the solidity of the world was mere appearance, and that spirits – like spiders – might easily be everywhere, cloaked by their invisibility but nevertheless powerful.

Awesomely powerful.

Gabriel, watching Harkender, saw that the farcical attentions of the young whore were arbitrary items of apparatus, of purely personal significance. Mrs Murrell thought that the magic ritual was only mumbo-jumbo to dress up the sexual encounter, but she was wrong. The sexual encounter was only a drama, and the magic was very, very real.

If Harkender's desire was to be a companion and confidant of demons and their kin, there was nothing in the limits of possibility to forbid him, so far as Gabriel could judge.

Is this why he has appointed himself my guardian? Gabriel asked himself. *Does he seek to ally my demon with his own?*

Again, he wished that he could draw Harkender's dream into his own, to see through Harkender's inner eye instead of Mrs Murrell's outer ones, which were still preoccupied with her own dismissal of Harkender's endeavours, and her own determination to call them meaningless.

Mrs Murrell had never told Harkender what she really thought of him. She was a whore, after all; it was her business to pander to the fantasies which conventional thought, conventional life and conventional marriage sought awkwardly to exclude.

Mrs Murrell sat down upon the chair again. The girl sat sideways on the floor, resting her head on Mrs Murrell's lap. Mrs Murrell began to play, absent-mindedly, with the girl's auburn hair. Meanwhile, she watched Harkender in the moment of his eccentric climax: the timeless moment of connection whose end would be the return to the mundane world and ordinary consciousness.

That return, Gabriel learned from Mrs Murrell's thoughts, was sometimes accomplished as easefully as a natural awakening from dreamless sleep, but on other occasions it was not. She was watching closely, curious to see what would happen this time.

She was not disappointed.

Suddenly, Harkender's thick lips were drawn back from his yellowed teeth, in a rictus of shock and pain. His closed eyes were squeezed, as though in reflexive reaction to a threat. His fingers, which had been displayed, began to clench – not suddenly or convulsively, but very gradually. Cold sweat stood out upon his brow, and his colour became pale, and then, by degrees, quite ashen.

It was as though, while Harkender had made himself naked to the universal soul, some other intelligence had tried to possess him or devour him; was trying even now to *become him* by means of some kind of material and spiritual metamorphosis. He seemed to be resisting, fiercely, with every atom of his being – and yet to be on the brink of failure, in danger of annihilation.

Madness, thought Mrs Murrell. *Utter madness*.

She had not the slightest doubt that Harkender was genuinely in distress, but she thought it self-inflicted, and did not care at all.

Gabriel, by contrast, was horrified. Harkender was already possessed, yet here – undeniably – something else was trying to possess him. Gabriel had not for one moment thought that demons competed among themselves for control of those humans who they inflicted with their corrupting knowledge and corrupting sight, and he wondered what it would feel like if his own demon were to be forced to fight for its tenancy of his soul – and what might become of him if the battle were to be fierce.

While Gabriel and Mrs Murrell watched, fascinated for very different reasons, Harkender's expression slowly cleared, and his muscles slowly relaxed. In the end, he awoke quite serenely, apparently without any consciousness of having been involved in a struggle – believing, it appeared, that he had done precisely what he set out to do, no more and no less.

But Gabriel knew – and was frightened by the knowledge – that just as Harkender's magic was real, so had been his peril. This man who sought to claim and use him had power, but was also vulnerable, and terribly so. How vulnerable he himself might be, Gabriel could only guess, but he felt that he had been shown – very clearly and calculatedly – that the demon which had him in its grip might one day be displaced, and he could not tell whether that was an eventuality to be hoped for, or dreaded.

5

His dream dissolved and Gabriel awoke. For a few seconds he was disorientated, unable to figure out who or where he was, but then consciousness reasserted itself with unnatural sharpness. He felt as if he had been touched, as though by a gentle hand. Although it was dark he knew that there was no one standing beside his bed, but he did not doubt that he really had been touched in *some* fashion, and he knew better than to cry out.

He knew that he had to get up; the touch was undoubtedly a summons. The night air was cold, but the summons could not be denied. It was Morwenna who was calling him; the time for his escape had come, much sooner than he had anticipated.

He was suddenly afraid. Morwenna and her promises had seemed dreamlike, and his contemplation of her seductive invitations had always been fanciful and abstracted. Now, abruptly, the prospect of escape was no longer a matter of idle fancy but a decision to be made.

He sat up, uneasily. Then he slipped out from beneath his blanket. He put on the jacket which he had laid aside on getting into bed, and picked up his shoes. He tiptoed in his stockinged feet to the door of the dormitory, and opened it very stealthily. It creaked on its hinges as it moved, but none of the others stirred. The Lodge was a creaky house, rich in uncomfortable timbers and murmuring water-pipes; tonight the sighing of the wind in the nearby trees added a further dimension to the background of small noises. Nevertheless, Gabriel was careful to stay at the edge of the staircase while he crept down, to minimize the sound of his passage.

It was by no means the first time that Gabriel had risen by night to go prowling about in the darkness, making his way around the house and out into the grounds. Sometimes he had gone wandering with Jesse Peat. They had never attempted to steal anything – not even food from the kitchen, because they knew how carefully Mrs Capthorn kept account of her possessions – but that had not diminished the adventure for them. Only once had he gone outside with Jesse, and their excursion had been short-lived; that was when Gabriel had realized for the first time how shallow was the mask of bravado which Jesse wore, and had understood that Jesse had begun to involve him in his exploits because he dared not undertake them alone.

Gabriel had not feared the darkness and the sounds of the night even then. Now that possession had given him the power to see with inner eyes, and the power of command over the small creatures of the night, he moved through the darkness with total assurance.

The back door was locked and bolted, but the key was on its hook and the bolt slid back easily and quietly. Gabriel's deft fingers made light of the task of getting outside.

Not until he was in the yard, putting on his boots, did Gabriel feel free to pause, in order that he might ask himself whether he was doing the right thing.

He was under no compulsion; though Morwenna had sent her summons by occult means she could not compel him. He had no idea what magical powers she had, but he was sure that he was not subject to them now.

He knew hardly anything about Morwenna. He knew that she was not acting alone, and that someone else had sent her to make friends with him, but who that someone else might be he could not guess. It was certainly not Mr Harkender; more likely it was an enemy of his. Harkender had spoken to Mrs Murrell of hiding Gabriel away, and of 'others' who took too keen an interest in his work, but why these others might want him, Gabriel could not imagine. Nor could he imagine what plans Mr Harkender had for him, though he now suspected very strongly that those plans must have something to do with the demon which had lately possessed him.

Mr Harkender had assured him that he was a friend, but Gabriel had learned well enough to be wary of mere words. Morwenna had made the same assurances, and might equally well be lying. If he were more inclined to trust Morwenna than Harkender it was only because she was more handsome, more loving, and more childlike. It was still possible, he supposed, that Jacob Harkender might be his father – the man had not explicitly denied it – while Morwenna was certainly not his mother, but there was nothing in Harkender's manner which Gabriel's uninformed instincts could associate with fatherliness, while there was something in Morwenna's bright and liquid eyes which promised care and kindness.

For the Sisters of St Syncletica and Mrs Capthorn he had not a thought to spare. He did not hesitate for long; the knowledge that he was possessed had conferred upon his spirit a fine recklessness.

Gabriel set off through the grounds of the Manor. His intention was not to go to the big gates, which he could neither climb nor unlock, but to find the particular part of the tree-screened and ivy-hung wall where Morwenna waited for him. This, he quickly divined, was in a more distant part of the wilderness than the place where he had earlier gone climbing.

As he crossed an open space Gabriel caught sight of something white in the direction of the Manor, and promptly halted in his tracks. For a few moments he thought, in spite of his dimly formed conviction that she was waiting outside the wall, that it was Morwenna come to meet him. When the figure came closer, though, he saw that it was not.

A small thrill of fear cut through him then, because he saw that it was the only person within the wall that he really needed to fear: the emaciated Sister Teresa, who wanted so desperately to be a saint. She alone might have the power to exorcise his demon, and he could not bear the thought of it, even though he suspected that it was only the demon's will which made him desire so ardently to remain as he now was.

Teresa was coming directly towards the place where he had paused, and he did not doubt that her inner sight was guiding her. By the light of the moon, which had not yet set and was temporarily free of obscuring cloud, Gabriel saw that her expression was blank. She might have been walking in her sleep, save that she moved so purposefully.

Gabriel moved into the bushes near by, trying to hide himself. But he did not crouch down, because he realized that it probably would not help him to evade her merely to hide himself from her outer eyes. His suspicion was correct; when she was within half a dozen feet of his hiding place she paused, and looked about her as if she knew that someone lurked near by. She was wearing a white nightshift, in some ways not unlike the garment which Morwenna had worn, though it was coarse and stained whereas the other had been sheer and clean. She seemed younger than Morwenna, but was very haggard. Her arms were so thin as to be hardly fleshed at all, and her face was gaunt.

As she looked about her it was impossible to believe that she was not looking for something, but it was difficult to believe that she could see, for her eyes were glazed. It was as though she were lost in a dream, and that what she searched for was in some other world and not in this one at all. As she moved her hands, with the fingers spread wide, he saw that there were dark and ugly wounds in the palm of each hand, from which blood was slowly trickling.

Gabriel wondered whether Sister Teresa too might be possessed after her own more saintly fashion, and might be driven now by *her* inhabiting spirit, which used her much more roughly than his own used him, despite the fact that hers was an angel instead of a devil.

She opened her mouth to speak, but at first no sound came out; it was as though she had a battle to fight before she could make her voice obey her. When she did force words out, what she said was: 'Help me, please! I beg of you!'

It was not what Gabriel had expected to hear, but he was not tempted to move. He watched her from the shadows as her glazed eyes softened, as though she was nearly waking from her trance, puzzled and terrified. He saw her shiver convulsively as she was struck by awareness of the cold.

'Help me!' she said again, in a tone more plaintive than any he had ever heard. Gabriel was certain that the words were addressed to him, and that she knew he was there.

He moved reluctantly from the bushes, coming into plain sight – but she could not see him with her outer eyes, which continued to peer into some dark infinity. He waited, and saw her gaze begin suddenly to roam wildly around, as though she knew that something was there to be seen but could not locate it. She looked at him not once but many times, without any sign of recognition. He wondered if he dared speak, but while he could not decide the matter he stepped forward, until he was less than three feet away from her. One of her arms, which she had begun to move before her, touched his hair.

Her reaction was utterly unexpected. Although it seemed that she still could not see him she recoiled as if she were terribly afraid. She looked at the hand in pain and dread, as though it had touched something slimy and horrid, and gave voice to her anguish in a low startled cry.

The words which Gabriel had almost begun to speak died

in his throat. The girl was staring right at him now, knowing exactly where he was, yet still not *seeing* him. He looked directly into her eyes, and knew them to be unseeing, and yet he was sure that she was not blind. She saw something, but it was not the frail human form of Gabriel Gill beside the bush. Her eyes were fixed on some further horizon, perhaps on some bright-lit world which was just as real to her as the gloomy world of trees and moon shadows which confronted him.

Could she see through him, he wondered? Could she see and feel the demon that was within him, although she could not see *him* at all?

It certainly seemed so, for she said, in a new tone: 'Go! Go, Satan! I will not hear you! O loving Christ, preserve me!'

When she called him by the Devil's name, all Gabriel's anxiety returned. He had not been horrified by Jacob Harkender's magic, though he had known that Mrs Murrell's contempt for it was ill-founded. Nor did he fear Morwenna, though he knew that she was in some way not entirely human. But as befitted a Satanic thing, he was prepared to fear this frail would-be saint, and he fled from her suddenly, racing away as fast as his little legs would take him.

She was lost in confusion, and did not follow him immediately. But when he had gone some thirty yards, and took time to look back over his shoulder, he saw that she had begun to move again, and that she seemed to float most gracefully over the ground, with her wounded feet hardly touching it at all.

As he climbed the wall, fierce with determination, the scratches on Gabriel's right hand were torn again, opened up and made worse – but the pain, though sharp, was like a cleansing fire, surging through him to clarify his purpose and justify his urgency.

But when he reached the top of the wall and looked down the other side, he found that Morwenna was not there, and he hesitated again.

He looked back, and saw that Sister Teresa was moving between the trees, reaching out with her thin arms as though imploring him to stay, to put his trust in the mercy of Christ.

Had Morwenna been there, he would surely have jumped down, trusting to her to catch him, but Morwenna was *not* there, and he had no faith in his ability to contrive a soft landing. He would have to let himself down carefully, searching for toeholds with his booted feet, but he did not know whether he had time for that; he already knew that Teresa could fly, and that the wall would be no barrier to her.

But then, while his anxiety was on the brink of turning to anguish, Teresa's pursuit was interrupted. A darkly dressed shadow ran from her left-hand side to seize her and hold her back.

It was Luke Capthorn, seemingly no less anxious than Gabriel himself.

When Luke took hold of the girl her curious effortless movement ceased instantly. She was brought down to earth, and though she had less than an inch to fall the return brought a complete change in her manner. She began moving her arms as she had before, again looking restlessly about. Gabriel could hear her tiny mewling voice, crying to Christ for help and instructing Satan to keep back. Luke did not stand on ceremony, but shook her insistently. Though this rough handling increased her terror momentarily the shaking seemed to bring her to her senses, and Gabriel saw that her eyes ceased to stare as though they looked upon another world. Her dream, if dream it had been, was banished.

'Sister Teresa!' said Luke, urgently. 'Sister Teresa!'

She responded to her name, and suddenly took hold of herself, calming herself.

'It was only a dream!' said Luke. 'You must go back to the Manor now.' Gabriel guessed that this was not the first time this had happened. He could feel no lasciviousness in Luke's thoughts, but only pure anxiety and the desire to restore normality. Luke was afraid of Sister Teresa, and if he had ever looked at her with dreams of using her as he sometimes used the children in his care, such ideas had been put away long ago.

Teresa looked at Luke, not staringly as she had looked into her other world, but shyly; she was still afraid, but in a different way.

'Go back!' said Luke, insistently.

'Satan was here!' she whispered, as if trying to warn him. Gabriel realized that Luke did not know that he was missing from the dormitory, and had not come searching for him. He knew that he must be visible, if Luke only cared to glance in his direction, but he felt no immediate inclination to hide himself, as he had when he first saw Teresa.

The wounds on Teresa's hands were bleeding more freely now, and Gabriel saw Luke start when he tried to take her by the hand.

'Go back!' said Luke again, more roughly than before. He thrust her away from him, and wiped his bloody hand on his trousers. 'There's no one here! Go back, damn you!'

It was the wrong thing to say, for she took the curse quite literally, and Gabriel saw how she flinched from the verbal blow.

'Go back!' said Luke again, this time imploring her in his desperation to make her obey him. 'In the Manor, you'll be safe. Safe! There's no one here!'

At last she went, moving away with some purpose. She kept looking back until she had gone ten or twelve yards – looking at Luke as if he was the devil – but at last she turned away, and hurried towards the dark shadow of the house.

Luke stood and watched her, breathing heavily. Gabriel still did not move. When Teresa was out of sight, Luke turned to go back into the Lodge, and Gabriel smiled at the sweet irony of Luke's failure to see him, or even to look in his direction. He took it as further evidence of his demon's power, believing that the demon had commanded Luke not to look and not to see, and that Luke had had no choice but to be commanded.

When Luke was gone, and all was quiet again, Gabriel turned his head to look down at the path which ran alongside the wall of Hudlestone Manor. Morwenna was there now, having appeared as if from nowhere to meet and greet him.

'Come down, Gabriel,' she said, a little breathlessly. 'It is time for you to meet my sister, who is most anxious to make your acquaintance.'

Without a backward glance, Gabriel leapt into her waiting arms. He found them uncommonly strong when they caught him and set him gently down beside her. The touch of her flawless fingers was as careful and as affectionate as he had imagined it would be, and he felt a flood of relief that he had not hesitated longer before obeying her summons. He felt sure that he had done the right thing.

No longer forsaken, and thoroughly beguiled, he let her take him by the hand and lead him across the road. Together, they moved away into the darkness.

6

Morwenna led Gabriel unhurriedly to the bank of the canal, which they reached at a place where it passed through a small wood. There was a barge waiting for them, and Gabriel could not help but think of Jesse Peat, slumbering peacefully in the dormitory which he had recently quit. There had always been a barge conveniently waiting in Jesse's fantasies of escape.

The barge was, at least in Gabriel's estimation, a gigantic craft, very much larger than he had imagined from Jesse's accounts of life on the waterways. It measured some seventy feet from stem to stern, though it was little more than six feet in width. Morwenna led him directly to the stern of the boat, so that he barely caught a glimpse of the huge grey horse which waited patiently to begin the task of towing it eastwards.

A single steersman waited behind the cabin, like enough to Jesse Peat in his appearance to have been taken for his kin, with the same dark features and black curly hair – but the man had also a black moustache and a gold earring. He was patiently sucking on a curved pipe. When Morwenna and Gabriel appeared on the towpath he beckoned them aboard without speaking, then guided them down the wooden steps into the cabin.

The cabin was lit by an oil-lantern suspended from a hook in the ceiling, but this was turned down low, and the windows were darkly curtained so that the faint yellow light would not show without. The walls were painted; each mural showed a landscape in which flowers filled the foreground and trees the middle-ground, and in each case there was a distant mountain-top fortress visible above the crowns of the trees.

The cabin's sole inhabitant was an old woman clad in a bright but rather dirty skirt, a white blouse and grey shawl, and a patterned headscarf. When Gabriel appeared, made to pause by trepidation, she signalled to him with a gesture that he should sit upon a bench opposite a coal-burning stove. Then she bowed slightly to Morwenna, and left the cabin to join the steersman.

Gabriel felt the lurch as the boatman cast off, and the smooth acceleration as the barge got under way. He could not hear the sound of the horse's hooves, for its feet had been muffled.

'This is what the halers call a monkey boat,' said Morwenna, her voice soft and musical. 'She carries coal to Paddington. We have always had friends among the gypsies, for they are *vargr*-folk like us, more restless than the common run of cold-souled men.'

Gabriel did not understand the greater part of this speech, but he did not ask questions. For the moment, he was intent on listening. A few minutes passed before he was satisfied that there were no sounds of pursuit. Morwenna, meanwhile, went to the front of the cabin and took two blankets from a cupboard beneath a bench and laid them out.

'Are you tired, Gabriel?' she asked.

Until she said it, he was not at all tired, but when he met her soft eyes, he felt very drowsy indeed. He resisted it, because he knew that it was magic, although he felt very strongly that she could not possibly mean him any harm, and only wanted to make him comfortable.

'Where will you take me?' asked Gabriel, in a conspiratorial whisper.

'First to Kensal Green,' she replied. 'There we will quit the barge, and go by carriage through the streets of London, which are very quiet now. We will lodge you in a big house, with a man named Caleb Amalax; you will not like him much, but you need not fear him. He is ours, and he is useful to us. As men make instruments of humbler beasts, so we make instruments of cold-souled men.'

'Are you magicians, then?' asked Gabriel, trying hard to maintain his curiosity against the seductive demands of his drowsiness. 'Like Mr Harkender?'

Morwenna smiled, and shook her head. 'My sister may be as powerful in magic as Mr Harkender,' she said, 'but we are no mere magicians. Do you not know what we are, Gabriel? I had thought you more gifted in the sight than that. I would not have you think that we had stolen you away by stealth and crafty lies. Look at me, Gabriel, and try to see me as I really am – for the human form is one I do not like, and not my own.' Her voice was soft and very soothing.

He looked at her very carefully: at her strong limbs, unconfined by the loose white garment she wore; at her liquid eyes and silken hair; at her red-lipped smile. All this, he knew, was mere appearance; he tried to look through and beyond it, with the inner eye whose sight he had not yet mastered, but which often seemed instead to be *his* master. And when he made the effort, he found that he could see – not clearly, but suggestively.

'You *are* a wolf,' he said, surprised to find that it was not so very strange a revelation. 'Your soul is the soul of a wolf.' He realized, though without any shock of surprise or alarm, that it had indeed been Morwenna that he had seen in the grounds earlier, and that the werewolves of London were real.

'Does that frighten you, Gabriel?' she asked, but so very

tenderly and lovingly that he was forbidden to be frightened.

'Is that what I am?' asked Gabriel, who had not quite made up his mind what kind of demon it was that lurked within him, and thought it not impossible that it might be a wolfish thing.

'Would you like to be?' she countered. 'Would you like to be a werewolf, and hunt with the pack through the dark city streets?'

There was a moment when habit nearly took over, leading Gabriel to offer a mechanical, 'Yes, ma'am.' He stopped himself. Even if it were the answer which was called for, he knew that he need not give it. Goodness was behind him now, and Morwenna's admitted unhumanity gave him permission to set aside all the expectations which had shaped his boylike appearance. Teresa had named him Satan, but if he was indeed of Satan's company, he surely need not seek to conceal it from the werewolves of London.

'I don't know,' he said, truthfully. 'I'd like to learn to change my shape, and I'd like to learn to fly. I'd like to learn all the powers of magic which my demon has.'

He assumed, tacitly, that she knew of his possession. It was a compliment to her, to let her know that he was not afraid of whatever she knew of his true nature. But she only looked puzzled. For a moment, he thought that she would ask what demon he meant, but she put a curb on her tongue, and when he saw that she was apprehensive it became clear to him that she did not know as much as he had supposed. It did not matter; after all, she was not the originator of this plan to rescue him from Hudlestone, but merely a follower of instructions and player of a part.

'Sleep now,' said Morwenna. 'It is only for a little while, but you must rest.'

He knew, when she said it, that she was a little bit afraid of him. He knew also that he could deny the pressure of her suggestion, if he cared to. His demon would keep him awake, despite the enchantment in her eyes, if he cared to invoke that fraction of its power which was subject to his mastery. Graciously, though, he consented to be affected by her spell. Patiently, he suffered himself to be made quiet.

But when he tried to make himself comfortable with the blankets, he could not help but feel that this was an uncomfortable place in which to sleep – and could not help but give his mind to wondering what might befall him in the company of the werewolves of London.

He tried to lie still, and keep his eyes closed, but his excitement was too much to contain, and he moved about in a restless attempt to be comfortable. The future, curtained as it was by uncertainty, had a more threatening face than when he had contemplated this adventure in daylight. This had nothing to do with his discovery that he had delivered himself into the hands of the werewolves; it was a more general unease born of the awareness that his past was not merely behind him but utterly cancelled out. But there could be no going back – not so much because he had run away, but because he had become something very different from the Gabriel Gill who had been lodged at the Manor as a babe. Whatever kind of devil it was which had possessed him, it had made the pattern of his life unsustainable, perhaps even unendurable. It was not just that he no longer belonged at Hudlestone Manor; he no longer belonged to the society of human beings at all.

Why, he wondered, did Morwenna say that men had cold souls? And why was she so certain that he had not?

Like the werewolves of London, he told himself, he was now a fugitive within the world of men – and like them, he had the power within him to hide or hurt as he willed it. He had been given the power to catch glimpses of that which was normally hidden – like the multitude of tiny spiders – from human sight; and in acquiring the power to see the world beyond he had been condemned to share it with all others who knew of it. This journey was not truly an escape at all, but merely a confirmation of his arrival.

It was a puzzling world in which he found himself, but having been cast adrift within it before he had found a desirable station in the one he had left behind he did not feel its lack of security and comfort too intensely. He was, after all, already skilled in the art of allowing himself to be led wherever others cared to take him, while keeping his real thoughts secret.

And so, with mixed feelings which somehow did not conflict as fiercely as they might, he whiled away the dark hours until the barge was brought to Kensal Green.

When, at last, Morwenna came to rouse him he got up with alacrity, enthusiastic to be taken out.

The bargeman appeared in the doorway, apparently anxious to hurry Gabriel along, and when Gabriel preceded Morwenna up the steps his arm was firmly taken, to give help which he neither needed nor desired – but he did not try to resist. He allowed himself to be hauled up the steps and on to the deck.

It was still dark, but the pale glow which preceded dawn was already visible in the starless eastern sky.

There was a road beyond the towpath, and on the road there waited a horse-drawn carriage. The driver was a young man, strongly built and clad in a big coat to keep the cold at bay. Gabriel felt that the man's shadowed eyes had fixed themselves upon him as soon as he had emerged from the cabin.

The driver leapt down from his station to stand before them. 'Hello, Gabriel,' he said, the cultured syllables belying the commonplace and rather dirty appearance of his coat. He was very different from the bargees in manner and physical type; the paleness of his skin and hair was evident even in the darkness, and now that Gabriel could see his eyes more clearly it was obvious that they were very unusual. They were blue, but of a bright hue which he had never seen before.

Gabriel clambered up on to the step, and was surprised when a white and slender-fingered hand reached out of the darkness within in order to help him board. He gripped the hand and was astonished by its smoothness and the firmness of its clasp. It was too dark inside the carriage to see very clearly who was waiting there, but he knew that it was a woman, and guessed that this must be Morwenna's sister.

'Gabriel,' she said, in a purring voice which was even softer than Morwenna's. 'I am so very glad to see you. Morwenna has told me a good deal about you.'

Morwenna followed him into the carriage, and took up a position with her back to the driver's seat, while the unseen woman drew Gabriel to the seat opposite, where he was set beside her. The arm which had helped him up now slipped around his shoulder, to hold him possessively and protectively. But neither the voice nor the hand, for all their softness, was as affectionate as Morwenna's. He sensed that this was a person of a much more calculating kind.

'Who are you?' he asked, in a low but urgent voice.

'Has Morwenna not told you my name?' the woman asked. Morwenna herself was silent, offering neither answer nor explanation. When Gabriel did not answer either, she said: 'My name is Mandorla, and I am mother and sister to the werewolves of London.'

The arm seemed to hug him more closely, and he could feel the touch of the slender fingers, trying to reassure him. He felt tired, but knew that *this* tiredness was authentic. 'It will be a long ride,' said the unseen lady, 'but it will pass soon enough. Don't be afraid – no one will harm you. We will keep you safe.'

'Why do you want me?' asked Gabriel, as the carriage began moving. 'Why did you send Morwenna to the Manor to take me away?'

'Because we know what you are,' replied Mandorla, very gently, 'and we knew that you were in danger, from those who do *not* know what you are, and from those who do and would seek to use you foolishly. Jacob Harkender would have used you brutally, to no good end, but we will not. We will teach you what the Sisters never could – the true history of the world, the true nature of mankind, and the true extent of the power which you have. We alone know your true destiny . . . and we alone can help you to discover it.'

'Are there many more of you?' he asked, still curious in spite of the exhaustion which was creeping over him by degrees.

'Oh yes,' said Mandorla. 'Perris is driving the carriage, and there are four others for you to meet: Siri and Calan and Suarra and Arian. Have patience, Gabriel, and in time you will meet us all – even those of us who are sleeping, if you will help us to wake them. Don't be afraid, Gabriel, of anything. You don't ever have to be afraid.'

The sky was grey now, and the nascent day was getting quickly lighter. He could see Mandorla's face. He had thought when he first saw Morwenna that there could not be a woman in the world more beautiful than she. Now, though he was not certain that he had been wrong, he was forced to think again.

Mandorla's hair was golden and her eyes were violet, and her face was as smooth as silk. She was more wonderful in appearance than any picture he had ever been shown, whether of the Madonna or the angels, but her finely drawn features were much harder than Morwenna's, and her expression was imperious. She was very conscious of her own authority, in a way that Morwenna was not. She reminded him slightly of the Reverend Mother.

Gabriel thought that he understood why Mandorla had sent Morwenna to befriend him, for Morwenna had an evident innocence and tenderness which Mandorla had not. But he did not resent the fact that the werewolves had sent the emissary who could most easily command his trust. He was not afraid of Mandorla; and when she told him that he did not *need* to be afraid – of anything, ever – he was prepared to believe her.

It was in Mandorla's arms, not Morwenna's, that he finally yielded to sleep, even though the carriage rocked and swayed as it bowled along the deeply rutted roads and gave him a rougher ride by far than the canal-barge had.

7

Gabriel stood at the attic window, looking down at the street-market far below. Night had fallen but the street was still brightly lit by the white glow of gas-lights, mingled here and there with the orange fire of grease-lamps; the crowd was still growing.

Gabriel had never seen such a pageant of confusion as was here displayed, nor ever dreamed that such a sight could exist. This, he felt, was the other world which should have been visible outside the walls of Hudlestone Manor but was not; this was the true tumult of modern life, of which he had heard the merest whispers of rumour, but which he could never have imagined for himself in this appalling detail. The movement, the noise and the crowdedness of it all were startling enough to take his breath away; he could not imagine how people made their way in such a crush, or achieved their purposes while moving in the midst of such chaos.

The throng in the middle of the street was faced by three ranks of merchants: first, the basket-sellers moving along-side their customers with fruits and whelks, ribbons and laces; second, the petty stallholders with their fish-friers and potato-baking ovens and chestnut-roasters; third, the shops behind the stalls where the butchers and bakers, stationers and tea-dealers displayed their wares. There were musicians' pitches in between the stalls, where men played flutes or concertinas, jogging about in a tired parody of dancing. Where the spaces were smaller there were beggars: blind men and lame men, and gaunt young women clutching wailing babes in their arms.

So fascinated was he with the spectacle that Gabriel could not tear his eyes away even when he heard the door open and shut behind him, and it was not until the person who had entered came to stand beside him that he turned to see who it was.

It was Mandorla. As she stood with him by the window the light from without made her milky skin glisten slightly.

'Are they not vile?' she asked him. 'They have the week's wage paid to them on Saturday and come to buy what they need; and when their needs are answered, or sometimes with their needs forgotten, they will follow their desires – which is to say that six in every ten will give every penny they can spare for the luxury of drunkenness or the excitement of the gambler's toss.

'It never changes, from one generation to the next or from one century to the next, and never need be remembered or forgotten. Whatever the name of a city, however are called the gods which its people worship, there is always the crowd – always the dirty, drugged mass squandering life and soul alike in a morass of misery. Look at them, Gabriel, and learn to despise them – for you are not of their kind, whatever they have told you in that pit of piety where Harkender hid you away.'

Gabriel looked up at her, curiously. There was something in her fervour to instruct him which reminded him of the Sisters of St Syncletica, but in every other way she was so very different. It was only to be expected. She, like him, was of the Devil, while the nuns were a regiment in the army of God.

'Why am I not of their kind?' he asked, faintly. 'I know now that I am not, but no one ever told me that I was anything else until Morwenna came, and of all the people at Hudlestone, only Sister Teresa knew when the demon possessed me.'

Mandorla had turned away before he spoke, and she did not immediately turn back. Instead she went to the small table beside his new bed, and lit the oil-lamp which stood thereon. It burned yellow, and not as brightly as the gas-lamps down below. Mandorla sat down upon the bed, and beckoned Gabriel to come to her, which he did, a little hesitantly.

'You must not be afraid,' she said, putting out her arms to draw him closer. 'I will make you my apprentice, and teach you everything I can about the arts of magic. You would like that, would you not – to have the power of command over the world of appearances?'

'Yes, thank you,' murmured Gabriel, feeling unusually ashamed of the easy, empty acceptance. He knew that he already had certain powers of command, or that his demon did, but he did not volunteer the information.

She picked him up – with surprising ease, given that she was so slim – and sat him on the bed by her side. She put her right arm around him and hugged him close, in a way that no one had ever done until he first sat beside her in the carriage which had brought him here from Kensal Green.

'You need no pretence with me,' she told him. 'I do not need to be appeased with courtesies. We are not of their kind, you and I. They are our cattle, put upon the earth for us to use as we may; though we use their form in order that we may move stealthily among them, we are very different, and when we deign to wear their appearance, we do so more skilfully than they can themselves. Our kind are beautiful, Gabriel, and we know how to use our beauty as a snare. In former times I have lived in palaces, but the comforts and luxuries which humans love are a danger to our kind, for they threaten to make us forget what we truly are. We are creatures of the wild, Gabriel – we are the *vargr*, the restless ones – and we must be careful never to forget the thrill of the hunt. Men like to think themselves civilized, and pretend to have banished wildness from their cities, but the dark streets of London are the greatest wilderness of all and the most perfect hunting-grounds.'

'Do you steal children to eat?' asked Gabriel, with a tiny flutter in his heart.

'We are wolves,' answered Mandorla. 'We eat as we desire, and human babes are no more and no less to us than rats or rabbits. We have no particular need of them, but we may take them if it pleases us. We kill as we desire, and if we take pleasure in our killing it is in our natures that we should.

Those who say that we prowl the dark streets searching for children to steal are liars, for we have no special hunger of that kind . . . but if it should delight us to dine on human meat, whether it be one night in ten or once in a thousand years, none can deny us the right, for we are wolves, and we owe nothing to the human herd.'

'And am I too a wolf?' asked Gabriel, haltingly.

'I think you might be,' she replied, 'if only you could learn the trick of it. But you are far more than that, my child, and even Jacob Harkender does not really understand what power you have, and how you might use it.'

'I am more like him than I am like you,' he told her, regretfully. 'For he has a demon in his soul, as I have one in mine.'

That seemed to annoy her a little, and she tilted his head in order to compel him to look into her violet eyes. 'You must not think,' she told him, sternly, 'that there is a demon inside you which is another and not yourself, no matter what the nuns have told you about the wiles of Satan. There are demons in the world, but the account of them which the nuns have given you is wrong in every particular. Their scriptures are as corrupt as any other of the lying appearances which preserve the image of the false past, and nothing written there can be trusted despite the feeble echoes of true history which can be found by wiser men. Do you honestly believe that you are possessed by some Satanic spirit out of the nightmares of the Sisters?'

Gabriel had believed it honestly enough, but when Mandorla told him that it was not true, he discovered that his belief had not the strength to resist her scepticism.

'No,' he replied, uneasily, 'but . . .'

He could not continue, but waited humbly for her to provide an alternative explanation for what had happened to him these last few weeks.

'If you are possessed, Gabriel,' she told him, 'it is the appearance of humanity which possesses you. Until now, you have been trapped by mere appearance, seeming human even to yourself, but now you are becoming a very different being, with the gift of inner sight and power over appearances. What you have thought of as a demon within you is your true self; the human carcass and the cold human soul which you thought of as your own are a mere husk, to be gradually shed as a dragon-fly sheds the husk of the crawling nymph which once it seemed to be.

'There are others besides ourselves which maintain some appearance of humanity although their inner nature is otherwise. Once, they had different forms, but all wear the mask of humanity now. The things of the world are losing their souls, and all the ancient folk must assume the guise of the soulless; we do not know why it is, but it is an evolution which we have so far been powerless to interrupt, because those who once had the power of Creation sleep far more deeply than those who were once their minions. It will not always be thus; a Millennium is coming which will be very different from the one which your pious nuns anticipate, and you might have a part to play in that joyous metamorphosis. Do you understand me, Gabriel?'

He longed to understand, and to please her with his understanding, but it was all too much. The wayward thing which was within him, demon or true soul, was capable of miraculous insight on occasion, but in other matters it seemed blind and stupid. He was not surprised to be told that it was only beginning to awaken.

'What am I?' he asked, doubtfully.

'Names do not matter,' she told him. 'You are something new in the world. It is a long time since there was something new in the world, except for dead and soulless things like the machines which men make. That is why we must hope for a new age to displace this dreadful Age of Iron which all our kind finds hateful. It will not be the Age of Gold returned, but we must hope that it will be an Age of Creation, and not the bleak and empty Age of Reason which the Clay Man has foretold.'

She paused then, obviously realizing that he could not possibly understand what she was trying to tell him. 'Forgive me, Gabriel,' she said, softly. 'We know so well how deceptive appearances are that we sometimes cease to heed them at all. It requires an effort, you see, to remember that you are one of us, yet have not lived through thousands of years as we have. I do not look as if I had lived ten thousand years, do I?'

As if to emphasize that she was once again mindful of the fact that he was a small child, she hugged him again. She was keen to touch him, and to stroke him. No one else had ever been so anxious to demonstrate affection for him, despite his prettiness and goodness. It was easy for him to believe, now, that those humans who had looked after him had always suspected – without quite knowing it – that he was of another kind. And yet, even Mandorla did not seem entirely sincere in her demonstrations.

With her free hand Mandorla ruffled his hair, then ran her fingers down the side of his face.

Suddenly, Gabriel began to weep – not to cry, or to sob, but merely to weep. Gentle tears ran down his cheeks, but he did not feel distressed, and did not know why he had felt such a surge of emotion.

'You must not be afraid,' she told him. 'There is a great deal to learn, but I am the one teacher who can tell you the truth.' She held him for a few minutes more, while the tears worked their way out of him, but when he sniffed to clear his nose and tried to sit up straighter, she let him go. He saw then that she had brought something with her, which she had set upon the table beside the lamp. It was a mirror in an oval frame.

'Watch!' she commanded.

He watched.

Mandorla held the mirror before her, and raised it to the level of her eyes. She stared intently at it, and moved it a little from side to side. She turned away from him, so that he too could look into the glass – and he saw that there appeared within it a tiny lick of blue flame, which curled and flickered and writhed about itself, growing and becoming brighter. The blue glow filled the glass, then blazed brighter and brighter until the blue became white and the radiance lit every corner of the room, outshining by far the yellow light of the oil-lamp, which now seemed sullen and murky.

Gabriel wanted to put up his arm to shield his eyes, but somehow he dared not.

Mandorla held the blazing mirror steadily, letting the light flow from it for half a minute and more. Her face, in that astonishing glare, seemed very white, save for her reddened lips and her fierce purple eyes. Her hair was lifted by some unseen force, which made it stand out from her head in undulating streamers, rocked by an invisible tide.

Then the white began to die into blue again, and collapsed upon itself, until nothing was left except a fugitive blue spark – and finally, nothing at all. The mirror was quite dark for a moment, before the reflection of the room returned.

Dazzled, Gabriel blinked, trying to get rid of the luminosity that was still in his eyes. The yellow faded gradually to ruddy orange, like the setting sun.

Mandorla took up his hand and touched his fingers to the surface of the looking-glass, which was very slightly warm to the touch – but that might only have been the warmth of her fingers which had held it.

'That is magic,' she said. 'Power to make light where darkness was. Can you do the same?'

It did not occur to him to deny it, though he had never tried any such trick. In a spirit of enquiry, he took the mirror from his patroness, and held it up as she had held it, looking deep into its centre. He silently commanded light to appear there, as imperiously as he could, but nothing happened. He felt disappointed.

'I can command tiny things,' he said, 'and shape the webs which spiders spin.'

'Can you?' she said, as though she was very pleased to hear it. 'That is good. Whenever you discover the working of such a spell, you must repeat it over and over, for only exercise will bring about improvement. I make you a gift of the mirror, so that you may try to find the trick which makes it glow. It is a useful instrument by which to measure your progress. Do not worry if you find it difficult at first; I promise you that the power will come, for it is rightfully yours as it is rightfully mine. Magic was made for our kind, Gabriel, not for the likes of Jacob Harkender; it is our inheritance from the Age of Gold, and when the wheel of time has turned full circle magic will bring us back to the full flower of our youth. That is our business, Gabriel – the task which we share. You think yourself newly born, but in fact you are only newly shaped, and the heat of your soul is that same primal fire which was the life of the Golden Age.'

She put the mirror from him, and set it down on the table again. The yellow lamplight washed over it, dappling its surface with flickering radiance.

'My mother died when I was born,' said Gabriel, uncertainly. 'Mr Harkender said that her name was Jenny.'

Mandorla laughed, and put her arm around him again. 'She was not the first cold-souled woman to bear a miraculous child,' she said. 'You must not think that you are human because you had a human mother. Men are our enemies, Gabriel, and Jacob Harkender is a worse enemy than all the rest.'

'He said that he was my friend,' Gabriel answered. 'He said that he alone could understand what I am.'

'He lied,' said Mandorla. 'He would have hurt you, Gabriel. In itself, that is not entirely bad, for the Dark Angel of Pain is also the Angel of Enlightenment. But Jacob Harkender, like all humans, can draw upon that enlightenment only with the utmost difficulty, and his ignorance would imperil you. None but I can properly teach you the ways of pain – there is none wiser in all this tawdry world, and none who longs so desperately for the transformation which will end it. I will teach you magic and I will teach you how to deal cleverly with the Dark Angel. I promise you that.'

Gabriel picked up the mirror from the tabletop where she had set it down, and cradled it in his hands. He looked deep into its heart, and wondered if he should try again to will it into dazzling brilliance. Mandorla watched him, curiously, as though it would give her great pleasure to see him succeed. But he put it down beside him, on the counterpane.

'The Sisters didn't want to hurt me,' he said, as though to himself – but really out of curiosity, to see what Mandorla would have to say in reply. 'I saw them whip other boys, and I saw some of them whip themselves, but they never whipped me.'

Mandorla looked at him, her expression unfathomable.

'Their kind have always hurt ours,' she said, 'and you may be certain that they would not have shrunk from hurting you, had they concluded – as you concluded – that you were possessed by the devil. But our kind need not be so afraid of pain as they are, and need not seek its worst extremes in order that we may see. Shall I show you another magic?'

He nodded.

Mandorla went to the door and went out, leaving it open. Gabriel sat patiently upon the bed, waiting, and as he waited he ran his fingers gently over the surface of the looking-glass which lay beside him.

When Mandorla returned, not bothering to close the door behind her, she had a knife in her hand. It had a very slender blade about a foot long, sharply pointed and doubly-edged.

'Be careful,' she said, as he reached out as though to touch it. She turned it, offering him the handle, and he took it, holding it very gingerly.

She placed her hair carefully behind her, and then ran her hand down the loose white shift which she wore to make it tight upon her skin below the curve of her breast. She pointed to a spot just below the left breast, and said: 'Place your hand here, to feel the beating of my heart.'

He did as he was told, and he felt the heart within, beating very steadily. His own was beating more quickly, and there was a catch in his throat.

'Place the point of the knife on the very spot,' she said, 'and slip the blade between my ribs, to penetrate the heart.'

He shook his head violently.

'Do it,' she commanded, 'for I am not a human creature,

and I cannot die. If the wound is clean enough, I need not even sleep.'

His hand trembled as he tried to place the point, and she had to guide it for him. She placed her other hand upon his, so that her fingers too could apply pressure to the hilt of the dagger. It felt to Gabriel as though they thrust as one, neither reluctant nor resisting.

The blade slipped smoothly into her body, penetrating to a depth of several inches. He saw blood well up about the wound, but only a trickle.

She sat very still, as though she dared not move while her heart was impaled. Then, together, they drew the blade out again.

A single sluggish drop of blood oozed from the wound, spreading out to stain her shift. When the stain was the size of a penny, it grew no more.

'You see,' she said, in a voice made slightly husky by effort or emotion. 'This is not a trick for you to try just now, but it is a power which most of our kind have. I cannot die, Gabriel, and I know the ways of pain. Jacob Harkender is all too mortal, and knows no more of pain than that poor deluded child at Hudlestone, who crowns herself with thorns so that she may hear the tender voice of her imagined saviour. I will teach you power and I will teach you pain – and the alchemy of transmutation too, given time. You must not be afraid, no matter what you may see in this house, for you are under my protection now, and nothing will harm you.'

As she spoke the last words she looked up very suddenly, and Gabriel looked up with her. Standing in the doorway was a man, uglier than any Gabriel had ever seen. He was tall and hugely rounded with belly-fat; he was quite bald, and the skin on his forehead and about his neck was gathered into rounded wrinkles. His eyes seemed very small, so puffy was the flesh around them, and there was filthy sweat upon his face. His clothes were as grimy as his face, but his boots were polished. He was leaning against the doorpost, watching them.

'What do you want, Caleb?' asked Mandorla, sharply.

'Calan is back.' The man's voice was as rough as his appearance. 'As drunk as a gin-house rat. He followed a man from Harkender's house, but was seen and challenged. He contrived to discover that the man was a doctor named Gilbert Franklin, but the fool was mad enough to brag about his true nature.'

Mandorla sighed as she took her arm from Gabriel's shoulder. 'Damn you for turning him into a drunkard,' she said, softly. 'But what can it matter? Do you think they will raise a crusade against us, because of some sneering joke? Harkender would tell the world who we are soon enough if he thought that anyone would believe him, but he knows how secure we are. Had news of the boy's disappearance arrived at Whittenton when Calan decided to quit his post?'

'No,' growled the ugly man. 'But what can it matter how soon he knows, given that we are so many, and he but one?'

'You do not know the kind of man Harkender is,' she told him. 'He is no fool, nor is he powerless. Do you know who this man Franklin is, by any chance?'

'A surgeon, I believe. And a friend of James Austen.'

'Austen! If Austen has been recruited to Harkender's cause, then Harkender may be more dangerous still – who knows how much he might have learned from the Clay Man and Pelorus, if he had the wit to see the truth within the Clay Man's madness? We must make certain that the Clay Man still sleeps in the grave which the doctor dug for him . . . and we must, above all else, discover where Pelorus went when he left England, and what he went to do. Go down – I will come now.'

The lumpish man shrugged his shoulders and turned ponderously away. Gabriel listened to the sound of his heavy footsteps descending the stair, and wondered how the man had come up so quietly.

'That is Caleb Amalax,' said Mandorla, briefly. 'He is *not* of our kind, but we, who are free and who live outside time, must still use mortal instruments to serve our ends. He is by no means our master, though he nurses the ambition that he might one day learn to control us. He has no understanding of the reality of power, and is no threat to you. Do not be afraid of him.'

Then she stood up, and went to the door. 'Good night, Gabriel,' she said. 'Sleep well.'

When she had closed the door upon him – without locking it – he looked down at the dagger which he still held in his hand, wondering if she had forgotten it. It was stained with blood, which he tasted – very carefully – with the tip of his tongue. The blood was warm, and sweet to the taste, but he did not feel the strange intoxication which he had felt when he scratched himself and sucked his own blood.

He set the dagger down on the table, and tested the softness of the bed. It was twice as big as the one in which he had slept at Hudlestone Lodge, and nearly as big as the mattress which he had shared with three others before he got a bed of his own.

He wondered, briefly, whether he ought to say his prayers; but he decided that he was done with prayer, now and for ever. Instead, he picked up the looking-glass, and looked long and hard into its depths, willing it to glow.

In the depths of the glass, there was a fugitive flicker of blue flame. Once it had been captured there, it soon began to grow.

As the magical light poured forth, Gabriel Gill laughed in pure delight, and soon had lost himself in a trance of his own making.

8

Gabriel huddled into the hollow of the armchair, sitting sideways with his legs drawn up. In his arms, possessively cradled, was the mirror which Mandorla had given him. He was still learning its uses, but had made rapid progress since the moment when he had contrived to awaken the first spark of light in its core. Now, he could see visions in the glass, as sharp and clear as those which he had earlier experienced more intimately; it was as though the glass had become a lens for his inner eye, focusing his secret vision. To commit such phantoms to the space behind the glass, where they were separated from his own thoughts and feelings, was in many ways preferable to permitting their invasion of his dreams.

In time, he thought, he might obtain such command of the glass that he could call up whatever images he required there. Perhaps he could put the whole world into that strange dimension which lay within and beyond the mirror, and change it according to his whim.

Mastery of the magic of the mirror was not the only achievement which he had won since entering Mandorla's house. He had increased his ability to link his inner eye with the sensations of others, so that this too need no longer trouble his dreams. He had tried to look into Mandorla's thoughts, but that end had so far proved elusive; it was easier by far to eavesdrop on the thoughts of Caleb Amalax, and Gabriel was gradually improving his skill in that regard.

He was sharing Amalax's eyes now – and was finding it a fascinating, yet strangely confusing experience, for one of the two people presently being watched by Amalax was himself; the other was Morwenna, who was stretched out languidly upon his bed.

Amalax was standing against the wall of a bare room, with his eye pressed to a spy-hole in the wall. He had made it the night before, investing his work with all the prideful delicacy of the practised craftsman, and thought himself utterly safe from detection – but Gabriel had known exactly what he was doing. The spy-hole was one of many which Amalax had contrived to place in the rough-hewn walls of the sprawling and ramshackle dwelling where he played open-handed host to so many robbers and housebreakers; information gained by such spying was one of the commodities in which he traded.

In times past, when Amalax's only means of support had been as a receiver of stolen goods and master of thieves, he had used his spy-holes solely to keep watch on his clients and employees, who had ever been as carelessly stupid as they were eager to conspire against him and cheat him. As time had gone by, though, he had become addicted to the practice of eavesdropping, which he now regarded as an end as much as a means. He was telling himself even now that a man who had the werewolves of London for accomplices must be doubly careful to maintain the means of spying on his friends, on the grounds that a very fine line lay between mastery and slavery when a man made pacts with such devils as they. Gabriel could see very clearly what a hypocritical excuse this was.

Like Mrs Murrell, Amalax had become more voyeur than actor. As she, in elevating herself from whore to bawd, had become a passive parasite upon the pleasures and humiliations of her fellow-creatures, so Amalax, in playing host to the werewolves of London, was now a dispassionate witness to their unholy schemes.

Gabriel, who had become suddenly and unnaturally familiar with the perversities of human thought and feeling, had quickly learned to be glad that he was no mere human child – though he had hardly begun to understand what he really was.

The purpose of Amalax's new spy-hole was, of course, to let him keep watch on Gabriel; the man had not the least idea that Gabriel was able to keep a much more intimate watch on *him*. Amalax did not know why Gabriel was so precious to the werewolves – which was a pity, because Gabriel would have been interested in any theory he had – but he knew enough to treasure whatever they treasured, and to be avid to learn from them whatever tricks he could. Gabriel noted that Amalax did not believe all that Mandorla had told him, and certainly not that the werewolves were immortal and had already lived for ten thousand years. As to the efficacy of their magic, however,

Amalax had no doubt at all; he was resolved that if Mandorla truly intended to instruct Gabriel in magic, then she must have a second pupil too, not one whit less willing to profit from her instruction.

At present, such instruction as was taking place within the room was of little practical use, but Amalax was not deterred by that from keeping his vigil, and Gabriel was glad of it, for he was sure that he could learn as much from Amalax's thoughts and reactions as he could from Morwenna's earnest conversation.

Gabriel was surprised to discover that Amalax did not like Morwenna at all, even though the sight of her supple body filled him with a grim and bitterly hopeless excitement. Amalax thought Morwenna stupid and relatively powerless, though he did not hold her in such contempt as the werewolf named Calan. Amalax had tried hard to exploit Calan and to learn from him what tricks of magic he knew, but had proved to be a far better teacher than apprentice; he felt strongly – and, again, bitterly – that he had worked wonders of his own to make the lad into a passable street-brawler and habitual drunkard, but had only discovered in himself an obstinate and unfortunate incapacity for conjuration and divination alike. Of all the werewolves, Amalax was now convinced, Mandorla was the only one who had not the heart and mind of a little child. Only Mandorla – and possibly Pelorus, who was known to him only by name.

Morwenna was lying down, supporting herself upon one elbow. She wore nothing but the long white shift which the female werewolves preferred when convention did not demand more formal attire – presumably because it did not inhibit their powers of transformation. The garment was itself provocative, and now, believing herself unobserved by any but Gabriel, she unthinkingly allowed herself the luxury of a relaxed posture besides.

Gabriel felt no desire or obligation to warn her that her assumption was wrong, for he was far too intrigued by Amalax's awkwardly mixed feelings; even while the grotesquely fat man revelled in the teasing of his lusts he was very conscious of the necessity to keep a tight rein on his extravagant fantasies.

Pity the man who would try to rape a werewolf! Amalax thought; Gabriel already knew enough to agree with him.

'Can you imagine,' Morwenna was saying to Gabriel, 'what it would be like to be a wolf?'

They have told him what they are! Amalax was thinking. *She seeks to soften the blow – but how can they be so artless, who claim to have lived for centuries? If they have always hated human beings, perhaps they have scorned to learn our lying ways – even Mandorla, who thinks that she knows them all too well.*

Gabriel did not look up, but he replied straightforwardly enough. 'I have tried to imagine what it would be like to be a bird,' he said, pensively, 'and to fly above the world. But a wolf . . . would be different.'

'It is not so *very* different,' she told him, in a patiently pedagogical fashion. 'What the joy of flight is to the bird, the joy of the hunt is to the wolf. What you must try to imagine is the *purity* of the joy, which is altogether unclouded by thought. I suppose you think that you know what enjoyment is, but the only joy which you can know is a *thinking* joy, which is very different. You might suppose that being able to know that you were joyful would be a good thing, but you would be wrong. To be able to say to yourself *I feel joyful* is to remove yourself from the joy itself, and to alter it. It is a gift to be able to hold conversation with ourselves – to know, and to know that we know – but there is a price which we pay in order to have that gift; what we gain in the power to reason and imagine, we lose in the power to feel, and to be what we feel, and to be what we are.

'To the thinking being, feeling is a source of trouble and pain, and joy is spoiled by the knowledge that we are not always joyful, and that our joy will fade soon enough. The wolf has only feeling: when she is joyful, joy fills her entire being; and even when she is in pain, she does not know that pain is what possesses her. For the wolf, pleasure is pleasure and pain is pain and that is all there is, without any consciousness that it might or will be different. For the human, pleasure is weakened by the knowledge that it might be otherwise and cannot last, while pain is made worse by the knowledge that it *is* pain, and holds the promise of injury and death. For the human, there is no pain without fear, and no fear without pain. The wolf, when she is miserable, has no redoubling of her misery; and when she is joyful, there is nothing which can take away the least measure of her joy. If you had the choice, Gabriel, you ought far rather to be a wolf than a man.'

Oh aye, thought Amalax, silently cynical. *But you have the choice, I suppose, and yet you exist in human form from day to day, transforming yourself into a wolf for brief periods.*

'I have been told that God made me,' said Gabriel, cunningly provocative, 'in His own image.'

'The Sisters at Hudlestone told you that,' said Morwenna, contemptuously. 'And they have told you, too, that man is born to suffer, that he should bear the burden of his own sins and those of his forefathers. But we are not of that kind, you and I.'

'They told us that Jesus came to suffer for us,' said Gabriel, reflectively. 'I could never understand why we also had to do it for ourselves.'

'You should not say *us*,' she told him. 'It was not for us that their saviour came to die, and we do not have to bear any share of his pain, if we can learn to avoid it. You might learn to be a wolf, Gabriel, if only you wanted it . . . and perhaps better than a wolf, if you learn well. And if you are as clever as Mandorla thinks you are, you might learn the most precious thing of all, which is to be a wolf *for ever*, and never have to be a thinking thing again.'

A dubious privilege, thought Amalax, unconvinced by the werewolf's account of how wonderful it was to be a wolf, *but if that is what you desire, do you hope that the boy can free you from your own half-humanity? Do you think he can learn to exercise his power over you as well as himself?* Gabriel was interested to overhear Amalax's speculations about why Mandorla wanted him, and what he might do for the werewolves, but Amalax clearly believed that Mandorla wanted more than a chance to be unhuman for ever.

'I don't know,' said Gabriel. 'I don't think I would like it.'

'You cannot know,' said Morwenna, softly. 'But that is innocence, and is easily lost. A wolf cannot ask herself whether she likes it or not, and the bliss of that unawareness is greater by far than any reward which can come from hopeful, fearful, precarious consciousness. The wolf cannot think; the wolf hunts. Her hunger is her will, which draws her on, and its satisfaction is her ecstasy, the taste of blood her glory.

'Did the Sisters tell you about Heaven, Gabriel? I dare say they told you a good deal more of Hell, which they are far better fitted to imagine and describe. I will give you a different account: Heaven is a wolf in the hunt, Gabriel; and Hell is simply to be human . . . even in joy, even in virtue, even in triumph. Hell is here, Gabriel, not down below in the bowels of the earth, and it was not made for Satan but for men. There is no Heaven for men, but only for the birds and the beasts – and for the Others like ourselves, who might learn to forsake that shadow of humanity which is upon their bodies and their minds, and enjoy the true rewards of transformation. Forget that saviour of which the Sisters told you; you must learn to be a saviour yourself, for all our sakes.'

From where he was standing, Amalax could not see Morwenna's face – only the curve of her beautiful back, and her long fine tresses. Gabriel felt a certain paradoxical gladness in the man's mind, born of a fugitive fantasy. Amalax imagined as he listened to this speech that her face must be rapt with visionary fervour, and though he was not certain that he would like the sight of it, still there was excitement in the image and its contemplation.

Amalax could not help but want Morwenna, just as he could not help but want Mandorla, but what they would not give him he could neither buy nor take by force. That filled him with a rage of helplessness – and amplified his determination to win what power he could, from them and over them. Because he was their ally, Amalax was the most ardent of all their many enemies, and he was clever enough to know what a paradox that was.

Gabriel, despite that he was only a demonic leech, greedily sucking in the cleverness of others, had dined well enough on intelligence by now to share in Amalax's convoluted insight.

They imagine that they have the boy, Amalax was saying to himself, resentfully. *But they are wrong. This is my house, and he is mine, and when I know what use he is, and what it is that he has the power to do, I will be the one who uses him, and the one who trades his favours.*

Gabriel knew, as Amalax could not, what ludicrous folly there was in this bravado. He knew that while the demon's powers were his – and he accepted now that they were truly *his* – no mere human being could use him. Already he had begun to wonder whether there was anyone in the world, even Mandorla, more powerful than he.

'I don't know,' said Gabriel, disingenuously. 'I can't be a wolf because I don't know how. I don't know what I am, if I am not a human being.'

'Don't be afraid,' said Morwenna, softly. 'You don't have to be afraid any more. We will take care of you now; Mandorla will teach you what you need to know. Although you are not a wolf, still you are of our kind, and not of theirs.'

'I cannot tell the difference between these kinds,' said Gabriel, with plaintive insincerity, and was surprised into a guilty start by the reaction in Amalax's thoughts: *That is a lie, little boy! You may not know what the difference is, but you know it. This is not ordinary flesh which parades itself before you like a painter's model of a courtesan, and you know in your heart that it is the stuff of legend. When you look at a man like me, you may think you see a devil, but you know in your heart that I am only a man.*

But another part of Amalax – strange how there seemed at times to be more than one soul in him! – was thinking that Gabriel Gill was as yet no werewolf or magician, and that despite his different flesh, this was one creature which might be raped and hurt, if only one need not fear the werewolves' reprisals.

That was lust again which spoke, for Amalax could not quite put lust away from him while the curve of the werewolf's body was visible beneath the flimsy chemise.

'You will feel the difference soon enough,' said another voice, cutting across the conversation from behind the door. 'You have learned to light the mirror more quickly than I could have hoped, and soon you will be able to begin to learn the way of pain. All fear will leave you then, and you will come into your true inheritance. Dream, child, dream . . . of such power as might end this hollow age of hollow men . . .'

What Mandorla said aloud stopped there, but Gabriel seemed to hear the continuing thought in the werewolf's head: . . . *and ravel up the vault of empty darkness which surrounds the earth, and build again the crystal spheres of Eden.*

He looked up in astonishment, and Mandorla met his startled gaze with her lovely violet eyes. She smiled, as if she knew by his reaction that he must have heard her silent words, which she had put deliberately into his mind.

'Oh yes,' she said, in a softer voice than she had ever contrived before in his hearing. 'That too. Until we know what bounds there are to your power, we may hope for *anything*, and if, in the end, you are a poorer angel than we hope, still there is the one which summoned you and the one which truly gave you birth. The gods are waking from their sleep of centuries, dear Gabriel, and all the world is trembling on the rim of the cauldron of Creation.'

9

The invisible webs which bind the world are miraculously made visible; every solid entity is wrapped by them several times over. The deepest layer, closest to the surfaces of things, is torn and tattered; but this decay is overlaid by layer upon layer of newer webs, strong and neat – gleaming now with a dew which is pure starlight fallen from the sky.

Every tree which stands alone trails half a dozen bridal gowns; where many grow together the wood is roofed over with misty whiteness which makes a dark labyrinth of what lies beneath. Every river flows beneath an infinity of silken bridges; every road is beset by countless traps which catch the souls from those who ride there on horseback, in carriages and carts. Every building is wrapped like a chrysalis, every door and every window tightly bound, though those who move within do not know how utterly they are imprisoned, or how securely their souls are entombed.

The spiders which spin these webs are made visible, too, by the same glittering encrustation; though their bodies are blacker than the deepest shadow they shine now with borrowed light, like great jewelled dragons striding over the fields and the houses. That strange eight-legged flow which is mysteriously repulsive to the eyes of men is here made majestic by size and slowness and scintillation; the spiders which are hunters of the soul are as awesome as any in that fabulous host of angels which are the true inhabitants of the world-as-it-is.

Within the candlelit rooms of Hudlestone Lodge and Hudlestone Manor life goes on as ever, for the miracle which has made the webs and their makers visible is granted only to those with inner sight, which even the meek and the pure in heart have not. With one exception, the foundlings in the Lodge are blind to this marvellous light; with one exception, the nuns in the old manor house see nothing. But even those with sight see very different meanings in the webs which bind the world and the dancing spider-angels, for wherever one may see a kind of Heaven, the other must find a kind of Hell.

And in the greater world beyond, in the cities which are the ant-hives and the termitaria of the cold-souled, those who are luxuriously blind race and rattle in their courses while the werewolves stalk the streets and the spiders spin their webs and the true masters of the world hatch out their gaudy schemes of death and transfiguration.

*

Gabriel . . .

  Gabriel . . . !

Gabriel woke with the conviction that while his dream had decayed to its inevitable end, someone had been calling him – but the voice had been somehow masked and muffled, as though it came from a great distance. His awakening made the summons no clearer, and the voice – if there had been a voice – was quickly lost amid the crowding sensations of consciousness.

He got out of bed, and reached out to touch the surface of the looking-glass which lay on the table near by. His fingers found it unerringly, and light blazed within it without an instant's delay. He dressed himself, as quickly and efficiently as he had for his nocturnal adventures at Hudlestone.

Although his door was never locked Gabriel had not so far chosen to stray from his room in Caleb Amalax's house. The passage of time had eroded his initial anxiety, but his curiosity had so far been wholly absorbed by the games which he played with the mirror, which allowed him access to sights far more bizarre than any he might hope to discover by mere wandering. Now, though he did not quite know why, he felt that it was time for a more mundane exercise of his faculties.

It had not for a moment occurred to him that he might make his first excursion by day, when he might be seen by any and everybody; the night was his time, as it had been at Hudlestone, and the suspicion that many of those who shared his new dwelling had a similar preference for the hours of darkness was no longer sufficient to make him timid.

The night was at its blackest. At Hudlestone, this had always been a time of silence and Stygian gloom, but here in London the streets were never entirely silent or lightless, and when he dimmed his magic lantern again there was still light enough to see by.

He did not put on the newest shoes that Mandorla had given him, which were too firm in the sole for him to move soundlessly, but crept forth in his stockinged feet – out on to the landing, and then along the corridor. Because he did not consider himself a prisoner, there was no thought of escape in his mind. He had not the slightest intention of leaving the house; he intended only to measure its extent and learn more of its inhabitants.

He had tacitly assumed that the house would be like the Lodge, with only a single staircase, but he soon realized that things were not so simple here. The corridor outside his room had no blind end, but turned at right-angles in both directions – nor was that the full extent of its winding. He counted a dozen doors, and found two flights of downward-leading stairs, as well as a shorter, upward-leading flight which led to a slanting trapdoor. Through a crack in the timbers of the angled door he could see the strange ruddy glow which the London sky always had, and he deduced that he could get on to the roof that way.

This was an interesting possibility, which he had not previously considered. He had planned to go downwards once he had made himself familiar with the layout of his own floor, but now he knew that there was an alternative he was seized by an unaccustomed temptation. He was no more afraid of heights than he was of the dark, and the prospect of studying the entire panoply of that strange sky was an intriguing one.

He tested the angled door. It opened outwards, and was difficult to lift, but it was not locked. His physical strength was tested to the full when he tried to lower it gently on to the slates, reluctant to let it fall with an audible crash, but he succeeded.

He had already guessed that the roof would boast a complicated landscape, for he had seen from his window what a confusion of gables and chimney-pots bedecked the buildings across the street. He was not disappointed by the profusion of slopes and turrets, and felt a prideful excitement in his discovery of this mysterious upper world. There were a number of tilted skylights set at regular intervals along the terrace, some of which were illuminated from within, one or two by golden lamplight, most by weaker candlelight.

Gabriel soon discovered that the houses on his street were

back-to-back with houses fronting on to another street. A curious valley ran between the roofs of these two conjoined sets of houses broken by skylights. Realizing what a remarkable opportunity for covert observation was presented by these inwardly lit skylights, Gabriel moved to the nearest one, taking care to move as silently as he possibly could – though he saw that there were birds' nests between the chimney-pots, and therefore guessed that small sounds from above would not alarm the people in the rooms.

The first room he looked into held little enough of interest. The man named Perris, who had come with Mandorla to Kensal Green, was lying upon his bed reading by the light of a candle. He could not tell what book it was, but the only books which he knew of were Bibles, missals, catechisms, and tracts, and so the question did not seem very interesting. He moved rapidly on to the next candle-lit window.

This time, he was not disappointed.

Mandorla was in the room, naked and not alone. There was a man with her, also disrobed. He was short and barrel-chested and had abundant black hair on his chest and back and legs. The two of them made a very strange contrast – she so pale, so slender, so seemingly delicate; he so dark, so muscular, so evidently coarse.

Mandorla lay supine on the bed; the man stood over her, with one knee balanced on the side of the bed, pausing to look down at her. He did not pause long, but lowered himself on to her, obscuring her breasts and belly, but not her face.

For a moment or two, Mandorla looked back at her lover, but as he altered his position she looked sideways, at the flame of the candle which burned beside the bed. Gabriel could not read her expression precisely, but it had amusement in it.

Suddenly, Gabriel found himself sharing the mind of the man; he was surprised, for he had not consciously tried to do it. He was amazed by the turbulent quality of the feelings thus exposed to him; it was as though he had been struck by a cataract of icy water.

He saw Mandorla as the man saw her, and realized with a

shock that he had never quite known what attractions beauty had. Amalax, watching Morwenna, had been lustful, but that had been a distanced kind of lust, a lust without prospect of satisfaction. This was something else, not merely something fiercer; this was lust in action, lust responsive, lust avid with anticipation. It was gloating lust, with all the perversities which gloating implied: triumph allied with a pure sensation of power; a contemptuous desire to impose, to be felt, to force, to be feared, to dominate. This was lust with a tightness in the throat, a stretching of the heart, a savage hardness in the prick.

To Gabriel, who was nine years old, it was alien and horrific. Amalax had seemed monstrous, but this was monstrousness grotesquely amplified.

And yet, it was not all fury, not all pride. There was fear in it too, and a failure of belief. This was a man well used to lying to himself – who had become so accustomed to deception that the truth had almost ceased to have meaning – and yet he knew when the world was out of joint. He knew whores and he knew fantasies, and he knew that whores were never the creatures of fantasy that men would have them be, and that it did not and could not make sense that here was something more fantastic than fantasy; here was something which even Mercy Murrell could not contrive.

Already within the whirlpool of emotion and sensation there was a bitter aftertaste, a self-betraying denial which would not trust the perfection of appearances or the fabulous good fortune of opportunity. Already there was fear that something would be required of him here which would put such a burden on his intelligence and on his soul that the dream must dissolve, that the moment, while incompletely savoured, must turn bitterly sour . . .

This man had no notion of how cold his soul was, for he did not know his soul at all, and had no sense which could show or suggest to him how much finer and warmer souls might be . . . and yet, it was in his mind that he was too lubberly and tawdry a thing to receive the gift of this moment . . .

Gabriel felt the connection made, felt smooth and silky liquidity . . . and surprise, that it should be so easy, so comfortable, so precise.

With his outer eyes Gabriel watched as the man began to move back and forth, his right hand roaming here and there about Mandorla's body. With his inner senses he felt the skin beneath the hand: its sheen and its texture, its softness and plasticity.

Mandorla hardly moved at all, languidly accepting the inquisitive probing of the hand. Her golden hair, spread upon the pillow like a halo, was stirred one way and then the other as she moved her head, first staring at the candle-flame and then at the ceiling. She never looked towards the skylight. The expression on her face changed by degrees, as the amusement in her eyes was gradually amplified. Her white teeth showed bright as she smiled. She whispered something into the man's ear, and though the words seemed to fill a curious emptiness inside him he did not properly hear them, and Gabriel could not understand their meaning.

It went on, and Gabriel felt himself filled with a terrible aching, as of resistance against the irresistible, as of a hopeless effort to make time elastic, as of a hopeless effort to concentrate all thought and feeling into a single instant of explosive transcendence . . . all failing, all crumbling, all decaying for want of skill and possibility . . .

There was a thunder in his head.

The man's movements became more urgent, more impassioned; Mandorla was still relaxed, receptive, moved by his insistent wriggling, but initiating no movement herself save for the tilting of her head from side to side. Her arms were thrown wide, her hands quite passive. She had the calm and calculating air of one well content with waiting, he the sickening surety of one who cannot wait.

There was a moment of interruption, of taut rigidity.

The man, having held himself sternly for a moment or two, let his full weight descend upon Mandorla's body. She did not struggle. She was still smiling. Gabriel's heart was pounding with a borrowed rhythm, his breath came in stolen gasps, his blood was dancing, but still there was fear and unbelief to spoil the silent cry which could only *pretend* to be triumph and joy and fulfilment . . .

. . . but was only, in the end, a cry.

After a pause, Mandorla eased her burden over to the left, and rolled him over on to his back.

Gabriel was possessed by dullness . . . by a thick and buzzing bluntness, as though all sensation had become heavy with saturation.

Then Mandorla sat astride the man, her arse upon his pelvis, and looked down at him. Gabriel could see her violet eyes with startling clarity, at second hand. Her hair cascaded down about her shoulders, tickling his face and making him close his eyes. His expression was a peculiar mixture of contentment and irritation.

She bent, as though to kiss his neck.

And then, quite without warning, her shape began to change. The other's eyes had already closed in anticipation of a kiss, but Gabriel saw . . . Gabriel *knew* . . .

And he knew, too, with startling suddenness, that all this was really for him, that it was all performance, to show him the ways of man and wolf, of hunger and passion, of nature and need.

Gabriel tried with all his might to separate his own feelings from the feelings of the man who lay supine on the bed, knowing that less than a second would pass before he opened his eyes to see what Gabriel already saw, to know what Gabriel already knew.

He could not do it. He was trapped. His own feelings were utterly submerged by the insistence and intensity of those he shared.

The swiftness of the metamorphosis astonished Gabriel, for it had somehow seemed to him – though the belief was unexamined – that it must be uncommonly difficult for human legs to shrink, for human hands to become paws, for the face of a beautiful woman to dissolve and a hairy canine snout to emerge from its dissolution. It would have been easier to believe in an instantaneous switch, accomplished much faster than the human eye could possibly measure, but it was not that either. There was an evident flow, a visible change of state from one thing to another. The long and silky tresses were somehow consumed; the pale grey fur which sprouted in its stead emerged; the bones altered and the flesh upon them melted and solidified again.

There was only one simile which came into Gabriel's mind, which was curiously apt, and at the same time absurd. It was as though, he thought, Mandorla had *caught fire* – as though some kind of divine or diabolic flame possessed and transmuted her; as though the wolf were somehow the *ashes* of the human being.

The man, supine beneath the wolf, opened his eyes.

Even in the feeble candlelight, Gabriel could see the surge of terror from his high vantage-point. It was as though the man too underwent a kind of metamorphosis, the human face which he had worn being suddenly transmuted into an awful mask.

Horror surged through him, and through Gabriel; it was as though their twinned souls were being ripped in two, as though some dreadful supernatural claw had reached out from a fold in time to seize their faces with its talons and drag them down to Hell.

And yet, within the horror and beneath the bottomless pit of fear into which they both were plunged, there was a sense of knowing that it *had to happen*, which was no mere echo of Gabriel's foreknowledge, but a defeated acknowledgement of the imperfect follies of human desire.

The man's panic did not last long. It did not last long enough for him to make any serious effort to dislodge the wolf from her position of advantage.

She ripped out his throat with quick efficiency, and her long rough tongue lapped at the blood which flowed.

Gabriel watched. He felt the man die, and shared his death.

For the man himself, the pain was only pain, but it was curiously numb and brief – as though his nerves, recognizing the hopelessness of the situation, had elected not to scream a warning, but had extended a welcome mercy in their refusal to transmit the impulses of agony. For Gabriel, the pain was a shock of exultation, like a donation of power.

I am a spider which feeds on souls, he thought, *and I have dined this night!*

He felt a little thrill of fear as he realized that Mandorla or Morwenna might just as easily have made a meal of *him*, but that fear was easily confined and subdued. He was confident that the werewolves did not intend to use him thus – and already beginning to be confident that he might be able to stop them if they tried.

Some minutes passed while the wolf did nothing but lick the blood. The dead man's eyes were open and staring, but the rictus of terror which had masked his face relaxed by degrees, as though soothed away by her caresses.

Gabriel felt nothing now.

The wolf which had been Mandorla – which was *still* Mandorla – looked up from her work. She looked directly at Gabriel, and though the room was lit from within, so that he ought to have been invisible behind a screen of reflected candlelight, he had not the slightest doubt that she could see him, and that she had known from the beginning that he was there.

He met her wolfish stare with a conspiratorial smile of his own, which said clearly enough that he not only knew, but accepted fully, that he was of her kind and not of that blind and cold-souled *mankind* to which her victim had belonged.

He was no blood-drinker, *yet*.

He was no monster, *yet*.

But he was not a human boy, or any kind of boy at all. His flesh was merely a mask which he wore to walk upon the earth, and within that shell he was a demon . . . or a god.

And while he watched the werewolf at her banquet, he felt no vestige of sympathy for the meat which she devoured, and knew by his transcendence of any such temptation that he was now a very long way from Hudlestone Manor, and from the goodness which the Sisters of St Syncletica had tried so hard to teach him.

10

When Gabriel returned to his room, abuzz with excitement, he found that the mirror which he had set down beside his bed was glowing, as though of its own accord. He approached it hesitantly, not knowing quite what to expect, but when he saw the image which was in it, he smiled.

The face of Jacob Harkender was caught within the glass, as though reflected there. Gabriel wondered whether Harkender could see his smile.

'Gabriel!' said Harkender, as though he had been calling the name for a long time, with no result. 'Gabriel, you must listen to me. Please!'

Gabriel was confident that he could dismiss the image from the glass with the merest touch. Perhaps he could do more than that; Harkender might have placed himself at risk by entering the imaginary space within the glass, which was the central arena of his own burgeoning power. Perhaps he could destroy the man who – only a few days before! – had planned to be his master; at the very least he might hurt and distress him. But he did nothing to begin the work of making these wild fancies real; instead he wondered what Harkender had to say.

'Why should I listen to *you*?' he asked, allowing the new identity which was emerging within him to declare itself, for the first time, in the boldness of his speech. 'You took me to Hudlestone Manor, and gave me to the Sisters, knowing full well that I was no ordinary foundling. You tried to blind me to what I really am, to hide me from those who would help me . . . to hide me even from myself.'

'No!' said Harkender, seeming very tiny within the mirror-space, though it was only his face that was visible. The face floated like a rubber mask, distorted by the slight curvature of the glass. 'You don't understand, Gabriel. You must not trust the werewolves – Mandorla is mad as well as evil, and she will not hesitate to lie to you in the hope of bending you to her will.'

For a moment, Gabriel was a nine-year-old boy facing the authority of an adult; goodness and duty almost reasserted themselves. But the demon which had brought Hell's fire to his soul had no need to observe the codes and barriers of politeness, and the intelligence which Gabriel had lately acquired could not feel humble or small or overawed. The moment hovered, and was gone.

'No one can lie to me now,' Gabriel told him, though he did not know whether it was true. 'Everyone has lied to me all my life, but now the lies must stop, for I have the power to find them out.'

'You *will* have that power,' said Harkender, quickly, 'and I was badly mistaken to think that those powers which you already have could not develop so quickly. But you are very young, and no matter what power you have to see, you cannot begin to understand what you might be. Mandorla will let you see only what she wants you to see – *you must not trust her!*'

'Why not?' retorted Gabriel. 'She has told me more of the truth than you did, when you came to Hudlestone with your kindly promises. I thought myself a child possessed by a demon then, but in a few short days she has shown me that I am a creature of a very different kind, and that what I appear to be is a mere masquerade. You say that she wants to use me. I believe you! But why should my ends be different from hers, if I am of her kind, and not of yours?'

'You are *not* of her kind,' replied Harkender. 'There are none of her kind in existence, save for the members of her pack, and one of them is a renegade against her schemes. Mandorla is opposed to man and god alike; she has no cause but destruction. She will use you, if she can, to wreak whatever havoc you can upon the human race – but if you do, it is not only the magicians of mankind who will strike back at you, for there are powers which have sheltered and protected human beings since the moment of their creation, and though you may think yourself a god when you use what power you have to look into the minds of lesser men or command obedience from spiders, you must realize that there are beings whose power exceeds yours as far as yours exceeds a spider's. Gabriel, I beg of you, *do not become Mandorla's instrument!'*

Harkender's strangely womanish features could not properly display the kind of urgency and sternness which the man was trying so hard to show. His wrath, upon such generous lips, was little more than petulance; his authority was blunted by the softness of his cheeks. And yet, there was no denying the strength of the man. But was there also something peculiar in his eyes? Was there an image magically reflected in his pupils, just as Harkender's face was reflected in the mirror?

Gabriel stared hard at the man who might or might not be his natural father, but whatever was hidden behind those eyes was as black as night and formless . . . a lurking demon, impossible to secure with shape and species.

'You want to use me too,' said Gabriel accusingly, his new-found voice rasping like metal on stone. 'But I have seen you at your work, through another's eyes, and now I am inclined to think as she does, that for all your magic tricks you are a posturing fool. I am not a human child, Jacob Harkender, for all that you have tried to make me one, and now that my soul's eyes are truly open, I am not afraid. In that, at least, I am content to be guided by Mandorla, for she is the only one who has ever told me honestly that I need not be afraid.'

'You are no human child,' agreed Harkender, 'but you do not know this world into which you are newly born. It is a world with many histories, none of which are true, and you can no more learn what it really is from the tales which the werewolves tell, or from the minds of those whose inner eyes are blinded, than from the doctrines of the nuns at Hudlestone.

There is only one way to the truth, Gabriel, and that is the journey of the soul, unhampered by the falseness of history – the unfettered flight of meditation, which alone can confront the higher reality. Only I can teach you that; Mandorla is imprisoned by the fantasies which she takes for memories, as all immortals are, and as angels and demons may also be if they are not wary of the seductions of faith.'

Gabriel did not understand what Harkender was trying to tell him, but he was not disposed to say so now. He had had his fill of playing the *ingénue*, now that he had a measure of command over the power of inner sight and the werewolves of London for his kinfolk.

'What have I to do with you, Jacob Harkender?' he asked, bitterly. 'You knew my mother, so you say, but you will not say what kin I am to you. You are a man and I am not, and you have no business with me, now that I know what a trick you played on me in taking me to Hudlestone.'

'If I was not your father,' said Harkender, 'I was certainly your midwife. Though I cannot claim to be your creator, I can say for sure that were it not for me, you would not exist at all. You would be a fool to cast me off so soon, for I know that which you direly need to know, and until you have the power to see it in my mind you can only learn it from my lips. Mandorla can only feed you lies and illusions, Gabriel – only I know the truth of the world, for I alone have undertaken the great voyage into inner space to touch the fabric of the universe. Take what you want from Mandorla, but you must return to me if you would know what you really are, and what you have it in you to become.'

Gabriel stared into the depths of the mirror, less confident than he had been when first he caught sight of Harkender's image trapped within it. He was no longer smiling, and the cruel excitement born in him when he had watched Mandorla feed had ebbed away now. It was as though the demonic force within him was becoming quiescent again, and struggle though he might against its indolence, he could not help but feel that perhaps he was only Gabriel Gill after all: a human foundling, who had been taught how to be good by the Sisters of St Syncletica.

'Leave me alone!' he whispered.

'Gabriel!' said Harkender, in a voice which was almost a cry of anguish. 'Listen to me! Mandorla cannot die, and thus is free to dream – whatever madness she may embrace, she cannot die. But you, alas, might be far more easily destroyed than you imagine. You are not human, but mortal you certainly are. Angel you may become, but in that becoming you might easily use yourself up in a single blaze of soulfire. You are in dire peril, Gabriel, and you cannot begin to understand the danger in which you stand.'

'Leave me alone!' said Gabriel again, turning away from that demanding stare.

'You're not alone, Gabriel!' said Harkender, speaking rapidly, as though he knew that time was limited. 'There is another which has come out of Egypt after you – I am certain of it! For the love of God, Gabriel, believe me! There is danger, deadly danger, from which that madwoman cannot possibly protect you . . .'

With a convulsive gesture of defiance Gabriel reached out to touch the surface of the mirror, as though to brush away the image which was captured within it. Harkender's features dissolved instantly, but somehow the image of the face lingered in his mind, as the mirror's bright light had once lingered in his eyes despite its banishment.

Gabriel wanted to trust the werewolves; he wanted to believe that Mandorla would do only what was best for him, and knew what destiny he had to fulfil. But that trust had been challenged, and in being challenged was already partly lost. Whatever he *wanted* to believe, he must now remember Harkender's warnings whenever Mandorla made him a promise, and whenever she invited him to be her partner in her strange conspiracy against the human race.

Where there had been, for a little while, the illusion of safety and certainty, now there was doubt again. And what, after all, had anyone really told him about what he was and how he came to exist at all? He could almost have wished to be a mere child of Sister Clare's stern God, miserably unpossessed and unredeemed.

The door opened and Mandorla came in. Having reverted to human form she was at her most radiant. There was no trace of blood about her lips, and her smile seemed pearly white even in the dim light which struggled through the grimy window-pane.

'Still awake?' she asked, knowingly.

'I like the night,' he replied, reverting unthinkingly to the voice and manner of the boy he appeared to be. 'And I had a dream, which startled me.'

'You will have many dreams,' she promised him, moving past him to stand by the mirror. She touched it, and yellow light flared within it. It was no brighter than candlelight, but that was her intention.

'Would you like to dream again?' she asked. 'I have bright dreams myself, and I have practised the art of making them. It is a gaudy kind of magic, but a very pleasant one. You and I can share our dreams, Gabriel, if you wish it. And in time, we might make our dreams come true.'

He lay down upon the bed, but did not undress.

'I can put my dreams into the looking-glass, now,' he told her. 'I do not need to live in them at all.'

'That trick is easy enough,' she assured him, 'but the best dreams must be lived, not merely watched – how else may we know which of our dreams we would like to come true?'

Her violet eyes seemed very large in the uncertain light, as if they glowed from within. He had seen her devour a man with that strange gaze, before she devoured him in fact, but he did not fear it – nor did he fear the landscapes of her dreams.

'Will you sleep now?' she asked him, in her honeyed maternal fashion. 'Will you sleep, if I give you a dream?'

He nodded, knowing – even though he could see nothing at all of the current of her consciousness – that she saw him for a brief moment as an infant, a cub to be cherished and protected.

Was she mad, as Harkender said? Or was it demon-haunted Harkender who should be reckoned mad?

He closed his eyes for her, and felt her gentle fingertips touch his forehead; and when a few moments more had passed, he allowed her to shape a dream for him, and condescended to live it for a while, but not, in his heart of hearts, to trust it.

The world is only dust, and the forces which hold it together are breaking down. Flesh, the weakest of its structures, decays in the wind of change more rapidly than anything else.

Faces are blown away, first to leave staring eyes and then to expose the mocking smiles of polished skulls. Where once a crowd of well-dressed men and women walked with pride there is now a host of skeletons clad in rags, and then a carpet of crumbling bones. At the last there is naught but a white and gleaming desert, sere and serene.

Flowers shrivel and greenery is blanched. Where once a great forest stood in patient confidence there is now a company of brittle trunks and bare branches, festooned with creepers like breaking cobwebs, and then a legion of melting husks. At the last there is naught but a great grey swamp, putrid and pathetic.

Buildings crumble slowly, smoke-blackened bricks scoured bloody red, glass windows flowing like sullen tears, tall chimneys keeling over like wheat before a lazy scythe. Only the pyramids of Egypt are shaped to resist the loss of form, dwindling by slow degrees; they are the last of the works of man to return to the cauldron of Creation, the rain of undifferentiated atoms, the formless chaos of primal fire.

Ashes to ashes; dust to dust.

All appearance is lost and all reality retained; time is ended and there can be no waiting. Clinamen – the infinitesimal swerve which is the new beginning; the word which will become the story which will become the ceaseless warfare of truth and symbol – is instantaneous.

The white and gleaming deserts produce a new legion of creatures; the great grey swamps dress the world in colour; the hands of the makers begin their work of shaping yet again.

But whose are the faces and whose are the eyes? Where are the angels and whose are the souls? The dust is dancing once again, and the ashes have once again begun to burn with the white fire of life. But the wind has not died, and will blow again, and again, and again, and all the faces are but masks created by the angels for their masquerades.

The dream evaporated and Gabriel slept; and throughout the empty interval before he woke it did not matter at all whether he was god or demon, allied with man or kin to wolves.

There was only darkness, and peace . . .

Until the morning came again, and forced him to confront the absurd and damnable world.

The Exploratory Imagination

The primary imagination I hold to be the living power and prime agent of all human perception, and as a repetition in the finite mind of the eternal act of creation in the infinite I AM.

Samuel Taylor Coleridge, *Biographia Literaria*, 1817

1

There are two ways in which the word 'werewolf' may have been derived. The simpler account, first given by Gervaise of Tilbury, is that it comes from the Anglo-Saxon *wér-wolf*, in which the prefix *wér* simply means 'man'. It has equivalents in Latin (*vir*), in Prussian (*virs*), and in Sanskrit (*vira*). But there is an alternative account in which the prefix derives from the Norse *vargr*, which means both 'wolf' and 'restless'; it has equivalents in French (*varou* or *garou*) and in Gothic (*vaira*). Certainly there is, or has been, more than one kind of werewolf, but if we are to speak only of the werewolves which Machalalel made, which are nowadays called the were-wolves of London, they surely owe their name to the latter derivation. They are the *vargr*, the *loup-garou*, the *vaira-ulf*: the restless ones.

The werewolves which Machalalel made do not change with the moon, nor can they change entirely at will. He made them to live their lives as if they were human beings, and it was not his intention that they should ever return, even for the brief intervals which fate permitted them, to wolf form. Alas, the will of Machalalel was insufficient to deny them this privilege, which they exercise most gladly. But it is their tragedy as well as their privilege, for they yearn to be wolves again for ever, and the echo of the wolf which is in them has caused all save one of them to hate humanity and the human form with a terrible fervour.

When they are in the form of wolves the *vargr* have the consciousness of wolves, though their nature is by no means entirely bestial. When they are wolves, the *vargr* have no access to their memories of being men or women, or to the language which they used as people; their nature is more rigidly divided than that, and when they are in wolf form they see and feel as beasts though the instincts and purposes which they have are polluted and perverted by mannishness.

Werewolves in wolf form are creatures of pure will, though the will which was written in the souls of the *vargr* when they were only wolves has been much modified by their long experience of divided nature. Before metamorphosis, the human intelligence of the werewolf may shape the wolfish will to a particular end – giving, as it were, an instruction to its other self – but once the wolf form is established, modification of this purpose is difficult, and the power of the instruction may prove inadequate if it is in conflict with the innate wolfish will.

It was this malleability of the inner wolfish nature which enabled Machalalel upon his deathbed to make the luckless Pelorus the executor of his own will, indelibly impressing by command his own purpose upon the soul of his favourite. The modifications of many centuries of experience as man and wolf have not yet proved adequate to the erosion or subversion of that will, which possesses poor Pelorus entirely – most urgently when he takes the form of a wolf – and which has made him alien to his own kin.

In truth, werewolves cannot help but despise and hate human beings – they of the dark hearts and cold souls, the meek inheritors of the world. The *vargr* cannot help but be resentful of what was done to them so long ago to make them what they were not intended by nature to be. Werewolves hate and fear their own remade nature, even though that remaking conferred upon them the gift of immortality. In this respect they are very different from the Clay Man which Machalalel made before them, who has no feeling for his creator but gratitude – for his manlikeness as well as his immortality.

In his creation of the *vargr*, Machalalel failed to accomplish what he set out to do. Their manlikeness is imperfect, for they have neither the cold souls of the humans nor the hot souls of the Others. They are no longer true wolves, and the she-wolf which leads them has come to believe that nothing less than an utter transformation of the world – which would obliterate mankind and manlikeness – would suffice to allow the *vargr* to be true wolves again. It seems that they have no place in the scheme of things, and for that reason they constantly ally themselves (save for Pelorus) with those – whether human or Other – whose purpose it becomes to break or alter the scheme of things. But they may be mistaken in their estimation of where their best interests lie, for the one thing we know for certain about the scheme of things is that it is not what it appears to be. The ultimate ends of truth and destiny are hidden, as yet, from all the best efforts of prophets and diviners.

Lucian de Terre, *The True History of the World*, 1789

2

The world is a whole and must be recognized as such. The magic of fragments and dissociated objects – sympathetic magic in all of its forms – draws upon the connections inherent in the essential integrity of that whole, but is essentially trivial. It is the level at which the alchemist, the hedge-wizard, and the witch-doctor work with some success, but the true magus must endeavour to go beyond the manipulation of materials and individual souls; he must aim to work upon the world itself, whole and entire.

Kant's *Critique* demonstrates that we can know the world only as an assembly of *phenomena* – things as they appear to our senses. Things as they are in themselves – *noumena* – we can know only by inference. Of course we readily assume that things really are as they appear – how can the imagination sensibly and comfortably accommodate the idea that appearances are grossly deceptive? – but the assumption is intrinsically hazardous.

The argument of common sense holds that it is thoroughly sensible to assume that things really are exactly what they appear to be, appearances are consistent, and that noumena will always, as it were, project the same phenomena.

If appearances *are* consistent and trustworthy, then science – which attempts to discover the hidden order of phenomena – is the only true and attainable wisdom. But if appearances are *not* entirely consistent in time and space (which are themselves phenomenal rather than noumenal), then science is limited to the observations of the moment, and the appearance of the world which it describes might at any time be completely transformed. Perhaps this has happened several times in human history. Perhaps it happens very frequently, for memory is itself an appearance, and it may be that when the world comes with its own 'past' shadowed within it, so that to each and every one of its inhabitants it appears to have always been what it now is.

If appearances really do change in this way, so that noumena continually project different sets of coherent phenomena, what determines the changes? Perhaps 'determines' is the wrong word. Perhaps one should ask what it is that *creates* one world instead of another.

We have answers of a sort ready to hand. 'God' was invented precisely to fill this explanatory void; He creates and His instruments are miracle and magic; Acts of Creation which require no cause or physical power, but only His Authority and Will. But what can we know about God, save that He moves in mysterious ways his wonders to perform? Can we really deduce – or even suppose – that he is immortal, invisible, omnipotent, and (hopefully) benevolent?

Though some of these terms appear to be positive they are all in fact negative, asserting only that that God is not phenomenal, is outside appearance – is, in fact, the fundamental relation between appearance and noumenal reality. God is only the confabulation which fills in the answerless void, and so is every imaginary division which separates Him into a pantheon, or opposes Him to a Satanic counterpart, or fills the universe with animistic souls and hopeful magics.

What is it, then, that our Inner Eyes see? Is it mere delusion which presents itself to us in dreams and nightmares, in visions and locutions? When the saints came to believe they held converse with God and his angels, were they simply mad? Is what we see in dreams a different phenomenal reality, much less stable than the one we see with our outer eyes – or is it a glimpse of the chaos which underlies phenomenal order?

There is no way to answer these questions save to admit their unanswerability. But there is one way, and one way only, to achieve certainty, and that is to say this: either the world really is as it appears to be or it is not, and if it is not, then it is a world which might in principle be different, and might in principle be made different, by calculated transformation and re-creation – in which case, the true wisdom is not science but magic, and the true end of wisdom is a kind of godhood: the true Authority of the Will.

If it is to be a matter of mere faith, one must surely prefer the magical thesis.

It is necessary to work with symbolic representations, because there is no other way for the mind to grasp the world, and without such a grasp there can be no possibility of control.

My world-symbol shall be the rosy cross and the Ptolemaic universe, the Wheel of Time and the Sephirotic Tree, all combined into a whole. The dome, illuminable in different ways, will admit and celebrate change and changeability in a way which the inscribed floor cannot. Dome and diagram *together* will map out the universe for my inner eye, allowing me to place myself at the very heart of Creation.

The business of invocation is essentially introspective, and must be directed within rather than without. If there is anything in dreams other than the froth and scum of everyday thought, this is the means by which the seeds of truth, authority, and power must be made to grow, and flourish, and bear fruit.

It is vitally necessary to go beyond mere visions and locutions to a deeper and more intimate level of inner perception.

We must beware of trusting our visions too well. True insight may require the stripping away of all the idol-makers which stand between the alienated soul which is man and the cosmic mind which is the sum of all Creators; but we must ask not only, *Is this possible?* but also, *Can it be endured?*

What I am doing is dangerous, in more than one way. The main dangers form a paradoxical pair, as with Scylla and Charybdis there remains only the narrowest of channels between them; they are the dangers of war and peace, of strife and its absence.

On the one hand, whenever I invoke the state of 'magical presence' I open my soul to a realm of conflicts, for whether I choose to characterize the universal soul as a single God or as many there can be no doubt that it is divided against itself in many different ways. Whichever names I call upon to aid me in this quest for insight and power, that call will commit me to the avoidance of others; to worship one god is always to deny another. And the generosity of one god may not outweigh the spite of another.

On the other hand there is a very different danger, which is that the reaching forth of my soul into the macrocosm might become an end instead of a means. The process of projection – which some have revealingly called 'ecstatic' – offers intrinsic rewards, so that those with considerable experience of it frequently lose all interest in the affairs of the material world, becoming addicts of transcendence. Perhaps that is the reason that the Others – who seem to have once outnumbered human beings very greatly – are now almost extinct; perhaps they found ecstasy too easy, the hurdle of pain being set in their case far too low to prove an effective restraint. But perhaps this is mere confabulation.

*

For the instruction of potential disciples: I have now mapped out all the familiar phases of detachment.

One must first lose the sensation of mass and location, so that the soul seemingly floats free; it is capable then of embarking upon an odyssey across the world and out into the realm of stars – but the seductions of *that* kind of confabulation are to be avoided.

Locutions flow most freely in this phase – the Babel of voices which others have taken for the voices of the dead, or the instructions of saints and prophets – but it is necessary to learn how not to be their victim either; theirs is a siren song, full of promises but without fulfilment.

The brightest visions follow resistance to locutions. They are inherently more difficult to disregard or treat with caution, by virtue of being phantoms of sight. Angels and dragons, marvels and monsters, Edens and Hells, are all ever-ready to spin their web of confabulation; their fascinations will gradually fade as the adept grows in skill.

The accomplished master may transcend locution and vision, reaching out for the horizons of the imaginable. There is a wilderness untracked by imagery; *there* is the unfolding essence which, flowering inside a human soul, might make him superman instead of merely man, and weave the texture of his being into a better reflection of the universal soul.

As above; so below – that is the statement and the promise, the potential godliness of man. The true magus must aim at nothing less.

Do I really need allies and collaborators? If I do, should I seek out others who have already traversed the path for themselves? My experiments in education have so far proved very disappointing – but where are there other adepts to be found? The spiritists are mostly charlatans, and those who are not are trapped by the demands of those to whom they pander. The Order of St Amycus draws those who have artistry from the ranks of the Church, but mires them deep within its own particular heresy. As for the fugitive Others which are described in *The True History of the World*, how and where can they possibly be found? The werewolves of London are mere grotesques, and not to be trusted.

It may be necessary for me to remain alone. Perhaps that is the only way to achieve true Authority; perhaps the Act of Creation is necessarily individual, and He who would be God must be a lonely and jealous God. Those of my friends and followers who have loved me most intensely, and submitted most willingly to my guidance, have suffered in consequence.

I must face the fact that I can no longer accept the love of others, and should instead prefer to deal with those incapable of love. Lovers make poor instruments; indeed, the perfect instrument can only be *created*, not discovered by chance in the routine of social encounters. If there were only some way to make a magical child, in whom the latent seeds of power were sown at the very moment of conception.

There is a way in which it might perhaps be done . . .

Jacob Harkender, journal entries recorded between 1848 and 1860

2

London, 23 March 1872

My dear Edward

I do not know whether this letter will reach you before you quit Gibraltar, but while there is a chance that you may receive it I feel bound to send it, and part of what I have to report is so odd that I feel a need to commit it to paper lest I become convinced that I dreamed it.

I have been to see Jacob Harkender at his house in Whittenton, as I said I would. I had expected the encounter to be a little odd, but I fear that it had an aftermath which was odder still – but I must not get ahead of myself, and must be scrupulous in the matter of order, or you will rightly chide me for my inadequacies as an observer.

I walked to Whittenton from Maidenhead station, and was very soon seized by the impression that I had crossed some invisible border into a more peculiar world. Harkender's house is the most curious dwelling I have ever seen; it has some kind of coloured dome built into the roof. I arrived without warning, and was duly informed by the butler that Mr Harkender was not at home, but I asked if I might wait for him; the man was reluctant but eventually condescended to accept my card. He showed me into the library and left me to wait.

Though the house is not very large, appearing from the outside to have no more than sixteen or twenty rooms exclusive of cellars, the library is a good size and very tightly packed with volumes. I was quick to seek out the section of the library which dealt with Egypt, and was not surprised to find Pettigrew's *History of Egyptian Mummies* rubbing shoulders with Wilson's *Lost Solar System of the Ancients Discovered*, while Alexander Rhind's book on Thebes sat alongside Piazzi Smyth's *Life and Work at the Great Pyramid*. I was more surprised to discover a very extensive collection of books of philosophy, including Bacon, Berkeley, and Hume as well as translations from the German of Kant and Hegel and from the French of Descartes and Rousseau.

For a little while I nursed the fond hope that I might discover the British Museum's lost copy of de Terre's *The True History of the World*, but could find no sign of it; my disappointment was quickly displaced by astonishment at the riches which were there, including many volumes in manuscript. Cornelius Agrippa was there, including the apocryphal text on black magic; Ficino was there too, and the *Clavicule Salomonis*; John Dee and Robert Fludd; and Pierre de Lancre's *Tableau de l'Inconstance des Mauvais Anges*; there were countless works whose authors I do not know, in Latin and in several vernacular languages. If these texts are not merely for show, then Harkender is indeed a scholar, and one whose interests are not merely fantastic.

I had less than an hour to wait before my unwitting host came in to greet me, and was not surprised to find him unenthusiastic to entertain me. He was accompanied by a woman whom he introduced as Mrs Murrell, though whether or not she was the person who has made that name notorious I do not know.

Although my presence was evidently unwelcome I was determined to ask my questions. I told him that I was acting on your behalf, and explained to him that you had lately been in Egypt. He recognized your name with some slight annoyance, but his attitude changed very markedly as soon as I mentioned that you had gone into that part of the Eastern Desert which is high on the sandstone plateau to the south of Qina. He asked who took you there, and I told him about your mysterious Father Mallorn. In reply to questions which he fired at me with great rapidity, I then explained what had happened to you, as you described it to me, and told him that I had been advised to approach him by Samuel Birch at the Museum. Only when I had concluded did it occur to me that I had come to ask questions rather than to answer them.

Harkender's reaction to what I had told him was unmeasurable, but Mrs Murrell seemed both surprised and disturbed by what I had said. Harkender saw this too, and immediately suggested – though I inferred that the suggestion carried the weight of a command – that she should withdraw. He then professed amazement at what I had told him, and stated that he had had great difficulty in persuading anyone to guide his own expedition into that region – a difficulty which had intrigued him sufficiently to redouble his efforts to reach it. Eventually, he said, he found less superstitious men who accepted the task, and was able to stay for some weeks in the valley where your own adventure took place, exploring among the mastabas.

The tombs, he said, had all been looted long ago – perhaps in the days of the pyramid-builders – and such artefacts as he managed to discover were humble ones, including potsherds and stone tools. He took leave to inform me loftily that even very small things have value to the antiquary, and reminded me that these explorations were carried out before publication of Sir John Lubbock's book *Prehistoric Times*. He claimed that news of his own discoveries had encouraged Sir John to go to Egypt himself, though he modestly accepted that his excavation was an utterly insignificant one by comparison with such marvellous work as Burkhardt's discovery of the great temple at Abu Simbel or Hoskins' explorations in Nubia. None of his own workers, he said, was ever bitten by a snake, and none suffered any kind of hallucination.

Although there was nothing very untoward in his tone, and what he said sounded perfectly plausible, I was quite convinced that Harkender was lying to me. I yearned to be able to disconcert the man – to shock him out of his composure, and so I said: 'Do you by any chance have in your library a book entitled *The True History of the World*, signed by one Lucian de Terre?'

There is no doubt that this shaft went home, for Harkender's astonishment was writ plainly upon his features, but I obtained no immediate advantage by it in so far as obtaining information was concerned. He merely observed that it is a very rare book, and that he had read it once in the Museum, but had never been fortunate enough to obtain a copy. He did ask, however, whether it had any relevance to the story which I had told him. I explained that it was possible that the man who called himself Mallorn had referred to the title of it, and this seemed to set his mind momentarily at rest. Then I remarked that an acquaintance of mine knew a man who claimed to have written it – and *that* information seemed to be as astonishing to Harkender as the mention of the title had been.

When Harkender asked me where the man was to be found I was determined to be as evasive with him as he had been with me, and I simply said that, alas, he was dead – but that I had heard that the book was a farrago of nonsense. Harkender smiled at that, and observed that I must be a sceptic, like you; he said that he had known you at one time, and still read your work, which he found interesting. You may be interested in his next comment, which was: 'Sir Edward was always an admirer of Bacon, sharing the great man's view that if only the mental idols which obscure and confuse our thoughts could be cast down, the truth would be manifest for all to see. Alas, I cannot agree with him. The truth never can or will be made manifest, for it is not a constant thing at all but something which shifts and changes, continually eluding our attempts to grasp it. Lucian de Terre knew that, which is why he wrote a book of poetic fantasies, in the hope of capturing the truth by concealment. It is perverse, I know, but it seems that hidden truths are not undermined and altered quite so quickly as those which are thought to have been made manifest.'

Harkender then said that he would like to meet you again, and would try to call on you when you are back in England. He added a promise that he would try to help your mysterious young man to recover his memory, employing his skill in hypnotism.

I had by this time grown impatient with the contest of wits in which we were engaged, and did not want to be taken entirely for a fool. I told him that although I had no right to demand information from him, and came to him perforce as a beggar imploring his help, I had nevertheless told him a story which he seemed very interested to hear, and wished that he could give me something in return, if only a trifle. I told him (not altogether sincerely) that I judged him an honest man, and was confident that he would see the justice in my claim.

Harkender admitted in his turn that I too am an honest man, but said that he had more of the market trader in him than I might suppose. He then promised to tell me the name of the Order to which Father Mallorn truly belonged, if I would tell him what man it was who claimed to have written *The True History of the World*, and where he lived before his death. Although I considered this bargain, I did not think I was free to make it, given that the man was the patient of a colleague, and that what I knew of him I had been told as a doctor. I told Harkender as much – and though he was disappointed, he seemed to desire that we should not part on bad terms. He asked me whether your priest had had a ring, and when I confirmed that he had, he asked whether it bore the letters O, S, and A. When I confirmed this also, he said that the letters stood for the Order of St Amycus. When I replied that I had never heard of any such saint he merely smiled, and said that few men had, but that they have a convent in London whose Superior is named Zephyrinus.

I confess that I had the ill grace to complain that this information was meagre reward for my trouble, but that did not please him. He said that he had only one thing more to say, and that was to warn us both that we are out of our depth in this matter. 'Sir Edward may have tried hard to persuade himself that what happened in the desert was mere hallucination,' he said, 'but he cannot sincerely believe it. His view of the world will never allow him to glimpse or to comprehend the roots of this mystery, and it would be better for all of you if you did not attempt it. Nevertheless, I would like to help the young man who does not know who he is, and will do so if you will permit me.'

I am sorry if you feel that I mishandled this meeting – as I suspect that I did – and I can only hope that if and when Harkender calls on you in London you will make a better fist of it; this letter will at least serve to forewarn you.

The day's events did not, however, conclude with my departure from Harkender's house; the most remarkable began with my leaving. I crossed the Thames at Hurley, heading towards Maidenhead, where I had to catch the train to Hanwell – I intended to break my journey there so that I might see Austen again.

I had skirted Prospect Hill and was descending the slope towards Stubbings Heath when I realized that I was being followed.

While we waited for the train, I edged closer to my pursuer

and studied him covertly. He was a young man, whose dress gave every indication of belonging to the city rather than the country. He was certainly not a labourer or a domestic servant, and his manner reminded me of a travelling salesman, though he carried no bag of any kind. He glanced in my direction occasionally, boldly and quite insolently, and the waiting seemed to make him very impatient.

When the train arrived, I put my bag into an empty compartment, and then looked back to see what the young man did. He met my gaze steadily for a moment, then got into a compartment in the next carriage. I had a book in my bag – Darwin's *Descent of Man* – but I made no attempt to take it out and read, being content to wonder about the curious substance of my discussion with Harkender. How did Harkender know about the ring which your priest was carrying? Could his word be trusted in the matter of the inscription which it bore? Why was Harkender interested in the man who had claimed to be Lucian de Terre? What *had* he discovered in the Eastern Desert, and what was its connection with the disaster which had later overtaken your party?

I made no attempt to invent possible answers for these questions, but as their number increased I became increasingly embarrassed about my failure to extract more information from the evasive Harkender, and I must confess that I dismounted from my carriage at Hanwell in a bad mood. I was further annoyed – but not at all surprised – to see the young man alight with me. Having become impatient with myself over past failures I now decided to take the bull by the horns, and I strode up to my pursuer while the queue to surrender tickets was forming.

'I believe that we have both come from Whittenton,' I said.

If he was surprised by my boldness, he did not show it, but simply admitted that we had. His voice was strangely soft and silky, but there was liquor on his breath and a certain agitation about his manner. He added that he had not the pleasure of knowing me, and asked my name. I felt suddenly foolish, having once again come to demand information and found myself being asked instead to surrender it, or at the best to exchange it. And yet – how could I refuse? I told him my name, and that I was a surgeon, but was quick to ask in my turn who he was.

He smiled, and said: 'My name is Calan, and I am a servant. Do you live in Hanwell, sir?' I could not remember having heard another voice remotely like it, for it was throaty and yet not harsh at all – but it was slightly drunken, and I had the impression that he was not entirely in control of himself.

By this time we had both passed through the barrier, and I stopped, determined to wait until the young man had moved off before resuming my own journey. I answered his question by saying that I was visiting a friend, and asked whose servant he was. He clearly knew why I had stopped and was unaccountably annoyed by it, as though I had no right to thwart his purpose. He replied, somewhat intemperately, that his mistress was called Mandorla Soulier. He looked at me curiously as he said it, obviously half-expecting that I would know the name. He did not go on his way, but stubbornly stood still, staring at me in his half-intoxicated fashion. His insolence made me angry, and with some asperity I asked him whether it was his intention to follow me all day, and whether that was the kind of errand on which his mistress usually sent him abroad.

He was very annoyed by this, and replied in astonishing fashion. 'I will follow you no further, since you obviously wish it so,' he said, 'but I bid you remember that you cannot hide from us. We can always find you, if we wish it, for we are the werewolves of London, and your friend Mr Harkender has not a tenth of the power which we command. You must warn him to stay clear of us, and not to try to find the boy.'

While I stood there, amazed, the young man turned on his heel and went quickly away, heading eastwards. I was still standing, as if rooted to the spot, when I was hailed by Austen, who was hurrying along the street from the direction of the county asylum, which he attends three days a week.

He asked me what news I had from the Hell-Fire Club, in a jocular manner which I could not bring myself to share.

When I told Austen what had just happened he was most astonished, but said that he could give a partial explanation of it – for he had heard only that morning of the disappearance of a child from the convent school at Hudlestone Manor, and that the child in question had been placed with the Sisters by Jacob Harkender! He was amazed, though, that the man on the train knew about the affair, because he did not think that the news was likely to have reached Harkender himself as yet. I was quick to ask him whether the Sisters in question belonged to the Order of St Amycus, but he assured me that he had no knowledge of any such saint, let alone an order named after him.

What on earth we are to make of all this, I have not the slightest idea. What began as a little puzzle seems to be expanding day by day into a Gordian knot of confusion. I tried to make good use of what time I had at Charnley by picking Austen's brains, but he is as mystified as you or I by the tricks and turns of the affair – though he does say that the werewolves of London are mentioned in de Terre's *The True History of the World*.

I can add, however, that Hudlestone Manor appears to be used at present by the Sisters of St Syncletica – a saint whose name seems as unlikely as the unknown Amycus, but one who does in fact exist.

Whether anything I have written here will help at all to unravel the mystery which has caught us in its meshes I cannot tell, and I hope that you will not think that I have conjured up a superfluity of mere melodrama. All that I seem to have gained from my endeavours is an inclination to look behind me, in case I am followed – and that is something which I share with an uncomfortable number of Austen's patients. I do not believe in the power of Harkender's magic, still less in the fabulous werewolves of London, and yet I cannot help but be a little bit afraid, lest we have unwittingly attracted the attention of those who might somehow do us harm. I pray that your return will introduce a keener eye and sharper wit into our enquiries than I have so far been able to provide.

Yours in anticipation
Gilbert

PART THREE

The Comforts of Blindness

Those who restrain desire, do so because theirs is weak enough to be restrained; and the restrainer or reason usurps its place & governs the unwilling.

And being restrain'd, it by degrees becomes passive, till it is only the shadow of desire.

The history of this is written in Paradise Lost, *& the Governor of Reason is call'd Messiah.*

And the original Archangel, or possessor of the command of the heavenly host, is call'd the Devil or Satan, and his children are call'd Sin and Death.

But in the Book of Job, Milton's Messiah is call'd Satan.

For this history has been adopted by both parties.

It indeed appear'd to Reason as if Desire was cast out; but the Devil's account is, that the Messiah fell, & formed a heaven of what he stole from the Abyss. . . .

Note: The reason Milton wrote in fetters when he wrote of Angels & God, and at liberty when of Devils & Hell, is because he was a true Poet and of the Devil's party without knowing it.

William Blake, *The Marriage of Heaven and Hell*, c. 1793

1

*H*ell's flames crackle and spurt beneath his golden body, each one a dart of pain and ecstasy which intensifies his sight, but all the revelations of his inner eye are tragedy and grief. As he weeps his bitter tears he longs for the comfort of blindness.

The unreachable earth above him is stained by sores and weals and scabs; it has seemed for a brief while to be slowly healing, coming closer to peace, but the prophetic sight of his cycloptic eye reveals shadows of awful possibility. The earth, like a sweet ripe fruit upon the branch of eternity, is host to cankers and parasites within, whose pupae squirm beneath the surface as if ready at last to crack and split, disgorging their black spiders and their yellow cats, whose bite is poison and whose claws are sharp.

If he could only reach out his healing hand . . .

His heart is beating within his breast, strongly and sturdily; he can feel its healthfulness, but he has long since learned that when he feels that inner strength the time is nearly come when the eagles will fall again from the fiery sky, riding the tides of the astral light, so that their talons may teach him what he needs to know: that man is no more than a whim of fate, all of whose vanities are mere vexations of spirit, for there is a time to rack and a time to rend; a time to harm and a time to hate; a time of war and a time of dark destruction.

He turns his head, desperate for aid, but God is helpless outside His Creation; He has made change, with its own inherent logic; He has made destiny, with its own inbuilt end; He has made time and space with their own intrinsic unfolding; but He is only surface, only image, only Alpha and Omega, Beginning and End, for ever and ever . . . Amen!

The wolves are running despite that their world has turned to ice, and though one has separated from the pack, and has turned his face to Satan's, with mercy in his bright blue eye, what can his tears matter or his stout heart achieve?

And in the cave the goddess smiles, and reaches out a beautiful hand to touch the face of the prisoner freed, to stroke his cheek and steal his eyes, and enslave his wayward heart. . . .

David Lydyard woke – or perhaps only thought that he woke – to that haven of comfortable darkness which could be won by the closing of his eyes. He was sweating feverishly, and he had a curious sensation of bedazzlement, as though his powers of sight had been overwhelmed while he slept by an unnatural profusion of light. This sensation was certainly an illusion, though, for when he opened his real and actual eyes they were startled by the relatively modest light which streamed through the porthole of his cabin. They were, in fact, so startled that three or four seconds must have passed before he saw the wolf.

The creature lay – or so it seemed – upon the floor. It was huge by the standards of its apparent kind, but there was nothing threatening about its manner; its body was quite relaxed and though its head was raised and turned towards him so that its bright blue eyes could watch him, its teeth were not bared. Its stare was placid and contemplative, not greedy at all.

Lydyard was surprised by his own reaction, which was to say silently to himself: *At last it has come and must now be faced. At last the madness has stepped from the shadows, to possess the world.*

Then, for the second time – or perhaps the third or fourth – he awoke, to the comfort of blindness.

This time, when he opened his fearful eyes, there was only Paul Shepherd, risen from his bunk and fully dressed, staring at him with evident concern.

It was not such a great surprise to find him thus, for the young man's condition had been improving for some days. His periods of wakefulness had grown longer, though they had until now been confined to the hours of darkness, and there had been clear signs of returning intelligence: expressions of bewilderment and anxiety; semi-coherent murmurings in which could be heard the occasional English word. Only the day before, Tallentyre had opined that whatever trauma had robbed poor Shepherd of his senses had now relaxed its hold upon him to the point where he might become himself again at any moment. That prophecy had evidently come true.

Those bright blue eyes – which had before seemed empty and innocent – were piercing now, startling in their authority.

'Is it over now?' asked the young man, reaching out to touch Lydyard on the shoulder. 'Is the dream quite gone?'

'Oh, yes,' said Lydyard, with a small laugh to signify his awareness of the irony that the other should be concerned for him. 'I am quite myself again, and not in Hell at all.' He threw back the sheet to bare his chest, and the blue eyes shifted to look at the porthole.

'What coast is that?' asked the young man.

'North Africa,' replied Lydyard, mechanically. 'We are not far from Tunis, *en route* from Alexandria to Gibraltar.'

The other nodded, as if relieved to find himself in a part of the world which he knew. But what he said was: 'Where Carthage once was, and where the Barbary pirates are.'

'Where the Barbary pirates were,' Lydyard corrected him. 'No doubt there are brigands in dhows who prey upon their own kind, but the *Excelsior* is a steamship, and the days of piracy are gone.'

'Of course they are,' replied the young man, softly. 'Dead and gone, and nearly forgotten.'

Lydyard extricated himself from the sweat-dampened bed-clothes and came down from the bunk. Strangely, it did not occur to him to be embarrassed by his nakedness. He had shared the cabin with his mysterious companion for several days, and was well used to the sight of the other's unclothed body. He dressed unhurriedly, carefully taking things in order. The turbulent anxieties of his nightmare were not yet completely calm, and he needed time to adapt himself to the grip of normalcy.

While he pulled on his clothes Lydyard felt the gaze of the bright blue eyes upon his face again, their curiosity almost tangible. He imagined that the young man was struggling with recalcitrant memories, trying to figure out what had become of him.

'Are you William de Lancy?' asked the young man, finally.

'No,' said Lydyard, shortly. 'De Lancy disappeared, in the desert south of Qina.'

'Then you must be Lydyard. De Lancy disappeared, you say – what about Tallentyre, and Brother Francis?'

'Tallentyre is in the next cabin,' Lydyard replied, carefully. 'The priest is dead. His heart stopped in that same place. Do you know what became of you there, Mr Shepherd?'

The remarkable eyes were steady enough, but they lost something of their intensity while he seemed to ponder the question. Finally, he shook his head.

'No,' he said. 'I cannot remember. Can you tell me?'

'We found you naked and badly hurt,' said Lydyard, continuing his dogged pursuit of the ordinary by ringing the bell which would summon the steward to bring a bowl of water. 'We found your horse near by, and certain personal possessions, but you had lost your wits. We brought you with us to Wadi Halfa, then to Cairo and to Alexandria – an enigmatic trophy, to remind us of the mysteries of the desert.'

This comment was met by the briefest of smiles, and a question: 'How much time has passed since you found me?'

'Nearly forty days,' Lydyard answered.

'Have I troubled you greatly?'

'Not greatly. We have contrived to feed you, and keep you clean, with the minimum of difficulty. Had I lost my own mind, I am sure that I would have posed far greater problems for those who had to look after me.'

'But you *have* looked after me,' said the other. 'I am grateful that you did not abandon me to some Egyptian asylum.' His voice was melodious and his diction very clear; he sounded like a cultured Englishman, but Lydyard could not put away an absurd suspicion that the language and his flesh were only masks that he wore.

'Sir Edward would not hear of that,' Lydyard said. 'We knew that you were no Egyptian, and such papers as we were able to recover said that you were an Englishman. Then again, you posed a question for whose solution he could not offer a sensible hypothesis. To a man like Sir Edward, that is like showing a red rag to a bull.'

'Of course,' said the other, smoothly. 'I have read one or two of Sir Edward's essays.'

'You seem to know a good deal about us,' Lydyard observed. 'Yet we know nothing at all about you, save for your name. Did you follow us without our knowing it, and if so, why?'

'Yes I did,' answered the young man, frankly. 'As to why . . .'

He broke off at this point because there was a knock upon the door. When the steward came in – showing some surprise at finding the cabin's second inhabitant awake – he paused again. Lydyard took the opportunity to excuse himself, and suggested that while he was gone, the steward should inform Sir Edward Tallentyre that the young man was awake, and able to talk. The young man nodded, readily accepting the postponement.

By the time Lydyard returned, Tallentyre had arrived, and had already struck up a conversation. The baronet, it seemed, had moved more quickly than Lydyard had to demand an explanation.

'It was Brother Francis that I was following,' the young man was saying. 'He and I had . . . similar interests. I was told that he had joined your party, and so I knew your names, but not your faces. I hoped to catch up with you in the valley, but it seems that I never reached it. I do not know what happened to me . . . it seems that I have lost forty days and more from my life. It seems . . .'

As the young man trailed off in apparent confusion, Lydyard was watching Tallentyre. The baronet's features were hard-set and his eyes were darkly suspicious. Tallentyre, Lydyard knew, was asking himself whether the young man was lying, and if so, why.

'Have you ordered breakfast?' Lydyard asked, as he began to wash himself.

'I have,' said Tallentyre, seating himself at the small table in response to a vague gesture of Lydyard's hand. Shepherd sat opposite, and they began to wait politely for Lydyard to dry himself. The burden of silence quickly proved too much for Tallentyre, though, and he turned again to the other.

'What brought you to Egypt, Mr Shepherd? And what set you on the trail of our friend the priest?'

'I suppose I am an antiquary, of sorts,' replied Shepherd, 'as was the priest. We each had our reasons to think that something of interest might be found in the valley, that something might have happened there, or might be about to happen there.'

'You are very vague,' observed Sir Edward. 'Will you tell us more precisely what you mean?'

A long moment passed while the two men stared at one another. Finally, the blue-eyed man said: 'Some things I cannot tell you; others I fear that you would not believe. I am very grateful for the help which you have given me, but there is more at stake than the simple repayment of hospitality. We were attacked in the valley, were we not? Something reached out to hurt us all, in different ways. With all due respect, Sir Edward, I do not think you could believe me if I were to hazard a guess as to what it was.'

'David was bitten by a snake,' said Tallentyre, drily. 'As to what became of de Lancy, I cannot tell. Mallorn's heart failed; perhaps it was caused to fail by terror, but neither I nor any other can say for certain. As for myself – perhaps I was attacked, by some dreadful creature of the night? So at least it seemed, and in a way I might be glad to know that it was true, for then I could trust my perceptions better than I have been able to do these last forty days. But there is also the possibility that I was deluded, and that what I thought I saw was only a phantom of my own mind . . . a creature of delirium and nightmare. Please do not tell me what I can or cannot believe, Mr Shepherd, because I do not know myself; but I want to hear your account of what befell us in that God-forsaken place. Even if it is the stuff of purest fancy, still I would hear it. And I tell you frankly that I do not like your casual statement that there are things which you cannot reveal.'

It was an impolite speech, but Lydyard was glad to hear it, and interested to see what response it would bring forth. Again, they were interrupted, though, because the steward brought their breakfast in, and lingered in order to busy himself with the distribution of napkins and the pouring of coffee until Tallentyre impatiently commanded him to be gone.

The young man commenced to eat as if he had been ravenous – though he had certainly been fed while his senses were gone, and he did not seem unduly thin. No matter how anxious Tallentyre was to hear some response to his provocations, he was forced to be patient. Not until he was perfectly ready did the young man offer any kind of explanation. A quarter of an hour went by before he consented to put his coffee cup aside for the last time, and began to speak.

'I owe you a good deal, Sir Edward,' he said. 'And I am sorry that I dare not tell you everything – but even if I did, you would not have your explanation, for there is too much that I do not know myself, and I fear that what was done to me was done to prevent my learning any more than I already knew. I cannot stay long in your company, but it would be wrong if I were to go without a word of thanks. I do not think you can believe what I have to say, but perhaps I should be grateful for that, and you are entitled to make up your own mind as to how mad I might be.

'I went to the valley where you found me for the same reason as the monk who called himself Francis Mallorn, who belongs to a company called the Order of St Amycus. We were both concerned to discover what it was that had awakened there, and how dangerous it might be. It is a creature newly made, whose like has not been seen on earth for some hundreds of years, and I do not know why its Creator has roused it now from a long inertia with which it had seemed content. I do not believe that the creature is evil, or that it attacked us with any intent to kill. It must have found the world a very strange and unfamiliar place, and its reactions were doubtless very confused.'

Tallentyre did not immediately reply to this, and Lydyard took the opportunity to say: 'It is not really dangerous, then, this creature?'

'It is more dangerous than you can imagine,' said Shepherd, flatly, 'because of the power which it has, and because it is like a newborn child in a world very different from that which it formerly knew. It probably has no innate malice against the world of men, but if its power were to be seduced to some destructive purpose, it could wreak great havoc.'

'You claim, then, that there actually *was* a creature,' said Tallentyre, as though stubbornly determined to take only one step at a time.

'There was a creature,' the young man confirmed. 'You saw it, and felt its presence. It was no delusion.'

'I believed, for a brief while, that I saw a creature,' admitted Tallentyre, 'but I could not sustain that belief, even while I felt its presence. I could not believe in a living Sphinx, and despite your assurances, I still feel compelled to hesitate.'

'Your hesitations are your own affair,' said the other. 'I have no ambition to convert you to any new faith. I can only tell you what happened, and I am happy to admit, if you wish it, that I might be utterly wrong. No one is immune from delusion, and I have greater cause than most to know how deceptive appearances can be. Shall I continue?'

'Certainly,' said Tallentyre. 'By all means tell me, if you can, where this enigmatic creature came from.'

'It was created, in the moment when you first saw it. It was probably not the first creature to be formed by its Creator, for the snake which bit Lydyard may have been its instrument too – and if so, that with which he was stung was certainly no ordinary poison. Whether the creature still exists I cannot tell, but if it does it may no longer have the chimerical form which it presented to you – that, I think, was an image borrowed from your own mind, or perhaps from the priest's. If it walks upon the earth now, it will probably have human form, for there is something about that form with which the world has become preoccupied.'

'I have never heard of any such saint as Amycus,' said the baronet, taking up another point. 'Nor did I ever hear the name from Mallorn.'

'Like the greater number of the saints,' said the young man, 'Amycus is a product of legend – though the legend has been long forgotten by all but a faithful few. It is said that another saint, who lived in Greece not long after the death of Christ, was befriended by a satyr, who assisted him in his merciful work, protected him from his enemies, and ultimately became a convert to his faith. In consequence, the satyr too was elevated to the company of the saints – and his name was Amycus. Brother Francis would not have mentioned the name because his Order is a secret one, hidden from Rome and from the world at large.'

'And how much of this do you ask me to believe?' said Tallentyre, calmly. 'Am I only to acknowledge that this Order might exist, or am I required to accept that there really was a saint who was a satyr?'

'Legend is often as reliable as memory,' said Shepherd, without any obvious irony in his tone. 'But whether the satyr saint existed or not need not trouble you. If you would have me play the scholar, I can do it well enough, and will only insist that Amycus was adopted as a symbol by a company of neo-Platonist Christians in the second century. Like many of the educated converts of the day they sought – long before Aquinas – to reconcile the dogmas of the faith with the wisdom of the Classical philosophers; they were declared guilty of a gnostic heresy. The followers of St Amycus have preserved their secret knowledge to the present day. They believe that they own a truer history of the world than the one recorded in the Bible, and a special knowledge of the nature and destiny of man. In the Middle Ages their company turned to alchemy and ritual magic, which tradition of research they have also preserved. With other gnostics they believe that the entrapment of the divine spark of the soul within an envelope of flesh was a kind of blinding, which brought it into a quasi-somnambulistic state. The world of appearances – which is to say, the world of vulgar matter – is not in their view the true world of God's Creation but a much inferior thing shaped by lesser Creators who were both corrupt and incompetent. These lesser Creators, tentatively numbered seven by association with the seven planets, are thought by the brothers to control the material world, and to have a predatory interest in human souls, which they seek to prevent from union with the Light of Heaven.'

'And will you now tell me,' said Tallentyre, 'that it is one of these seven Creators which has recently been awakened, having previously slumbered for centuries beneath the ancient sands of Egypt?'

'That is undoubtedly what Brother Francis would have told you,' said the young man, agreeably, 'had he seen fit to break his vows of secrecy. But the Order of St Amycus is by no means alone in its belief that it preserves the truest history of the world. There are many other histories kept in writing or in memory, all of which share the notion that the world of appearances is but a shadow of some greater reality, vulnerable to the interventions of those who have creative power. The Order's faith is one among many distorted images of the past, no better and no worse than most.'

'And why did these beliefs bring Mallorn to Egypt, and to his death?' asked the baronet.

'The Order embraces a Millenarian faith, which anticipates the end of the world as prophesied in the Book of Revelation. Its members believe that Christ will return as redeemer to transform the world into an unimaginable paradise, and they assume that this return must be a glorious and warlike one, in the course of which the malevolent shapers of the material world will be crushed. Their Christ is pure spirit, who could not deign to clothe himself in actual flesh, though he might condescend to present a human appearance to the eye of observers – and they believe that his reappearance will follow the arrival in the world of a false Christ made by the shapers, who will represent the last desperate throw of the evil angels. They are ever on the lookout for that Antichrist and his minions, and for signs of the coming end.

'In Brother Francis' eyes, the creature which you saw was made by a fallen angel, and might have come into the world to play the role of Antichrist. He must have believed that his righteousness would protect him from harm while he came to find it, but it seems that his convictions may have failed the crucial test.'

'It is a failing of religious men,' said Tallentyre, in a voice hardly above a murmur, 'that they commonly put arbitrary faith in place of reasoned belief. I am sorry to think that a man's heart may be stopped by so little a thing as a loss of faith. A man of science, on the other hand, must always be willing to be proven wrong by the evidence of his senses – an open mind requires a bolder heart.'

'I am glad to hear it,' said Shepherd. 'But in truth, Sir Edward, you have not been very severely tested by what happened to you in the desert or by what I have told you just now. It is, I fear, your friend here who is endangered – for though he has a mind as open and a heart as bold as your own, he has also a poisoned soul.'

And so saying, the man turned to David Lydyard with such an expression of pity in his bright blue eyes that Lydyard felt his blood run cold.

2

Lydyard had been virtually unmoved by all that Paul Shepherd had said, until the moment when the young man spoke in such vivid metaphorical terms of his own predicament. All the talk of awakening Creators and gnostic heretics had washed over him as though it were merely a rippling wake left by the strange events which had occurred in the valley south of Qina; whether or not there might be any truth in it had hardly seemed to matter. But when the explanation was suddenly expanded to take in his continuing condition of disturbance, he felt an unexpectedly strong sense of invasion and threat.

Lydyard had said little to Tallentyre of his trials and tribulations. To that hardened realist, a man who could not stand fast against his nightmares was to be reckoned weak of will – and Lydyard had every reason to wish that his guardian continue to hold a good opinion of him. For this reason, he had made light of his sufferings, and had been dismissive whenever Tallentyre had noticed that something was amiss with him. Although he had made occasional reference to the content of his visions – especially to the curious readiness with which his dream-self identified with a suffering and innocent Satan – he had always done so with a calculated contempt which suggested that they were mere follies unworthy of serious attention. In the privacy of his own thoughts, though, he had contemplated his experiences in a very different way, wondering whether it might actually be possible, after all, for a man to be possessed by a malefic demon which could plague him with vicious fancies.

Lydyard really did feel as though some strange eye had opened within him, to whose gaze all his thoughts, sensations and memories were mercilessly exposed. Worse than that, he sometimes felt that this strange inner vision looked outwards in its own extraordinary fashion, and that by some mysterious process of leakage its extra-sensory perceptions were polluting his own consciousness. If only this magical inner eye cared to concentrate its efforts, he suspected, the secret thoughts of other men might be as open to inspection as his own, and he feared that he had hardly begun to see what might in the fullness of time be revealed to him.

He was afraid of this, not so much because he feared what he might find in the minds of other men, but because he feared what might become of himself as a result of that discovery. He did not believe that he had yet gone mad, but he did fear that madness was lying in wait for him, and might claim him if his firmness of mind were to be further softened or shattered by the fearful weight of unwelcome revelation.

When Paul Shepherd looked at him, therefore, with what seemed to be understanding of his predicament, Lydyard felt a very profound shock in which fear and hope were intimately alloyed. For forty days he had thought of Tallentyre's mystery as something intriguing but peripheral – a potential distraction from his private woes rather than an extension of them. He was now abruptly made to see that this had been a foolish attitude. He cursed himself for having to be so unkindly forced to recognize that his condition was at the very heart of the mystery, and that its cure might depend on the solution of the puzzle.

In spite of all this, though, Lydyard said nothing in reply to the young man's observation. Tallentyre was still present, and Lydyard could not abide the thought of confessing the extent of his desperation to the man whose daughter he loved. Nor did Tallentyre recognize any need for interruption in what Shepherd had said, for he let the reference to Lydyard's poisoned soul go by as though it were nothing more than empty rhetoric. The baronet simply passed on to his next questions, which were: 'If you do not share Father Mallorn's anxieties about the advent of the Beast of Revelation, what was your interest in the valley? And how did either of you know that anything of interest would happen there?'

As though in a daze, Lydyard heard the answers given, but he could only store them away in his memory for future response.

'The Creator who shaped me left me no option but to take an interest in the others of his kind,' said Shepherd, in a gently ironic tone which testified that he knew full well how odd the statement sounded. 'He had become very interested in the problem of mankind, and he commanded me – in a fashion which permitted no rebellion – to be a friend and protector to men, whatever forces might threaten them. Whether or not the creature which emerged from the tomb is the one whose advent was prophesied by the Book of Revelation its arrival in the world must be reckoned ominous. As to how I knew of the awakening of its Creator . . . I can only say that I have my resources, though you might not be prepared to recognize their validity. Despite that the world has changed so profoundly since it was made, some magic can still be made to work, even by cold-souled men – and there are those who nowadays have human form, yet are other than human, whose dreams are sometimes to be trusted as glimpses of the future.'

'That is riddlesome talk,' complained Tallentyre, 'of a kind which I have too often heard from men who pretend to esoteric wisdom. England is full of charlatans who claim that they can converse with the dead and obtain intelligence of the future – but I think that they are all tricksters and fantasists.'

'The dead are dead, alas,' admitted the other, 'and those who try so hard to hear their voices are deluded by hope. By the same token, many of those who would dearly love to be inheritors of ancient wisdom are too eager to believe that they have found what they seek. And yet, the way of pain is not completely closed, even to human beings, and there are others whose inner sight has not been blinded or exhausted. If I say that I am not free to speak of them more forthrightly, you will think me guilty of mere mystification, but it is true. Some would argue that I have already said too much, but I have a reason for telling you as much of the truth as I dare.'

'And what, pray, is that reason?' demanded Tallentyre, satirically.

'Whatever that creature which attacked you may really be, and whatever the intentions of its Creator, it is still at large in the world. If it is dangerous, you stand in greater peril than other men, and the will of Machalalel will not let me leave you naked to that peril. If you intend to pursue this matter further – and I cannot believe that a man like you could possibly let it alone – then you deserve such enlightenment as you are capable of achieving. If it is a man who has succeeded in awakening this Creator, then he is a very dangerous man indeed, and I warn you now to beware of him. If the man is but an instrument, then whatever it is that has used him is more dangerous still. You, Sir Edward, have no power but knowledge and intelligence – and the only way in which I can try to protect you from the possible consequences of your inquisitiveness is to give you information. That is what I have done; whether you believe me or not is entirely a matter for you to decide.'

'I am in your debt, of course,' said Tallentyre, but Lydyard could see that the baronet was impatient with what he considered to be mere bluster. He could see clearly enough that Tallentyre's entire battery of sceptical suspicions was roused now. For himself, he could only stare mutely at the young man's handsome face, in unexpressed sympathy.

Shepherd turned abruptly away from both of them. 'If you will forgive me,' he said, 'I must rest for a while. I am still not quite myself, and I need sleep. Do not be afraid that I will regress to my former condition. We will talk again, I promise you, but for now . . . I must ask to be excused.'

Tallentyre made no attempt to persuade him to continue, but stood up promptly and signified his consent with a too-theatrical bow. 'Perhaps we both need time to consider what has been said,' he said. 'And I fear that David is still suffering a little from his misadventure. We will go on deck, before the sun climbs so high that it becomes unbearable.'

Lydyard consented to be led from the cabin, though he looked back from the doorway in great perplexity to meet those ice-blue eyes with his own.

As soon as the two of them were safely ensconced in canvas chairs on the shaded side of the deck, Lydyard was quick to ask the baronet what he thought of their reawakened guest.

Tallentyre needed little prompting. 'He is a most remarkable person,' he answered, judiciously. 'But in all that farrago of nonsense there was precious little which could qualify as honest explanation. It is all blusters and evasions, and I must confess to the hope that when he has had time to think about it, he will concoct a better story.'

Lydyard cast about for a suitably diplomatic way in which to phrase his next question, and eventually said: 'Is there any truth at all, do you think, in what he told us? Does he honestly believe it himself?'

'I cannot tell,' answered the older man, 'but I think that may be the least of all the conundrums which he has set before us. We live in an age of would-be magicians and Rosicrucians, spiritist mediums and mesmerist healers. Many there are who claim to hear the voices of the dead, or to draw upon the power of mysterious godlings. Simple incredulity is no help in dealing with such phenomena, and our friend knows that well enough to tantalize us with his refusal to care whether we believe him or not. He dares us to open our minds while he teases us with gaudy fantasies, but in one sense he is right – if we want to play this game which has snatched us up unawares, then we must be prepared to set our established beliefs aside, at least for the time being.'

'He has at least given us an account of the mysterious Father Mallorn,' observed Lydyard. 'He did not know about the ring we found, whose initials might indeed stand for the Order of St Amycus.'

'We do not know that he has never seen the ring,' Tallentyre pointed out, 'for he has admitted that he came to Egypt following the same trail that led the priest here. But it does not seem to me to be so very interesting that a company of heretics might have survived into the present, for the dogmas of the orthodox Church are not one whit less silly.' He paused then, as if lost in painstaking contemplation of what he had been told.

'What do you intend to do with him?' asked Lydyard, quietly.

'It is not for me to do anything with him, now that he has recovered his senses,' said the baronet. 'He may go his own way, as and when he pleases. On the other hand, I assume that we will have the pleasure of his company at least until we dock at Gibraltar.'

'Will it be a pleasure?' asked Lydyard. 'I thought that he had begun to annoy you.'

'There is a certain masochistic pleasure to be found in annoyance,' said Tallentyre, lightly. 'And even if he is nothing but a silly fantasist, still he might prove to be intriguing. And after all, *something* happened in that valley, which has cost the life of one man, and perhaps a second.'

'But you will always refuse to accept that there was an actual creature, despite what you saw,' said Lydyard, colourlessly, 'and if this man insists on asserting that there was, you will surely have difficulty finding common ground.'

'I hope I am more honest than that,' said Tallentyre. 'However we are to account for it, we have seen what we have seen, and it was very strange indeed. But there is a great abyss between the supposition, for the sake of argument, that there was an actual thing which had the semblance of a Sphinx, and an acceptance of all this talk of Creators. I am reluctant to accept that the world of which I have knowledge is a mere illusion of appearance, and that the history which is implied by that appearance is no more accurate than the fantasies of the monks of St Amycus. If appearances are as untrustworthy as that, how can men ever plan their lives? What makes us rational beings is the ability to plan for our own advantage, which necessitates that we are able to calculate – roughly, at least – what the consequences of various possible actions will be. All such calculations are based in our understanding of what the world is like, and how it has previously behaved; if our understanding is false, how can we explain the continuing success of our calculations? It is, you will surely grant me, a manifest truth that human intelligence succeeds, at least to a degree, in ordering the affairs of men and in securing some measure of moral and technological progress.'

This speech helped to set Lydyard's seething mind at rest, for it was a return to a mode of discourse with which he was very familiar, having listened to Tallentyre expound his views on many occasions. It offered a way for him to return to the familiar ground of hypothetical argument. 'And yet,' he found himself saying, 'when all Europe believed implicitly in those dogmas of the Church which you now deem false in every particular, still there was an order in the affairs of men, still there was rational action, and still there was progress. The enlightenment of which you are so proud was initially born out of ignorance and error.'

Tallentyre smiled, for the first time since the conversation had begun. 'I take it as a compliment,' he said, 'that you should try to confound me with rhetoric, for I fancy that you have had a clever teacher at home as well as those you met at Oxford. You are right, of course; false belief need not be a barrier to progress – but I insist that the progress of intellect occurs in spite of false belief, and not because of it. If the Church had not sanctified Hippocrates and Ptolemy with the stamp of faith, how much sooner might we have had the scientific medicine and the scientific cosmology which are only now emerging to displace their bold but unhappy guesses?'

Lydyard was tempted to point out that the falseness of the ancients' cosmology had not prevented the priests of Egypt from using their astronomical tables to predict the flooding of the Nile, nor the Church from revising its calendar, but he resisted temptation. 'Shall we treat this whole affair as an intellectual game, then?' he asked instead. 'Is it only a pleasant folly, notwithstanding that one man has died, that another has disappeared from the face of the earth, and that we ourselves may have come very close to death?'

'It is a mistake,' Tallentyre replied, soberly, 'to think of games as frivolous things. Many men have died for sport, whether their pleasure be hunting big game or playing cards. There is an element of mummery and play in our most solemn enterprises – in the working of the law courts, and in the conduct of wars. Britain's glorious empire is, after all, a kind of game, played out to written and unwritten laws, in all manner of fanciful costumes. If it were not that we had nearly died, I would let this thing alone, but I have been hurt, and I wish to know how and why. If I must listen to tales of imaginary Antichrists in order to discover what is going on . . . so be it.'

'And you expect no less of me,' Lydyard added, dully.

'Do not play the hollow man with me, David,' said Tallentyre. 'I know you too well. You could not turn away from the attempt to discover how you came to be cursed with these nightmares, even if I desired it. You too have been hurt, and I know that you must be as avid for an explanation as I am.'

Sir Edward spoke, Lydyard thought, more truly than he knew.

Later, Lydyard returned to his cabin. He was not entirely surprised to find that Paul Shepherd was not asleep. Apparently, the young man had been waiting for him, desirous of an opportunity to speak to him alone.

Lydyard felt that there was little point in wasting time. 'Tell me,' he said, 'what happened to me when I was bitten by the snake.'

The other seemed relieved to be asked so directly. 'It is not easy to explain,' he said. 'And what I know of your condition has been inferred from very meagre evidence. You have delirious dreams, I believe?'

Lydyard nodded.

'You feel, perhaps, as though you are *possessed* by some alien entity?'

'That is precisely how I feel,' confirmed Lydyard, dolefully. 'Do you mean to tell me that it is true?'

'In a manner of speaking, it is. By means of the snake, the being which created the beast which attacked Mallorn and Sir Edward has injected a little of itself into your own being. In so far as there really are devils and demons, this entity is one of them – but you must not be too alarmed by that, because it might equally well be called an angel. It is not evil in any simple sense, and though the Christian Satan may be a representation of something like it, his image is much distorted by human hatred.'

'In my dreams,' said Lydyard, reluctantly, 'I have often seen Satan in Hell, and have thought that in some way he is my own self, and by the same token, I have thought him misunderstood.'

'There is sometimes truth in dreams,' said Shepherd. 'The dreams with which you have been afflicted may have more truth in them than most – but they are not on that account to be trusted without question. Everything which you see is filtered by your own concepts, your own beliefs, and your own fears. Men who seek enlightenment often forget that, and far too many have succeeded only in discovering a grotesque magnification of the anxious fears and ambitious hopes with which they began. It is true of saints, and of Satanists too. Never surrender your scepticism.'

'Can I be cured?' asked Lydyard, coming to the point with brutal determination. 'If I am indeed possessed, can this thing within me be exorcized?'

'It cannot be driven out,' said the other, in a tone which suggested that he was sorry to be the bearer of bad news. 'It may let you go, in its own good time, or it may not.'

'Are you saying that there is nothing I can do?'

'That depends on what the being which has intruded itself into your soul intends to do with you. In all likelihood, it seized upon you as a means of gathering information about the world

– it seeks to know what you know, and see what you see. It has been quiescent for so long that the world into which it has awakened is very different from the world in which it went to sleep. It has power, and it has intelligence, but it is at present an innocent struggling to comprehend what it has become, and what has become of the world. I do not believe that it is Satan, or the Beast of Revelation, but that does not mean that I know exactly what it is, or what its awakening really signifies, or how powerful it is. What I do know is that the chain of events which led to its awakening seems to have begun in England, and it is probable that the solution to the mystery is to be found there. If and when I can discover what is happening, I may be able to help you further. It may even be possible that you can help me. Do not despair if you should lose me, because I will come to you again when I can. But you must beware of certain others, who have appointed themselves enemies of mankind, and beware also of the man to whom Sir Edward's enquiries will inevitably lead him.'

'Are we likely to lose you?' asked Lydyard.

'Very likely,' admitted the other. 'I may be in danger myself, and this forty-day sleep of reason has certainly not been to my advantage. But I am your friend, and I will do whatever I can to help you to deliver yourself from your unfortunate predicament. Alas, you may discover sooner than I can what the thing which has elected to use you has become during its age-long sleep, and how it may exercise its power now that it is awake.'

'You are overfond of that word *alas*,' said Lydyard. 'And you are distressingly vague about what it is that this angel or demon might intend. Has it, in fact, the power to bring about the end of the world of men, as Mallorn's gnostic brotherhood believes?'

'I honestly do not know,' answered the other. 'I doubt it. Everything I know about its kind urges me to believe that time may have robbed it of some of its power while it slept, and that it will be very reluctant to waste what remains. But I dare not take that on trust. It *may* have been awakened in order to wreak destruction, or to become the hapless prey of some other being of its own kind, which seeks to take it unawares, but I dare not say too much, for whatever I say is heard not only by you, but by the being which has trapped you in its web. I only beg you to take care, and to be strong, and to be patient.'

What fine advice! thought Lydyard. *I come to him for reassurance, and he redoubles my fears. Before, I was only afraid that I might be going mad; now, I must be more fearful by far of the possibility that I am not!*

'If you are right,' he said, softly, 'then I may indeed be damned – I am condemned, at least, to find out what becomes of men who fall into the hands of a living god. I would rather disbelieve it, if I can.'

'"As flies to wanton boys are we to the gods,"' Shepherd quoted, '"they kill us for their sport." I wish that I could tell you that it is not true, but when beings with godlike power last walked the earth, they certainly did not scruple to destroy mere men . . . and there were those among them who believed that the extermination of man would be no bad thing. But there were others who believed differently, and it may well be that another belief is true: that cold-souled men have it in them to become more powerful by far than the gods once were, and – unlike the gods – need not be destroyed by the exercise of their own creativity. You have no magic, David, but you are neither powerless nor helpless, and I wish you would always remember that.'

Lydyard looked at him bleakly. 'Who are you, really?' he asked. 'I do not believe for a moment that your name is really Paul Shepherd, or that you are the kind of faddish mystic Sir Edward takes you for. In fact . . .' But he broke off then, unable to say any more.

'You are right,' answered the blue-eyed man. 'The name is a mere flag of convenience, and so is the pose which I struck for Sir Edward. But I dare not tell you who and what I am, if your inner eye has not yet allowed you to see it. I can only give you warnings, which you may heed or not as you please.

Beware of the creature when you meet it again, no matter what disguise it wears. Beware of the man who visited the valley before you, and who dares to dabble in the affairs of fallen angels. And beware of the werewolves of London, who will surely know as much as I know, and probably more.'

3

When Lydyard woke next morning he found the lower bunk empty. His first reaction was to assume that Paul Shepherd was simply keeping irregular hours, but when the other did not reappear he and Tallentyre mounted a discreet but careful search. It quickly became obvious that their erstwhile companion was no longer on the ship – and it proved, on investigation, that the remainder of his belongings had disappeared from the hold in which they had been stowed.

Tallentyre dismissed Lydyard's suggestion that only a madman would leap over the side of a vessel at sea, pointing out that the African shore was no more than four or five miles away, and that there were many other boats in the vicinity. Tallentyre, in fact, seemed oddly unconcerned by the disappearance of their visitor – as though the incident served only to confirm his suspicions about the man's veracity. Lydyard, by contrast, felt the loss keenly, not so much because he believed everything that he had been told, but because Shepherd had at least held out the hope that his inner predicament might be comprehensible. Despite his reluctance to believe that he was possessed, he had come to find the notion less dismaying than its obvious alternative. So great was Lydyard's fear of being mad that the possibility that he was instead possessed by some alien intelligence – whatever the likely outcome of the possession – now seemed like a saving straw to be grasped.

The *Excelsior* continued to make its slow way to Gibraltar, where they found two letters from Gilbert Franklin awaiting them, which set everything in a new light. Then even Tallentyre began to regret that Shepherd was no longer available for further cross-examination.

Tallentyre read the two letters in turn, passing each one to Lydyard as he finished it. Tallentyre's reaction, as ever, was superficially cool and thoughtful. Lydyard's, on the other hand, was full of an excitement which he barely succeeded in controlling for the sake of propriety.

'What do you think?' asked Tallentyre, as soon as his companion had laid down the second letter.

'They corroborate what Shepherd told us about Mallorn's affiliation,' said Lydyard, beginning very warily. He dared not confess his reaction to the reference to the werewolves of London which was in the second letter, because he had not cared to give Tallentyre an exact account of the strange warnings which had been given to him alone.

'They also offer us a possible source for some of his own statements,' Tallentyre observed. 'I will be very interested to read this book, if a copy can be found – and I would like to speak to Franklin's friend about his mysterious patient. But as for Harkender . . .'

Lydyard knew how unusual it was for Tallentyre to leave a statement unfinished, and was surprised to hear the sentence trail off.

'Do you know the man well?' he asked.

'I feel that I know him rather *too* well,' the baronet confirmed, his voice full of distaste, 'though I have not seen him for years. I have often heard his name bandied about when conversations have turned to the fancies and follies of modern occultism, but I have not met him face to face since I came down from Oxford. He was a student there – not in my college, but well-enough known in the town. He was a bitter man, who had learned too well how to hate and sought to make a virtue of the fact that he was hated. He was clever, and sharp of wit, but he was an outsider – the son of a businessman who had entertained social ambitions for him which were perhaps more optimistic than realistic. Fearing that he might be scorned, he protected his feelings by insisting upon his own hatefulness, and tried as hard as he might to hurt others as much as they hurt him. He refused to admit the basis of any orthodoxy at all, whether social, religious, or scholarly – he would certainly have relished the prospect of becoming an Antichrist. He did not graduate, but whether that was a failure or a refusal is a matter of opinion.'

'And he is now a magician?' asked Lydyard.

'He poses as one,' said Tallentyre, scrupulously. 'It seems that he chooses to conduct his rituals in very strange places.'

'With very strange results,' Lydyard added, though he did not like the way Tallentyre looked at him when he said it. Quickly, he added: 'What do you make of this curious matter of the abducted child and the self-declared werewolf?'

'I cannot take self-declared werewolves seriously,' said Tallentyre acidly. 'If such mythical beasts have lived quietly in London for centuries, I wonder why they now consent to be lured from hiding. On the other hand, although I am reluctant to believe that a man like Harkender is capable of turning his occult learning to any practical purpose, it certainly does seem that others have become sufficiently interested in his affairs to offer dark and reckless warnings to casual callers at his home.'

'Can we doubt that our experiences in the valley are in some way connected with his earlier expedition?' asked Lydyard, feeling that he at least could not. Though Paul Shepherd had not mentioned Harkender by name Lydyard was certain that he must be the man of whom he was supposed to beware – and that this person named Calan, however his lurid claim was to be construed, was one of the others against whom he had been warned.

'The phrase *in some way* may cover a considerable range of possibilities,' commented Tallentyre.

'And are you prepared to count among those possibilities the awakening of some slumbering demonic demigod?' asked Lydyard, with ironic asperity.

'I suppose I must,' said Tallentyre, with equally ironic generosity, 'if no simpler explanation can be found. But in the end, Occam's razor must rule here as it does in any quest for a satisfactory explanation.'

'Will you go to see Harkender yourself, when we return to London?' asked Lydyard, and was surprised to see the expression of distaste renewed in Tallentyre's features.

'Perhaps, or perhaps not,' answered the baronet, his voice implying that the negative was more likely than the positive. 'He and I had a quarrel once, and though Gilbert suggests that *he* is more than ready to forget it, I am not so sure that I am. Nor do I like the tone of the little lecture which Gilbert quotes – which was presumably delivered in the expectation that it would be quoted. No doubt Harkender thought it amusing, but I do not.'

'Have we much chance of finding answers to our questions if we refuse to address them to Harkender?'

'How can I possibly tell?' Tallentyre retorted. 'But he is the last man in the world from whom I would expect an *honest* answer. If he is the only man in the world who knows the truth, then I suspect that there is little chance of that truth being fully disclosed. Nevertheless, I suppose that we must be prepared to hear what he has to say.'

'Shall I visit him alone?' asked Lydyard. 'It might be easier.'

Again Tallentyre looked at him rather sharply, as if the suggestion were less welcome than it should have been. 'He seems to have been less than generous in replying to Franklin's questions,' he observed, 'though Gilbert, in his customary fashion, has forgiven him for it. With all due respect, David, I think you might be too polite to penetrate the man's evasions. I will see him myself, if and when the opportunity arises.'

'And will you also seek out Mandorla Soulier, and the werewolves of London?'

'If I can,' said Tallentyre, as though he could not consider it seriously as a possibility. 'If she or her eccentric servant can be found, then I will be very pleased indeed to hear what they have to say.'

Lydyard, remembering the warnings which he had not passed on, reflected that he could not endorse the word 'pleased', but that he would be most interested to discover whether the werewolves of London really did exist, and what they were if they were not true werewolves, and what they might have to do with the mysterious Jacob Harkender, and the equally mysterious Paul Shepherd.

That night – possibly because his imagination was now fuelled even more fully than before – Lydyard dreamed a nightmare more vivid and more easily remembered than any which had visited him since the night of his first fierce delirium.

The vision began very quietly, with a series of images. The images were neither bright nor very sharp and they had little colour in them. Most were tall buildings seen from close range at ground level, so that their roofs and towers soared vertiginously into the murky sky. Some he recognized: the new Palace of Westminster, Notre Dame de Paris, the dome of St Paul's. Others were chimerical, compounded by the imagination out of borrowed fragments; here the familiar spires of Oxford mingled with uncommonly ugly French gargoyles, with Turkish or Muscovite minarets, and stranger edifices known to him only through works of art. At some point he began to see these domes and towers as human hands and fists reaching out in a vain attempt to grasp the star-filled sky, and from then on the shapes seemed to lose something of their solidity and become fluid.

From contemplation of these lofty heights his viewpoint shifted to the horizontal, and to images of streets thronged with people. At first the crowds were distinct and identifiable: the night-birds of Piccadilly; the Sunday riders in the Row; the beggars of Cairo; then the crowds, like the buildings before them, began to merge and overlap. It was as though his mind's eye strove to find within these individual crowds the Platonic Ideal of a crowd: an archetype infinitely greater in claustrophobic confusion than the tens of thousands who flocked to Epsom Downs on Derby Day or any human herd driven from its land by the fire of war.

Lydyard normally had no fear of crowds, no horror of people in the mass, but in this nightmare the sheer profusion of human bodies became appalling.

His dreaming self withdrew into a night-lit desert where nothing was to be seen but rock and sand. The sand was gently stirred by a warm wind, its tiny motes sparkling with reflected starlight as they drifted in the heavy air.

Lydyard began to walk across the derelict landscape, each step carrying him for thirty yards. And when he saw ahead of him a great ruined city he knew that this was not his own world – or, at the very least, not his own time – for the buildings half-fallen into ruins were greater by far than any of the petty edifices which he had earlier remembered or constructed.

Here were columns a thousand feet high, and statues six hundred feet from top to toe. Some of the statues had human heads, others had human torsos or human legs and feet, but all of them were chimeras of one kind or another.

Eventually, he came to the very centre of the city, where the towers had been taller still before they had fallen into ruins. Here there was a steep-faced pyramid which had not been toppled by age and time.

The apex of the pyramid was at least a mile above the base, and each of its steps was taller than a man. To scale it would have been an extremely difficult task for a group of men, but the floating dreamer drifted lightly up its face as though he were nothing more than a mote of sand tenderly carried by the capricious wind. He entered the interior of the pyramid through a great arched portal. He began to drift downwards then, through slanting corridors and vertical shafts, and into such a maze of catacombs that he lost all sense of direction.

This journey into the darkness became frightening, for the dreamer could not imagine how he would ever escape, but the fear did not last long, for the flight began to slow down, and he soon saw light ahead of him. As the light came closer, reassuring in its yellow brilliance, his movement gradually ceased, until he found himself standing once again on booted feet, at the threshold of a great lighted chamber.

As he stepped forward into the light he felt the weight of his own body, the dry warmth of the air against his face, the grip of his clothes about his chest, the slow beat of his heart. He was uncomfortably material, distressingly alive.

The chamber was vast. Its ceiling was more than two hundred feet high, and its floor must have measured four or five hundred feet on either side. In its centre was a throne, and on the throne – fifteen or twenty times as tall as a man – sat the cat-headed goddess Bast, looking down at him with her huge amber-coloured eyes. There were no other human or semi-human figures to be seen in the carpeted chamber, but there were thousands of yellow cats variously occupied in sitting, strolling, grooming, or playing. None of them paid the slightest attention to the dreamer as he moved forward.

Lydyard was very conscious of his own tininess as he approached the seated figure. Although the cats were much smaller than him, their size being perfectly normal by comparison with his own, he felt that he was no bigger than a beetle, and they no larger than ants.

With every forward step he took, the interested scrutiny of those huge eyes seemed to become more terrible and more threatening. He looked around as though to seek help, and though he saw no one he was terribly conscious of the *absence* of certain individuals. Cordelia Tallentyre was not there; William de Lancy was not there; Sir Edward Tallentyre was *almost* there, but not quite. In the absence of these particular persons he felt an extra burden of loneliness and anxiety, which made him cry out in anguish.

The words which he cried aloud were: 'What do you want of me?'

The last word echoed eerily from the walls, and he was forced to wonder whether it would be worse to be met with silence or to hear a reply which would fill the empty space with unending sound. He had not time to form a conclusion before the echoes died, answerless.

He looked wildly about him, desperate for help, but there was no other human being to be seen.

He was seized by a very powerful feeling that Sir Edward *ought* to be here, and that if only Sir Edward *were* here, everything could be saved: his life, the world, his soul, the soul of the world. If the Sphinx with her dreadful riddles were truly the Beast of Revelation, he felt, and cat-headed Bast her Creator, then Tallentyre and Tallentyre alone could find the answers which she required; Tallentyre and Tallentyre alone could play Messiah and deliverer to his beleaguered self and the world unhealed.

But I too, he told himself, *am Sir Edward Tallentyre – for the kind of wisdom which is his does not belong to him alone, but to everyone. It is not secret and it has neither unsolvable mysteries nor any esoteric doctrines. If the need is ever there, I can bring Sir Edward to answer it.*

But still, the goddess had to be faced. Still he had to suffer the gaze of her yellow eyes. Still he had to question her, to demand to know what she truly was and what she wanted of him.

And so he met her gaze, and asked his question.

'Why?' he cried – and though he sounded the word once and once only the echoes threw it back at him in absurd multiplication, draining the meaning from it by converting it into an empty ululation, which filled his ears so painfully that he was cast out of the dream altogether, and woke in a cold, cold sweat, appalled by the dreadful stillness of the night.

4

*S*atan *writhes upon his bed of fire, as fiercely as the restraining nails will let him. He tries with all his might to deny the insistence* *of sight, for he cannot bear to see that firmament in which the earth is set like some polluted and unpolished jewel. Once, the sky was all fire and fury, but now it is dark and starry, and amid the stars strange shadows are stirring, which sometimes glide like great black cats and sometimes scurry like hirsute spiders. The stars are their eyes: the eyes of stalking predators . . .*

Satan longs for the cool darkness of the cave of illusions, for the heavy chains of merciful confinement, for the gentle play of firelit shadows upon the secluding wall. Even there he could hear the howling of the wolves, and sense the icy touch of the bitter wind upon their fur, but there was a measure of safety in that cave, and a kind of peace. Here in Hell there is only pain, and the sight that comes with pain, and the knowledge which comes with sight, and the fear that comes with knowledge.

Satan has many names, and one of them is Shepherd, though the shepherd has lost his flock and fears for the wolves that may come into the fold to drink their fill of thick red blood, but the shepherd is only one more wolf himself, and knows too well the thrill and taste of warm rich blood, and how can he accuse the spider and the cat of wickedness, when he is they and they are he and there is none at all who has clean hands?

And Satan's other name, for now, is David of the poisoned soul, whose petty slingshots cannot after all prevail against the immensity of Goliath and the uncaring impotence of the God who is Outside, in the dark beyond the dark, where time is not, and space is not, and life is not, and hope never was . . .

Pity Satan, in his misery and desolation; pity he who would repent and redeem, who would save and release, who would wash away the stains of his guilt, if he only could, were he not lost and damned.

Were he not lost, and damned . . .

Lydyard woke with a start, ashamed that he should have slept when he intended only to rest his tired eyes, while he was fully clothed and the hour was not yet late. After the shame came a tear of regret, because he had hoped, with all the fervour of one who has little hope left, that in the familiar surroundings of his own room, upon the familiar mattress of his own bed, he would once again be able to sleep the restful sleep of ordinary life, free from the nightmare which had snatched him up in an Egyptian tomb, and had not let him go.

Alas, though he had come home whole and safe, he had brought his demon with him. It possessed him as fiercely as it ever had, and mocked him as loudly. There was to be no easy escape from its demands.

His homecoming had not been successful. Though he had looked forward to it with all the eager anticipation of which he was capable, he had not risen to the occasion. He had played his part, he remembered now, with appalling awkwardness. If there had been a chance, however slight, to leave Hell behind and return instead to the comforts of custom and affection, he had lost that chance by his own ineptitude, by his own failure to seize the moment as he should have seized it.

The moment was still horribly fresh in his mind, and dreadfully uncomfortable. As the carriage had turned into Sturton Street a shaft of dewy sunlight had shone briefly through the side window, illuminating his face; he remembered how his eyes had blinked in startled response, and how he had tried to sit upright. He had been very tired, but well enough aware of the need to preserve appearances. He had glanced at Sir Edward, whose face showed not the least sign of laziness, and envied the immunity to fatigue which the man seemed to have.

He had leaned forward so that he could look out of the window. Sturton Street had been exactly as he had always known it: the pale façades of the terraces to either side, the narrow 'gardens' caged by iron railings in the centre. Its familiarity had been momentarily reassuring, but even then his self-betrayal had begun, for that very familiarity had somehow seemed bizarre, as though the house in Sturton Street – and for that matter, the whole of London – could not really belong to the world which he had been led by misfortune to inhabit.

As Tallentyre strode majestically up the steps and into the house, Lydyard had felt a strangely sharp sensation of being under observation. He had turned immediately, and looked directly at a person who was standing on the opposite pavement, leaning against the railings, apparently caring nothing for the rain. The man's face was shadowed by a broad-brimmed hat, but Lydyard did not think that he would have recognized it. The man made no attempt to conceal himself, or to pretend incuriosity – but Lydyard, feeling nauseously uncomfortable, had only turned away, to go leadenly into the house.

Once they were inside the returning travellers should have abandoned themselves to the pleasures of reunion. Lady Tallentyre had greeted them with an easy formality which did not eclipse the radiance of her affection, Cordelia with calculated extravagance, the servants – led by the indomitable Summers – with sturdy bonhomie. It should all have won broad smiles from Tallentyre and Lydyard, but Lydyard could not remember having smiled at all . . . or if he had, he had smiled with glassy falsity, with his lips alone and not his fevered eyes.

Somehow their coats had been shuffled off and spirited away, and the entire party had moved towards the sitting-room. There, while they had waited for tea to be served and while Tallentyre was receiving the loving attentions of his wife and daughter, Lydyard had stood aside, feeling very much alone. Summers had spoken to him, but he had not even heard what the butler said, let alone responded in any fashion which befitted a civilized man.

Then it had been Lydyard's turn to be greeted by Lady Rosalind and her daughter. 'I hope that you are quite recovered from your adventure?' had said the lady, to whom precedence gave the right to speak.

'Oh yes,' Lydyard had said, as lightly as he could – though his words must have sounded horribly hollow and insincere. 'Indeed, I am ashamed of myself. To be bitten by one snake was careless enough; to be bitten by two seems awkwardly symptomatic of a developing predilection. Happily, I survived both injuries.'

'Your journey home cannot have been easy,' the lady had said, with the utmost politeness.

'Not so very difficult,' he had replied. 'Our amnesiac took well to the schooling required for his care, and his eventual recovery and departure simplified matters further. Since we left Gibraltar it has all been . . . plain sailing.'

Lady Tallentyre had excused herself then in order to give instructions to the servants, though her true purpose was to give Cordelia the opportunity of exchanging a few private words with Lydyard – but his awkwardness had only increased, his foolishness magnified.

'Awkwardly symptomatic of a developing predilection,' she had quoted, in teasing fashion. 'What a monstrous phrase! And then to slip into such deadly cliché as *plain sailing*. You really must learn how to talk to my mother in a better fashion than that.'

She had demanded – nay, pleaded – for a witty reply, to be turned with deftness to a compliment, to open the way for affection. How well he understood that now! But what he had said was: 'Agreed. I really must.'

Disappointed but valiant she had continued, her voice soft with authentic concern. 'But how are you, really?' she had said. And he had replied, hollowly: 'Fit and well, and very glad to be home.'

She had frowned, and who could blame her? She had looked upon him as though she had discovered a stranger in his guise, a wolf in sheep's clothing, an imbecile where a lover should have been. 'I can forgive you the banality of the first remark,' she had said, 'but not the apparent insincerity of the second.'

He could still feel, even now, the fever of the blush which had crept upon him, and the agony of the stutter through which he had tried inarticulately to assure her that he certainly was *extremely* glad to be home.

'In that case,' she had said, 'there must be some other cause of your confusion, for there is something awkwardly unspoken behind every word you utter.'

She was right, of course. She was right, though he had
not told her – for his letters to her had somehow assumed
the same shroud of secrecy that cloaked his conversations
with her father. In fashioning a wall to hide his visions, his
nightmares, and the poisoning of his soul – though he must
have done it very ineptly – he had built a barrier between
them. He had committed his love for her to prison, so that
he could no longer find the way to express it. In the face
of her disappointment, he had only been able to murmur
something about telling her everything, in time – a remark
whose incoherence had only annoyed her further.

He had not known what to say to begin to save the situation,
and knew now that his helplessness must have been embar-
rassingly obvious to everyone. He had been rescued, after
a fashion, by the movement of the little crowd into another
room, but that had not redeemed him from his misery.

He had heard Lady Rosalind say to her husband that a man
named Jacob Harkender had called, and that another, named
Shepherd, had also come in response to an advertisement
which Gilbert Franklin had placed in *The Times*, but that both
of them had been asked to return at a convenient time, and
that Franklin would be there for dinner . . . and so on, and
so on . . . and with his head spinning, Lydyard had at last
found the courage to ask for permission to leave, in order to
come to his room and lie down.

He had *not* intended to sleep, but had been kidnapped by
the nightmare which would not let him go.

He sat up, just in time to call out an invitation to enter in
reply to a knock at the door.

It was Tallentyre, fortunately more concerned than annoyed.

'Are you recovered, David?' he asked. 'I cannot blame you
in the least, for that was a damnably uncomfortable ride, and
though it is spring the London air has not lost the touch of
winter. If anything was calculated to bring out the heat of
that poison which lingers in you, it was certainly that filthy
fog which descended in the night. Will you be well enough
to come to dinner?'

'Oh yes,' said Lydyard, faintly. 'I will dress – most certainly, I will dress. What hour is it?'

The last question needed no reply; even as he spoke the words he looked at the clock on his mantelshelf: the old clock; the old shelf; the old fireplace. He felt, for the first time, a pang of reassurance, a ripple of that kind of glad homesickness which needs no cure.

'Gilbert is here,' said the baronet. 'Shall I send him to see you?'

'Oh, no,' said Lydyard. 'I do not need a doctor. It was foolish of me to lose my wits in that sorry fashion, and doubly foolish to fall asleep. Forgive me, please.'

Tallentyre only nodded, as if satisfied that the refusal of a visit from the doctor was an infallible guarantee of good health.

'Did I hear that Harkender had called?' asked Lydyard, to make conversation. 'And someone with the same name as our one-time companion?'

Tallentyre nodded again, and said: 'They will return, no doubt.'

'And what does Franklin say?' asked Lydyard, as he searched his wardrobe for a dinner suit, wondering if he could still remember how to put it on. 'Has he news to add to his letters?'

'Little enough,' replied the baronet. 'He regrets that he has not been able to ascertain whether Harkender was speaking the truth when he said that the ring which we described was significant of membership in the Order of St Amycus. I assured him that we had heard as much as we needed to know about the Order of St Amycus from another source, and asked about the man who followed him from Whittenton to Hanwell; but he has been unable to trace Mandorla Soulier, if she exists. He does say, though, that his house was recently broken into, and miscellaneous papers stolen – including the letters which I sent to him from Cairo and Alexandria.'

'Little enough, as you say,' said Lydyard, while changing his clothes.

'Oh, he said far more, as he invariably does,' Tallentyre told him, airily, 'but it is all of no consequence. With Austen's help he set out to make discreet enquiries of local tradesmen about the boy who went missing from Hudlestone. Local gossip assumes that the child is Jacob Harkender's illegitimate son, but that is the kind of conclusion to which uninformed speculators always jump. The people at the Lodge claim that the child was kidnapped, but there was no conspicuous evidence of abduction, and the common opinion seems to be that he simply ran away. There are the usual rumours of ill-treatment, but Austen told Gilbert that the home has a good reputation, and was certainly not notorious for cruelty before this unfortunate incident occurred. He observed that all such institutions inevitably have problems with runaways.'

'All of which,' said Lydyard with a sigh, 'merely adds to the labyrinth of dark hints, in which we cannot yet see a guiding thread.'

'And so we must set it aside,' said Tallentyre, 'and make haste to enjoy our homecoming dinner. Cordelia is very anxious for you, and I am sure that you have a great deal to say to her.'

While he was speaking, both men heard the sound of the doorbell. Lydyard had completed his costume before Summers appeared at the door, full of gestured apologies.

'There is a gentleman who wishes to see you, Sir Edward,' he said. 'He has no card, but he says that his name is Shepherd. He has been here before, in reply to the advertisement which Dr Franklin placed in *The Times* at your request. He says that he is most anxious to have news of his brother, who travelled with you from Egypt. He is with the doctor in the drawing-room.'

Lydyard took note of the fact that although Summers' tone was light and level, he stressed the word *gentleman* as if to imply that the caller was no such thing.

Tallentyre and Lydyard went down together to see the visitor, and found him confronting Gilbert Franklin in awkward silence. When he saw the man, Lydyard could not suppress an audible gasp, and was glad to see that Tallentyre seemed no less astonished. The visitor might easily have been mistaken for the man they had found in the desert. His hair was similarly tawny, his complexion equally pale, and he had the same remarkably bright blue eyes. He was dressed much as a lawyer's clerk might have dressed, and yet had a little of the *élan* which Paul Shepherd had briefly displayed before his disappearance. Lydyard noted that although he had handed his bowler hat to Summers he had not surrendered the stick which he carried, which was made of black polished wood with an ornate silvered handle.

'Sir Edward,' said the stranger, with studied politeness, 'I am very pleased to make your acquaintance, and offer my apologies for interrupting your homecoming, but I really am anxious to have news of my brother Paul. I came earlier, when I first saw your advertisement in *The Times*, and I was asked to come back tonight, when you were due to return.' He favoured Lydyard with a small bow, but his gaze remained fixed on Tallentyre.

'I fear that the young man is no longer with us,' said Tallentyre, blandly stating the obvious. The baronet met the other's stare very frankly, but Lydyard could imagine well enough what curious thoughts must be swirling in his brain. Lydyard remembered the warnings which Paul Shepherd had given to him in that last, secret interview, and wondered whether and how this person fitted into the list of those whom he was supposed to beware.

'Can you tell me how you parted company?' asked the blue-eyed man. 'I am sorry to press you so soon after your return, but you must have observed that my brother is subject to protracted bouts of mental derangement. He is not always as he was when you found him, but even when he has his wits about him he suffers from very strange delusions.'

'I fear that I know nothing of that,' said Sir Edward, smoothly. 'There was some improvement in his condition while he remained with us, but he disappeared soon after seeming to have recovered his wits. He quit the *Excelsior* while she was under steam and it seems probable that he simply stepped overboard. Whether he drowned or not I have no way to tell.'

The second Mr Shepherd studied Tallentyre very carefully while he listened to this speech, and it was plain that he did not know whether to accept it at face value or not, or how he might further pursue his enquiries without giving offence.

'I am very sorry to hear that,' he said, eventually. 'You say that he did seem to have recovered his wits?'

'He did,' said Tallentyre, 'but very briefly. I am afraid that I could not make much sense of what he told us. Can you inform us, perchance, how he came to be wandering in the desert where we found him? It is a puzzle whose solution still eludes us.'

'As I have said,' the blue-eyed man replied, a little unsteadily, 'poor Paul was continually subject to strange delusions and strange fits. I cannot blame you for failing to keep a proper watch over him, when we have so obviously failed to do so ourselves.'

'We?' said Tallentyre, innocuously. 'Has he other relatives in London besides yourself?'

'Oh yes,' said the other, uncertainly. 'But he has been estranged from his family for some time.' As if he could no longer meet Tallentyre's stare the young man shifted his gaze abruptly to Lydyard, at whom he looked with a very strange intentness.

'Did my brother say anything to you, Mr Lydyard?' he asked. 'We really are very anxious to find him, if there is a chance that he is still alive.'

'Why, no,' said Lydyard, trying with all his might to feign innocent surprise, though he did not quite know why he felt such an urgent need to dissemble. 'He woke for only a few hours each day, usually after dark, and though he consented to be fed by me I saw hardly a glimmer of human intelligence in him, until the day before he disappeared. I fear that your brother was very ill . . . but I am sorry that we could not bring him home.'

'Have you been ill yourself?' asked the young man. Lydyard was surprised by the apparent sincerity of his concern.

'I was bitten by a snake,' said Lydyard, evenly, 'but I am fully recovered now.' He congratulated himself silently on the development of his skill in falsehood. He did not like Paul Shepherd's brother at all, and felt curiously uneasy in his presence.

'I fear that I did not catch your first name, Mr Shepherd,' said Tallentyre, amiably.

'It is Perris,' said the other, whose speculative eyes were still on Lydyard.

'An unusual name,' commented the baronet. 'If you would care to give me your address, and those of your brother's other relatives, I would be more than pleased to write a full account of our dealings with him, which I will send with my most earnest condolences.'

'That is very kind,' said Perris, 'but I think that my cousins would rather hear the news from my own lips. Do you think it likely that Paul is still alive?'

'We certainly cannot be certain that he is dead,' replied the baronet, 'but a man who is not in full possession of his faculties, who disappears from a steamship in the early hours of the morning, has little chance of survival, even in a sea as benign as the Mediterranean. I could not advise you to raise your hopes too high.'

'Of course,' replied the visitor. Without warning, his gaze suddenly shifted again, this time coming to rest briefly on Gilbert Franklin's face before returning to Tallentyre's. 'I am very sorry to have troubled you,' he said, again. 'It was very kind of you to take care of my brother, and I am sorry that your solicitude did not have a happier result. Alas, he had been ill for a long time, and we were told that there was little hope for his complete recovery.'

The visitor put out his hand then, and accepted his hat from Summers. Then, with a small bow, he turned abruptly on his heel. No one moved until they had heard the sound of the main door closing, followed by the sound of footsteps clattering away down the steps into the street.

Tallentyre glanced at Lydyard before saying to Franklin: 'Did you recognize that man? He looked at you then as if he knew you.'

'Why no,' said Franklin. 'Nor do I know how he came here, when mine was the address which was given in the advertisement which I placed in *The Times*.'

'I did not like him at all,' said Lydyard, in a puzzled tone. 'Which is most odd, for I felt no such dislike for his brother, who is certainly his twin.'

'I felt something of the same dislike,' admitted Tallentyre.

The doctor, who had knitted his brow in concentration, suddenly said: 'I have not seen him before, but I *have* seen someone very like him.'

'Ah!' said Tallentyre. 'Perhaps, then, his brother is alive after all, and has reached England before us.'

'Alike, yes,' said Franklin, ruminatively, still following his own train of thought. 'And if madness runs in the family, perhaps also akin.'

'What do you mean?' asked Lydyard.

'Why,' said the doctor, 'I mean the young man who spoke to me at Hanwell station. He was certainly not so like Mr Shepherd as to be his twin, but still there is a sufficient resemblance to make me think that they might be members of the same family.'

'The werewolves of London!' said Tallentyre, sarcastically. 'I should have guessed.'

Lydyard too had remembered what the young man in question had said to Franklin – and he remembered also that Paul Shepherd, whose real name was surely not Paul or Shepherd at all, had urged him very earnestly to beware of the werewolves of London. He had the feeling that a vital connection, which he had been led by his dreams to suspect, was now securely forged – and though he knew full well that he had not a shred of evidence which Sir Edward Tallentyre would recognize as proof, he was certain in his own mind of one astonishing fact.

Paul Shepherd *had* been the wolf in Sir Edward's dream, which had saved him from the Sphinx. The family from which he had later claimed to be estranged were the werewolves of London.

And Lydyard knew full well that once he had accepted *this* – and he did not, could not, doubt it in the least – then there was a good deal more that he must not now deny.

The creature, his demonic possessor, was certainly real. And real danger did in fact threaten him, from all the directions in which the manwolf of the *Excelsior* had told him to look for it.

He had, in a way, always known the truth of these things, but now, he admitted it too. He was neither mad nor deluded, and if the riddle of the new sphinx could not be answered in a satisfactory way, then far more might be lost than Sir Edward Tallentyre's pride in his own ingenuity.

5

Their second visitor presented himself at Sturton Street that evening, when dinner was barely over. Tallentyre consented to see him, though Lady Rosalind and Cordelia were by no means pleased to be deserted.

Lydyard anticipated an interview no less peculiar, and hoped for one which would be far more enlightening. But it started very awkwardly; there was a tangible embarrassment in the way that the four men arrayed themselves upon the chairs in the smoking-room, patiently waiting to speak until Summers had poured brandy into four glasses and departed.

'I was not certain that you would admit me,' said Jacob

Harkender, looking up furtively from the glass which he was warming in his fingers.

Tallentyre seemed to be studying his visitor carefully. He had earlier confessed to Lydyard that although he had not seen the man for twenty-five years, he still had a memory of Harkender's face, as sharp and fresh as if it had been etched upon his mind: he had described it as a frail and effeminate face, its pale skin ever likely to take on a hectic flush, yet capable of a fearsome stare, possessed of an infinite reserve of malevolence. It was difficult for Lydyard to imagine the Harkender who sat before him, much marked by age and discipline, as a monster of bile and wrath, but there was something faintly volcanic about him, as if he might still be capable of erupting with wrath. And there was still a certain effeminacy about the man. There was something else, too, which Lydyard found hard to define – some shadowy superimposition of his second sight.

'Why should I not admit you?' the baronet answered. 'Do you think I am the kind of man who would remember with rancour a quarrel which took place more than twenty years ago?' His tone, grotesquely out of tune with his words, suggested that he was exactly that kind of man.

'To be frank,' said Harkender, 'I used to think you excessively meticulous and unyielding – and I cannot believe that you have changed. The actual quarrel we had was merely a symptom of a more deeply seated mutual dislike. Given the kind of man which I have become, and the kind which you have always been, I suspect that you loathe me now as completely as you ever did.' Harkender's tone was level and silky, but he did not seem to be mocking his antagonist. It was rather as though he were trying too hard to be frank and open.

Lydyard's eye was caught by the odd movement of a shadow cast on the wall behind Harkender's chair by a combination of firelight and lamplight; it seemed uncannily dark and ominous, and somehow reminded him of a hunting spider lying in wait for its prey.

'If that is your judgement,' said Tallentyre, 'I wonder that you should ask to be received in my house.'

'I came here,' said Harkender, who seemed also to be watching the play of the lamplight as it was reflected in his wide-bellied glass, 'in pursuit of the principle that the enemy of my enemy might be my friend. The ironies of fortune have made stranger compacts. I know that you cannot think of me as a gentleman or a scholar, but I believe that you might be kind enough to think a little better of my veneer of quality and learning if you compare it, not with the manners of those you most greatly admire, but with the manners of those whose enmity you have lately earned.'

As he spoke these words – which Lydyard judged to be a carefully rehearsed speech, Harkender glanced uneasily at Lydyard, as though puzzled by some aspect of his appearance.

'I am not aware of having made any enemies of late,' said Tallentyre, placing a slight but deliberate stress on the last two words.

Harkender seemed unimpressed. 'May I ask what happened to the young man you found in the desert south of Qina?' he asked, abruptly.

'He made a full recovery,' said Tallentyre, airily. 'And we will be pleased to tell you more about him, if you wish. But first, we have questions of our own which you must answer. Dr Franklin has put some of them to you before, but you were evasive then. Will you tell us now why you went to the place where de Lancy disappeared and David was hurt – and what connection your visit there has with the child who was in the care of the Sisters of St Syncletica until he ran away?'

Harkender did not seem surprised to be asked about the boy – nor did he seem overly displeased. The shadow behind the visitor's head seemed to Lydyard to have increased its resemblance to a predatory spider, though he was not sure how much of the increase was due to the creativity of his own imagination.

Harkender licked his lip then, and sat back in his armchair.

The shadow behind him disappeared as though sinking out of sight into some secret lair, but the fire in the grate was burning fiercely against the chill of the blackthorn winter and it continued to light his lower features redly and rather eerily. Lydyard amused himself with the conceit that Harkender had the kind of face which a Romantic painter might give to Milton's Satan, but the amusement faded when he realized that Harkender was not unlike the Satan of his own vision, with whom he had so strongly sympathized.

'I doubt that you would believe the truth,' said Harkender to Tallentyre, 'even though you are clever enough to ask the question.'

'I doubt everything,' countered Tallentyre, 'and believe nothing until I am certain of it. Nevertheless, I would like to hear what you have to say, no matter how incredible it might be.'

Harkender stared at him steadfastly for a few seconds, then shrugged, and said: 'How much did Pelorus tell you?'

'What makes you think he told us anything?' retorted the baronet – but Lydyard noticed that Sir Edward was careful not to disclaim any knowledge of who Pelorus might be.

'Your attitude,' said Harkender, 'your curiosity, and your willingness to trade information tell me that you have a hand to play, and that your best cards are concealed. When Dr Franklin came to Whittenton he knew nothing – now you feel that you know enough to taunt and tempt me. I must warn you to be careful, though, for Pelorus has a family in London whose members are ill-disposed towards those who help him.'

'We have met his brother already,' said Tallentyre equably. 'He came this afternoon.'

Harkender nodded, though he did not seem altogether unsurprised. 'Mandorla knows that her game is a dangerous one,' he said, half to himself. Then, he said: 'Do you know what Pelorus and his family are?'

'They are the werewolves of London,' replied Tallentyre, promptly. Lydyard saw Franklin give a small start of surprise. Lydyard permitted himself a small smile, knowing that although Sir Edward was playing a game, what he said was no less than the truth.

Harkender pursed his lips. 'You must have seen him change,' he said. 'Either that or you do not really believe it, and assert it only by way of experiment. It hardly matters. Pelorus has presumably explained to you already what I have tried to do, and why the interference of his kinfolk is so very unwelcome.'

'Perhaps he has,' said Tallentyre – and Lydyard could imagine how delighted the baronet must be with the success of his ploy. 'But this is a matter in which I hesitate to take anything on trust, and I would prefer to hear what you have to say from your own lips.'

Harkender drained the brandy from his glass. 'Sir Edward,' he said, grimly, 'I think you can guess how reluctant I was to come here – but what Franklin told me of your adventure in Egypt led me to hope that it was Pelorus who saved you. I have never met him, but I know something of his kinfolk, and I know that he is opposed to them in the one ambition which has driven Mandorla to steal Gabriel Gill. I am sorry that I asked Franklin to warn you to stay out of my affairs, for now that you are involved, I would rather have you as an ally than an enemy. But I must say, frankly, that Pelorus might be far more useful to me. If you wish to be rid of me, you need only tell me where Pelorus is.'

'I will tell you what became of him,' Sir Edward replied, still taking acute care in the turning of his phrases, 'if, and only if, you will tell us why you went to that valley in the Eastern Desert, and what you sought to do there.'

'I went in search of enlightenment,' said Harkender, flatly. 'Like the follower of St Amycus who was with you, I know that the Creators which struggled to impose their will upon the world in the remote past did not die when the Age of Miracles ended. Transformed by the thrust of evolution they might be, but dead they are not; their power remains, and one day they may choose to return. Unlike the followers of St Amycus, however, I do not believe that there is any underlying war between good and evil in this matter – that is a mere conceit of pious men. Nor do I believe that there is any divine plan whose plot is already written in the scriptures. The future is not yet decided, and it may not be decided by the Creators, if only men can learn how to take control of their power for themselves.

'That is the path which I have tried to follow. I went to the valley in order to undertake a rite which borrowed a part of the power which lay dormant there, and I incarnated that power in a newly conceived child. Once, there were many such quasi-human beings, but they are almost extinct now, and there are many reasons why it was more to my advantage to bring one into being than to discover one which already existed. I placed the child in the custody of the Sisters of St Syncletica to keep him safe until the moment when his inner eye would open, so that he might become my oracle and fount of secret wisdom. I sought to hide him, it is true, but not because I thought that anyone would want to steal him away. I did not reckon with the intervention of the werewolves.

'Mandorla does not want the child for a fount of wisdom – I can only suppose that she seeks to use his power in a very different way. Perhaps she thinks that he can take away her unwelcome half-humanity, to make her a wolf again. Perhaps she is more ambitious, and desires to bring the Creators back in order to upset the world which has been crafted by the humans she hates. She must know that Gabriel cannot restore the Age of Miracles, but she may be nursing some scheme to hurt the race of men. What Gabriel might achieve in that regard were he to learn to control and channel his powers I cannot tell, nor can I tell whether Mandorla could persuade him to do it. Whatever she intends, though, the child would be infinitely safer with me.

'In my belief, Pelorus is steadfastly opposed to Mandorla's ambitions, and is therefore certain to try to release the child. We would both stand a far better chance of success were we to combine our efforts, and that is why I ask you to tell me where he is.'

While he was speaking Harkender had gradually leaned forward again, so that it seemed to Lydyard that the shadow spider emerged by careful degrees from its covert behind the chair, to loom grotesquely over the magician's head. It looked more menacing now than it had before, and Lydyard had a momentary thrill of fear as he imagined that it might at any moment take on substance, then leap from the wall to seize one of them and sting him with its fangs.

'Who was Gabriel's mother?' asked Tallentyre. The baronet's voice was still quite colourless; he was trying with all his might to imply that nothing he had heard was new to him, and to avoid giving any hint of his reaction to it. Only Lydyard knew how cleverly his friend was lying – and he could guess what a complex mixture Tallentyre's motives were. It was not simply that Tallentyre wanted to hear everything which Harkender might be tempted to tell him; he also wanted to exercise power for its own sake.

'A common whore name Jenny Gill,' said Harkender, unashamedly. 'She did not long survive the birth. That is not important. I have told you what you wanted to hear, now I ask you again: where is Pelorus?'

'Alas,' said Tallentyre, 'we do not know the present whereabouts of the young man we discovered in the desert. He left the *Excelsior* secretly, some time before we reached Gibraltar. He may have drowned, as I suggested to his inquisitive brother, or he may already be in England. We do not know.'

Harkender was severely displeased by this casual dismissal, and Lydyard could sense something of the wrath seething within him. Lydyard could not help but feel that the magician was entitled to be annoyed, for he had been blatantly tricked. But Harkender controlled his temper, and contented himself with a baleful glare. 'That is a poor reward for my honesty,' he observed.

'It is the way of the world,' replied Tallentyre mockingly, 'that honesty often goes unrewarded while deception leads to success. And what you have said, even though you may believe it to be true, is certainly not the whole of the truth.

Whatever you began in the valley has not ended, and if you have really succeeded in making some kind of supernatural chimera, it is not the only one. What of this other creature which robbed the man you call Pelorus of his senses, and caused the priest's heart to fail? Did you make that, also?'

'No,' said Harkender, 'I did not. Nor do I know why it was made, or why it has been sent to earth. Zephyrinus will probably tell you that it is the Beast of Revelation, come to play its part in the Apocalypse – and he might be right. I am not such a fool that I do not fear this new entity, but nor am I so fearful as to take it for granted that it means to do me harm. And if we are taking census of chimeras, Sir Edward, let us remember that there is one other to be counted, who sits beside you.'

Harkender looked directly at Lydyard, who could not help but flinch under the gaze, though he felt ashamed of himself for doing so.

'David is quite recovered from the bite which he sustained,' said Tallentyre, sharply. 'His delirium did not last long.'

Lydyard said nothing to contradict him, but he saw clearly enough that Harkender – like Paul Shepherd or Pelorus before him – knew better. The shadow-spider behind Harkender's head seemed to be staring at him with a predatory fascination which frightened him even though he knew that the monster did not really exist at all, but was simply a trick of the light.

Harkender did not press the point. Instead, he said: 'I wish you would agree to help me in this, Sir Edward. I cannot believe that you are happy to leave Gabriel in the hands of the werewolves, now that you know what they are. I am, after all, the boy's legal guardian, and I will gladly swear any oath you care to name that I mean to use him more kindly than those who have him now.'

'That,' said Tallentyre, with a deadly coldness which surprised Lydyard, 'would surely depend on one's idea of kindness. You must remember that I know how you have used others in the past.'

Harkender's posture was as stiff as ever, and his firelit

features were suddenly contorted with such bitterness that other eyes seemed to be peering out from behind the mask which was his face: hot eyes, angry and malevolent.

'Oh yes,' said the magician, his voice little more than a whisper. 'The quarrel. I had forgotten it for a moment. Do you think I want the boy for a catamite, then? If only you knew the truth, Sir Edward – the *real* truth! And now, I am not speaking of science, or religion, or philosopy, or mysticism, but only of ourselves and what we are. But you could no more see it than you can see what kind of world we really live in – the blindness of your class is utterly comprehensive. You do not see the chaos which is masked by your systematic physics; you do not see the England of the poor, which exists outside your Utopia of aristocratic comforts; you do not see the perversions of the soul which are walled up by your polite hypocrisies. You think I am a monster, and yet you are blind to the true monstrousness of the world, of the state and of the self. Comfort makes all men blind, but I think that *your* class revels in blindness for its own sake, and has forgotten how to feel ashamed.'

The volcano, thought Lydyard, *has erupted*.

It was now Tallentyre's turn to be astonished, and not merely because he was taken aback by the sudden change in Harkender's mood. 'What on earth has my class to do with it?' he retorted.

'To do with what?' countered Harkender, with bitter irony. 'To do with your uncompromising materialism – more than you realize. To do with your iron-clad moralism – everything.'

'To do with ourselves,' Tallentyre shot back. 'To do with the dislike for one another which we have nursed so long, and which seemingly has not withered at all.'

'Oh, everything,' said Harkender. 'Everything. But of all the things we might debate, that is surely the least.' Then he paused, and looked at Tallentyre more steadily for a few seconds. 'But perhaps not,' he said, with a sigh. 'I had thought to place before you rational arguments about our common interest, but it occurred to me that you might not hear them if the dead past came to life in your mind when you saw me again. That is another feature of your class – it never forgets, not because it prides itself on the perfection of its sense of history, but simply because it never forgives.'

'You remind me of something Franklin once told me about James Austen's observations on the subject of persecution mania,' said Tallentyre. 'He referred to the ready claim made upon a weak mind by the delusion that conspiracies are everywhere. No doubt you envy my class because you do not belong to it, but you must not imagine that the aristocracy of England exists solely for the purpose of falsifying truth and depriving you of the status to which your fancied occult wisdom and powerful wizardry would otherwise entitle you.'

It appeared to Lydyard that Harkender fed upon Tallentyre's sarcasm; it was as though he grew stronger by being attacked. A few moments ago, he had been distressed, but now he was supremely controlled again.

'Perhaps it was a mistake to come here,' he said, with a mildly self-reproachful air. 'I could not expect any kind generosity from you, whether in matters of belief, or courtesy, or feeling. Were I to show such meanness in return, however, I would simply drive us further apart, and it really is my opinion that we should become allies against a common enemy. As Pelorus has doubtless explained to you, no good can come of allowing Mandorla to control the powers which Gabriel has, because her motives are at best selfish and at worst destructive. If you are interested in helping to prevent tragedy, my house is open to you, and I will be glad to add the resources of my magic to whatever resources Pelorus has.'

Tallentyre would not consent to smile, but Lydyard found himself liking Harkender a little in spite of the baronet's distaste; of the two, it certainly seemed that Harkender was the more generous in his attitude. Lydyard wished that Tallentyre might let go now, but knew that he would not; the baronet could be a very stubborn man.

'For one who despises my class,' said Sir Edward to his

unwelcome guest, 'you try hard to ape its manners and affectations.'

'The two are not unconnected,' Harkender assured him. 'And the movement from cause to effect goes both ways, though I know your scientific mind will not entirely approve of such a confusion.'

'Whatever did we do to you?' asked Tallentyre, striving to find an insult which could break through the wall of defiance. 'Did your mother die in a workhouse, or was she simply a victim of the *droit de seigneur*?'

Lydyard caught his breath at that, and saw that Franklin too was becoming very unhappy with the manner of the argument. Perhaps even Tallentyre regretted having said it once the words were out, for he was not by instinct a callous man.

Harkender's face was seemingly quite bloodless. 'Are you so determined to hurt me?' he asked, with deadly gentleness.

'Gentlemen,' said Franklin, interrupting for the first time, 'may I beg you to leave this quarrel alone? Whatever your differences may be, it surely serves no purpose for you to harry one another in this way.'

Lydyard could imagine how reluctant Tallentyre must be to show repentance, but he was glad to see the baronet nod curtly.

'You are right, Gilbert,' he agreed. 'I apologize for what I have said, Harkender; it would have been better had I been able to forget what cause I once had to dislike you.'

Harkender did not immediately reply, but when he did his composure was intact. 'I suppose that is the best apology one can expect from a Tallentyre,' he said. 'But if it will please you, I will admit that I did harm. Others had harmed me, and I sought to even the score by harming others in my turn – I would have harmed you, had I been able, and done so with a ferocity which you would have considered inexplicable. But I have since learned that there is sometimes truth even in platitudes. Two evils cannot cancel one another out, and yet good can come of evil. I suppose, in a way, I should be glad that your class has taught me the value of pain and suffering, though it certainly did not set out to teach me anything but the folly of my own aspirations, and that cruelly.

'To answer your earlier question, my mother died in a well-made bed, not ignobly, and I was the legitimate issue of a marriage which was not entirely unhappy. It was not the poverty of my family which nurtured my hatred but its relative wealth, for my father became rich through luck and industry when that clever machinery which you worship transformed England into a powerhouse of progress. He adored the aristocracy, and was ambitious to make me fit to take a part in its privileged society – as if mere wealth could accomplish such a miracle of alchemy! He sent me to school, and then, as you know, to Oxford. If you would think about it, you might be able to imagine what forces combined to form the mind and spirit which seemed – and seems – so vulgarly diabolical to your refined sensibility.'

'I believe that I can,' answered Tallentyre, tactfully.

'It is my turn to play the sceptic,' said Harkender, humourlessly. 'You might deduce the facts of the matter, but I do not believe that you can truly imagine the reality of which those facts are the mere surface.'

While Lydyard was considering the implications of this statement, Harkender had turned towards him, and now spoke directly to him. 'Sir Edward knew me at the time when I first became old enough to do harm as well as suffer it,' he said, conversationally. 'I would gladly have brought the Devil himself to earth then. I am sometimes compared by rumour to Dashwood even now, but whatever hell-fire burned in Dashwood's soul was nothing compared to the inferno seething in mine. Now, I have diverted my energies in other directions; I am a builder rather than a destroyer, and for that reason I am set against the werewolves. If Sir Edward intends to involve himself further in this affair, I am certain that we might oppose our enemies better by combining our efforts. If you have truly recovered from your experience in the desert, I am glad – but if you have not, I am certain that I can help you. Come to Whittenton when you can.'

Lydyard nodded awkwardly. Politeness compelled him to be grateful, but he could not help remembering Paul Shepherd's warning. Nor could he ignore that strange shadow upon the wall.

Harkender did not seem dissatisfied with his awkwardness, and turned his disconcerting gaze back to Tallentyre. 'Consider my words very carefully, Sir Edward. I mean no treachery. Indeed, as an earnest of my good faith I am willing to tell you how to find those who consider me to be damned, so that you may compare my case with theirs.'

Harkender tore a leaf from his pocket-book and scribbled on it with a pencil, resting it on the arm of his chair. As he handed it on – not to Tallentyre but to Lydyard – he said: 'It is the address of the house which the Order of St Amycus keeps in London. If they tell you what they know of the werewolves you may be more inclined to be anxious about the fact that Mandorla has Gabriel in her custody.'

Lydyard accepted the piece of paper silently, and Tallentyre stood up in order to ring for the butler. Lydyard was pleased to see that the mysterious shadow on the wall lost all resemblance to a spider as Harkender stood in his turn, but he could not suppress a painful thrill of premonition which told him unmistakably that his business with that paradoxical creature of darkness was by no means finished.

6

The address which Harkender had given to Lydyard proved to be a secluded house surrounded by a high wall, set in a gloomy avenue overhung by sycamores. Lydyard dismounted from his hansom and asked the driver to wait for him. He had come alone, because long-delayed affairs of business had claimed Sir Edward's attention.

The wall had no proper gateway, but only an arch with a double door. There was a bell, which Lydyard rang, but when it was answered the door did not open – instead, a square spyhole at head height was uncovered, so that he could be inspected from within. He bore the inspection tolerantly, though it seemed to him that an unnecessarily long interval elapsed before a voice within said: 'May I help you?'

'I would like to see Brother Zephyrinus,' he said. 'My name is David Lydyard, and I have something to tell him concerning the death of a member of the Order.'

'I am sorry,' said the invisible other, 'but this is a religious house, and it is not permitted for laymen to enter.'

'I know what kind of house it is,' replied Lydyard, 'and I would not normally ask that its rule be broken, but I do need to speak to your Superior. One of your number died in an attempt to discover the information which I now bring to you, and I have some items of property which I should like to return, including a ring which bears the initials O, S, and A. The man who had it gave his name as Francis Mallorn.'

'Wait,' said the voice, in an annoyingly peremptory fashion. The spyhole clicked shut. At least three minutes passed before it was opened again, and Lydyard braced himself for another inspection, but this time there was only a brief interval before a key turned in a lock, and the door was opened inwards.

There stood within two men in habits. One was tall, middle-aged, and lean – very much the same physical type as Sir Edward Tallentyre; the other was shorter and younger, with jet black hair around his tonsure. The shorter man looked at him with open suspicion, but the taller was more welcoming.

'Mr Lydyard,' said the older man, extending a hand – not to be shaken, but rather to usher him through the doorway. 'I am the abbot of this house; my name, as I think you already know, is Zephyrinus.'

'Thank you for agreeing to see me,' said Lydyard.

'It is we who should thank you,' replied Zephyrinus, courteously. 'We had heard through other channels of the sad death of our brother, but the details of his end were distressingly unclear, and it is kind of you to return his possessions. I wonder whether you would mind very much if I did not take you into the house. I suppose that I may bend the rules if I will, but I would rather you walked with me in the gardens at the rear instead. It would set a more acceptable precedent.'

Lydyard agreed, whereupon the abbot turned and led him along the side of the house. The other monk, conspicuously unintroduced, entered a door at the rear of the house while they went on.

At the rear of the house was a series of neatly kept plots planted with vegetables; the paths between the plots were made from irregularly shaped paving stones. The abbot led the way to a bench near to the centre of the open space, where he indicated that his guest should sit facing away from the house. Lydyard did as he was bid and Zephyrinus sat down beside him.

'May I have the ring?' he said.

'Certainly,' said Lydyard.

The older man accepted the ring and the packet of papers with it, placing them in a pocket inside his robe. He glanced briefly at the amulet displaying the *utchat*, but took no particular interest in the design. He said nothing, apparently being content to wait for Lydyard to speak, but Lydyard found himself at a loss for words. Sir Edward, he knew, would have been incisively inquisitive, but he had always found it harder to cut through the barriers of common politeness to the heart of an issue, and though his faith had been fatally weakened by exposure to Tallentyre's scepticism he was still inclined to feel anxiously humble in the presence of the officers of the Church.

'I was brought up a Catholic,' he said, tentatively, 'but I have never heard of your Order, or the saint after whom it is named.'

'Our existence and purpose constitute a secret which few are privileged to know,' admitted Zephyrinus, amiably enough, 'and I admit that we have no warrant for existence which the present Pope would recognize. Nevertheless, we are good Christians, and are confident that in the eyes of God, the saint from which we take our name is worthy of our respect.'

Lydyard found nothing in this answer which could serve as a thread to develop the conversation, and knew that he must steel himself to ask questions. 'Did the reports of Father Mallorn's death which reached you include my name?' he began.

'They did,' Zephyrinus answered. 'In any case, the last letter which we received from Brother Francis explained that he had cultivated the acquaintance of three Englishmen, and gave all of your names. He was particularly glad to have recruited the aid of Sir Edward Tallentyre.'

'That seems strange,' said Lydyard, feeling slightly resentful of the implied element of exploitation in the strategy. 'Sir Edward may have been a Catholic once, but that ensured that his conversion to atheism would be attended by a devout desire to expose the follies of his abandoned faith. Why should a priest be glad to combine forces with such a man? And why should he wish to deceive us, when the Church asks us to be honest?'

'I believe that you will find, if you remember his words carefully, that Brother Francis told you no lies,' Zephyrinus replied, 'and if there were matters which he kept secret, he did so because he was bound by vows forbidding him to speak. I am sure that the Jesuits who taught you respect for the truth taught you also that obedience to vows is a virtue. Brother Francis was glad to have a man like Sir Edward with him because of the respect which we have for the power of sceptical reasoning. He did not know what he might find at his destination, but he was afraid that his own credulity might forbid him to see clearly enough, and was glad to be in the company of a man whose beliefs were very different. It is sometimes the case that two men who see differently can arrive at a better understanding than either one of them alone.'

To Lydyard, this sounded suspiciously heretical. The Jesuits who had taught him had possessed a very different attitude, in which the view of the faith was supreme and unchallengeable. Tallentyre was equally convinced of the unchallengeable supremacy of the scientific world-view.

'Will your vows of secrecy prevent your telling me why Brother Francis wanted to go to the valley?' asked Lydyard. 'And will they prevent my asking for your advice on certain matters which arose from our adventure there, which continue to disturb our lives? I have come here under instructions from Sir Edward to ask certain questions.'

Zephyrinus expressed polite surprise. 'Has Sir Edward sent you in search of our advice?' he enquired, as though it was hardly credible. 'I thought he had ventured the opinion that men of superstition – in which category he would surely include our community – live in a world where fantasy makes them free to declare whatever they like? What use could our advice be to a man like him, who has told the world how bitter and disappointed he would be were he forced to share the insights and opinions of such wretches as believe in miracles?'

Lydyard could not help but be amused. The abbot's tone, though mocking, was also very gentle. 'I did not realize,' he said, 'that monks took the *Quarterly Review*. I believe – and Sir Edward agrees – that we do stand in need of your advice, and would be pleased to receive it. After all, your Order must take a little of the blame for the embarrassment of my presence, for it was Father Mallorn who sought us out and involved us in his scheme. Are we not entitled to some kind of explanation?'

'Perhaps,' agreed the abbot. 'I am sorry that Brother Francis used you – doubly sorry because it seems to have cost the life of William de Lancy, and may also have caused undue pain and difficulty to yourself. You were bitten by a snake, I believe, and badly hurt.'

'I was bitten,' agreed Lydyard, 'but strange as it may seem, I do not know how badly I have been hurt. That is one of the matters on which I hoped to obtain advice – for my own sake rather than Sir Edward's. I believe that I have information to offer in exchange, though I do not mean to imply that you would be interested in vulgar trading.'

The abbot smiled, willing to be amused in his turn, but did not reply.

'I will not break any vow of confidence to which you swear me,' said Lydyard, 'although I ask your permission to convey what you tell me to Sir Edward, and to his friend Gilbert Franklin. What I offer you is a full and honest account of what happened on the night of Mallorn's death – and what I ask in return, as I have said, is your advice in the matter of increasing our understanding of what happened to us.'

Zephyrinus looked steadily at him for a moment, and then said: 'Who told you of the existence of this Order, and where to find this house?'

'Jacob Harkender told us where to find you,' said Lydyard, with meticulous honesty. 'But the man who first informed us of your existence called himself Paul Shepherd. I believe that he is also known as Pelorus.'

'Ah,' said Zephyrinus, softly. 'Do you know what Pelorus is?'

'He is one of the werewolves of London,' replied Lydyard, calmly. 'But it seems that he is estranged from the others of his kind.'

'That may be true,' said Zephyrinus. 'The example of our own patron saint instructs us that there are those among the unhuman who serve God, and whose souls are equal to ours in His regard. The history of our Order advises us that Pelorus is not an evil creature, though the others of his kind undoubtedly are.'

'Will you consent, then, to advise us?'

'I will answer your questions as fully as I may,' the abbot replied.

Lydyard was well aware of the evasiveness of this answer, but he accepted it, and asked: 'Why did Brother Francis want to go to the valley which Jacob Harkender had visited some ten years earlier?'

'Because,' said Zephyrinus, carefully, 'we believe that Harkender is among those whose task it is to prepare the way for the coming of the Antichrist, and it seemed that his mission might be part of that preparation.'

'How did you discover what his mission was?' asked Lydyard, quickly. He had anticipated the first answer.

'We have our visionaries,' replied Zephyrinus. 'Our magicians, if you will. Their locutions and visions became redolent with warnings of imminent change, which referred us not only to Harkender but to Egypt.'

'And to Hudlestone Manor?' Lydyard asked.

Zephyrinus was not to be drawn so easily. He turned his pale eyes – which had been staring into infinity – to Lydyard's face, and said: 'What do you know about Hudlestone Manor?'

'We know about the boy who was placed there by Harkender,' said Lydyard, flatly. 'We have been told that he was conceived during Harkender's expedition to Egypt, and that his conception was connected with some magical rite of Harkender's. We know that he has been lured or taken away from Hudlestone, perhaps by the werewolves of London.'

'Then you know all that I can tell you,' said Zephyrinus.

'Except for one thing,' said Lydyard, soberly. 'We do not know whether you believe that the child is the Antichrist.' As he pronounced the words he was uncomfortably aware that they sounded bizarre – and uncomfortably certain that this curious monk would take them utterly seriously.

'We do not know what he is,' said Zephyrinus, levelly. 'But what you have suggested is a real possibility. Jacob Harkender does not believe it, but he does not know whose power it is which feeds his vengeful will. Nor, Mr Lydyard, do you believe it, in spite of your careful attempt to play a neutral part for my benefit.'

'I have an open mind,' countered Lydyard, 'which has lately become more open than I could desire. But I honestly do not know what to believe about the reality of werewolves or powers of magical sight. Since I was bitten by the snake, I have had visions of my own, but I dare not entirely trust what I see or what I have been told. Whatever I do or do not believe, Brother Zephyrinus, I would be glad to have your advice about what I might do in this matter of Harkender and the boy. Harkender has come to us asking for our help in recovering him from the werewolves.'

Zephyrinus stood up for a moment, smoothing the creases from the rear of his habit. Then he resumed his seat, and touched a contemplative finger to his lips. 'Do nothing,' he said, firmly. 'There is nothing you can do which will alter the destined result of this affair, and nothing you need to do, save to make your peace with God. Be reconciled to the faith, Mr Lydyard, and urge Sir Edward to do likewise.'

'Do you mean that you also intend to do nothing?' asked Lydyard.

'That is a matter of which I may not speak,' replied the abbot.

Lydyard was frustrated by the refusal to say more, but knew how futile it would be to pursue the matter. Instead, he said: 'What troubled Pelorus and myself also, is the matter of the second creature which emerged from the valley in Egypt. What has it to do with the child, and with us? If the child is the Antichrist, what is the other? Is it the Beast of Revelation, or Satan incarnate?'

'We cannot be certain,' said Zephyrinus again, 'but the coming of a Beast is clearly prophesied, and there may be nothing in this event to surprise us. We might be better able to judge if we knew exactly what happened before Brother Francis died. That, I think, is the information which you promised me.'

Lydyard was by no means satisfied with what had so far been offered to him in exchange for his information, but he did not hesitate. He explained what had happened in the valley, adding brief accounts of his own delirious nightmares, and of Pelorus' eventual awakening.

'I have an open mind,' repeated Lydyard, but could not resist adding: 'in spite of the efforts which the Jesuits made to close it. The Jesuits claimed too much, you see, when they said that a boy who is theirs in his impressionable years is theirs for ever. I do not know, even in that covert of my soul which my teachers tried to make their own, any of those things which faith instructs you to believe in, and I think you will understand what a turmoil of uncertainty I am in.'

'You may have set aside what the Jesuits taught you, but you have not escaped them,' Zephyrinus said. 'Even Tallentyre has not escaped them, as may be seen from his contributions to *The Quarterly Review*, notwithstanding their hostility to the doctrines of the Church. The beliefs of the Jesuits he has cast aside, but their rhetoric and their fervour he has not. When the day comes on which you and he must make the choice in earnest between faith and oblivion, you will both know well enough what choice it is which faces you. If ever God calls you to the faith again, as He called Saul on the road to Damascus, you will take everything that the Jesuits taught you, bold and entire. You are theirs, if you are anyone's, doubt it as you will. I advise you to be prepared, for the day might not be long in coming.'

Lydyard was not impressed by this sermon in miniature. 'And suppose the end can be averted?' he said. 'Or suppose, at least, that there is yet a role for men to play, in shaping the event?'

'Pelorus might believe that,' replied Zephyrinus. 'And Harkender too, but you must not. Faith and hope testify that Christ will come again, to reign upon the earth for a thousand years. Pray to him for your salvation, and you will have it. Do not attempt to play with Harkender's magic, for it is an instrument of Satan, and will seduce you to your own damnation.'

'The visions I have lately had,' said Lydyard, in a low voice, 'might easily be seen as such a seduction, for they reveal in me a greater sympathy for Satan than I thought I had. But Sir Edward could never agree.'

'Indeed not,' said Zephyrinus. 'The coming transformation of the world is exactly that kind of Act of Creation whose contemplation so frightened him in that essay which he wrote. It was clear that he found the prospect horrific, though he tried to conceal his feelings in charges of absurdity. Atheism is his defence against the horror of a world which can be remade – but there can be no defence, as all true men of science know. Have you read Hume, Mr Lydyard?'

'I have,' answered Lydyard, accepting the implicit invitation to play devil's advocate. 'He was the man who proved that the reality of a miracle could never be established by evidence – one of many philosophers whose reasoning impelled him towards an atheism which diplomacy in the face of intolerance prevented him from openly declaring.'

Zephyrinus smiled. 'Perhaps,' he said. 'But was it not the same Hume who showed that all the grand, bold laws of science were just as frail as miracles, on the grounds that no amount of evidence could ever suffice to make them certain?'

'To make them logically certain,' agreed Lydyard. 'But no man of science nowadays believes that the nature of the world can be logically deduced. It is true that we can only observe a finite number of instances of a universal law – but still, such laws refer to what any and all men may see in the world, with their own eyes; and any regularity which all men with eyes may see, often and invariate, is preferable as an item of belief to something which was never seen, save in the dreams of some self-appointed prophet. What we *see* is a world which moves and changes according to processes of cause and effect, and that is all that we can truly *know*. I must say that I cannot fault this case, even though it seems to me that a new eye has been opened inside me, which threatens to deluge me with dreams of another and less certain world.'

'But you must know your limitations better than that,' countered the abbot, smoothly. 'You know well enough what kind of image the lens of your eye must cast upon your retina.'

'An inverted image,' answered Lydyard. 'What of it?'

'What of it? Why, only this – that your mind's eye, your *inner* eye, turns that image right way up again, so that you may see that the sky is up and the earth is down. It is your *inner* eye, Mr Lydyard, which brings the truth out of the illusion which your organ of sense has created. It is an Act of Creation, is it not, which turns the whole world upside down, so that you may see it right way up? Yet you will mock me for believing in a transformation of the world!

'The world which is visible to our limited, fallible senses is not the world as it is, but only the world as it appears. Its dimensions, its stability, its solidity, and its connectedness are products of our inner eyes, which will one day be allowed to see it otherwise. Sir Edward is still comfortable in the world which his senses and his science have made for him – comfortable in the belief that up is up and down is down, and that that is what he sees – but comfort blinds us all, and when by some stroke of chance or genius we catch a glimpse of the world as it really is, we must recognize that there is nothing secure in it – not its dimensions, nor its stability, nor its solidity, nor its connectedness. Appalling that may be, and horrific, but it is the truth, and the only hope we have is that the guiding hand of Creation is something which loves us.'

'Sir Edward would call that sophistry,' said Lydyard.

'It is advice,' retorted Zephyrinus. 'It is what you came here for. Trust your inner eye, Mr Lydyard, for what it sees is real – but you must beware of its seductions as you must beware of the seductions of doubt, for there is evil in the world, and Satan is ever anxious to draw the souls of men to his own vain cause. Faith alone can tell us what sight cannot. I am sorry for you, because you must bear the torment of vision without the armour of faith, but I can offer you no other answer. We are but men, Mr Lydyard, and however much we may aspire to be Creators, it is not for us to usurp that privilege – all who try to do so are servants of Satan, whether they know it or not. Go home and pray, Mr Lydyard, and leave Gabriel Gill to the werewolves which are his spiritual kin. You need not fear the boy, or that Beast which you met in Egypt, for they cannot steal away that heritage which is yours by virtue of Christ's mercy, which is the Kingdom of Heaven, now at hand.'

After a pause, he added: 'Thank you again for bringing Brother Francis's ring, and for your account of his death.

You must leave now, for there is nothing more I can tell you.'

Lydyard allowed the abbot to lead him back along the twisting path to the arched doorway. But there was one more question which he was determined to ask, before he left. As they reached the doors set in the archway he turned once more to the monk and said: 'Do you believe that a man can be possessed by the Devil?'

'Most certainly,' replied Zephyrinus. 'And I believe in the power of the rite of exorcism as well as the power of prayer. But that sight which has been granted to you is not in itself evil, Mr Lydyard; it is not some imp of Hell sent to punish you. Your salvation is your own responsibility, and cannot be threatened without your permission.'

The doors closed behind him then, and he heard the bolt shoot home. He turned towards the place where he had dismounted from the hansom, with head lowered – but he looked up very suddenly when he realized that the carriage which stood there now was not the same, being considerably larger and drawn by a pair of stout bays.

Looking out at him through the window of the carriage was the most beautiful woman he had ever seen. Her hair was very long and fair, her complexion pale and perfect, she had very remarkable violet eyes. Her teeth, which showed in a quizzical smile, were white and smooth.

'Mr Lydyard,' she said, in a cloyingly sweet fashion, 'I took the liberty of sending your cab away. I will take you wherever you wish to go, and would be very grateful for the opportunity to talk with you.'

Lydyard did not know why he did it, but he instantly stepped back, and looked warily around. He looked up at the coachman, but even before he recognized the man he had guessed who the woman was.

'Mandorla Soulier,' he said, feeling slightly foolish because he could think of nothing further to add.

The woman in the carriage only smiled, but the coachman – who was Perris, the brother of Pelorus – picked up the silver-capped stick from the seat beside him, and drew back the head from the polished black shaft, just far enough to show Lydyard that it was a swordstick.

'Get in, Mr Lydyard,' said Mandorla, her voice still honey-sweet. 'We mean you no harm, I promise you.'

Lydyard looked from side to side, wondering whether there was any possibility of his being readmitted to the house of Zephyrinus if he should thunder upon the door in panic – or whether he might simply run away, with the carriage in hot pursuit.

While he looked wildly about, another man stepped from hiding, appearing almost as if by magic from behind one of the sycamores. In his right hand, extended before him, was a pistol.

'Put down your stick, Perris,' said Pelorus, 'or I will send you to sleep for a long, long time – and Mandorla with you. And lest you are tempted to be foolish, may I point out that this is no silly duelling-piece, but an American revolver. With its aid, I can easily send you both on a journey into the distant future, if that is what you wish.'

Lydyard, in spite of his amazement, was quick to turn to see what Mandorla's reaction would be. He caught the briefest flash of emotion in her face, in which cold anger and dreadful hatred were alloyed – but then her composure returned.

'Why, Pelorus,' she said, in a tone even sicklier than that she had employed on Lydyard, 'I have so looked forward to this meeting. My heart has ached to see you for so many years, and you cannot imagine how sad I am to find that you are still so tragically enslaved. If only you had the strength to turn that weapon on yourself, how happy you might be!'

Pelorus showed not the slightest sign of having heard her. His eyes were on his brother, and so was the gun.

'Drive, Perris!' he commanded. 'Drive, lest the will of Machalalel should tighten my finger on this trigger.'

And Perris, without waiting for any order from the woman within, snatched up his whip and cracked it loudly, to spur the horses into instant action. The carriage clattered away down the shadowed road, while Pelorus pointed the gun after it as though it were in truth an effort to refrain from firing it. Not until it had turned a corner and passed out of sight did he lower the weapon.

Lydyard stared at his rescuer, still at a loss for words.

'Go home, Mr Lydyard,' said Paul Shepherd, in a harsh and bitter tone which could hardly have contrasted more strongly with Mandorla's, 'and in future go armed whenever you go abroad. My cousin is afraid, and eager to know what that creature which disturbed your mind intends to do. In order to find out, she would hurt you – and Harkender would do the same. But remember that while Mandorla cannot be killed, her plans will come to naught if she is put to sleep. A bullet would do it – it need not be silver.'

The blue-eyed man spun on his heel then, and made as if to run off, but he halted when Lydyard called to him to wait. When he turned back, though, there was an expression on his face which frightened Lydyard almost as much as Mandorla's seductive invitation had frightened him. 'Go home, Mr Lydyard,' said Pelorus again. 'I will come to you again, if I can do it safely – but you might regret it when I do. I would be a better friend by far if I could only let you alone.'

And with that paradoxical parting shot, the man who might or might not be half-wolf broke into a curiously unsteady run, and was very soon lost to sight.

Lydyard had no alternative but to hurry away himself, looking over his shoulder all the while lest he find himself again pursued by a carriage pulled by two strong bays.

7

While he and Cordelia walked along beside the Serpentine, heading towards the Long Water and Kensington Gardens,

Lydyard could not help looking back occasionally to see if they were being followed. There was no evidence of it, but he was nevertheless unable to relax. He was beset by a sensation of constant unease which manifested itself physically as a faint dizziness; it had visited him often, ever since that fateful night among the tombs, but had never been as persistent nor as strong as it now was.

On the previous day, Lydyard had consulted Franklin about his troubles, but his veiled and somewhat embarrassed account of his nightmares had left the doctor at a loss, with no recourse but to mutter about 'nerves' and suggest mild doses of laudanum to facilitate sleep.

Lydyard had taken no laudanum; his dreams were quite vivid enough without such encouragement.

'This is monstrously unfair,' remarked Cordelia. 'We have come away from the house in order to save you from your brooding and your incessant discussions with father and Dr Franklin – and yet you pay far more attention to some phantom behind us than you do to me. To add injury to insult, you seem to be determined to endorse my father's casual refusal to explain to his wife or daughter what this mystery is which occupies so much of your time and effort.'

'I'm sorry,' said Lydyard. 'I had hoped to leave misfortune behind when we left the valley of tombs and vipers for Wadi Halfa – and had fully expected that such mystery as remained would be a mere puzzle on which Sir Edward and I might exercise our minds. Alas, my troubles did not end when we reached the foggy shore of England, and I fear that I still suffer from the fevers which I caught in Egypt. It is not uncommon, and you must not worry about it unduly.'

She paused, and he paused with her, half-turning towards her. She reached out a white-gloved hand to touch his cheek, gently and briefly, but she did not seem to be pleased with him. 'Poor David,' she murmured, in a tone which had more complaint in it than sympathy. 'Your troubles are not uncommon, you say, and so you instruct me not to worry. Yet it seems to me that your troubles are so very uncommon that you dare not let any of us know their nature and extent. Father is anxious about you, you know – and he is not a man to bear anxiety lightly.'

'He must think me very feeble,' replied Lydyard, quietly.

'He thinks that you still carry some poison within you,' she corrected him. 'He knows that you have frightful nightmares. David, you must not be ashamed of being ill – no one will blame you for it.'

'Fever is no fault in itself,' he answered, 'but any kind of testing may reveal flaws in a man. A nightmare is only a dream, yet it has power to taunt and tempt – it threatens to fill the world with phantoms, to destroy the foundations of belief and sanity. In dreams it is all too easy to believe the impossible, and when dreams acquire too great a force within the mind, they may spill over into waking, like a corrosive acid which eats away at the roots of wisdom. Every day I wake in the hope that my condition will improve, and every day it seems to be worse. I do not know how to fight this poison, if poison it is; I do not know how to defend myself against its ravages.'

'But I must not worry *unduly*, you say?'

He flinched at the grievance in her voice. 'None but I can stand against the torments of my own nightmares,' he told her. 'In such a contest, a man is bound to be alone.'

And that, he thought as he pronounced the words, *is the very heart of it. In the arena of my dreams, I am alone. Whatever monsters visit me there have to be faced alone. If only . . .*

'But when you wake,' she said, 'you need not be alone, and should not be. When you are awake, you must not retreat into the private world of tortured thought, from which others are closed out. You must not try to hide, David – not from my father, and not from me. Or have your dreams transformed me in your eyes? Do I seem in your nightmares to be a harpy or a gorgon? Is that why you can hardly bear to look at me?'

She reached out to him again, using her hand to turn his head very gently towards her, so that he had to look her in the eye. She had her father's eyes, sober and brown, but her features followed the softer contours of her mother's face. She had nothing of the sleek and brilliant glamour of Mandorla Soulier, but she was consummately handsome after her own gentle fashion.

He blushed at the touch, and smiled wryly. 'By no means,' he said, with a sudden flood of affectionate warmth. 'In my dreams, you are ever the bright angel of mercy who comes to stand over me, and guard me from the dark angel of pain. I am never so well as I am when you are with me, even in my dreams.'

She started walking again, making a small clicking sound with her tongue, which was a token recognition of her obligation to make a show of dismissing the compliment. But she too shied away from the rush of intimacy which she had brought forth. 'I have never seen you so well suntanned,' she said, teasingly. 'While we have been in England, suffering the snows of winter and the fogs of London, you have been in Egypt glorying in the sunlight. You come home to find the cold north winds blowing even in April, with your face as brazen as a Greek god's, and still you protest your infirmity!' She sounded uncomfortable as she said it, and he knew that she was annoyed with herself – just as he was annoyed when he betrayed himself with lapses into similar fatuity.

'I am no coughing invalid,' he assured her, 'I am only poisoned, after all. I have become unduly attractive to snakes, it seems, and I expect that every adder in England is hurrying to Lancaster Walk in the hope of meeting us there.'

'For adders,' she said, 'one must go to Regent's Park.'

'Except for those which Medusa had for hair,' he countered.

'For those,' she answered, in the same light tone, 'I believe Green Park is best – especially after dark.' He could not help but colour slightly as she said it. There were things which young women were not supposed to know – and were required to disregard, if they did know them.

They stopped by the bridge, and watched the people on the water plying the oars of their little boats. The park was very crowded, for this was the first bright Sunday of spring, and though the wind still carried a slight chill it was by no means fierce enough to keep people at home; Rotten Row and the Ring were busy with trotting horses and parading popinjays, and the music of the military band could still be faintly heard, competing with the murmurous hubbub of a thousand conversations.

Is this the world, thought Lydyard, *which is soon to end? Do the demons which will snuff it out walk among these crowds even now?*

It was impossible to believe; the sheer ordinariness of the scene constituted a tyranny which defied deceptive subversion. Here, Brother Zephyrinus and Jacob Harkender could only be remembered as madmen and fantasists. But what, then, was he?

'I am sorry that our homecoming has been spoiled by my illness and our idiotic intrigues,' said Lydyard, in a more serious way. 'I would certainly have preferred a merrier reunion.'

'Oh no,' she said. 'I have not seen father so fervent for years; he is never happy, you know, unless his sensibilities are sufficiently offended to rouse his powers of indignation. But mother fears that his mundane affairs will suffer if he continues to attack his duties with such ruthless impatience.'

Lydyard laughed. 'For a man of letters,' he said, 'Sir Edward has an unusually aggressive manner. He takes the same delight in riding down and demolishing a folly or a frail conceit as lesser men take in following the hounds or tracking lions on the veld. But it is not merely the routines of his mundane business which are making him impatient. The mystery of what happened to us in Egypt, and why, is becoming a Gordian knot of absurdities, and it distresses him that he can see no hope of finding a satisfactory solution. He abhors an unsettled question as much as nature is said to abhor a vacuum.'

'But you feel differently, do you not?' she said, sharply. 'While he becomes impatient, you become anguished.'

He could hardly deny it, though he wanted very much

to shield it from her. 'I wish that your father and I were more alike,' he replied, obliquely. 'I crave his good opinion – but I cannot quite respond as he does to the matters which enthuse him. I marvelled with him at the wonders of Egypt, as all visitors must, but the heat and the sandflies sapped my capacity for awe to an extent I am ashamed to admit. He is an explorer and an explainer by nature, whereas I . . . do not know quite what I am, or what I may become. He has been kind enough to treat me like a son, and I would not like to disappoint him, but I fear that I may not have it in me to live up to his expectations.'

He knew, as he said it, that he sounded overly morose; he felt that he ought to be making a better effort to be bright and amusing, for his own sake as well as hers. He was awkwardly conscious of the fact that Sir Edward expected Cordelia to be left out of the affair completely; the baronet's code of behaviour specified that wives and daughters were to be protected from all kinds of stress and strife.

'Alas,' said Cordelia, in a voice hardly above a whisper, 'I failed to live up to his expectations from the instant of my birth. And my mother failed too, in carelessly rendering herself incapable of bearing other children, and maliciously refusing to leave him a widower.'

'You should not say that,' Lydyard told her, genuinely offended on Sir Edward's behalf.

'No,' she answered, 'I should not. And has not fate provided what the marriage made in Heaven could not, in giving him as good a son as any man could wish?'

To that, he could say nothing.

After a brief interval of silence, she asked: 'Does that dark angel of pain visit you often in your dreams?'

'Often,' he echoed, soberly. 'But he cannot touch me while my bright angel of mercy stands in his way. I do not quite understand why I am so very conscious of his nearness.'

'Father showed me the snake which bit you,' she said. 'It seemed such a tiny thing – so easily crushed beneath his heel.'

'I suppose it had the worst of our encounter,' Lydyard conceded. 'Does he still intend to send it away to be identified?'

'He said that he would, but he has had to put it aside for now. Why did Jacob Harkender come to see him the day before yesterday?'

Lydyard did not allow himself to be taken by surprise by the sudden question. 'I think he came to heal some ancient quarrel,' he said, vaguely. 'Sir Edward would not tell me exactly what the quarrel was about, but I think he is half-persuaded to forgive the man.'

'I cannot believe that was the whole of it,' said Cordelia, in an annoyed tone, 'but if you will not answer me, I suppose I must be content. No doubt I can discover something from the gossip of the servants, as women are usually forced to do.'

'Then I hope the servants can make more sense of it all than I can,' he said, in a petulant fashion. 'But I wish that you would not try to prise out of me what Sir Edward has forbidden me to reveal. I brought you here in order to escape from it all.'

She frowned. 'I am sorry that you have not found me a more convenient vehicle for your escape,' she said, tartly. 'And you must not think that I hold you to be at fault for merely obeying my father. I suppose I am still resentful that it never so much as crossed Sir Edward Tallentyre's mind that his daughter might be as pleased to see the wonders of the ancient world as his surrogate son, and now that I find myself excluded from your dour discussions of what befell you there I feel that insult has been added to injury. I am doubtless wrong to be annoyed by the presumption of my irrelevance, and I should be humbly glad to be of service to you while you seek distraction from your anxieties. We are probably both in dire need of a walk in the park, dedicated entirely to witty conversation and flirtation.'

It was such an accurate summary of what Lydyard thought they *did* need that he flinched again, and while he floundered in embarrassed confusion could only echo the last item in her register of veiled accusations. 'Flirtation!' he exclaimed. 'Why, I had no . . .'

But then he stopped, realizing belatedly that whatever he chose to deny would make him seem ungracious at best.

'Alas,' she said, sarcastically, 'I know only too well that you did not come here to flirt with me. You have not yet learned the art of it. But you should not let it make a hypocrite of you. Everyone expects you to make love to me by slow and polite degrees, moving inexorably from cousinly signs of chaste affection to an eventual proposal of marriage. My father knows it; my mother knows it; and you know it yourself, even though you are still wondering how and when you could ever pluck up the courage to see it through. No doubt we all have our different reasons for approving of the scheme, if we approve at all, but we all know that it is laid out before us, paved with as many good intentions as the road to Hell – though we must hope that time will bring it to a more hopeful destination. Please do me the favour of refusing to feign shock or protest innocence.'

Lydyard would have liked to laugh. Indeed, he would have liked to make buoyant laughter an overture to a joyous litany of compliments which would properly capitalize upon the opportunity which she had given him to be clever; but embarrassment stopped him still, and tied up his tongue. He had to turn away, as though he had caught sight of some exceptionally fascinating event, unhappy in his conviction that any one of the countless strolling swains passing back and forth across and beneath the bridge could have done better.

When he finally contrived to answer her, it was only to say: 'I confess that I had caught a glimpse of such a chart – but I did not know that it was open to such wide exhibition.'

'And I have hurt you by declaring it,' she replied, 'and now must refrain from teasing you lest I hurt you more. How sharper than a serpent's tooth it is to have an awkward lover!'

'I had thought *that* Cordelia was unjustly chided as a thankless child,' he said, feeling that there was safety in Shakespearian exegesis; but then he spoiled it by adding: 'but if we are lovers, and one of us is awkward, it is certainly not you.'

'That was a very churlish *if*,' she observed. 'Although you have never taken the trouble to tell me that you love me, it can only add injury to insult to pretend that you might not.'

'I withdraw the *if*,' he said, immediately, while fervently wishing that he could discover enough belated fluency to repair his position. 'And now I know that the map of our destiny is as fixed and clear as the map of the Underground Railway, I will certainly ask your father's permission to pay court to his favourite daughter.'

'You must ask my permission first,' she said, less lightly than he might have hoped. 'And I must carefully consider whether I wish to be courted by a man who keeps so many secrets, and prefers the cultivation of mysteries to the company of one he is supposed to love.'

He saw that she meant this more seriously than she had intended to imply when she set out to say it.

'I cannot tell you,' he said, flatly. 'Even if I had not been forbidden, it is too bizarre. We have heard several explanations of what happened to us in Egypt, but they are so very fantastic that there seems no hope of ever reaching the truth of the matter. Sometimes, I am half-convinced that I must still be writhing in my hammock in Egypt, and that my every awakening since then has merely been an extension of my nightmare.'

'And am I also to be reckoned no more than a figment of your nightmare?' she asked, pointedly. 'Am I only a merciful angel, a mere phantom of your delirium?'

'No phantom,' he replied, with feeling, 'and certainly not mere – for whether I dream or not, your nearness is the one thing which matters more than any other, and I believe that I could stand to see the world come to its destined end, if only I could be with you in the hereafter.'

'If that is a figure of speech,' she said, 'then I must thank you for a pretty compliment; but I have the strangest suspicion that it is not. For father, of course, it would be the end of the world if once he was proved wrong, but you are not so brittle. Is the world to end very soon, do you think?'

'You are too clever this time,' he told her, trying not to sound resentful, 'for the simple truth is that I do not know. I met a man yesterday who assured me that it will, but he is a scholar monk of a very peculiar sect, and I do not think that his opinion can be trusted. Now I have told you more than I intended, and I hope that you are glad of it. I would be glad myself if only I could be certain that I am not mad, or close to becoming mad.' After a pause, he added, in a lower tone: 'If I could be certain of your honest affection for me, setting all plans and schemes aside, I would be glad of that, too.'

He felt, as he said it, very daring.

'You can be sure of that, at least,' she said, but not with the breathless tenderness which he thought appropriate to such a declaration.

'You are already certain of me, it seems,' he said, suddenly feeling that he might, after all, be capable of lightness and an attempt at charm, 'but for what it is worth, I declare it: I am in love with you. For your sake, I will make what shift I can to decide what kind of life I intend to make for myself, so that I might show you what it is that I will ask you to share – if it should transpire that the world does not end after all.'

'Thank you,' she said, plainly. He was perversely glad to find her somewhat at a loss for words, now that she had obtained the declaration which she sought.

'All this mystery will come to an end very soon,' he assured her, ardently. 'There is nothing which can come of it, so far as I can judge. My nightmares will cease, in the fullness of time. Jacob Harkender will continue to practise his esoteric magic in the privacy of his own home, troubling no one. The essential ordinariness of the world will assert itself, and the silly game with which we have become involved will simply dissolve into a scattering of inexplicable incidents altogether unworthy of further thought.'

And the werewolves of London, he added, silently, *will be banished to that nursery rhyme which is where they truly belong, and never again will trouble honest folk with the thought of their dreadful metamorphoses.*

'And we will escape the dark angel of pain,' she added, in her turn. 'He will return to his own places – to the streets where the poor people live, where disease and the rats kill far more children than any pack of werewolves ever could.'

But I have not mentioned werewolves at all! he protested, being suddenly made aware of the fact that she somehow knew more than she should. He could not believe that she had been eavesdropping herself, but she had only recently reminded him that a house with servants was a house without secrets, and 'werewolf' was a word which gossips were ever avid to repeat in London.

'You have been reading the socialist tracts which your father brings home,' he said, refusing to give anything more away by a careless acknowledgement of her remark.

'If I were in truth an angel of mercy,' she said, sourly, 'I would have such an abundance of work to do that I would not know where to start, and could never rest. I need no tracts to tell me so.'

She did not wait for a reply, but walked on into Buck Hill Walk. He could not be entirely sure that it was not mere optimism, but Lydyard thought that she stood a little straighter, and strode a little more confidently than she had before.

We are lovers now, he told himself, savouring the echo of the words within his mind. *She has told me so, and I have told her in return.*

It seemed to him a very vital beginning, and he was joyously surprised that it had taken such a tiny measure of good intention to set his feet on a pathway which would surely lead to Heaven, and not to Hell.

The dizziness in his head was not quite banished, but it was transformed for a moment or two into an intoxication for which no man would have wished to find a cure. And while that intoxication lasted, he could not bring himself to care overmuch about the existence or the schemes of the werewolves of London.

He began to hurry after her, and in his haste he did not

see or hear the horse behind him and he barely had time to hear the warning cry uttered by its child rider before the flying hooves collided with his ankles and sent him tumbling to the ground.

Though he tried to break his fall with his arms he could not do it, for the shoulder of the beast thrust him heavily down – and though he lost consciousness soon after his head struck a sharp-edged stone he had time to see the dark angel of pain descending upon him like an eagle from the fiery sky, sharp talons splayed and black eyes ablaze with cruel triumph.

8

His unconsciousness did not last long – barely long enough, in fact, for him to be brought to the carriage and placed inside. He was able to sit up while the wheels clattered and leapt over the rutted roads. He was able to hold a handkerchief to his bleeding temple, able to grit his teeth against the aching of his limbs, able to look into Cordelia's dark eyes, whose soft expression was flooded now with pity and concern.

Later, he was able to be still while Gilbert Franklin examined him, able to agree when the surgeon assured him that no bones were broken, able to reassure Lady Rosalind that he would be able to present himself for dinner in the appropriate costume at the appropriate hour.

He was perfectly able. There was nothing wrong with him at all, save for the bruising of his dignity and his poor afflicted flesh. There was only the pain.

Only the pain.

Despite the juddering and jarring of the journey back to Sturton Street, with all its stops and starts and lurching turns, the immediate agony of his small catastrophe soon faded. That forked-tongued fury with poisoned talons which was the dark

angel of pain had him in her most intimate and untender grip
for just a few fugitive moments before she was forced to retreat
into the shadowed walls of the world. Afterwards, she reached
out on occasion to rake his elbow or his calf with a careless
claw, but could not securely imprison him within the folds of
her stinging wings. And while she could not, he could not be
forced to see the fissured floor of Hell or suffer the ignominies
and regrets of the crippled golden angel.

Instead, he had the power of his outer eyes to sustain him
– the covetous enthusiasm of his greedy gaze, which reached
out to seize the real world and all its fugitive firelit shadows:
first among them dark-eyed, sweet-natured Cordelia.

All through the day he kept the angel of pain at bay, and
would not be conquered by his inner sight, even though
his heart ran slow when once he heard the mewling of the
kitchen cat.

But when the night came, and he lay in cool soft sheets, and
felt the calm caresses of the empty dark . . . Then the chains
which he craved fell away once more, and he turned his head
towards the fabulous light which transfigured all the world and
showed him the shapes of the risen gods. These gods came not
crowned with thorns and weeping for mankind, but dressed
with the hearts and souls of predatory beasts, saying: *Nothing
is hidden, nothing is dark, nothing is forgotten, nothing is denied,
nothing is for ever fixed, nothing is what it seems, nothing is ever
honest, nothing cannot be changed* . . .

And then, with the borrowed eyes of some lost and lonely
angel, he saw . . .

He saw in a fashion very different from any vision or nightmare
that he had previously experienced. It was as though that inner
eye which had opened in his soul could no longer be content to
look upon the marvellous and infinite vistas which were there
exposed to its fascinated gaze, but instead took wing within the
world of men, to visit other souls which were cold and
blind, to share their comfortable being-in-the-world.

Given that his magical sight should go a-roving at all,

Lydyard could not be surprised that it elected to follow Sir Edward Tallentyre – who was not at home that evening – but he was both astonished and distressed to find that the view which his magical sight adopted for its own, and brought as a perverse gift to him, was not Sir Edward's at all, but that of the mistress which the baronet kept in Greek Street, whom he had never been privileged to meet.

He had never known her name before, but now he discovered that she was called Elinor Fisher, and within minutes of his dream's beginning he felt that he knew more about her than any man had any right to know about the sensations and emotions of any other person.

He knew, for instance, that the lovemaking in which she and Sir Edward had recently indulged had been less furious than she had anticipated after such a long time apart. He knew, too, that although Elinor had tried to put that awareness from her mind in order that she might abandon herself entirely to the pleasure of intercourse, she had not been able to do so. He was privy to her suspicion that Tallentyre had devoted his first and most ardent attentions to his wife – and also to her disappointed expectation that a greater enthusiasm should have been reserved for one whose relationship with him was quite unsullied by any matters of duty or heavy courtesy.

It was as though he could hear her private thoughts as clearly as she could herself: *Why should a man want a mistress at all, save to give himself the freedom and luxury of pure passion? And if that passion is now inhibited, what can it signify but that the mistress is no longer adequate to invite such surrender; that the man is bored by her?*

The memory of their lovemaking, fresh as it was in her mind, was no more shocking to the passenger in her consciousness than the seemingly cynical undercurrents of thought which surged within that memory. She had always known, it seemed, that one day she must be 'cast aside' or 'put away' – or whatever cliché was nowadays used as a polite evasion of the horror of it – but was amazed to find the beginning of such a process in a man who had been abroad for several months, whose absence ought surely to have sharpened an appetite blunted by familiarity.

Could it really be true after all, she wondered, that the fabled whores of Paris and Rome were so expert in their art as to make any English bitch appear to be no more than a shabby mongrel?

Lydyard, helpless to detach himself, found the awareness thrust upon him that Sir Edward's unsteady thrusts had pricked and pummelled her uncomfortably, while anxiety prevented her reaching even that pitch of excitement to which she normally aspired. Tallentyre could not possibly have guessed what kind of thoughts were running through his companion's mind – *I am too old to begin again in this routine, and should this be the end, I am naught but waste and jetsam, with nowhere to go!* – and Lydyard felt it to be a terrible burden that the awkward knowledge should be thrust upon him.

It was not difficult to believe now what Zephyrinus had assured him: that this was the work of the Devil himself, angling for damned souls with the fruit of the Tree of Knowledge as bait.

When Tallentyre had finished, and while her heart was still hammering – though not with any passionate fever – he had remained inside her for a while, circling her with his long arms and hugging her to him almost as if she were a daughter to be cherished. She had felt safer then, for there was always more honesty in what a man did with his arms than what he did with his bloated member, but now he had released her again, and Lydyard could feel the doubts cascading through her thoughts as though they were hailstones.

That eye which was Lydyard was helpless to do aught but see; it could not tell this suffering woman that what was wrong with Tallentyre probably had nothing to do with her. Had he been able, Lydyard might have kindly reassured her that she had not lost her place in the secret world of Tallentyre's imagination as a vision of desire; that she still had the power to cast her little spells, englamouring his soul; that it was not some rival siren song that had made him deaf to hers; that it was some other, unconnected trouble . . .

But sight was silent, and comfort was only for the blind.

It was useless even to wish that he could soothe her fears, for if by some miracle he *had* been able to speak to her, the mere fact that there was another voice besides her own which could be heard in the auditorium of her mind would have terrified her, and convinced her that she must be mad.

She was now stroking Tallentyre's body, very gently. She was reaffirming with the delicate familiarity of her touch the strength of the compact which bound them, by which she kept herself for him, and he in his turn kept her. The pleasure which she gained from the action was innocent enough, yet Lydyard could not feel it at second-hand without a horrific sensation of shame. He was pathetically glad when she stopped and got out of bed, putting on a silken dressing-gown embroidered with coloured dragons in the oriental style; but still he was forced to observe and share her concern as she took care that the garment would not conceal the whiteness of her thighs and the curve of her breast while she went to fetch more wine.

In the warm aftermath of lust expressed, she was telling herself, Tallentyre might be made to notice her again, and be pleased with what he saw.

Through Elinor's eyes, Lydyard watched Sir Edward Tallentyre sit up in his mistress's bed, and accept the wine which she gave him. He and she watched as Tallentyre took the first few sips very greedily, with a hand that might have shaken had he not exerted stern control.

'What is it, Edward?' she asked, knowing that there was a void which only a solicitous question could fill. 'Did you catch some fever in Egypt which the bitter English spring has brought out of you again?'

'No,' he replied. 'I am of the favoured few who thrive in the dry heat and the brightness. Poor David was ill, when the bite of a snake distressed him, and I think the cold makes him more miserable than he might be, but I am very well.'

Poor David! thought Lydyard; and was instantly privy to the very strange awareness which Elinor Fisher had, that she had never met David Lydyard but had heard so much about him that she hoped that one day she might – for there came, she had been told, a time when every man showed off his mistress to his son, or such substitute as he had for a son. Lydyard was unwillingly conscious of her savouring the possibility – or idle fantasy – that Sir Edward might one day require her to 'educate the boy', knowing that in the mean time he was only a rumour: a faceless entity of whom Tallentyre spoke overfondly.

Lydyard had never heard Sir Edward speak overfondly of anyone or anything, but he supposed that a mistress was for a man's indulgence, and that indulgence might easily include sentimentality as well as lust. Men like Sir Edward were never sentimental with their friends or their sons, and rarely with their wives. But with their mistresses, they were free.

'I am well myself,' Elinor assured the baronet, though he had not asked. 'I had a cold at Christmas time, but I am better now.'

'I am glad to hear it,' he told her, though his manner made clear to her as well as to Lydyard that he cared not a whit whether he heard it or not. 'I took some kind of fever myself, very briefly, and dreamed of hostile darkness, and a living sphinx, and a great grey wolf – but I am better too, though the dream, in some mad and perverse fashion, refuses to fade away.'

'It is a way which dreams have,' she assured him, 'though men rarely find it out.'

Her irony, which she thought uncommonly clever, went completely unnoticed by Tallentyre, and she could not know that there was another listening whose position made it impossible that he should miss her implication.

'One man died,' said Tallentyre, 'and one was lost – but in his place, we found another, who had not his wits about him at the time. When he recovered, he recited a pretty catalogue of nonsense – and exerted such a spell upon me that I hear such babble now from nearly everyone I meet. Perhaps that is only to be expected, for it seems, if we can trust to rumour, that he was one of the famous werewolves of London – what say you to that, dear Nora?'

This, thought Lydyard, *he would not have his wife or daughter told – and he cannot be honest even with his mistress, for he tries to imply that it is all mere amusement, though I know full well that he has a different attitude.* But he did pause to wonder, very briefly, whether Tallentyre too might be a little bit afraid.

'I say that my name is Elinor,' Miss Fisher replied, lightly, 'in case you have forgotten it and think me a mere Nora. But if you have truly crossed the path of one of the werewolves of London, I think you had better take care not to annoy him, for I never heard anything but ill of their kind.'

Tallentyre frowned, but she was glad to see that he looked at her then, and to Lydyard's intense embarrassment she watched proudly as his eyes took in the sight of her pretty gown, and her sleek hair in its engaging disarray, and the smooth contours of her body.

'Did you miss me?' he asked. Though it did not sound plaintive at all, it was a plaintive question, and Lydyard had never thought to hear one like it from the lips of his benefactor.

'I did,' she said. Ironic impulse would have made her give a different answer – *Oh no*, she thought she might have said, *for I had a dozen other lovers whose hearts I had to break most carefully, one after another* – but she dared not say anything of that sort, for she was convinced that men were almost as jealous of their mistresses's freedoms as their mistresses were of the secure positions held by wives.

'And I you,' he assured her. But he had not told her yet what it was that had somehow come between them, and made their licentious tussle less than it should have been, and Lydyard saw Elinor's anxiety renewed.

Somehow he has come to doubt himself, just a little, she thought, *and for a man like him, that is probably a very new experience, for he has always traded on the certainty of his convictions.*

It was, thought Lydyard, a perceptive observation.

'There is a story of a woman who fell in love with one of

the werewolves of London,' she said, musingly. 'He loved her too, it is said. But though she longed to be his mistress, it could not be. "I can feed as a man or as a wolf," he said, "and I can drink as a man or as a wolf, but I can love only as a wolf, for honest passion will not let me remain in human form." It is a sad story.'

'I have not heard it,' said Tallentyre, with an odd note of puzzlement in his voice. 'But I remember that I heard a different one, when I was a very little child. It was the tale of a man who fell in love with a female werewolf, but it could not have been consistent with yours, for I feel sure that the man married the wolfwoman, and kept her with him for many years until he thoughtlessly broke some promise he had made to her, whereupon she left him for her own kind.'

'It is not at all inconsistent,' she told him, airily.

'Oh?' he said. 'Do you tell me that a man would quite happily share his marriage bed with a wife who became a wolf whenever passion seized her?'

'A wife,' she replied, 'can bring herself to the marriage bed as often as she likes, without ever being troubled by passion. Now, if there were a tale of a man who took a werewolf lady for his mistress, that might be a different matter, might it not?' Lydyard knew, though, that she did not think so.

Tallentyre had the grace to laugh, but she felt that his laughter was inhibited in much the same fashion that his lovemaking had been inhibited. Whatever the matter was which was clouding his quest for a proper release, she thought, it was still near to the surface of his thoughts.

Being a true believer in the creed of *in vino veritas*, she brought him more wine.

'Is it true?' he asked her, when she had filled his glass. 'Does passion always make wolves of men? Are men so utterly helpless in their lusts?'

'Do you doubt it?' she asked.

He made no immediate answer, but eventually said: 'Can you believe in werewolves, Nora? Can you believe that there are fallen angels in the earth, ready to erupt to plague man-kind?'

'It does not matter what I can or cannot believe,' she said. 'I have never been to school, and know nothing at all.' Secretly, she said: *Once he came to me only for pleasure; now he asks me for my untutored opinions. How can I possibly pay him, in coin so worthless?*

'There is something which someone said to me two nights ago which has troubled me,' said Tallentyre, slowly. 'It was a man I hated, and thought I had cause enough to hate, for a kind of wolfishness which he once displayed. He said that I could not possibly understand what he had suffered, and until he said it, I did not realize that I had put it from my mind without ever trying to understand it.'

Lydyard knew that Tallentyre was speaking of Jacob Harkender, but Elinor had no way to guess. There was a moment's silence before she said: 'It is a pretty riddle, but I fear that you will have to unravel it for me.'

'It was a man who believes in werewolves,' he said, after taking more wine. 'Hypocritically, I once thought, though I now believe him to be perfectly sincere. When I was at Oxford, many years ago, I thought him to be the most evil man I knew – very handsome, capable of immense charm and wit, and yet so horribly cold within that he seemed literally fiendish. He seduced men and women alike – to affectionate feeling if not to actual sexual intercourse – and he took pleasure in hurting everyone who thus became vulnerable to him. He drove one girl to suicide; I knew her very slightly, and though she was little or nothing to me but a glimpse of a sweet smile I thought at the time that it was an act of such unremitting cruelty as to beggar explanation. Had I not already given up the faith, I might have fancied the man possessed by a demon, and when others called him wizard and Satanist I thought I knew why they did it, though for myself I considered his actions no more than a frightful revelation of the capacity for ugliness and cruelty which men have. I remember that I actually thought of challenging the man to a duel, and told myself that I could not

– not because I did not want to kill him, but because *he was not a gentleman*! I quarrelled with him in a less violent, but more contemptuous way, and was always proud of it . . . until last night.'

'Why?' she asked, softly – for she knew, as Lydyard did, that he was waiting to be asked. 'What explanation did he give?'

'He said that he was sent by his father to school, in the hope of making him a simulacrum of that gentleman which birth had not made him.'

'What of it?' she said. Lydyard, fascinated, felt that there was here some kind of purpose for his dream-odyssey, and he waited for Tallentyre to confirm the conclusion to which he had jumped himself.

'What indeed?' said the baronet. 'No doubt he learned his Latin and his Greek, his rhetoric and his mathematics, and the proper modes of speech and dress. His father may have thought it all a great success, though what he thought of the direction in which the imitation gentleman subsequently developed his powers of scholarship, I hesitate to think. But he reminded me what price he had to pay for that education, and asked me to imagine what forces there combined to make him what he was.'

'I have heard that your schools are cruel places,' she said. 'There are half a dozen brothels in the city which cater to those who have a peculiar taste for the birch. I was with Mercy Murrell myself once, as you know – and might have been with her still, but for the grace of God and Sir Edward Tallentyre.'

Tallentyre laughed – very shortly, very sneeringly, in a way which bruised her a little, and which Lydyard found equally uncomfortable. 'Did you know a woman there named Jenny Gill?' he asked, as if on a sudden whim.

'I know the name,' she said. 'She went away, I think – there were rumours that she had been killed, or died in awkward circumstances, but they were only rumours. I was young then.'

I was pretty then, Lydyard heard her say to herself. *But now* . . .

Tallentyre nodded, and set the digression firmly aside.

'Our schools are not so bad,' he said, reflectively. 'Every pretty boy has a female nickname, but it is mostly play, and the system which enslaves the younger boys to the elder is not so black as it is painted. Anyhow, a discreet measure of beating and buggery is held to be healthy for a boy – something to be suffered in silence as a test of fibre, and then forgotten for ever. But it is true that some get more than a measure, and that those who cannot find a protector, or who find a protector more vicious than the rest, can be shared so freely and cut so deeply that . . . well, he was right to argue that I cannot properly imagine what effect it might have. I suppose that ruined and disappointed girls have no monopoly of suicide.

'None of that really matters, though it startled me to hear him speak of it. What really cut me was a contemptuous assumption that I was somehow guilty of it all myself, by virtue of my class, and that I must somehow know what purpose his treatment had served as a kind of education. I could not help but wonder whether there might be a connection, as he alleged, between the fact that I had never asked myself a question of that sort, and the fact that I could so easily refuse to believe in werewolves, in Satanists, in magicians, and in God . . . while he finds it all too easy to believe in any and all of them.'

Lydyard felt that this was a Tallentyre he had never seen before, and was uneasily aware of the fact that Elinor Fisher felt the same. She did not reply, and Sir Edward went on: 'Is there really a wolf in men, Nora – a wolf which men cannot resist, though women can? Do our schools whet the appetite of the wolf while they strive so hypocritically to civilize the child? And when the wolf within the child is fully trained in cruelty, what can we expect of the man, but that he take his wolfishness to man and woman alike, and leave them bleeding if he can?'

Elinor did not know, and Lydyard did not know either. She had not been able to follow the argument as well as Lydyard, who had been privy to Harkender's bitter speech of two days before, but she had picked up the thread of it well enough to be sure that Tallentyre's preoccupation with werewolves was no idle whim.

'I had always thought,' she said, 'that if there was a truth hidden in the myth of the werewolves of London, it was that all men are wolves beneath their masks of painted politeness.'

'So had I,' said Tallentyre, softly. 'And now that I am beginning to believe that there might indeed be truth in the myth, I cannot help but wonder whether that is one of the truths which is in it.'

Lydyard saw, by means of his miraculous sight, that Tallentyre was genuinely troubled by the labyrinth of fantasy into which he had been led. With a shock of insight, he realized that just as he himself had taken infinite pains to conceal from Sir Edward what he really felt, so Tallentyre had taken pains to do the same. The baronet too had heard the mad beating of angels' wings, and could not bring himself to deny it as fervently as he desired to do.

I am not alone! thought Lydyard, with a strange flood of relief. *He is with me, as I once dreamed that he would be.*

But even while Elinor Fisher looked so fondly at her lover's doubtful face, that face dissolved and became another face, which was infinitely more handsome, infinitely calmer, and infinitely terrible. Elinor Fisher dissolved with it, and Greek Street, and London itself, until at last there was only the face, superimposed upon the cold light of the stars in the infinite void.

It was the face of the Sphinx.

I am coming, it said to him, although its red lips did not move at all, *and when I come, I will know what to do.*

9

While Lydyard waited for Sir Edward Tallentyre to come down to the study he stood by the window looking out over the thin strip of shrubbery which divided the two halves of Sturton Street. There was no one stationed directly opposite the front door of the house, but there was a man leaning against the railings some twenty or thirty yards away, who glanced sideways with what seemed to Lydyard mechanical regularity, twice or three times a minute. If any carriage were to draw up in front of the house, or if any caller were to ring the doorbell, the watcher would know.

Lydyard presumed that there was another spy stationed in the mews at the rear. He would have liked to seize and capture one in order that the man might be forced to tell anything that he knew. He had even mentioned the possibility to Tallentyre, who felt the surveillance to be an insult as well as an irritation, but Tallentyre had simply shrugged his shoulders, saying that the men were probably hirelings who knew nothing.

Tallentyre entered the room then, and came to stand beside him at the window. As Lydyard had earlier done, the baronet swiftly scanned the street with his eyes, and noted the presence of the loiterer.

'This is becoming intolerable,' Tallentyre murmured, in a low tone. 'I suppose they will follow us to Charnley, if they can. We must try to evade them, if only to annoy them.'

'They know enough about Franklin to look for us there,' Lydyard pointed out. 'If we are to hide, we must do it cleverly.'

'There is nothing from which we need hide,' said Tallentyre, with some annoyance. 'If they are waiting for Paul Shepherd to come calling, I suspect that they will wait for a long time.'

'That may not be their only purpose,' said Lydyard, quietly. 'I fear that they may be more interested in me. I think I know now why Pelorus took the trouble to keep me out of their hands when Mandorla Soulier issued her invitation to me – and I suspect that his interference has more than redoubled their determination to seize me.'

'You are too anxious,' Tallentyre told him. 'They cannot possibly wish to do you harm.'

Lydyard looked up into the baronet's eyes, uncomfortably. He had given his friend a full account of his interview with Zephyrinus and the incident which had occurred afterwards, but he knew that Tallentyre had inferred nothing more from the story than a supposition that Mandorla Soulier had wanted to question Lydyard about 'Paul Shepherd'. At the time, even Lydyard had hoped that there might be no more to it, but now he no longer found it possible to entertain such optimism.

'Edward,' said Lydyard, uncomfortably, 'I have not been entirely honest with you.'

Tallentyre's expression was by no means unkind. 'If you mean that you were more badly hurt by the snake than you have been prepared to confess,' he said, 'I know it. I have heard you calling out in your sleep, and I know about the feverishness of your nightmares. You need not be ashamed, you know.'

'There has been more to my secrecy than that,' said Lydyard wearily. 'I have long since ceased to believe that it was any ordinary snake which bit me, or that what I have suffered is any commonplace delirium. Perhaps the new sight which I now have is all deception, but even if I believed that, I could not refuse to see. I believe in the werewolves of London, Edward – in their actuality, and in the threat which they pose. I believe in this reawakened power which we met in Egypt, though I do not know whether to call it a god or a devil, an angel or a demiurge. I believe that the sphinx which hurt you was a real and solid creature, which still walks the earth, and though I cannot accept that the end of the world is nigh, I fear that something may soon happen, which might easily be terrible. You may think me weak or deluded if you will, but I cannot help but believe these things, and I can no longer stand to be alone with my belief. I need your help, Edward – and I do not mean that I need reassurances that I will recover if I only give myself pause to rest.'

Tallentyre studied him for a moment or two, then pointed to the armchair which stood beside the bookcase. Lydyard sat down, while Tallentyre placed himself on the chair behind the desk.

'What help do you want, David?' he asked. 'I will give it gladly, if I can.'

Lydyard shook his head. 'I am not so sure of that. I think I can prove that my visions are indeed a kind of sight, but I do not think you will like my proof. For now, I can only ask that you will listen. Later, I wish you would help me to decide what to do.'

'I will certainly listen,' answered the baronet, neutrally. 'I will be most interested to hear your proof, and you should not be anxious that I will not like it. No honest man is ever distressed by a proof.'

Lydyard licked his lips, and took temporary refuge in procrastination. 'What I have come to believe,' he said, 'I have pieced together from the accounts which others have given to us, with the aid of the oracular dreams which I have had since I was favoured by the snake. I have, you see, become an oracle of the kind which Jacob Harkender sought to create for himself when he went to Egypt. Perhaps I am not exactly the same – and I cannot pretend to know how many kinds of oracle there are – but I am sure that I am an oracle of sorts. The spiritists, no doubt, would call me a medium, but it is not the innocent dead whose voices I hear.'

He paused. Tallentyre inclined his head slightly, and said: 'Go on.'

'The werewolves of London stole Harkender's wonder-child because they believe that he might have the power to change as well as the power to see, and they wish to seduce or force him to use that power for their own ends. Pelorus, acting under some compulsion which sets him at odds with his own kind, is determined that they shall not do that; he would steal the child back again, if he could, but he is very anxious about the destructive potential of the more recently spawned creature which appeared to us as a sphinx. Harkender, knowing that Pelorus has an interest in removing the child from Mandorla's care, wants to make an alliance with him – but Pelorus is very reluctant, perhaps because he is afraid that Harkender may be the unwitting tool of another powerful entity, whose intentions might also be destructive. The other werewolves would like to eliminate Pelorus from the game – and though they may not be able to destroy him utterly they can certainly hurt him badly enough to render him impotent – but they too are anxious about the new creature. They are interested in me because they believe, correctly, that I am the creature's instrument.'

'An excellent summary,' said Tallentyre, drily. 'To which we might add that the monks of the Order of St Amycus believe that the destructive power of one or all of these mysterious creatures is destined to be released, bringing about the end of the world as prophesied in the Book of Revelation. If that is true, there is nothing any of us can do; if it is not true . . . I cannot tell what might be achieved by any of the contending parties, least of all ourselves. But I have not been touched by the goddess, as you have, and I do not have delirious dreams which might be taken as visions of the truth. I fear, David, that I cannot believe this when it comes from your mouth, any more than I can believe it from the mouth of a man like Harkender. I fail to see how you can persuade me that there is more in this than fevered delusion.'

Lydyard smiled thinly, knowing – or believing that he knew – that this wall of scepticism was but a mask, behind which might be found a much more credulous man.

'There remains my proof to add,' he said. 'But I must warn you again that you may not like it.'

'Why ever not?' asked Tallentyre, genuinely aggrieved. 'I

am a reasonable man, and you may be sure that I lend to you a more sympathetic ear than I lent to Jacob Harkender.'

Lydyard felt his heart quicken in trepidation. 'Would you accept, as proof of some power of sight far beyond the ordinary, an account of the conversation which took place last night between yourself and a woman named Elinor Fisher, which could not have been witnessed by any other person?'

In all his life, Lydyard had never seen Sir Edward Tallentyre completely astonished. Now he saw the man struggle with all his might to be calm and clinical, and fail. He watched the blood drain from his friend's face, and saw an ugly anger spring nakedly to his expression. For two or three seconds the fact that Lydyard had dared to say such a thing to him overwhelmed any merely scientific interest in the means by which the young man might have come by the information. For those few seconds, Lydyard was afraid of the man – but then the moment passed, and Tallentyre's rational intelligence reasserted its dominion over his being.

'Go on,' he said, icily. Lydyard flinched before the hostility of the tone, though it was not unanticipated. Nothing else that he could possibly have discovered – no matter how incredible it might be – could better serve the purpose of convincing the baronet that normality had been transcended than the intimacy of this revelation.

'Last night,' said Lydyard, only a little unsteadily, 'you recalled that someone had once told you a tale of the werewolves of London – a tale of a man who fell in love with a female werewolf, and married her, and kept her with him for many years until he broke a promise and she returned to her own kind. When you remembered it, you thought it inconsistent with a tale that Elinor Fisher had just told you, but she pointed out that it was not inconsistent at all, because women can easily make love without passion, whereas men require arousal. This was the prelude to a discussion of the wolfish behaviour of Jacob Harkender and its probable explanation, which I can give in full if you like.'

Tallentyre simply stared at him – as though, Lydyard fancied, he were some monster of legend. He did not think that he could have had a more profound effect on the man had he turned into a wolf himself.

'Is there any need to go on?' asked Lydyard. 'I could multiply the detail by a factor of ten, if you wish – but I am as reluctant to do so as I was to be a witness to these events in the first place. I can assure you that I would have withdrawn, had I only known how to do it, but I have not yet learned the art of controlling my magical powers.'

There followed a long silence.

'Have you had other such visions?' asked Tallentyre, eventually. He seemed to be trying hard to make his tone less wrathful, so that he might properly play the part of the rational man which he had claimed to be.

'Not of the same kind,' Lydyard answered. 'But there have been others more honestly dreamlike. For a long time I thought them a mere aftermath of my delirium, products of my own imagination. Now, I can no longer be sure. I have no control over what I dream, and I am perfectly certain that not everything which I see in my dreams is true, even if it be construed as allegory, but I know – and last night my knowledge became indubitable, if what I have just told you is true – that I have some power of sight which was lent to me by the snake which bit me in the tomb, and which links me still to that sphinx-like phantom which hurt Pelorus and nearly destroyed you. That is why the werewolves want me, and why Jacob Harkender would be glad if I would consent to visit him at Whittenton. Whether anyone else could control my powers of vision better than I can myself, I cannot tell, but I believe that they desire to make whatever use of me they can in order to discover precisely what the newly created creature is, and why it has been created.'

'Why did you not tell me about these earlier visions?' asked Tallentyre. 'Why did you take the trouble to insist that you were cured, save for a few lingering symptoms of no importance?'

'I did not want you to think of me as the kind of man who could be troubled by bad dreams,' answered Lydyard frankly. 'I wanted to appear in your eyes as a man of strength and unconquerable reason, because I was certain that was what you wanted me to be, and because I am in love with your daughter.'

Again, Tallentyre responded with a long silence – which seemed to Lydyard poor reward for such courageous honesty.

'And now?' said the baronet, eventually.

'Now I want to appear in your eyes as a man who knows when to abandon dissimulation,' said Lydyard, 'and as a man who is capable of admitting a mistake. Now I want to be a man who can honestly ask for your help, because I really do stand in need of it.'

Tallentyre had the grace to smile at that, albeit half-heartedly. 'I suppose,' he said, 'that I do not appear in your eyes to be quite the man I was before.'

'On the contrary,' said Lydyard, very conscious of his own daring. 'I see no contradiction between the way you treat your mistress and the way you deal with the rest of the world. Where honesty serves, you are brutally frank, and where dishonesty is required, you are perfectly adept – and you are always sure in your own mind of what the truth of the matter is.'

Tallentyre was unimpressed by such a perverse compliment. 'And now, I suppose, you expect me to believe that you are imitating me in the hope that I will take your imitation as flattery?'

'I am grateful that you acknowledge my sincerity,' answered Lydyard, pleased with himself for thinking of such a nice parry.

There was a further silence before Tallentyre murmured, as much to himself as to his companion: 'And if the world should prove to be other than we have believed it to be, still we must live in it, as best we can.'

'Of course,' said Lydyard, lightly, 'the mere fact that I have an inner eye which can see in such a curious fashion does not prove that all the rest is true. Perhaps, after all, these dark angels who have woken from their long slumber have not the slightest wish to upset the world. Pelorus suggested that they might be quite uninterested in destruction. But he also suggested that what was newly awakened in a much-changed world might be lost in confusion – open to manipulation by any who are clever enough to do it . . . perhaps easily thrust into conflict.

'In my dreams, I have begged that cat-like goddess who first confronted me in Plato's cave to tell me what she wants of me, and she has never answered. I do not think that she knew what she wanted, or what she ought to want, until these last few days, and I am fearful to know what she has now decided. Edward, I would dearly like to have your help – to discover what use might be made of me, what power I might have, because I fear that if I cannot master whatever gift has been granted to me for myself, others will make shift to master it for their own ends.'

While Lydyard was still trying to measure Tallentyre's reaction to this speech – while Tallentyre may still have been trying to formulate a reaction, in fact – there was a polite knock at the door. The baronet called out a half-articulate invitation to enter and Summers came in, carrying the morning post on a silver salver. For Sir Edward there was a neat pile of half a dozen items; for Lydyard there was a single handwritten note.

While Tallentyre took the opportunity to retreat into a cursory examination of his correspondence Lydyard tore open his missive with a fervour which was born of frustration rather than anticipation.

The message which was scrawled on the single sheet of paper within seemed to have been written hastily, though it was the work of a well-schooled hand.

It said: *My intervention has only served to make you more interesting to your enemies. If you wish to know more, and are capable of believing what you hear, come to the Surrey side of the Vauxhall Bridge at eight. Avoid those who will follow you, or you will increase the peril in which we find ourselves.*

It was signed: *Pelorus.*

Lydyard held out the note to Tallentyre, who put down a letter of his own in order to scan it. When the baronet had read the script, he said: 'We cannot know that this is his hand. It may be a trap.' By the time he had said it, though, Lydyard had decided upon his answer.

'I know that,' he said. 'But I will go armed, and will not risk myself until I have seen his face.'

'I will go with you, of course,' said Tallentyre, softly. 'In this matter, as in any other, you will have all the help from me that you need.' It was, of course, no more than Lydyard had expected, and he was very grateful to see how quickly the baronet had put aside the annoyance and anxiety which had followed the revelation that his privacy had been unwittingly invaded.

'Thank you,' he said. 'But the wolfman trusts me, a little, and he is concerned for me. He may speak more freely if I go alone, and I will listen with a readier ear. Only say that you will be ready to hear me when I return – and that you will not insist that I must be mad, if I tell you things which are strange and dreadful.'

'I will be ready,' promised Tallentyre. 'This is my affair as much as it is yours, and I am determined to know the truth, even if it should transpire that the world I have believed in is not the world that is. Wherever the truth lies, David, we will pursue it unrelentingly; you have my word on that. And whatever help you need from me is yours for the asking.'

'Thank you,' said Lydyard, again. 'With you to help me, I am infinitely stronger than I was when I felt myself to be alone, and I know that if the truth is to be found by my magical sight, I could not have a better friend to guide my eye.'

'Let us only hope,' said the baronet, 'that the riddle of the new Sphinx is not too deep for us to fathom.'

10

The room to which Pelorus led Lydyard was at the rear of a tall tenement more than a mile away from the bridge where they had met. It had not occurred to Lydyard to ask himself where a werewolf might live, or how sumptuously, but having seen Mandorla and the carriage in which she rode he had made the tacit assumption that the werewolves of London were not without means. Apparently, Pelorus was the exception; Lydyard had never been in a place as poor and shabby as this one, and he realized as he entered it that it was, in a way, hardly less alien to his personal experience than a world where werewolves co-existed with the Beast of Revelation.

He took leave to wonder, as he surrendered his coat and hat, how the werewolf earned the money to maintain himself, even in a place like this. Pelorus spoke and conducted himself in the manner of an educated man – and his brother could assume the appearance of a clerk as easily as that of a coachman – but Lydyard could not imagine him in steady employment.

'Were you followed?' asked Pelorus, as he ushered his guest to a seat by the fireside. The night was not as cold as the previous one had been, but the room was still in need of warming.

'Only as far as I consented to be,' Lydyard assured him. 'London crowds and London traffic are becoming the substance of nightmare, but they are invaluable to a man who wishes to evade unwelcome pursuers.'

'I have sometimes found them so myself,' admitted the other. 'Will you have a cup of tea to warm you?'

'Certainly,' said Lydyard, who no longer found anything particularly bizarre in the notion of taking tea with a werewolf.

When Pelorus had set a kettle by the fire to boil, he said: 'I was surprised to receive your note, when you have twice refused better opportunities to tell me what you now wish me to know. Why did you change your mind?'

'Because I have seen Jacob Harkender – and I saw in him that which I had feared to see. Something is using him.' Pelorus paused, then, to look long and hard at his visitor, and then he said: 'Do you know what I am?'

'Certainly,' said Lydyard, though he had to swallow to overcome a slight lump in his throat. 'You are one of the werewolves of London.'

Pelorus nodded slowly, lowering as he did so the gaze of his startling eyes.

'But I am not sure exactly what that implies,' Lydyard added. 'How are you descended from those of which legend speaks? Are you victims of the moon, as some say, or do you control your transformations? How do you find your prey in a great city like this?'

'My family is but distantly related to the other manwolves of legend,' Pelorus replied. 'I have not seen one of the other kind for many years, and never in England. My own family has lived ten thousand years, and we cannot be killed; no matter what is done to us in terms of violence, we survive to live again – though the harsher accidents of fate may let us sleep for a thousand years, and sometimes we are grateful for it. We are not victims of the moon, and yet we are not entirely creatures of our own will – not even Mandorla. We have a need to be human which we cannot deny, and the freedom of being a wolf is granted to us very meanly. We prey, as wolves do, on rats and mice and anything we find it easy to kill, and though Mandorla has taken care to cultivate a taste for human flesh, it is not for reasons of hunger that she has done it, but for reasons of hatred. Her feasts of that kind are more ritual than reward. I am forbidden such meat by the will of Machalalel, so you have not placed yourself in danger by coming here.'

Pelorus paused, apparently hesitating over something else

he might have added, but in the end he decided not to say it. His blue eyes seemed to be measuring Lydyard's reaction, but for the moment, Lydyard had none to show. Instead, Lydyard said: 'What is it that is using Harkender?'

'Something not unlike the being which is using you,' the werewolf replied, bluntly. 'God or demon, angel or monster – who can tell what time has made of it? I may have known it when the world was young, but what it made of itself when it ceased to play the Creator, I do not know; and how the tides of change have used it I cannot tell. I am sure that it cannot properly know itself, for all its wisdom and faith were frozen with its power, and if I who have been awake through the greater part of these ten thousand years have found this new world far too strange for my liking, how much stranger must they find it who have but recently awakened?'

'But they have their own means of discovery,' said Lydyard, quietly. 'What Harkender knows his master must know – and if Harkender's picture of the world is utterly false, as Sir Edward would insist, can it not elect to see through a thousand other pairs of eyes? Surely nothing can be hidden from a being like that!'

'Sight and understanding are not the same,' said Pelorus, gravely, 'as I think you may have come to understand. The power of Creation is not without its penalties, for our mind's eye changes what it sees, and the hungrier we are for enlightenment, the more easily we fall victim to the seductions of confabulation.'

'But once, at least,' Lydyard murmured, 'I have seen that which I could not doubt – and it was something that I could not have invented, and certainly would not have chosen to see.'

Pelorus turned away, because the kettle had begun to boil. He paused to spoon tea into a pot, and then to add the boiling water, carefully swirling the mixture around.

'You are no Creator,' he said, eventually, 'and you may see more clearly than some by virtue of your ice-cold soul. And yet, you claim that only once have you seen the evident truth.

The gods need oracles more than men do, David, for the gods often see far too much, and not always enough.'

Pelorus poured the tea into cups and passed one to his visitor before settling back in his chair. He deliberately looked away from Lydyard, at the flames which danced and flickered in the grate. 'What are your plans?' he asked, in a deliberately casual fashion.

'We had intended to go to Charnley Hall tomorrow,' Lydyard told him. 'Sir Edward is anxious to meet Dr Austen, and to hear his account of the mysterious patient he once entertained there, who claimed to have written *The True History of the World*. Franklin says that you knew the man.'

'He has long been my only friend,' Pelorus answered. 'The world is lonely without him, but though he left it by choice, I do not think he will be away for long. Now there was one who came very close to understanding, and if there is anyone who can unravel the mysteries of time and space, it is he. When he has slept for a while, to salve his disappointment, he will return. I wish he were here now, for he would know far better than I what might and ought to be done. Perhaps I should go with you to Charnley, and try to rouse him from his temporary grave.'

Lydyard could only shake his head in bewilderment. 'I cannot follow this,' he said. 'Did you ask me here to confuse me with riddles?'

Pelorus shook his own head, by way of denial. 'On the contrary,' he replied. 'I brought you here so that I might do what I can to explain what it is that has made a prisoner of your soul. But there is much that I do not know myself – and it may be that you cannot begin to believe it.'

'I have suffered so much madness,' said Lydyard, 'that I will try to believe anything, if only it will help me. Once, I could never have believed in a werewolf, but now I do not find it difficult at all.'

'Have you read the Clay Man's *True History*?'

'Alas, no,' said Lydyard. 'We cannot find a copy to buy, and the one which the British Museum had to lend was stolen. The last person to see it was Jacob Harkender. Austen will doubtless tell us what he remembers of it, but he only read one volume of the four, and for the rest he must rely on his memory of what his patient said to him. Do you tell me, then, that this fantastic history is really true?'

'In so far as the truth can be captured by remembrance,' said the werewolf, with a certain meticulous emphasis, 'what the Clay Man wrote is true. Our memories are not invulnerable to the tides of change, but I think they are more to be trusted than the language of rocks and artefacts. The Clay Man's story is the *truest* history which can be written. There is more in the book than I can tell you now, but I must say as much as time permits, for you could not otherwise begin to understand what you are, and what may yet become of you.'

Lydyard sipped tea from his cup, and found it much more bitter than he was used to. He shifted in his chair, too well aware of the stiffness of his limbs and the pain of his bruises. The drabness of the room seemed oppressive, and the light given by the yellow oil-lamp was dim and unsteady.

As soon as Pelorus began to speak, however, Lydyard somehow slipped away from the moment which surrounded him, as though it had become too much to bear – or as though the dark angel of pain, from somewhere in the unimaginable reaches of the void, had reached out to take advantage of his weakness and his folly. It seemed to him, absurdly, that he did not hear what Pelorus said to him while it was actually being said, but afterwards, he remembered it in a curiously vivid way, as though he shared the knowledge of it which Pelorus had in the most intimate possible way.

There had been a time before men, which may have been a uniquely happy time, when joy was unalloyed and unconfined. In that time, human form was but a whim – one of many appearances to be worn for an hour or a year, but always something which could be put away.

It was, as the Clay Man called it in his book, a Golden Age. None who had any knowledge or memory of that innocent time could avoid regret for its passing, though that regret might have been foolish. Only the Creators – the demiurges and the fallen angels – could really remember the Golden Age, and when they acquired the gift of memory its purity was already tarnished.

The true Golden Age must have been an age without individuals, in which it would have made no sense to talk of greater and lesser beings possessed of different kinds of power, but in time – certainly in the aftermath of man's emergence – that was the way in which creativity came to be weighed and calculated. From the freedom of flux emerged persons in conflict, and their notions of self were carefully described and refined and bounded.

By the time men appeared, each being which existed knew how it was bounded, knew whether it stood among the most or least powerful, and had begun to harbour ambitions and anxieties appropriate to its station. Those which were the greatest knew that they were gods, those which were the least knew that they were merely Others – *not-men* – and there were many creatures in between.

When true men first appeared, they seemed to the legions of Others which inhabited the earth to be a silly jest of some cruel Creator. Creatures bound by constancy were new and strange, and stranger still was the fact of their dull mortality. These new creatures came, and were, and went, and all the creativity which they had was in their loins. It was not true creativity at all, but merely the ability to reproduce; to copy, to multiply.

In the true Golden Age, Creators merged and divided, and did not know or care whether they were many or one – but in the aftermath of man's emergence, they had perforce to speak of division and descent, of Ones becoming Many. In that time some began to think of increasing their new-found selves by absorbing others, and gods which thought themselves not great enough became ambitious to grow. So difference grew into conflict, and the joy of the Golden Age gave way in part to fear.

When the beings of the Golden Age began to think in terms of children they did not at first condescend to copy men; their offspring were subject to their own whims and their own powers of transformation. Even had their forms been fixed, they would not have chosen to make their children like themselves, for they were Creators, whose souls were burning with the fire of shaping power, and they would always have wanted something better, something newer, something brighter, something to show what power of imagination they had.

Those who lived in the Golden Age had a kind of mortality too, but the idea of death made no sense to them. The power by which they changed themselves was gradually used up, so that they spent their substance and their energy and ultimately became nothing at all, but they did not at first consider this an end or loss of self, but merely as a merging with the world – neither ashes to ashes nor dust to dust, but life to life and change to change. Their hot souls consumed themselves in the blaze of their creativity, but they did not think of their destiny as oblivion, because they could not think of themselves as any one thing of fixed duration. In the beginning they could not have had the idea of identity, but must have thought themselves mere aspects of the world's hectic business of incarnation and reincarnation, nor could they have had the idea of history. They must have lived each moment as it came, and their memories were fragile, fickle things very clever in the art of forgetting.

But it all changed.

Paradoxical as it may seem, no being of the true Golden Age could have known or understood that the world was changing. When all is flux and all is freedom, and anything may be transformed by effort into anything else, the notion of an evolution – of a fundamental movement in the way things are and can be – can make no sense. And yet, the world was changing. All the flux and freedom was framed by the state of being which consented to it; the Creators had themselves been created, and their creativity given to them.

There had been a beginning, an ultimate Act of Creation; the gods had been made by a further God, who was outside Creation, outside its restless soulfire, its exuberant rejoicing in the fact of being.

When time had come into being, so had change; the world would not always be the same, but had had some pattern of development built in at the very instant of its first imagination.

When this phenomenon of fundamental change was first discovered, it was thought to be a flaw in Creation. Some argued that it must be a necessary flaw, and that any Creation must be in some way limited, vulnerable to decay and exhaustion; others argued that it was a whim or fault of the Creator, an error or a failing. But whatever might be guessed or supposed, the fact remained. The Golden Age could not be for ever; creative power could not be infinitely renewed; there was change, and one aspect of that change was the gradual erosion of creative power.

Because of this, some came to see the emergence of men not as a jest at all, but as a prophecy. Some saw in men the shape of a new way of being to come – a cold-souled way of being which, because it was not wasteful of creative power, might endure when other ways of being became impossible. Some speculated, even in the very early days of man's appearance, that there might come a time when everything which lived would have a fixity of form, and the power to reproduce itself endlessly. Some guessed that whichever Creator had made man – from the substance of his own being, it was presumed – had found a transformation which would permit its endurance long after all the other Creators had wasted themselves and become nothing at all. In discovering constancy, some argued, this Creator had defeated the logic of flux; in discovering death and birth, this Creator had defeated the logic of dissipation and decay. But no one knew which Creator had made man, or how, or why.

There was a danger in all this supposing, which was that whatever came to be believed might become true because it was believed. Some said that the pattern of change which underlay Creation was not fixed at all; a few claimed that it was an illusion of fear and faith. These cried out to one and all that the tarnishing of the Golden Age was a failure of the Creators, and that the future which seemed to be written in the image of man would be the actual future only if the Creators were weak and foolish enough to believe it.

But the world changed.

The race of cold-souled men thrived, and multiplied; and the world changed around them, to be remade in the image of their way of being.

By far the greater number of the Others, who had worn human form upon a whim, or had combined its aspects in chimerical fashion, surrendered to the pressure of inevitability, or what they thought was inevitability. Some took care to save themselves from mortality, and some retained a little of their power over shape and form, but almost all of the lesser beings of the Golden Age ultimately consented to be human, or something very like it, when the end of the Golden Age came.

In the true Golden Age there were no puzzles and mysteries, no questions to be asked and thus no answers to be found, but when the Golden Age began to pass away, the world became full of enigmas and secrets and dilemmas. Why was there change? What opportunities did it offer and what dangers did it pose? Was the failure of the greater Creators to take charge of destiny a necessity or a weakness? Should a Creator use what power it had for the sake of the sheer joy of its use, or should it instead begin to hoard that power.

Those Others which regarded the human state of being as crippled and horrible became bitterly fearful that the world would be slowly and inexorably altered until it would be filled with human beings, mechanically reproducing their lowly kind while their own more perfect and more precious kinds would slowly disappear.

These individual Creators – some of them great and others

small – became inquisitive. They sought knowledge by their own means: by intuition and revelation, by the sight of the inner eye. But what was seen still required to be interpreted, to be understood, and to be made coherent, and the work of the inner eye was no less subject to the distortions of false belief than the work of the outer eye.

In order to see clearly, and to see further, the inner eye required a discipline of its own, and that discipline was very painful. It was through suffering and self-denial that the wizards and sages of that world achieved their enlightenment. Pain was found to be the means by which the sight of the inner eye could be purified and increased in power.

For the Others, as for men, pain was commonly unpleasant, and in its extremes was agonizing – and yet its unpleasantness was counterbalanced by a strange kind of intoxication, which was the pure thrill of enlightenment. The unhuman beings of that early world were not at all like men in their vulnerability to injury and disease. Ease of healing was the first corollary of the ability to change shape – or *vice versa*. A being hacked into two or a dozen pieces might regrow from any one of them, reconstituting itself without overmuch difficulty; or might, instead, grow into as many new and different beings as there were pieces. Such beings had no need of pain as a warning, to serve as an indicator of danger or damage, and therefore their pain was free to be a very different thing, with a very different purpose.

But when human beings came into the world their nature forced the phenomenon of pain into a very different adaptation, which robbed it of its rewarding aspects, and made it into a thing to be conscientiously avoided: a spur to guide the new emotion of cowardice.

Cowardice was unknown to those who were other than men – but it was not until men were also in the world that they could claim its absence as a badge of merit; this is why, in the story which is told in the *True History of the World*, the Golden Age was followed by an Age of Heroes. Until there was cowardice, there could be no heroes; until the pain which was sight was transmuted into the pain which was only pain, there were neither noble sufferers nor cruel torturers.

From the viewpoint of human beings the tarnished Golden Age might have seemed a very evil – which is to say painful – time, but it could not have seemed so to the Others, who had a very different experience of pain, and hence a very different idea of evil. But the Age of Heroes was an evil time for all, human and unhuman alike.

There were a few beings in the world even before the coming of man who sought knowledge not by inflicting pain and deprivation upon themselves but by visiting these things upon others, imprisoning oracles from whose testimonies they sought avidly to glean new understanding; but this was not seen by those involved as cowardice or cruelty, until cowardice and cruelty came into being. It was not seen in those terms until humans, observing that other ways of enlightenment were virtually closed to them, began to mimic the practices of these Others.

In later times, a small number of human beings contrived to open their inner eyes, and found a difficult and treacherous path to enlightenment, which might be followed for a little way with the aid of discipline and self-denial, but for the great majority the effort expended was entirely incommensurate with the reward obtained. Very few achieved true vision, and even those who did were inclined to elaborate a vast amount of confabulation about a very meagre seed of true sight; illusion and false belief remained paramount. Human beings, alas, were so constituted that they had far better access to the rewards of intuitive knowledge by tormenting Others and forcing them to speak than they had by their own efforts.

For this reason, the least of the Others became the enemies of the men and other creatures with whom they shared the world. They began to shun them, perhaps not so much because they feared to suffer, but because they hated what human beings became when they turned their hands to such work. As for their greater kin, who had no need to fear the strength of human hands and tools, they too began to hide. They became miserly with the use of their power, or became predatory, so that the lesser Others, if they desired to be selves and individuals, had to hide from them as carefully as they hid from men.

And in time, the world became quiet and cold of soul. The fugitive Others were gradually lost, and the Creators themselves, who thought themselves gods, and yet had found greed and fear and uncertainty and confusion, hid themselves away to wait, and wait . . . to wait for what, no one knew, least of all themselves. . . .

And the world changed, and changed, and changed.

Whether there might be one predestined end to change, or many possible ends, no one knew; and what the end might be, if end there was to be, no one knew; and what those Creators became who hid in the substance of the earth, or what they might do, or what they might hope to become, no one knew.

But some there were who yearned for an end, or a transformation. Some there were who yearned for one more Act of Creation which would set the world to rights again. Some there were, and some there are, but they cannot know what Acts are still possible, nor do they yet know in their inmost hearts what ends are truly to be desired.

And in their confusion, in their ignorance, and in their fear, they are dangerous – to men, and perhaps to the world itself.

11

When Pelorus stopped speaking the cataract of thoughts and images which had flooded Lydyard's mind dwindled away, until there was nothing left but a few fugitive echoes.

Only then could Lydyard see again – only then did he become conscious of those gleaming eyes, as blue as the Egyptian sky.

He knew that he had not merely *listened*; he had linked his consciousness with the werewolf's, not quite in the same way that his dreaming mind had inserted itself into Elinor Fisher's thoughts, but in a fashion not dissimilar.

'Do you tell me that all this is literally true?' he asked, weakly. 'This is what you remember, of your own origins and the early history of the world?'

'That is what I *know*,' Pelorus answered. 'And though the greater part of what I have described happened before I came into the world, I have shown you how it is in my mind, whence it came by the same means that I have given it to you. If you are determined to tell me that it is a fairy tale, or a tissue of delusions – which is what James Austen told the Clay Man – I will not be able to deny it with any certainty, for there is much of the dream about it, and I know as well as anyone how fallible memory is. Perhaps it is not true at all, or holds the truth in some encoded form – but it is what I know, and what the Clay Man knows, and we have seen enough of the world to be certain that the history recorded in its rocks and relics is mere semblance. It is the truest history which remains to be told, truer by far than the one which you own.'

'What is it that you seek to teach me?' asked Lydyard. 'Why do you take the trouble to show this to me?'

'The day of the great Creators is long gone,' said Pelorus, quietly. 'The majority exhausted themselves by profligate use of their power; all that remains of them has been accommodated to the human kind of mechanical reproduction, whereby plants and animals make copies of themselves over and over again. A few sought immunity from that kind of dissipation, hoarding their power and hiding themselves away, seeking to preserve their potential by inactivity.

'Some became predators, consuming the creative power of others by absorption; all became mistrustful of other beings, and more mistrustful still of others like themselves. These are the angels fallen to earth – fallen *into* the earth and become part of its substance – which are remembered in the myths of your own people and others. When they might return, or in what form, or with what purpose, no one has ever truly known, though some have entertained hopes and fears. Mandorla and the followers of St Amycus have both hoped, in their very different ways, that their return is inevitable and must be followed by a wholesale transfiguration of the world of appearances. The Clay Man and I, on the other hand, have hoped that they would never become active again, or that if they did, they would be impotent to bring about real change.

'I have not abandoned that hope, but I am afraid that I may be wrong. I had hoped that this new awakening was merely for the purpose of enquiry and exploration, in tune with the spirit of the age – but now that I have seen Harkender, I believe that his master has some darker purpose. That master may have helped Harkender to create Gabriel Gill merely in order to steal the power which is incarnate in the boy, but I fear that it may be spinning a more complicated web. The child may only be the bait in a trap, into which the second creature – and perhaps the Creator which made it – are to be drawn. If that is so, then you too are in great danger.'

'Do you warn me for my own sake, or are you speaking through me, to whatever it is that has opened its eager eye within me?'

'Both,' said Pelorus, frankly. 'But my primary concern is with you and your kind – for there may be as much reason to fear your master as there is to fear Harkender's. I cannot tell.'

'It seems to me that you cannot even tell whether what you believe is true,' said Lydyard. 'You share your memories with the Clay Man, and presumably with the others of your kind, but it may simply be that you are all sharers in the same mad dream.'

'Memory is fallible,' admitted Pelorus, 'and even cold print is merely one more set of appearances, as subject to the tide of change as any other. The Clay Man, when he wakes from that sleep which simulates death, may have forgotten that he ever posed as Lucian de Terre or Adam Clay, and his book may have disappeared from the face of the earth. He and I might then remember an altogether different history, and be quite convinced that it was the only history we had ever known or lived. I cannot deny it, knowing as I do how uncertain the world of appearances is.'

'It must be uncomfortable to live with such uncertainty,' said Lydyard, in a neutral tone.

'Knowledge and sight are uncomfortable as well as uncertain,' Pelorus agreed. 'By now, you must know that very well.'

'I am uncomfortable in my dreams and nightmares,' admitted Lydyard, 'but I have not yet surrendered hope that I may separate truth from delusion. And I find the utmost difficulty in believing that all appearances – from the magnitude and physical laws of the universe to the words upon a printed page – are subject to change by arbitrary acts of creation. Is there not a paradox in what you say? Your claim to know that the history in which we believe is false is based in your having a different memory of it, and yet you admit that your memory is equally likely to be false.'

'I am sure that Sir Edward Tallentyre would argue it thus,' answered the werewolf, unrepentantly. 'And I have no defence that would satisfy him. But he is not the one who has been cursed with the inner sight and the power of dreams. You are the one who must decide what you are, and what might become of you. I have tried to give you what warning I can – I think you understand what I mean.'

Lydyard took up his cup, unsteadily, and tried to take one last sip from the dregs, but the liquid which remained was quite cold.

'I am an oracle,' he said, offhandedly. 'There are those who will try to hurt me, in order to stimulate my powers of sight. Mandorla and Harkender – and whatever entity it is that has given me this power in the first place. But what is it that they want me to find out for them?'

Pelorus shrugged. 'Mandorla will be eager to know about the second creature, whose eyes you are. Beyond that – she has Gabriel to help her in her grander plans, if she can only keep him, but that is not to say that she might not also find a use for you. Harkender's master, too, must desire to find out more about its adversary. As for the one which made you what you are, first it needs your thoughts, your sight, your understanding of this world – but when it has wrung you dry of those, who can tell what you might be made to see, if only . . .'

'If only I were hurt enough?'

'If only your sight could be exploited to the full. You are yourself a novelty of sorts, an intriguing experiment, though I am sure that your maker did not think of it in that fashion. Jacob Harkender set out to follow the way of pain long before his inner eye began to see, and though his powers of sight have lately been augmented, he is largely the instrument of his own shaping. Your sight was more rudely thrust upon you, and you are possessed of a kind of scepticism which none who have come by the sight by nature or by effort have ever had before. I cannot tell whether this will make your sight truer than another's, but it would be interesting to know what you could see, if . . .'

'If,' repeated Lydyard, sourly. 'Am I then in danger from you, also? Or do you merely suggest that I might care to hurt myself, in order to fuel the fires of my heated soul?'

Pelorus shook his head. 'I cannot hurt you,' he said. 'You are as safe from me as from the good priests of St Amycus, who only offer invitations to their would-be visionaries. Nor can I advise you to commit yourself to the way of pain, for I have known too many who followed it – some of them voluntarily – and I am unconvinced that the ecstasy which some claimed to have discovered on the far side of pain is worth the price which they paid to attain it. They are the pure in heart which see their gods, but the Clay Man always believed that in such a moment of climax, hope might so far triumph over reason that the gods which they see are merely their own selves writ large upon the sky.'

'You do not have to give me that advice,' said Lydyard, in a low voice. 'I am not such a fool as to nurture these nightmares by hurting myself, nor am I such a fool as to believe all that I see when I am hurt and fevered. If it is not all madness and illusion, still there is too much madness and illusion in it. No matter what power of sight this inner eye has, still I prefer the conclusions of science and reason – and I think the world would be a better place if all men had my preference.'

'I wish that the Clay Man could have heard you say it,' said Pelorus. 'For that was his own plea, and his own hope for the salvation of the world. His own Golden Age – the only Heavenly Kingdom which he could bring himself to desire – was to be built by the toil and intelligence of cold-souled men, when the day came that the fallen angels would be laid to their eternal rest. His faith was invested in evolution, not in Acts of Creation.'

'A thousand pities, then, that he never knew Sir Edward. A thousand more that the snake which bit me did not choose a better target – for it would have been a better experiment by far to burden his scepticism with this curse of sight.'

Pelorus made no answer to that, but made an odd gesture, as though he were trying to draw his clothes more warmly about him, to ward off the chill of the night. Perhaps, thought Lydyard, the hairless flesh of a human did not suit him well enough in this dank and dreary isle.

'What do you want from me?' asked Lydyard, suddenly. 'I thank you for your warnings, of course, but I suspect that there is something which you want in return.'

'I ask only this – that if your sight should give you any of the answers that I lack, you will call on me. You have the means, now.'

Lydyard did not have to ask him what he meant. Lydyard had shared his consciousness, his dream-laden memories. There was a link between them.

'And what would you do,' asked Lydyard, 'if either of these Beasts of the Apocalypse were to turn its hand to destruction?

What could you do? I have not forgotten what the sphinx did to you in Egypt.'

'Machalalel is dead,' replied Pelorus, 'but his death may only be the kind of sleep which has the Clay Man in its grip. If so – well, I alone am the bearer of his will, and I alone might be able to raise him from his rest. He was by no means the greatest of the great, but even such as these would have something to fear were he to wake. That is one of the reasons why Mandorla is so anxious to remove me.'

Lydyard shook his head tiredly. 'Too much,' he said. 'It is too much.'

'I ask nothing,' said Pelorus, softly, 'not even your trust. I only say that if and when you cannot help but see, I will be listening. And if you stand in need of my help, I promise that you shall have it. You are not alone, and though I may be a feeble ally, still I would be your friend.'

Not alone, Lydyard repeated to himself. *Not alone.*

'Can you not lend power to your own sight?' he asked, curiously. 'Can you not feed your own dreams with that educative pain, which would tell you what you need to know about these phantoms of the past?'

'I can feed as a wolf or as a man,' said Pelorus, regretfully, 'and I can drink as a wolf or as a man – but I can dream only as a wolf, for in my human guise, my soul is as cold as Sir Edward Tallentyre's. When I am a man, I am nearly incapable of wolfish joy, but when I am a wolf, I am nearly incapable of human thought, and must follow my will in animal fashion. Even Mandorla, who is capable of making love as a woman, cannot dream as a woman. Her powers of magic are paltry, no matter how she may pretend to the contrary. That is why she needs Gabriel Gill; and that is why she will surely try again to capture you.'

'To use me as an oracle by hurting me. But Gabriel Gill, if what is said of him is to be believed, is hardly human at all, and must be an oracle more powerful by far than I am.'

'He is,' said Pelorus, dolorously. 'But Mandorla is too wise to risk inflicting hurt on one who has power as well as sight.

She will try to seduce him into use of both, but that might not be easy. We may have cause to be grateful that he is incarnate as a little child, and not a full-grown man, for Mandorla can be difficult to resist. She is very dangerous, for even if she cannot guide Gabriel's creative hand, still she may try her utmost to procure a violent conflict between Harkender's master and the Beast made in Egypt, without any fear for herself – she is immortal, after all, and cannot be destroyed no matter how she plays with fire.'

'And yet,' said Lydyard, provocatively, 'if I were unfortunate enough to fall into her hands, and forced to see whatever there is to be seen, you would doubtless be glad enough to know what I discover.'

'I do not want that,' Pelorus assured him. 'I would far rather see her forced out of it, and I pray that you will use that gun you carry, if the chance arises.'

'Perhaps I should be glad of that,' said Lydyard. 'At least, if you desire me to be hurt, you would rather that I hurt myself.'

'You mistake me,' answered the werewolf, patiently. 'I will sincerely regret any suffering which comes to you. I would redeem you if I could from that unkind fate which has overtaken you, and heal your burning soul. But I cannot do it – all that I can do instead is to tell you what I know, in the hope that it may help you to understand, and hence to manage, your affliction. Believe me, David, although I am a wolf as well as a man, I am your friend.'

Lydyard remembered the first and most frequent of his recurring visions: the sad and suffering Satan, roasting in the fires of Hell, who reached out his hand in the hope of redeeming the world from its plague of troubles, only to see the earth move obstinately away from the touch of his healing hand. He had thought to see himself in the plight of that helpless angel, but now he realized that there was another whose fate might as easily be measured therein . . .

There was no way to know whether it was irony or prophecy, but he remembered the other vision which had followed the first, to which his fervent prayer had seemed to bring him: the vision of God as the boundary of the universe, utterly impotent to intervene in it.

'I think I see now,' he said, 'why you told me that you might be a better friend to me by far, if only you could leave me alone.'

'And you will also see,' said Pelorus, 'why I am so often drawn to use that word *alas*.'

Later, Pelorus walked with Lydyard to Vauxhall Bridge, where they had met earlier in the evening. It was past midnight now, but the city had not fallen silent, and the river was still alive with the myriad barges which moved between its countless wharfs.

'Will you be able to find a cab?' asked Pelorus.

'I doubt it,' said Lydyard, drily, 'but I need not fear to be robbed while I walk. I have a gun in my pocket as you have one in yours, which will serve to hurt men as well as werewolves. The fog might choke me, but if I take a chill and fall into a fever, I will go with as brave a heart as I can into the wilderness of my delirium.'

Pelorus turned away, uneasily, to look out over the water, in the direction of Lambeth Bridge and Westminster.

'Do you really think,' asked Lydyard, 'that there is any hope for me? If what you have told me is true, what chance have I of escaping this affair alive?'

'Never despair,' said Pelorus, looking down at the turbid waters of the Thames. 'Whatever it is that possesses you will not easily let you die. I cannot promise you that it will not hurt you, or let you be hurt, but while it needs you it will sustain you; and if the time should come when it no longer needs you, it may simply let you go. And if you should discover for it what it needs to know, if you can see that which it truly needs to see, in order to know what it is, and what it might be, and what it should make of itself . . . it may be capable of gratitude.'

'I should think of it as a trial, then – a test of fire.' Lydyard paused, then said abruptly, 'Why is the Clay Man so called?'

'Because he was fashioned out of clay, as my family was fashioned from a pack of wolves. We were, I suppose, the world's first experiments, and like most experiments, we failed. With luck, you may do better. Believe it, David, I beg you. *You may succeed*. I dare not promise you that you will not be hurt, but you must not think that because you are a man and not a god you have no power to influence this matter. Courage and intelligence are not to be despised.'

'I do not despise them, I assure you,' Lydyard replied. 'I only doubt that I have them in adequate measure.'

Pelorus did not reply, but looked up from the dark water to the lights along the river's shore. 'Once,' he said, 'I saw this city burn. I saw it consumed by angry fire. It was the last time I saw Mandorla happy, the last time I saw her ecstatic with honest affection. I cannot help but love her, you know, for she is the centre of my wolfish world, the commander of that infinite animal joy which my soul craves.

'But Mandorla's happiness soon turned to disappointment when she saw that the world was unaltered. The city of wood was rebuilt as a city of stone – a colder and more powerful testament to the soul and toil of humankind. London will never burn again, David, and I pray that it will never crumble into dust and desert like Heliopolis and Memphis, Carthage and Troy.'

'It is more likely to drown in its own stinking wastes,' said Lydyard, in reply. 'There is too much poison in its water and its air, and too many of those who crowd its streets are little more than human waste themselves. We have far to go before we can make a heaven on earth, and there are those who think that cities are running sores on the face of civilization. There was a plague, I believe, before the Great Fire – did you see the people dying in the streets before the flames came to cleanse and cauterize?'

'I have seen worse,' said Pelorus. 'I was in England when the Black Death came. But disease can be conquered, and madness too – and they will be, if men like Gilbert Franklin and James Austen are allowed to have their way.'

303

Lydyard set off across the bridge. He did not say goodbye to the man who stood and watched him go, nor did he thank him for such meagre hospitality as circumstance had allowed him to provide.

12

By the time Lydyard arrived back at Sturton Street the fog had thickened, softening the glare of the gaslights into a diffuse, almost magical glow. As he approached the house he looked sharply at the railings across the street, which were at the very limit of visibility, but there was no sign of any watcher keeping vigil.

Knowing that Lydyard was out, Summers had left the front door unbolted; he let himself in with his key and bolted it behind him. The butler had also taken care to leave a nightlight burning in the hall, which he took upstairs with him when he had divested himself of coat, scarf, and hat. He moved as quietly as he could; clearly, Sir Edward had not troubled to wait for him.

He paused once in his ascent, when a small noise startled him – but the old house was forever creaking and groaning when the temperature dropped at night, and he went on immediately, cursing himself for his nervousness.

The corridor in which his room was situated had six doors, but one was a bathroom and one a water closet. Cordelia had the large room at the end, and the dressing-room next to it, while the room facing his own was used as a guest-room.

The door of the unoccupied room opposite his own stood ajar, and he frowned at the error of omission before closing it himself. Then he went into his own room and sat down on the bed. He felt exhausted after his long walk, but he was not particularly sleepy. He felt as though his heavy limbs were as yet unequal to the task of taking all his clothes off, but he removed his jacket and threw it on a chair once he had taken his gun from the pocket and placed it carefully on the bedside table. Then he took off his boots, and pulled the socks from his aching feet; but after that he simply extended himself upon the bed.

Despite that his exhaustion seemed absolute he was very restless in his thoughts. He lay back on his pillow and listened patiently to the small sounds of the night. His thoughts, which were for once untainted by visionary unease, were all of Pelorus and the werewolves of London. The manwolf was so strangely melancholy, and yet it seemed to Lydyard that it would be an incomparably marvellous thing to know that one could not die, and might live to see the end of the world no matter how and when it came.

Sleep would not come – but to his chagrin, a kind of vision did. Gradually, his mind was invaded, as the thoughts of another began to be confused and entangled with his own. He felt his own heartbeat quicken in response to an anxiety which was not entirely his.

There is no pain! he protested. But it was not quite true, for the dull ache left by his bruises was still there, and seemed suddenly to intensify as the vision began, though whether his sensitivity was cause or effect he was too confused to know.

Once again, he was prisoned in another person's skull, seeing as the other saw, feeling as he felt. But this was no discontented mistress full of ambivalent warmth; this was a man almost rigid with tension, despite that his body was by no means built for rigidity. This was a man ardent with determination, literally gritting his teeth against the unkind attentions of creeping fear. This was a man whose thoughts were full of names, cascading with the consciousness of others near to him and under his direction.

His own name was there, hard held in his mind almost as though he feared to forget it.

He was Caleb Amalax.

Amalax had no such sharp awareness of where he was –

not, at least, in any fashion which gave it a name. Lydyard could not tell, for several chaotic seconds, whether the other was close at hand or half a world away. Without making any connection in his mind he observed as Amalax signalled to one he knew as Calan and another he knew as Jack to go to a certain door in a certain candlelit carpeted corridor – which they did, and on testing it, found that they could open it.

He knew that door – knew the feel of it upon his own hand – and for a moment or two memory and observation overlapped and became confused.

Why?

He struggled to think, but the knowledge that his own hand – *David Lydyard's hand* – had touched that same door in that same candlelit corridor not half an hour ago was so peculiar that he could not make a sensible connection with what was happening now to some other very different man.

He watched the one called Calan turn from that door to another, and cross the carpet. But this was even stranger, for he had touched *that* door many times, and knew it more than well, and this seemed to add to the terrible tangle of sensations, making them into a tight and ugly knot which he did not like at all.

Lydyard seemed to hear the sound of the door opening not once but twice, and though one reaction was to freeze him for half a second as Amalax froze there was also a curious echo, by which he reacted in a startled and far more anxious fashion.

The door opened wider, and again there was an audible sound – a scratch and a scrape. Again, it seemed to Lydyard that he heard it twice, and had mixed reactions; he both heard and felt a response, as someone within the room moved. He heard that the movement was a rustling sound, made by the friction of clothes and quilt, but he also felt it as a pressure upon his skin.

Only then did he realize that Amalax and the others with him were very close at hand, and that the room whose door had just been opened was his own.

Lydyard was less conscious of his own actions than he was of Amalax's observation of them. More keenly than his own movements he sensed Amalax's judgement that an unknown person had moved upon the bed, and might rise at any moment. He knew what a dark shadow he must present to the other's night-adapted vision, for the candle was still shielded by the bulk of the door. More keenly than his own alarm he felt Amalax's urgency as the intruder drew back, then pointed – with the finger of a hand which held a long knife – to the far side of the doorway, instructing the man who had undone the catch to position himself there.

Lydyard did not stop himself from rising, although he was fully aware of Amalax taking up a position on the other side of the doorway, waiting for him.

The door stood ajar by no more than the merest crack, but Lydyard could see it and simultaneously understood that Amalax knew that it must be visible, however well-shadowed his candle was. When he picked up the revolver which he had placed beside his bed there was no quickening of Amalax's fear – how could there be? – and yet Amalax's anxiety ran high enough almost to drown out his own. His observation of himself seemed as passive and helpless as his observation of the other, and his consciousness of danger proved no check at all as he went to the door, took hold of the handle, and pulled it open.

Despite that he had the gun in his hand, and had intended to be ready, he was unprepared for the surge of panic which he felt at second-hand, and stupidly unready for the assault which came.

It was a reckless assault, but they did not know he had a gun. Amalax was at him in a trice, snaking one long arm around his neck and bringing up the blade which he held. Lydyard felt the fat man's urgency so strongly that it swamped his own belated feeling of foolish wrath. As both captor and captive, on the one hand wide awake and on the other half-fuddled by fatigue, he struggled convulsively against the strangling arm.

Amalax, he knew, could not see the gun in his hand, but

someone did. Calan or Jack or one of the others – there seemed
to be five in all – struck out at him with some kind of cudgel,
and the impact was sharp enough and forceful enough to
knock the heavy weapon from his grasp and send it tumbling
away into the shadows, clattering loudly as it went.

He heard the noise through Amalax's ears and Amalax's
brain, feeling in harmony with his assailant the awful thrill
of fear which it evoked.

He discovered, at second-hand triumphantly and at first-
hand despairingly, that the sheer bulk of Amalax's body made
him master of the situation; the brute was far too big a man
to be thrown back. Lydyard felt himself hauled – but also
hauled himself – out into the corridor, with the constricting
arm choking off any cry he might have tried to make, until
he could see what in some sense he already knew: how many
his opponents were, and how the candlelight gleamed upon
the blade which Amalax put up before his eyes.

'Be still!' Amalax hissed into his ear, the words echoing
eerily as it seemed that he both spoke and heard them. 'Be
quiet now, and no harm will follow – defy us, and I'll slit
your throat.'

But Lydyard could hear the thoughts behind the words as
well. There was a desperate, irrational prayer that quietness
now might somehow cancel out the clatter of the object –
Amalax still had not guessed that it had been a gun – which
had skidded almost to the corridor's end; alloyed with it was
a fervent hope that Lydyard would believe a threat which
really had no substance, for Amalax's task was to capture
Lydyard alive, and only mortal fear would make him carry
out his threat.

Lydyard's reflexive response was to tense himself, but he
knew as he did so that Amalax had anticipated him. When
he quickly relaxed, he did not know himself whether it was
a simple failure of the reflex, or whether what he knew
as Amalax was fusing at last with what he knew as his
own self.

Although he knew that Amalax did not want or intend to

kill him, Lydyard could not hold at bay the cold tide of his own fear, which mingled crudely with his perception of his captor's feelings, and made him so giddy he thought that he might faint.

'Good,' said Amalax, more to himself than to Lydyard. Lydyard saw in his captor's mind that the other was still hoping, against all probability, that the sound of Lydyard's fallen weapon would go unheard, but upon the foundation of that hope there was building the conviction that with Lydyard as his hostage he could in any case walk free.

Lydyard glanced at the door by which the revolver had come to rest, not knowing whether to hope that it might open, or to pray that it would stay closed. If only it had been Tallentyre's room, and not Cordelia's! If only Franklin had still been here, lodged in the room whose door the invaders had tried at first!

Another name floated in the turbulent sea of the collective consciousness which he shared with Amalax: *Mandorla*. It was a name which trailed clouds of anxiety for both of them. Amalax knew what Mandorla was, and though he thought himself his own man, Lydyard could see – perhaps better than the man himself – the true extent of his enslavement.

Jack and Calan, whose anxious faces were clearly visible by the light of the candle which Jack held aloft, seemed not to know which way to go. Panic had frozen them, too.

Calan's breath reeked most unpleasantly of meat and gin. Jack took a step sideways, towards the stairhead, but as he did so Calan, like some mad mirror image, took a step the other way, towards the corridor's blind end. Lydyard, afraid for Cordelia, moved as if to stop Calan – but as soon as he moved, Amalax's hand clamped tightly about him again. Lydyard felt his own alarm savagely undercut by his consciousness of a new determination forming in his captor's mind.

'Come with me now, and quietly,' Amalax hissed in Lydyard's ear, 'and no one will be hurt. Fight me, and I loose the wolf.'

Until Amalax said it, obviously expecting him to understand,

Lydyard had not quite realized who Calan was, but when Amalax called him wolf he was suddenly privy to all the connotations which that held for Amalax, the werewolves' pawn.

Amalax knew well enough what might be involved in 'loosing the wolf' and Lydyard could see with his own eyes as well as the other's how loose were the garments which Calan wore, how easily they might be shed.

There was a sound from within Cordelia's room – no tiny click or creak of the floorboards, but a duller and more substantial sound. The noise of the falling gun had awakened her, and though her bed was doubtless warm and the night very cold, still she had decided to get up, to see what it was that had fallen.

'Silence, or thou'rt a dead man,' whispered Amalax, with his lips very close to Lydyard's ear. The words echoed as they were formed and spoken, heard and understood.

Lydyard knew how sorely Amalax was tempted to prick him and make him bleed, to show how determined he was. If only the man could have guessed how abundantly clear his determination already was!

Lydyard tried to look into the eyes of his captor – which he had not yet seen – but was abruptly prevented by some fugitive impression of Amalax's which made him look the other way instead, where he caught double-visioned sight of Calan's gleaming eyes, feverish with intoxication and frustrated wrath.

Amalax wished that the werewolf would be still, but feared that he might not be. Amalax wished with all his heart that the door at the end of the corridor would not open, but feared that it might. Amalax wished as mightily as he could that he could get away from here, but dreaded that—

Amalax licked his lips, and Lydyard's head reeled with the tumultuous confusion of his anxieties. Lydyard could not believe that there were ever such vilely mixed motives in his own actions, and was astonished by the sheer rawness of Amalax's self-consciousness.

He had thought men more alike than this, all cold-souled replicas of one another. But they were not alike.

They were not!

The blade shifted against the side of Lydyard's windpipe, applying pressure – not enough to draw blood, but enough to signify that a flick of Amalax's wrist could do murder. Lydyard felt his own body become rigid with strain, and felt Amalax's fanciful supposition that he could feel a fear in his captive sufficient to grip him like an icy wind – but if there was any icy wind at all, it blew from Amalax's soul, not Lydyard's.

The handle of Cordelia's door began to turn.

In that instant, the double consciousness ended, and Lydyard abruptly found himself alone in his own skull, with his own fear – and, he discovered, his own reckless bravery. Having so recently shared Amalax's thoughts he was surprised to find how pure his wrath was against the vicious creature which held him.

Lydyard saw Calan's lips form a snarl, and saw that the werewolf's hands were at the knot which secured the cord at his waist. He was painfully aware of the danger which seemed to be welling up irresistibly from some deep, dark reservoir of evil circumstance. He was terrified that when Cordelia opened the door, Calan would attack, and though he was no longer present in Amalax's mind he could feel that his captor was anxious too.

'Jack!' said Amalax, as soon as they all were sure that the door was opening.

But Jack did not know what he was being asked to do. Cordelia was visible now, dimly silhouetted in the widening crack of the door by a tiny light in the room behind her, which must have been burning by her bedside. She peered out into the corridor, which must have seemed brightly lit to her, but then looked down at the object which had come to rest no more than half a dozen inches from her door.

Perhaps none of the three intruders, until that moment, had actually realized what the thing was which had been so unceremoniously struck out of their prisoner's grip. But they could see it clearly enough now.

Cordelia, having seen the company which waited in the corridor, illuminated by their single candle, immediately knelt down and snatched up the gun. She could not have moved quite as swiftly as it seemed to Lydyard that she did, but the others were no quicker to react than she was. While she picked up the weapon and levelled it, without troubling to rise to her full stature again, nobody moved.

Lydyard could see that his beloved was white with fear, but he knew well enough that she had handled guns before. They had been out shooting together on more than one occasion, and though the pistol was very different from a shot-gun, still she had the confidence to point it, and he did not doubt that she could fire it. He knew – as Amalax must also know – that the candlelight made ready targets of them all.

But Amalax must have seen a doubt in her eye which Lydyard had not. Amalax must have known that she could see the knife at Lydyard's throat, and must have guessed what that sight signified to her.

'Don't fire, my lady,' said Amalax, quietly. 'I have your friend for a shield, and you would be sure to kill him.' Lydyard saw the barrel of the revolver move, as though she was sighting along it at his face, and then, to his relief, it moved jerkily away again. But she was simply shifting her aim, to point the gun at the man named Jack, who had no shield at all. Jack fell back another pace, ready to hurl himself at the stairhead. Calan could have taken that position before him, but did not deign to do it. For that reason, the gun moved again, to point directly at Calan.

Everyone – including Cordelia, as Lydyard presumed – was still listening, to see if anyone else was coming. No one was. Sir Edward's room was too far away, and if the pistol's fall had disturbed his sleep at all, he must have concluded that the noise was of no significance. There were too many sounds in the house, too many ways to reach the conclusion that a distant clatter was nothing that need concern its master.

Lydyard knew that Calan could not be made afraid by any mere firearm. He wished that it were otherwise. Calan might be confident that he could not be killed, but if he attacked, others might be.

'Stay where you are, Calan!' said Amalax, who must have reached the same conclusion. Then he spoke again to Cordelia, in a tone which was probably as polite as he could achieve.

'We are too many for you to shoot, my lady,' he said, still whispering tautly. 'Even with as many bullets as you have, and even if you could miss your friend. We only wish to leave. We will go downstairs, very carefully. When we reach the door – but not before – I will release Mr Lydyard.'

Lydyard did not need to read the other's thoughts to know that the promise was a lie, and yet he hoped that Cordelia would believe it, for her own sake.

But Calan did not move in reponse to Amalax's undertaking – and now, very belatedly, there came a sound from the floor above, which said that one of the servants must now be up and about.

'Go, Jack!' said Amalax quickly. 'All must flee, and none must stop!' Instead of heeding his own advice, though, Amalax paused. He still held Lydyard firmly, keeping him as a shield. The small man took the candle which had lighted the invaders' way, so that a blanket of shadow quickly fell upon those who remained in the corridor.

Lydyard sensed rather than saw the wrench which Calan made at his waist, but there was light enough to see the way his shirt went sailing away as he thrust with his arms, and cried, 'No!' – as much to Amalax as to the werewolf.

But Cordelia must have fired at the movement, and her aim was good.

The blast took Calan while he was still in human form – but in the near darkness Lydyard could see that the change was already begun, and was only interrupted by the bullet which bowled the werewolf over and threw him backwards. The force of the recoil drew a cry of pain from Cordelia, but she had known that it would come, and did not lose her balance. She levelled the gun again, and gripped her right wrist with her left hand in order to steady it.

Calan, writhing in the shadows, was no shape at all, and blood was founting out of him.

He howled, and in that frightful howl there vanished any fragile doubt which Lydyard might have nurtured as to whether the werewolves of London were really what they claimed to be. It was a demon's cry rather than an animal's, and Calan now had become a huge four-legged thing, monstrous and mad.

The wounded manwolf hurled itself forward again, and Lydyard could see the vivid green eyes which caught and magnified the dying light.

Cordelia fired again.

Exactly where the bullet hit there was no way to tell, but hit it did, and though the landing was full of shadows now, there was light enough to see how the bloody, furry and furious mess which was Calan was still in dreadful flux, as his human nakedness still erupted with coarse wolfish hide.

What will happen to the bullets? Lydyard found himself enquiring. *Will they be expelled, or will he take them inside himself? And what of all the blood he has lost?*

The shots would have killed any ordinary man or any ordinary wolf, and the effect which they had on Calan was by no means trivial. His flesh was only flesh, whatever exotic powers of reconstitution it might possess. It was as though the violence of the wounds and the swiftness of his metamorphosis combined into a strange explosion of being, which sprayed blood in all directions, and left a tortured mass of limbs and fur which could not quite complete its change of form.

The house was full of sounds now as the echoing shots brought others tumbling from their beds.

'Run!' howled Amalax, desperate to be obeyed. 'Flee for your very lives!'

Lydyard, brought to action by a combination of courage and terror, sank his teeth into the arm which Amalax still clutched about his throat, and thrust hard in the hope and expectation of breaking the other's grip. How close he came to being stabbed to death he could not guess, but the ploy failed. The blade cut a long but shallow wound from his neck to his temple, sawing painfully across his ear. Amalax still had sufficient presence of mind to hold him hard, and then to bring down his huge and meaty fist upon the top of his prisoner's head, knocking him silly.

Lydyard's head spun and he had to fight to stay conscious, but he knew that Cordelia was still there, with bullets still to fire. Amalax was now the only target left, and dared not let Lydyard fall, but dragged him insistently backwards towards the stairhead, keeping the slim body between his much greater bulk and the gun. Lydyard could feel warm blood coursing down the side of his head, and his ravaged ear prickled and burned, but the pain was not yet intense, and was subdued by the stress of it all.

Somehow, the wreckage which was Calan tumbled and squirmed ahead of them, wriggling down the stairs.

Amalax followed, and Lydyard was heartily glad that he was no longer able to share in the other's thoughts and fears, and wrathful fulminations. It was enough that he could hear the man cursing so volubly, so viciously, so angrily, and he thought, in an oddly detached fashion, that it was almost a miracle of sorts which enabled the string of curses to go on and on and on . . .

For such a very long time . . .

13

*L*ondon is afire with uncanny light, its buildings dissolving into coloured smoke as the stars tumble from the sky like bright rain. The people are frozen where they stand, and as the transforming light dances about them it smoothes away their features; they are melted into awkward lumpish shapes, in one and twos and whole crowds, mothers and babies melting together, lovers becoming one at last.

Through the changing streets the wolves are running. They are white and silver-grey and black, fleet of foot and light of heart. And the fallen angels which hate mankind parade across the sky like wheels of fire, exulting in their freedom from the darkest prisons of matter, space and time.

In Hell, Satan weeps, watching helplessly as the world above him is lit from within like a crystal ball, all flame and flux and fury. He would reach out and touch it, if he only could.

Outside Creation, God's image shifts; helpless in his omnipotence, he is remade, and cannot call to judgement those whose very souls are consumed in the cauldron of potentiality.

The man in the cave confronts the smiling cat, whose jaws gape wide and whose eyes are ablaze with dreadful wrath, and who speaks to say: What you have stolen from my soul I will take back, else I will poison all the world and wreck Creation itself.

And the man cries: Sed libera nos a malo, sed libera nos a malo, sed libera . . .

Unheard.

Lydyard opened his eyes, which were awash with tears of pain, and said: 'Cordelia?'

There was no answer.

His head was pounding and he felt sick to his stomach, but the inner sight had let go of him, and left him to the unalloyed misery of his discomforts. The bright imaginary light which had been dazzling him faded into mere yellow lamplight, and he saw the walls which confined him, and the bed on which he lay.

His wrists were closely bound together by thin cord, whose coils were also knotted about one of the iron bars which supported the bedhead. His ankles were bound in similar fashion and tightly tied to a bar beneath the lower rail which was at the foot of the bed, so that his bare feet projected beyond the rail. He was held in such a way that he could not make himself comfortable no matter how he squirmed or tried to change his position. The mattress upon which he lay was very uneven.

He was not alone; beside him, sitting on the bed and looking down at him, was the awesomely beautiful woman he had seen once before. Her neatly formed teeth were just visible between her gently smiling lips; her eyes, which had violet irises, were fixed upon him. Her expression was mockingly affectionate. In the lamplight her silken, glimmering hair seemed more honey-coloured than when illuminated by pale sunlight.

He could not take his eyes from her face.

'You would not come with me when I asked,' she said, in a teasingly reproachful fashion. 'You let my jealous lover take you away. Poor Pelorus has lately become quite mad, as you must have guessed – his will is not his own. My will is entirely my own, and cannot be denied by mere mortals, as you see.'

'You are the queen of the werewolves, I presume,' he said, gritting his teeth to sustain the angry irony, 'and I dare say that you have learned much by the example of our own dear queen.'

She laughed, in a curiously mock-polite fashion. 'Have you a queen of your own? It is so difficult to keep count of your ephemeral monarchs that I no longer try. I have not been entertained at court for . . . some time.'

Lydyard looked about him, at the walls darkened by soot and fungus, which nevertheless contrived to gleam in the lamplight because they were so enslimed. The mortar between the bricks was crumbling, and the brick itself gave the appearance of being rotten to the core. The floor was as brightly lit as the walls, because an oil-lamp stood upon it; it was dirt, not even flagstoned, and it stank of excrement. The chair upon which Mandorla Soulier sat was sturdy and plain. Apart from the bed on which he lay the only other piece of furniture in the room was a low table by the bedhead, on which stood a candle-tray; its candle was lit but had already burned low, and its coarse wax had melted into a bizarrely misshapen lump.

In the midst of all this squalor, Mandorla Soulier was ostentatiously costumed in coloured silks, like some Drury Lane actress dressed to play Cleopatra – or Salomé.

'If this is how you entertain at your own court,' he said, 'I hope that as many years might pass before I am invited again.'

This time, her smile seemed more genuinely amused. 'There have been times, Mr Lydyard, when I could have welcomed you to a finer place by far. But a beautiful woman who does not age is too often flattered by accusations of witchcraft. You do not know what it is like to burn, my darling David, and if you were ever to find out, you could not wake again to cherish the memory. I know, and I sometimes wish that I did not. It is an experience which might teach Pelorus a salutary lesson about those who he holds in such foolishly high regard.'

'We never burned witches in England,' said Lydyard, fighting against the many pains in his cut and aching head, and also against an insistent nausea in his belly, 'and we have not hanged one for a century and more. Had you kept in better touch with our affairs, you might know that.'

'I had slept for a while,' Mandorla said, regretfully, 'and those who guarded me were obliged to be careful. The world had changed when I returned, more than I had thought possible. It had become black and ugly, choked with smoke, flatulent with steam, and drenched with cheap gin, with manners and morals to match. And yet, it has greater potential for its own destruction than I have ever seen before. In these crowded streets, famine and disease are ever close at hand . . . and there is cause for hope that a glorious transformation of the business of war might increase the toll of its slaughter in a most pleasing manner. There is such a wonderful profusion of new engines of destruction!'

'How is Calan?' he asked, bluntly.

'Asleep,' she replied, easily enough. 'Asleep, and dreaming. Do not think that your leaden bullets can poison or corrupt him, even though your vile liquor had begun to make him stupid. He will wake again, refreshed and renewed, and if I can, I will refresh and renew the world for him, so that he may have a more joyous awakening than he has ever had before. It is the way of the wolf pack, you see, that I am mother and protector to my siblings and my cousins as well as my whelps. We are more faithful and loving than your own kind.'

Lydyard yanked at the cords which secured him, squinting against the shock of pain, and said: 'I cannot believe it.'

She smiled yet again, more coldly than before, and said: 'But this is just appearance, my darling David. I am not really human at all – I am a wolf, and humans are my prey, as little to me as rats and frogs. I am loving with my own kind, as you are with yours, but you are as little to me as the beasts which you send to your own slaughterhouses. I might make a pet of you, if the whim took me, and favour you with the kind of affection which you might give to a sleek and pretty cat, but I could not offer you that purer love which a she-wolf feels for her kin.

'I ask you to understand this, David, for I know that you are clever by the standards of your kind, and capable of philosophical detachment. I would not have you think me cruel, when I am a reasoning creature like yourself. You do understand me, David, do you not? Unless you do, you will not understand your own situation, and I want you to see that however I may use you, I do no wrong. I owe you no mercy, no pity, no charity, for I am a wolf, David, no matter what I seem to be in the sight of your poor deluded eyes.'

The earnestness of it was somehow more appalling than the implication. If cattle had the power of speech and thought, would human beings approach them in like fashion? Would the predator expect his prey to understand the logic of the abattoir? Would he have the right to demand that his explanation be accepted – that the justice of murder be admitted, that the rectitude of the slaughterer be recognized?

'Whatever you want from me,' he whispered, 'I will deny you. By torture you might make me see, and you might also make me speak, but if you hope to separate truth from delusion, reality from dream, you will surely be disappointed. It has ever been the way with oracles, has it not?'

'I know far more of oracles than you do,' she told him. 'Has Pelorus told you about the way of pain? Even if he did, I doubt

319

that he told you enough. With me to guide you, you will learn to dream the truest dreams of all, and in the end, you will be grateful for the chance to serve my ends. I know the way of pain, you see, far better than any of your kind ever could. I know its persuasiveness as well as its rewards.'

He could not doubt that she did, and was forced to swallow a lump in his throat.

Mandorla was still smiling. 'Do not be afraid,' she said. 'You are a little more than human now, and you must not think as a cold-souled coward. I ask for your understanding, and that is not something which I have asked of many men. Different we are, but still we might be allied. I am honest with you because I hope that you might be honest with me. I do not seek to use my disguise in deception or seduction, not because you know what I really am – the power of your eyes to see falsely is so great that I could deceive and seduce you in spite of what you know – but because I see in you authentic intelligence and genuine curiosity.'

He knew that it was a lie. He knew, beyond the shadow of a doubt, that it was a mere stratagem, a seduction which sought to succeed by disowning the intention to seduce.

He knew, too, that it was a kind of play. She did not speak to him thus because she truly thought it to be the best way of attaining her end, but rather because she rejoiced in her own deceptiveness. Behind her flattery there was a special contempt.

'Do not lose yourself in delight,' he told her, with sufficient asperity to take her by surprise, 'for something is coming after me, and there is none who can bar its way or force its hand. Neither you nor Harkender can keep Gabriel from the one to whom his soul truly belongs – and it is not for you to command the conflicts of the gods.'

She was taken aback, but only for a moment. 'Poor oracle,' she said. 'The poison in your soul will hurt you, if you cannot contain it better than that.'

He shook his aching head, as though he might clear it by throwing off his confusion. Unsurprisingly, the shaking worsened his distress. The world seemed to fade and blur. Even through his clothing he could feel the coarseness of the blanket on which he lay, and the chafing of the cords about his bleeding wrists, and these sensations were very sharp indeed – but the face of Mandorla Soulier had lost some fraction of its glamour, and the dismal walls of his prison seemed to have retreated into a distant haze.

'Was any other hurt?' he asked, more harshly than he had intended.

'No,' she replied. 'Amalax panicked, but his foolishness was contained by his determination to escape. Sir Edward and his daughter are safe and well – for the time being.'

Lydyard heard and understood the implied threat, but did not react.

'It may not be as easy as you think to keep me here,' he said. 'Sir Edward is an influential man, and kidnapping is a serious crime. There is also Pelorus to be reckoned with.'

'The police cannot find us here,' she assured him, so casually that he believed it, 'and if Pelorus cares to come to your aid, he may indeed meet with a reckoning of sorts. I would not hurt him for the world – he is one of us, by nature and by true inclination, and I love him as dearly and inescapably as he loves me – but he must be protected from the alien will which works its evil way within him. He regrets as bitterly as any that his will is not his own. He cannot surrender to me, no matter that he longs to do it, and so I must capture him, as any who loved him half as much would be bound to do. If he comes to save you, his dearest and most secret wish will be to fail, and to be allowed to fall into the sleep of centuries. I would be a poor she-wolf if I did not seek to grant that wish.'

Lydyard breathed carefully and deeply, trying to prevent his hand from trembling and his teeth from chattering. The pain in his head was dull but all-consuming. Everything which Mandorla said seemed to reek of mockery and deceit.

'Pelorus may not come alone,' he said. 'He might make common cause with Sir Edward. And you must not forget

321

the other who might come to help me – that Sphinx whose toy I am. It reduced Pelorus to helplessness in Egypt, and it will do the same to you, if the whim takes it. I will do all I can to bring it here – that I promise you – but I will not bring it to be seduced or teased, I will bring it to exercise its wrath!'

He was glad to see that Mandorla's eyes narrowed then, and knew that he had frightened her, a little. She could not know what measure of mastery he had over his power, or how intimate his connection was with the Sphinx.

'Do not overreach yourself,' she murmured. 'You might fall into the trap which has claimed poor Harkender. He thinks himself a stealer of souls, but his own soul is imprisoned in a web which he cannot begin to comprehend. Do not think yourself the master, or even the favoured slave, of that thing whose eyes you are. I have tried to show you what you are to me, but you are less than that by far to the being which has warmed your soul. You cannot command it, or even dare to hope that it will listen to your prayers.

'Poor manchild, you think that you have only dreamed of being in Hell, but you do not know how real your dreams now are. You are hostage to the powers of Creation and Destruction, whose reality is unimagined in your knowledge and your language. What owns you now had vanished from the reach of outer sight when the world was very young, perhaps before the race of men had been created. Reincarnate, it is free to make what it can of this dreadful, cold and desolate world, and my hope and expectation is that it needs only to see what men are, and what they have made, to be persuaded to turn its power to the breaking and the withering of everything which exists.'

He knew that she dared not really believe it. Hope was speaking, not conviction – and even the hope was reaching far beyond her expectations, no matter what she said. In her own way, she was afraid – not of death, but of her own helplessness. She had stolen Gabriel Gill to give her the illusion of power, the illusion of control, but in her heart of hearts she knew that she was no commander of Creation, but only a wolf denied the joy and comfort of her own true being.

She had asked him to understand her, but he suspected that he understood far better than she had intended him to. He had the power of sight, still growing within him. He was a magician, however reluctant, and his power to dream the truth – and know the truth when he dreamed it – was greater than she knew. But his wrists were tightly bound and his body was racked with miseries, and whatever powers she claimed without having, she certainly had the power to deliver him into the untender arms of the dark angel of pain.

She reached out her hand, and put it to his forehead. The ache in his head flared up again, as though the contact had sent a shock through his brain, which seemed unjust, for he believed that she had genuinely sought to soothe and not to inflame. Wolf though she was, there was sufficient humanity in her to corrupt the wholeheartedness of her desire to hurt him. But then she ran her fingertips along the line of the cut which Amalax's knife had made, and there was no doubt that she meant to hurt; her sharpened nails opened the cut again, and he felt blood trickling into his ears.

He tried to move away, but found that he could not. He was too well secured; she and not he had control of his movements.

For the first time, he felt the extreme of fear: all loneliness and pain were in it, all misery and desperation, though first and foremost it was helplessness. That ultimate fear froze him, made him a mere toy of external force, forbade him to act, or even to exert his will against inaction.

'It is not for my own pleasure that I do this,' she said to him, 'but for your own education. You must learn the way of pain, and I know that you have not the courage to tread that path alone, as Jacob Harkender has.'

She took up the grotesquely molten candle from the table, and stood up. She moved unhurriedly to the foot of the bed, so that he would see and understand what she intended.

'It is only a candle,' she said to him. 'A very tiny flame, which cannot really hurt you. Do you know how long it would take to burn a man to death, if one had only a candle to accomplish the task? It would be a long time, David, whether measured in hours or by the intensity of pain. That pain is best which can be most cleverly prolonged, which hurts without destroying, so that it may be constantly renewed.'

She set the flame to the naked soles of Lydyard's feet. She moved it up and down, teasingly, so that the pain would grow slowly.

For a few seconds, the sensation was so dull and distant that he was more inclined to laugh than to scream – but then it began to build, and its sharpness grew in a gradual crescendo. The calluses on his feet were singeing, the dead skin shrivelling away to expose the living flesh beneath.

He could not tell how long he fought before he finally screamed. As soon as he cried out, though, she took the little flame away. The pain did not stop, but the crescendo began to wind down again.

She came back to the bedhead, and put the candle close to his face so that he could look into the heart of its tiny malevolent flame. She let him look at it for a minute or more, while he hoped fervently that her intention was to set it down and let him rest. But the hope, too, was part of her scheme, encouraged in order that it might be dashed and when she was ready she moved again to the foot of the bed.

'Dream for me,' she said to him, in a seductively pleading tone. 'Fear not that there will be an end, for I will not let you die. But when you have dreamed, you must be more honest with me than you have so far been. Think on my beauty, if you can, and learn to love me just a little, for that will make the path of pain much easier to bear. Only dream for me, and you will find that I can reward as well as punish.

'I need to know the Sphinx's riddle, David – and more than that, I need to know its answer. Find your other mistress for me, and then return to tell me what and where she is. Tell her that I have lived ten thousand years, and that if there is any on this earth who has the wisdom which she needs it is Mandorla the she-wolf. Tell her that, David, and I might ease your hurt for a while. I promise that you will not hurt too badly, for this is only the beginning, and in time, even the harshest of hurts might cost you less, if you will only condescend to learn what I can teach you.'

But the reality was harsher than the promise. The pain had not died away before it began to build again, and this time the crescendo was not so soon interrupted.

Lydyard's vision of Satan in Hell was suddenly before him again, in all its dreadful detail, and no matter how he sobbed and cried for the dream to die and fade into the darkness, it would not.

14

The sky was full of eagles, which swooped upon him one by one to tear his belly open slit by slit, to lay bare his white ribs and his coiled gut, and his beating, beating heart. And as the flesh was lacerated by the talons and the beaks, it was moved to wild and eager growth, so that the beating heart swelled inside his breast, and his ribs gleamed as though with white fire, and the pain . . .

He screamed in anguish, and the extremity of his agony dried up his scalded tears and mocked his hopelessness, for how could he hope to heal the world when he could not save himself from the punishment of his treason?

He opened his mouth to cry for help, but at first the words would not come. Was he not in Hell, beyond hope, beyond salvation? Surely he was beyond the reach of any angel of mercy, and likewise beyond the reach of any regret or repentance of that uncaring and unfeeling God who was without the limits of Creation, unable to interfere with the destiny which He had set in train?

He did not doubt it — yet still he sought to cry out, to scream, for whatever mercy blind chance might provide. And so he screamed, and his plea for help echoed through eternity and was miraculously heard.

And though the eagles continued to tear and rend him, and would not let him be, still he slipped away into some dark and velvet covert of time and space.

He escaped into the safety of another's thoughts – thoughts which belonged to the settled past, which had been scrupulously laid to rest for patient and painless examination by curious historians who would seek only to understand and not to change, only to describe and not to create, only to watch and not to be. . . .

As the darkness slid away, he became conscious of a sensation of slight unsteadiness. For one brief moment he thought, absurdly, that the earth might be rocking drunkenly in its orbit about the sun, as if it were in imminent danger of losing its position entirely and falling into the infinite dark void. Then he remembered that there was nothing as safe as the good earth, nothing as unchangeable as the rising and setting of the inexhaustible sun.

The sight of a porthole above his head informed him that he was aboard a ship which was yawing and heeling because it was in the grip of stormy weather.

He felt a surge of relief which was as absurd as his former anxiety, but it possessed him so completely that he could not immediately ask himself any of the sensible questions which might have come to mind: What ship? Whither bound?

He sat up in the bunk, and the loose covers fell away from his naked torso. He looked out of the porthole at the far horizon, where the setting sun was neatly caught between the grey sea and a bank of cloud which was no less grey and no less solid. Rain was already falling, blurring the ruddy face of the sun, and he wondered how glorious the rainbow might be that must be visible from the cabins on the port side.

He knew by deduction that the boat was heading north, but it seemed so strangely fascinating to watch the slanting rain falling upon the slow great waves, lit from the side by the dying daylight, that he still did not ask himself those questions it was entirely reasonable to ask. Paradoxically, he was aware of the fact that he was avoiding some vital issue – perhaps several – in the interests of tranquillity. He knew that he was clinging to his moment of delight and freedom from anxiety as a shipwrecked sailor might cling to an item of flotsam, so intent on surviving the moment that the future was immaterial and insignificant.

The relief ebbed away. He was dimly aware that he had forgotten his name and his purpose, and could not tell whether the eyes with which he saw were his own or another man's.

He touched his breast where dark hair grew, and wondered who he was.

Then he looked away from the red-lit porthole, to inspect his berth. There was someone else in the cabin, standing by the closed door, watching him. For a moment, it seemed to him that this other was not human, but rather some kind of great cat, contorted so as to stand erect like a human being, yet retaining its tawny mane and amber eyes, its black snout and lips, and its carnivore's fangs. For an instant only that was what he saw, or seemed to see.

Then he felt a strange flicker of sensation – as though another piece of the jigsaw that was the world had been slotted into place, bringing him one step further forward in the quest for coherence and normality.

It was a woman who was looking at him. Her eyes were most certainly amber, and there was something of the feline in the way she stared at him; but her hair was black, not tawny at all, and her nose was aquiline and her lips were full and red. When she smiled, he saw that her teeth were quite perfect. She smiled the way a lover might smile: pleasantly and possessively. She wore an evening-dress whose peacock-blue brightness was startling.

'Memories are fickle things,' she told him. Her voice was low and musical, and had in its quality something of the purring of a great cat. 'You have forgotten yourself, but I think you remember the world well enough.'

He looked out of the porthole again. The world had not,

after all, fallen into the bowels of the universe: sun, sea, cloud-filled sky, and falling rain were all in place. So, he imagined, must Paris and London be, and Wadi Halfa and Rome and Timbuktu. Victoria was on the English throne, Charles Darwin had published his account of *The Descent of Man*, Barnum and Bailey had opened the greatest show on earth in New York, and Bismarck had engaged the Catholic Church in *Kulturkampf*.

It seemed that he was, indeed, on tolerably familiar terms with the world. But who on earth was he? And who was she?

'I, on the other hand,' she told him, as though it were a matter of no great concern to her, 'know well enough what I am and what time and chance have made of me – but the world is so utterly new and strange to me that I almost despair of understanding it and fear to hurt it by enquiry.'

It was an enigma that he could not yet face squarely. 'What ship is this?' he asked.

'The *Popinjay*, bound for Southampton from Cherbourg. The crossing will be very rough, I fear, but we will be safe and well.'

He noticed that she was speaking English, as he had been. 'Are we homeward bound, then?' he enquired.

'No,' she answered. 'I have no home here, and yours was forfeit when you met me. I am not part of this scheme of things, and have taken you outside it, in order to use you.'

He was beginning to suspect that he was somehow incapable of feeling alarm. Something had been done to him, to make him as much marionette as man, and it was unjust that he could not care about it, or rail against its injustice. He was a prisoner of his own enforced complacency.

'What are you?' he asked, though he could not quite remember why it was an important question.

'Call me Lilith,' she replied. It was not an answer, but he was content with it.

'And what shall I call myself?' he asked.

'You must call yourself Adam,' she told him, 'as all men do

when they find themselves newly made. You are entered on the passenger list as Adam Grey, and that is the name which is shown on your documents, but I will not hold you to it if you think it does not suit you.'

'I was someone else, once,' he observed, laconically.

'Once,' she agreed, 'but not any more.'

He could not fight his indifference. It was all he could do to bring to his lips the most ominous question of all: 'Why?'

'I needed your mind, your memory, your voice – and *your compliance*. I am a stranger in the world, in need of guides. Something there is which seeks to use me, and I cannot yet tell what it is, or where my own interests lie. I still need you, Adam Grey; I need your blindness, for I cannot read appearances honestly enough, when my Cyclopean eye is open. I need you because I am afraid – not of death or destruction, but of change; I need your knowledge of the world, which can tell me better than my own clear sight what it is that the world would will me to become.'

For one fleeting moment he came close to grasping a fugitive memory, and felt that he had nearly remembered something of importance – not who he was or had been, but a memory of somewhere he had been, and something he had done. Its substance evaded him, but it stirred some kind of association in that part of his knowledge which had been restored to him.

'Paris,' he said. 'We have recently been in Paris.'

As he said it, he felt a tiny prick of triumph, knowing that he was not entirely the captive of her shaping. He was a man and not a marionette; his will was free though his memories were not. With effort, with luck, with what vestiges of desire he could muster, he might yet remember who and what he really was – or had been, before he was Adam Grey.

'Yes,' she said, equably, 'we were in Paris a little while ago. It is an interesting city, where I learned a good deal about the world which has become, but we are bound for London—'

'Where the werewolves are,' he said, interrupting her. He did not know why he said it, but for the second time he had the feeling that it was his notion, and that he had fished it up from the depths of his concealed self.

'Where the werewolves are,' she agreed. 'But you need not fear the werewolves, my Adam, for I have made you much cleverer than they are. I have breathed such Promethean heat into your cold soul that the werewolves cannot hurt you at all.'

She unhooked her evening-dress, and let it fall from her shoulders. He was oddly surprised to see the underclothes beneath it, assertively ordinary.

The ship rocked upon the waves. The sun had set, and the grey clouds had all but extinguished the twilight. There was a vibration in the body of the ship, conducted into the rods and sinews of his bunk, so that he might feel there the stalwart throbbing of the ship's steam-engines. The whole world was shaking, and lurching while it shook, shivering and staggering, but it was only a rough crossing, by no means unusual in the English Channel. Surely he had felt the like of it before?

She had placed the blue dress on the lower bunk, neatly. Now she was removing the rest of her garments, unhurriedly and unashamedly. Had he seen the like of this before?

He searched within himself for more elusive memories.

He remembered the world well enough; he remembered how to talk, and what a joke was, and the rules of the game of cricket, and he knew well enough how to make love, and how to do it with sufficient finesse to pass for a man of the world. But he could not remember ever having done it. He could not remember the name or form of any woman he had ever bedded. He did not know whether he had been a married man, and though he remembered Piccadilly well enough, and the kinds of night-flying creature which fluttered back and forth along the borders of Green Park, he could not tell whether he had been the kind of man who would buy the kind of whore who could be had for half a crown.

But what, he wondered, did she remember? And when had her memories been laid down in her mysterious mind?

For a moment he thought that she might climb into the lower bunk, but she had no such intention. And whatever she did or did not remember of the world and its ways, she showed no confusion or shyness as she bestrode him; and as her yellow eyes stared into his own from the gathering shadows of the falling night, he thought he saw a kind of rapture there – an exultation in the wearing of flesh, which somehow implied that whatever she had been before she was Lilith, it was something much colder and far more forlorn than man or cat or god incarnate.

And he found, to his astonishment, that something of that exultation was in him too, perhaps conveyed by the warmth which she had bestowed upon his feeble soul. He wooed her with such delirious fervour that he quite forgot to wonder who he might have been, and what he might become, but was contentedly Adam, not grey or grave at all.

But when their ecstasy was done, and comfort should have come, and merciful blindness to save him from himself, there was instead a flutter of eagles' wings, which threatened to throw him forward in time and into the world as it truly was, as hideously bright as only consuming fire could be, and he knew then that he must pray, must pray as fiercely as he could, for a higher God to save him from the loving grasp of the Sphinx whose riddle his other self had not yet solved, nor even heard in full.

So he prayed, and felt his prayer fall into the well of eternity, as all prayers do.

But the words had not disturbed her in the least. He was glad of it, in a way, for he no longer felt that he could say the Lord's Prayer honestly. In his dream he had been Satan, and Satan had been Prometheus, and Lydyard had pitied him and shared the burden of his pain.

'It is kind of you,' he whispered, 'to wait by my bed. I wish that you would bring me water, for I have a thirst which makes it difficult to speak.' He was conscious, now, of the pain in his feet, but it seemed dull and distant again.

'What did you see?' she asked, neither teasingly nor threateningly. 'Tell me what you saw, and you may have water. Only be honest, and you shall have food, and better clothes. Only trust me, and the way of pain will become less hard and less treacherous. But first – what did you see?'

'The Sphinx is coming,' he told her. 'It wears human guise now, as you do. It seeks the same privileges, has the same seductiveness. But like you, it is not truly human, and is contemptuous of its humanity. You cannot force me to see more, if it does not choose to show itself, for it has the power to free me from distress. I am its pawn, and you may not use me against it.'

He tried to sit up, but on the instant that he moved his discomforts began to return.

'Be still,' she said, softly.

He licked his lips, and said: 'You would do better to give me what I need, and let me go. The Sphinx is no friend to your kind, and you have no part to play in what it has come to do.'

'That has yet to be determined,' she told him. She contrived to bring the smile to her face again – and he read the hope which was in the smile. She did not intend to let him go. While he and Gabriel were here, any who wanted them must come to fetch them, and must be prepared to fight for the privilege of taking them away.

Mandorla did not know what would follow from that conflict, if conflict there was to be, but she knew that she had nothing at all to lose. At the worst, she would be laid to rest, for ten years or a thousand, and Lydyard could see in her dark eyes how little that prospect frightened her. He could not entirely blame her for her wanton hope that the infinite sheet of ice which bound her soul to earth and human form might one day be dissolved in cleansing fire.

The smile was suddenly twisted into a scowl; perhaps she had seen the pity in his eye.

'You are a fool, David Lydyard, to try to mock me. Always remember, frail man, that I can hurt you – far more than you might imagine possible, and any release from pain which you are ultimately to receive is in my gift. *My* gift, unless and until your Sphinx can spirit you away.

'Remember that you are human, after all, and I am not. I can show you suffering that you could not endure – and you may be certain that whatever your protector may do for you, it cares not a whit for those you love. I am fond enough of the flesh of men to drink your blood if the mood should take me, or the blood of any you hold dear. Fear me, my darling David. *Fear me!*'

It was a command which made him lick his lips again. He knew only too well that she could hurt him, and he knew that when she condescended instead to play with him, it was in the same way that a cat might play with a mouse.

There is a bolder cat at large, he said silently to himself, *who might play with you in like fashion, and hurt you in ways which neither you nor I can quite imagine. But how would that save me, if the fury of Hell were let loose upon the earth?*

'I fear,' he said, gruffly, 'that I cannot yet be grateful for any mercy you might show in deciding not to hurt me. Will you give me water, or will you only use my thirst to make me dream again?'

She accepted the rebuke with surprising grace, neither smiling nor scowling.

'You are no weakling,' she said, in a low voice. 'I cannot like you for it, for I am not of your kind – but I have lived too long among humans to hate the best of them as much as I hate the worst. I will not hurt you merely for the sake of it, but hurt you I must, when it is time again. I will send Amalax with water, and a blanket to keep you warm.'

She stood up then, and turned to go. The renewed ache in Lydyard's head was sufficient to make him want to rest its weight upon the mattress, and he was glad to see her go up the stone steps which led to the door, so that he might lay himself down, and surrender himself to exhaustion. But when he had relaxed himself, he began to sense the nearness of that hell which so often came to claim him. The cold dankness of the room mingled with the heat of his soul's unnatural fire and the pain which gnawed at each of his feet from toe to heel. The slimy walls of his prison were all aglitter, as though with the promise of a brighter light beyond.

In order to keep the visions at bay, he began to recite, very softly: '*Pater noster, qui es in caelis . . .*'

But he no longer knew to whom his prayer should be addressed.

15

In due course, Caleb Amalax brought Lydyard the cup of water for which he had asked. The fat man looked at his wretched prisoner as though he would rather throw it in his face than let him drink it – and for a moment or two he held the cup teasingly beyond Lydyard's reach, taunting him. Lydyard only waited, patiently, and in the end Amalax put the vessel to his lips, and held it so that he could take the liquid at his own pace. It tasted bitter and metallic, but Lydyard gulped it down gratefully.

'Thank you,' he said, when he had finished, but Amalax did not want his thanks, and would not do him the favour of speaking to him. Having delivered the water, he left. To add calculated injury to insult, he took the oil-lamp with him. Lydyard had only to glance at the dwindling mass of candle-fat in the tray by his head to know that he would soon be left in Stygian gloom.

The blanket which Mandorla had also promised him was never brought.

Lydyard lay still for what seemed like a long time, determined that he would not sleep. He tried for a little while to loosen the cords which bound his wrists, but he could not do it, and became impatient with himself when he realized that he had caused the chafed skin to bleed again. The pain of the cords which held his hands and feet seemed greater by now than the sullen excrucation of his burnt feet.

His resistance to sleep came initially from his reluctance to dream, but a more practical reason was soon to be found when the candleflame finally guttered and died. Only a few minutes more had passed before he heard the sound of the rats scampering across the floor of the darkened cellar. They became increasingly active, and more than once an invisible creature scrambled up on to the bed, forcing him to kick out against it. He could easily imagine how it might feel if a rat should sink its yellow teeth into the round fleshy pad of one of his seared toes, perhaps beginning a frenzied attack in which a horde of the verminous beasts would strip the flesh from his bones.

He soon ceased to pray. He called out once or twice when he heard people moving along the corridor outside the high-set door, but no one came in to see what he wanted. When no food came, and no more water, he could not help but wonder whether Mandorla's sullen friends had decided to let him provide food for the rats. But the likelier explanation was that it was part of a process of calculated demoralization. Mandorla could not be content with simply hurting him – she needed his co-operation. She intended to make him so desperate that when she came again he would be glad to see her, glad to listen to her soothing voice. Her plan was to make him utterly dependent on her favours.

Or perhaps, he said to himself, in a moment of morbid humour, *I have been appointed to be the bait in a trap, intended to bring the rats to this place, so that the werewolves may pounce upon them, and feast upon those they kill.*

Another rat climbed on to the bed, this time near to his head. Though his hands were useless he contrived to push the creature back with his elbow. It squealed, more in annoyance than in fear, and Lydyard was certain that it had only consented to a temporary retreat, being cunningly prepared to bide its time.

Overhead, the house was by no means silent. It was seemingly full of people who walked this way and that across the creaking floorboards. They must have numbered dozens, and yet none could be found who would respond to his calls. He supposed that he must be in a part of the world where cries in the night were commonplace, and none cared to ask whence they came.

Weariness made him pause in his writhing and lie still. Barely ten seconds afterwards he felt the snout of an inquisitive rat soft against his heel. Gripped by a sudden paroxysm of anger, he kicked out, and simultaneously wrenched hard against the confinement of the cords which bound him. He knew full well that he could not break free by sheer brute strength, but felt that he must make some demonstration of his frustration, even if that demonstration could only consist of writing his wrath upon the record of existence in the fierceness of pain.

And when, in that moment of perversity, he accepted the pain and welcomed its caustic fire, he slipped again through some mysterious fold in the substance of the world and the texture of time.

Time passed, and he lost himself in its passing – yet he somehow managed to retain that ghostly inquisitiveness which had not been entirely eradicated from his intelligence.

Once again he shared the petrified consciousness of the man who had lost his name, and had become another in an indefinite series of appointed Adams.

We were in Paris, the man was thinking, in a strangely slow and glutinous fashion. *Something happened there. . . .*

To concentrate his reluctant thoughts, Adam Grey meticulously brought to bear those visual memories of the city which his mind had been permitted to retain: the façade of the Louvre facing the Seine; the Champs Elysées; Notre-Dame de Paris. Nothing sounded a chord; the hook which dangled from his thread of thought, carefully lowered into that part of his mind which was cold and submerged, encountered nothing.

He was not dismayed; the indifference which his strange mistress had forced upon him was as much a gift as a curse when patience was required. He went on calling forth remembered images, as dim and blurred as drab watercolours or sepia daguerreotypes: the Pont Neuf; the gold-plated dome of the Church of Saint-Louis rising above the hospital; Les Halles; the Church of Saint-Sulpice and its halo of shops hawking tawdry devotional statuary . . .

It was, improbably, the Saint-Sulpicerie statuary which struck a sudden spark, and touched off a curious small explosion in his mind. For the second time in a few minutes Lydyard, this time as passenger in another man's soul, found himself detached from the advancing moment of the present, falling through time.

He found himself immediately within a church – not Saint-Sulpice, or any of the great churches, but some minor Gothic edifice, unnaturally cold and eerily lit by throngs of candles, whose tiny flames were reflected in the complex leaded windows, faintly coloured by the stained glass. He stood on a balcony above the congregation, whose members were by no means numerous. He was alone.

There was some kind of ceremony in progress, but at first he did not take it for a Mass because the robes of the officiating priest and his assistants were so strange, their chasubles being black and silken. Nor were the Latin phrases recognizable, and though he could hear the intonations of the celebrant quite clearly he could find no sense in them. There was a low table placed between the altar steps and the communion-rail, leaving only narrow margins in which the priest could move before and behind it.

Then it was that his eye was caught by two statues which had been placed at the ends of the altar, and he realized how the cunning link in his memory had been forged. They were every bit as crude as the cheap plaster icons of the Latin Quarter; the resemblance of style and technique were unmistakable. But the subjects were strange, for one showed the goat-headed president of the witches' sabbat and the other a demonic gargoyle.

Then, and only then, he noticed that the cross above the altar was inverted, and that the chalice was as black as jet.

Adam Grey – and Lydyard with him – melted back into his earlier self, and shared the dulled emotions of the curious watcher. Among the detritus of his knowledge of the world was rumour of the perverted Masses of the Yezidees. Thus, a slow realization was able to dawn within him that he was watching the rite of Asmodeus and Astaroth: the dark communion of the latter-day Satanists.

When this understanding dawned he scanned the congregation more closely, seeing that they numbered between thirty and forty. The women went bare-headed but the men wore caps; otherwise they were dressed in an ordinary manner, in clothes of reasonable quality.

While he watched, one of the assistants went to the vestry, and returned leading a girl, no more than fifteen or sixteen years old, masked but otherwise naked. She did not shiver against the cold, and her bearing was odd, as though she moved in some kind of daze or trance – a recognition which made him feel uncomfortable, for he was aware of some such modification in his own state of being. She got up on the table and lay down supine upon it, her arms straight at her side. Then the priest brought the chalice, and began to mark her body with something taken from it, which the watcher in the balcony could only take for blood. He marked her forehead and her breasts, and drew a cross whose intersection was her navel and whose foot was rooted in her pubic hair. Then, having placed the chalice by her head, he brought the paten carrying the host, and placed it upon her belly.

The Mass proceeded with due solemnity, now seeming more familiar as it echoed the conventional offertory. The watcher saw the host offered up, and wine added to the chalice, but the name in which the bread and wine were dedicated was not that of God, and some other incantation – no mere reversal – was substituted for the *Pater noster*. He watched the host broken and a particle of it placed in the chalice, but knew that the symbolism intended by the act was not that enshrined in the proper Mass. This worship was addressed to the Creators of matter and the body, and intended to exclude that Creator of the soul who was the Lord of the orthodox Church. It was, according to the orthodox, a black Mass – a homage to the Devil – and yet it was, he saw, an act of solemn worship, of reverence rather than calculated blasphemy. There was no lewdness in it, despite the presence of the naked girl, and no kind of sacrifice, despite the blood which had been contained in the chalice. These people thought themselves good, and respectful, and dutiful after their fashion.

As the people now gathered at the communion-rail bowed their heads, the priest – who had ascended with the host to the altar – turned first one way and then the other, and said: '*Ecce Asmodeus; ecce Astaroth,*' and more which the watcher could not understand. Then the celebrant turned again to face the congregation, intending to come down the steps. Before doing so, he looked back, quite casually.

He froze where he stood, unable to take that first descending step, for there had appeared above the body of the naked girl, as though standing weightlessly upon her, a huge and awesome figure. The would-be worshippers, many of whom must have closed their eyes, did not at first realize that it was there, but the shock of its presence was communicated to them one by one, and one by one they looked up, to gasp in wonder and horror at its magical appearance.

It was by no means similar to either of the images which had been placed upon the altar; its basic form echoed more closely that of the body on which it seemed to stand, for it was naked from the neck down, and unmistakably female. Yet it was not simply a copy of the nubile girl, for its figure was much fuller and more rounded, maternal rather than virginal in its amplitude. Nor was its face a mere reproduction of her plain black mask, and if it was a mask at all it was an inordinately clever one, for it was furred like a cat's and capped with half a dozen curling horns, and its great eyes blazed like glowing coals. From top to toe it was fully twelve feet tall, and that awesome head was a yard and more from crown to chin.

Then it spoke; and what it said was: '*Ecce Astaroth! Ite, missa est!*'

All of a sudden there was the sound of screaming in the air, as the people at the rail rose to their feet and shielded their eyes and tried to run away, colliding with one another in their panic.

The priest had dropped the host, and was likewise shielding his eyes in alarm and disbelief. The only person in the church who seemed unmoved, as though caught by rapt and naked admiration, was the girl who lay flat beneath the feet of the self-proclaimed dark angel, her face hidden by her mask.

Then the church was filled by the sound of wild laughter, which seemed to spring from the stones themselves; and the windows blazed with coloured light as though the night outside had been abruptly turned to gorgeous day. The images in the stained glass were no longer pictures of Christ and the company of the saints, but were instead a riot of demons and monsters, cavorting madly and comically about.

The people ran, including the priest and his assistants; all except for the girl upon the table, who was as still as if she had died and her soul gone to purgatory, where it must hear whatever judgement fate might pronounce upon its heresy and folly.

The man who had been commanded to be Adam opened his eyes abruptly, to look upon the comfortable dreariness of England's green and pleasant land from the window of a train. His ears were filled with a rapid clickety-clack which was suddenly cacophonous.

Am I, then, in the grip of Satan himself? he thought, with a sudden sickness in his stomach which penetrated the curtain of carelessness that had enshrouded his feelings.

But Lydyard, imprisoned with him, knew that this was no confirmation of the fears and hopes of the priests of St Amycus. The imagery was all borrowed – it came from the minds of those whom the fallen angel had possessed. The angel had played Astaroth for the devil-worshippers merely as a jest . . . an amused exploration of human contemptibility.

And when the angel replied to Adam Grey's unspoken anxiety, it seemed to Lydyard that she was not speaking to her more helpless instrument at all but to the prisoned Lydyard whose body still lay in the lonely rat-haunted darkness.

'Why not?' she said, from the corner of the carriage where she sat, beautiful and completely human. 'Men should be made to face their gods, to see what cowards ignorance has made of them. And as for the gods; may we not be content to be what men would make of us?'

'Is that your true form?' asked Grey, in a tone hushed by temporary alarm. 'Are you truly a giant, with the face of some monstrous creature and eyes of fire?' Even before she answered, he realized – as Lydyard already had – that she was playing with him, teasing him with a little flutter of fear. He could feel nothing without her permission, and when she withdrew it, he felt indifference descend upon him like a stifling cloak.

'When the angels walk upon the earth,' she told him, 'they must choose the forms which will best facilitate their ends. They must be beautiful and stern, but they must also be what men expect of images of power. Men are the caricaturists who make gargoyles of their imagined tempters, and dress their goat-faced adversary in shaggy shanks and a forked tail. It is men who love ugliness in those they desire to hate, and wish that beauty spoke honestly of good and generosity. And so they give form and substance to the angels which visit them from the depths of time.'

She paused to look out of the window at the dewy fields and the sullen sky, but soon continued. 'O my Adam,' she said, with affected weariness, 'this is a very silly world which I have found. Those humans which were hairy fools when last I walked the earth have found such clever ways to display their brutishness! Do not hunt within yourself for what you truly are, for all that you will find is a sorry ape with remarkable delusions of gentility. Ask instead what you might be, if I should choose to make you the parent of a better kind.'

Adam Grey struggled for understanding, but the mind which had been capable of such understanding was too deeply submerged. His thoughts were entrapped, as though wrapped tightly about by webs of spidersilk – and yet he knew that he must not struggle to escape, that there was some reason for his being here.

Lydyard could not tell whether or not his own thoughts and sensations were somehow leaking into the other's mind.

'You are no doubt kind,' said the body which was Lydyard's host, 'to let me remember the world from which my sad and sorry self has been erased. But I fear to dream of a glorious future while I do not know whose foolish dreams have made you captive, and I fear to trust your promises while I have only seen Astaroth and have yet to meet Asmodeus.'

Hearing these words, Lydyard became certain that his presence as passenger within the other's thoughts was having its effect. If only he knew how, he thought, he might take charge of this encounter, and confront the creature directly, with all the questions which were in his mind, and all the pleas and prayers which one with godlike powers might answer; and with warnings, too, against the hapless wiles of Mandorla Soulier and the spider which lurked in Jacob Harkender's shadow.

But he could not quite break through.

'I have seen what passes for everyday Creation in this world of yours,' she told him, and it still seemed that she knew full well that she was speaking to two men and not to one. 'I fear that the others of my kind are sleeping more soundly than they know. They have locked themselves into its substance and its space, and cannot know how the toll of change is slowly perverting their being.

'I am grateful to whatever freak of human boldness it was which dared to disturb me, for I could never have guessed when first I lay down to bide in time just what the results of my patience would be. Your world is fully ripe for Acts of

Creation, my Adam, and I dare say there is none who would stay my hand should I decide to alter it. And yet, there is much that I cannot see or understand, much that is unfathomable to the eyes and minds of those whose sight I have stolen.

'What is truly strange about this world of yours, my lovely consort, is that it defies the imagination of those who live in it. But then again, it is not so very strange, given that the world has been left to cold-souled men who have not the power of vision. What men are within themselves, I can see for myself, but I have hardly begun to comprehend the science and the society which are their world of appearances.

'If only you might be allowed to see what your world is really like, what news would you then bring back to earth? The tide of change has accomplished more than I could ever have thought possible, and I fear – yes fear, despite what I am – that there is something in the power of change which might yet deny the power of Creation. Nor should you, my Adam, rejoice in that anxiety, for you dare not hope to be free from your gods until you know what kind of freedom that would be!'

'I might be more useful to you, not less, if you would let me remember who I am,' he said. But it was only Adam Grey who spoke, for Lydyard could have made a better answer by far – or so he believed.

'I fear not,' she replied, ironically. 'It would confuse you, and I value your clarity of thought and observation. Do not struggle against my will, my beloved. Love me, my Adam, and you will find yourself capable of questionless surrender, and the purest joy. Only love me.'

Lydyard realized, as his captive host studied the woman's perfect features, that beauty – skin deep or not – was very difficult to resist. Mandorla Soulier had tried to play with him in exactly the same way that the Sphinx was playing with Adam Grey. Grey could not hate her for this; it was an honest compliment of sorts. Nor could Lydyard, in his heart of hearts, hate Mandorla Soulier, despite that she might kill him with her playfulness.

And Cordelia? thought Lydyard, with a painful shock of cynicism. *Is the play of her own beauty no more than a shadow of the playfulness of lovely monsters?*

He put the tormenting notion from his mind, and tried to concentrate instead on what the englamoured Adam Grey was saying to his stately mistress.

'The world was a smaller place by far when last you walked within it,' he whispered, his voice nearly drowned by the discordant song of the broken rails. 'It may extend too far in space and time to be as easily altered as you think it is. The power that would bring about its end may not exist at all, and if it does, it may be greater than any petty tribal godling could imagine. You may do well to fear, in spite of what you are.'

'Perhaps,' she said, scrupulously careful in her hesitation. 'But magnitude is like beauty, contained in the eye of the beholder, and I have yet to be convinced that I cannot stop the stars in their courses, and bring them raining down upon the earth, if I so choose. There are those among you who devoutly desire an end – and if that is what they ask of their gods, why should I not provide it?'

But even as she spoke, Lydyard saw something strange through Adam Grey's eyes. When the morning sun was suddenly exposed by the shifting clouds, there sprang into being behind the Sphinx's head a curious shadow, like a predatory spider lying in wait for its prey.

And though Lydyard tried to shout a warning through Adam Grey's reluctant lips, he could not do it, but fell instead into a web of dazzling light and all-consuming fire.

16

*H*e was in Hell, and he was Satan, *raging against the ignominy of his confinement, raging against the cruelty of God and the indolence*

*of man, raging against the hot lava which bubbled up beneath him
and scorched his incorruptible flesh, which could not wither or
blacken or decay, and whose immortality condemned him to pain
for all eternity.*

*The world was no longer visible above him, nor was his right hand
free, nor did the eagles circle about him in the fire-filled sky, for this
was the night of time, lit only by the eruptions beneath him, and he
was crucified by circumstance and sin, helpless to rewrite the scroll
of history despite the fact that nothing existed which could not be
remade, and nothing had ever happened which could not be erased.*

*He raged against the nails which were driven through his palms,
straining to tear himself away from them, even if it should leave
such gaping wounds in his hands that they would take a thousand years to heal. Heal they would, for he was an angel and
not a mortal being; and knowing that, he knew also that he could
change himself, if only he knew the way . . . could free himself,
if only he had the trick of it . . . could redeem himself if only
. . .*

Light faded to darkness, and agony to mere pain, and yet he
was not free of Hell, but only taken to another part of it,
which was not better but in its cunning way much worse.

He could hear the rats, and the stench of decay was so fierce
in his nostrils that he could almost believe himself dead and
putrefying where he lay. He moved his lips and his sluggish
thoughts as if to form a prayer, but then . . .

Fiat lux, said something – a whisper in the walls of his
dungeon; a voice from nowhere.

And there was light: magical, miraculous light.

There was also a small boy, like a fair-haired angel, carrying
an image of the world in the crook of his frail right arm. The
world was alight with silver radiance.

The good angel reached out with the fingers of his left hand,
and brushed the cords which held Lydyard's wrists, which
promptly fell away without any necessity that they should be
cut or unravelled.

And then the good angel held out the world to him, so that

he might touch it at last, and have that chance to redeem it for which he had yearned so long.

Lydyard took the mirror which held the world in both his hands, ignoring the blood which ran from his wrists, and stared deep into the magical light which flooded from the frame, as if to seek his own reflection within its depths.

For the merest instant the light flickered, as if fading and dying, but then it flared up again as brightly as ever.

'I can do it,' he whispered. 'I have stolen the light of the gods, and it is mine to command.'

The child said: 'Who are you?'

He answered: 'I am Lucifer Prometheus, who tempted cold-souled man with enlightenment and fire, and was blamed for all the punishments which men have suffered in consequence of the destiny which was written for them in the tides of change.'

He was not surprised at all when the angel said: 'My name is Gabriel.'

But then the illusion collapsed, for what the child said next was: 'Are you a werewolf?'

Lydyard swallowed suddenly, and discovered a nasty lump in his throat and a vile taste in his mouth.

'What kind of light is this?' he asked, desperately puzzled by the glowing object which he held. Then the light did begin to die, as his consciousness of its impossibility obliterated the effulgence.

The child took the light-source back again, and hugged it to his chest to save the dying radiance and make it bright again. The darkness returned, but only for an instant.

'You didn't have to let it die,' said the boy, in a vexed tone. 'You could make it glow; you saw that you could. I can do a lot more, not just with the mirror. Even the glass in the window and the dust on the rug. I can see, and I *do* have the power to change things. I began with the little things: the woodlice and the spiders – but that was only the beginning. I belong to the Other kind, like Mandorla . . . like you.'

'Not I,' said Lydyard, in a whisper. 'I was only a man, until

I was bitten by the snake. It was the serpent which was Satan in disguise. The demon isn't me, not even part of me. I want to be rid of it. I want to be a man again, blinded by merciful comforts.'

'I thought the same, at first,' said Gabriel, matter-of-factly. 'But it isn't a demon at all. It's only me. It's what I am.'

It was only then that the last vestiges of Lydyard's confusion finally fell away, and he realized belatedly who it was that he was looking at.

'You're Gabriel Gill!' he said.

'Who tied you up?' asked Gabriel. 'Was it Amalax?'

'Yes,' said Lydyard, gruffly. Suffused with new hope now that some of his bonds had been loosed, he said: 'Where are we, Gabriel? Can you take me out of here?'

'I can see with Amalax's eyes,' said Gabriel. 'I could see with Teresa's too, and just for a few moments Mandorla let me see with hers, when she turned into a wolf. It wasn't until then that I understood what Morwenna had tried to tell me.

'They have joy, you see, and we don't. No one does, except them. Teresa could fly, and see Heaven, but she had to hurt herself so badly . . . like Mr Harkender. Pain's different for me, but I don't have joy, not really . . . not yet. But when I learn how to turn myself into a wolf, I'll be a wolf for ever, and I'll help Morwenna and Mandorla to be wolves for ever too.'

'Who's Teresa?' asked Lydyard, utterly confused by this torrent of speech.

'One of the Sisters. They think she's a saint, because she can fly and talk to Jesus. She called me Satan, but I'm not.'

'No,' said Lydyard, wondering now what he could possibly say to the boy to cut through this knot of bewilderment. After a pause, he said: 'They're not your friends, Gabriel. Whatever she's told you, Mandorla's not your friend. She'll hurt you the way she wants to hurt me. Help me, Gabriel, and I'll help you. Get me out of here, and— '

He stopped suddenly, and looked up. The bright light which the boy nursed in his arms had dazzled him, and despite the

lighted candle which the shadowed figure in the doorway held,
Lydyard had not seen him arrive. It was Amalax, as huge and
obese as ever. How long he had been standing there Lydyard
could not tell.

Gabriel turned, and moved the mirror so that its radiance
bathed the eavesdropper. Lydyard could see the man quite
clearly, all the more dreadful in his lighted ugliness.

'You should not be here, Gabriel,' said Amalax, in a tone
whose kindly concern sounded hollow and false.

'I can go wherever I want,' replied Gabriel, calmly.

'Mandorla would not like you to be here,' said the other,
seemingly unperturbed by the child's insolence. 'If she knew
that you were here, she would be angry. You must go to your
room, and leave this man to me.'

'He's thirsty,' said Gabriel, 'and his feet are hurt. He was
alone in the dark, with the rats.'

'Gabriel,' said Amalax, steadily, 'you must try to be a good
boy. Mandorla will come down here soon, and she will be
angry if she finds you here. Please go to your room, and
let me look after this man. I will leave this candle by his
bed, and will bring him more water. The rats won't hurt
him.'

'I don't have to be a good boy any more,' said Gabriel, in
an oddly self-satisfied tone. 'I never had to – I just didn't
know that I didn't have to. You can't hurt me, Mr Amalax.
You daren't even try.'

'I don't want to hurt you,' said Amalax, stubbornly – though
it was obvious to Lydyard that what Gabriel said was true. 'No
one wants to hurt you. But this man is your enemy. He wants
to take you away, and that would be bad for everyone. Please
leave him to me.'

'I'm no one's enemy,' Lydyard said. 'Gabriel, try to see with
my eyes, as you have seen with this man's. I know what you
can do, and I want you to know all that I know. I want you
to know everything. I don't know if you can understand, but
I want you to see. You don't have to stay here – don't worry
about leaving me. But you must try to see with my eyes, so

that you will know better what the world is really like, and who your true friends are.'

'Shut up,' said Amalax, harshly. 'Let the boy alone.' But it was a futile gesture, and Amalax knew it as well as Lydyard did. Gabriel looked into Amalax's eyes, and then into Lydyard's, measuring and calculating with an intelligence which belied his childish appearance. Lydyard nodded, to encourage the boy.

Gabriel nodded in his turn, then condescended to go up the steps to the door where Amalax waited. The big man drew aside to let him pass, but as he went by Gabriel looked up in such a way as to make it clear that his was no mere act of obedience, and that he was his own master.

When he had gone, Lydyard lay back on the bed, and did not resist when Amalax came down to tie his hands again.

'She cannot keep him,' said Lydyard, as Amalax turned to go, after replacing the extinguished candle on the table with the other one as he had promised. 'He is too powerful – and he sees too clearly now to be hoodwinked for long. Whatever you hoped to gain by playing lackey to the werewolves, you will be disappointed. You are in great danger, and would do well to let me go.'

'Oh, no,' said Amalax, looking slyly back at his captive. 'You are too precious for that. Remember how the rats flooded into the cellar to seek you out! You might even be bait for direr beasts than that – for a werewolf who is traitor to his kin, let us say. And while you wait for him, Mandorla is curious to hear about your dreams.'

Lydyard forced a smile. 'You dare not even dream of the beasts which I might bring,' he said, in a tone as softly menacing as he could achieve. 'For I have a part of the Sphinx's soul twinned with mine, and with that power I can summon the Sphinx – and perhaps the spider too – and though it may be Mandorla's dearest wish to contrive a violent meeting between them, I doubt that she has told you what that would involve. She has paid you with promises of power, but she intends the annihilation of all your kind, and all your petty gains will return to dust and ashes if she has her way.'

'And would you save the world of men, if I let you go?' sneered Amalax. 'Could you defeat the werewolves, and these others of which you speak? What power do you have, to make better promises than those I have received?'

What power indeed? thought Lydyard.

But what he said to Amalax was: 'I have seen through your eyes, Caleb Amalax, and so has the boy. He and I know your most fervent hopes and most secret fears, far better than Mandorla can. You know well enough that you are a pawn, likely to be sacrificed without a thought – and I assure you that if there is any hope at all, for you or any of us, it lies with Pelorus and not with Mandorla.'

Amalax spat contemptuously upon the cold floor. Lydyard knew, without requiring to see through Amalax's eyes, that the gesture was a poor substitute for a reasoned answer; but he knew also that Amalax dared not turn against the werewolves. He was far too fond of the loathsome flesh on his bones to tempt them with any act of treason.

'Go then,' said Lydyard. 'Go to your doom, like all the other fools she has englamoured with her prettiness.'

But his final words were drowned by the sound of a sudden volley of shots.

'Pelorus!' he shouted – and though he could not for the life of him understand why, the name brought tears of joy to his eyes. *You are not alone,* he said to himself, as Tallentyre and Pelorus had earlier said to him. It seemed that he was not, after all, to be surrendered to Mandorla's malevolence.

More shots rang out, and through the floorboards Lydyard heard the sound of cries, both anguished and angry. He saw Amalax look up, and with triumph in his heart he saw the big man turn pale and hesitate.

He is a coward after all! thought Lydyard. *The fear is surging through him like acid in his veins. Already he is thinking of flight, of escape!*

'Free me!' said Lydyard, urgently. 'Free me now, and I will do what I can to see that you do not die. Free me, or you are doomed!' He had not time, he knew, for reasoned argument. He had to hope that pure melodrama would win the moment.

It did not. Amalax made no move in any direction, neither towards the stairs nor towards the bed, but simply stood where he was, content to wait. From a sheath at his belt he took the blade which he had earlier held to Lydyard's throat. It gleamed in the candlelight, more like a flaming sword than a dagger. Lydyard could imagine the single thought which possessed the giant's mind – the determination to wait until the shooting was over and done.

Lydyard and Amalax both looked at the door which Gabriel had left ajar, direly anxious to know who would come through it.

They had not long to wait; it was Mandorla.

Lydyard heard Amalax's grunt of satisfaction, but heard it also change into a squeal of rage. Mandorla stood at the head of the stair for just an instant before she was thrown down from behind, and she did not tumble down the steps but over the unrailed edge, to fall like a stone to the filthy floor.

Lydyard could see the expression of her handsome face as she fell, which was fury unalloyed – until the moment of her landing, when it turned abruptly to hurt and humiliation and bitter hate.

She was not hurt; even in human form, encumbered by clothing, she knew how to fall. She came swiftly about into a curious crouch, tensed like the predatory beast she was, but she did not launch herself at the person who had pushed her, and simply made herself ready for the threatened spring. She dared not do more, for the figure at the top of the stair was brandishing a gun: an American revolver like Lydyard's own.

It was Pelorus: blue-eyed Pelorus, who had come as bravely as a wolf into the den where his enemies lay in wait.

'Thank God!' said Lydyard, aloud.

But Pelorus, having closed the door behind him, had paused where he was, looking first at Mandorla and then at Amalax, as if he did not know where to point his gun.

'He has but one shot left,' whispered Mandorla, in a voice which was breathless with urgent concern. 'He dare not kill you, Caleb, or he is doomed. The others are waiting, and there is no way out.' To Pelorus, she said: 'Throw down the gun, dear heart. You have done what the will of Machalalel commanded you to do, and you have failed. You are free now to do what your secret self desires. Throw down the gun, and I promise you peaceful sleep. Fire, and I swear that I will do what I can to ensure that you never wake again, until the crack of doom is sounded!'

There is no time for reason, thought Lydyard, *and she must hope as I did that melodrama will suffice.*

Pelorus was stilled by indecision, and his startling gaze went first to Lydyard, then to Amalax, and came finally to rest upon his wicked cousin.

'If I fire,' he said, 'then I will fire at you, Mandorla. Amalax must cut the boy free, and he and I must be allowed to leave – for if you will not let us go, you must go to sleep, for a hundred or a thousand years. Let us go, and you might have your chance to sway the Sphinx – prevent us, and you will wake into a very different world.'

Mandorla laughed, but she darted an anxious glance at Amalax, to make sure that he had not moved. The fat man stood as still as he had since the first shot was fired.

'Perris is beyond the door,' said Mandorla. 'Siri and Suarra too. I doubt that you hurt Arian badly enough to make him sleep, and you were not wise to shoot Morwenna, for Gabriel likes her very much – and if Gabriel cares to punish you, you might truly learn what it is to suffer pain. Give it up, Pelorus. *Give it up!*'

Pelorus only smiled, but the smile was grim and very anxious. 'Cut Lydyard loose!' he commanded.

Amalax made no move to obey.

Pelorus pointed the revolver at Amalax's head, and said: 'Well then, if I am lost, there is one I may shoot who cannot rise again. *Cut Lydyard loose!*'

Lydyard could see that one shot was far too little for an

effective threat. No doubt the manwolf had more bullets in his coat, but he had not time to break the gun and put them in – Mandorla would be at him in a trice. Amalax, alas, could see it too, and he did not move.

And while the fat man stood where he was, Lydyard knew, there was a stalemate which could only be broken by some outside force.

Sphinx! he said, with a silent fervour which would not admit to the absurdity of the prayer. *Sphinx, if you can hear me now, I pray that you will come to save your servant!*

But there was only silence, only deadlock.

Then Caleb Amalax reached up reflexively with his free hand, to brush something away from his hairless pate. Lydyard could not see what it was, but even in the dim candlelight he saw that something else dropped from the wooden rafters as soon as the pass of the hand was complete, and then something else . . .

Amalax looked up, then came to pick up the candle again, so that he might see what it was that was falling. While he held it up, his other hand brushed away at his head, despite that the gesture was made clumsily ineffective by the knife which he held. The fat man frowned in obvious puzzlement, unable to see anything lurking among the shadowed beams which should not have been there.

All that Lydyard could see from where he lay was a host of grimy cobwebs.

Then another little spider dropped from the shadows on to Amalax's bloated head, and another, and another . . .

Even Mandorla gasped in alarm.

Amalax ducked, then moved quickly sideways, but it did no good. The spiders continued to drop from above on to his head and his shoulders.

The big man dropped the candle-tray, but it fell the right way up, and though the flame fluttered and flickered it did not die. By its light Lydyard saw that Amalax was now the centre of a veritable deluge of spiders – thousands of them. Not one of them was bigger than a fingernail, but there were so many that they covered his expansive form completely, clinging to his flesh and his clothing no matter how hard he tried to brush them off.

Amalax screamed in terror and desperation.

Lydyard knew that the spiders could not possibly have been hiding in the rafters. He knew that they were not falling from the ceiling of the cellar, but from somewhere else entirely – unless they were being created for the first time out of the substance of the shadow, produced from thin air to form a living cataract.

Had the Sphinx answered his prayer? Or was this the work of that other fallen angel – Harkender's master – which had such a strange affection for the power which arachnids had to horrify mankind?

As Amalax screamed again, Lydyard was possessed by wild and cruel laughter. He was exultant with the discomfort of his enemy, enraptured by the sound of anguish and terror.

But then he realized that the spiders which could not cling to Amalax were flooding the floor of the cellar, spreading out in all directions like a great dark stain, and remembered that his own hands and feet were tied.

Mandorla came to her feet and backed away. Pelorus stood as still as if he had been turned to stone, his weapon useless in his hand.

Amalax was nothing now but a great silhouette, so blackened by the awful deluge that the creatures which continued to fall from nowhere had nothing to which they could cling. They rained instead upon the floor, which was by now alive from wall to wall, and though Lydyard huddled up as best he could, the crawling creatures were already swarming on the mattress, and upon his body.

They did not sting or bite, but the touch of their scurrying legs on his body filled him with repulsion and dismay.

He heard Mandorla cry out, howling like the wolf she was.

Knowing that there was no escape, that Hell was all about him once again, and no less dreadful than before, Lydyard closed his eyes and tore with all his might at the iron rail to which his prisoned hands were tied, knowing at last that the only freedom there was, the only freedom that there could ever be, was the freedom of pain and vision, the freedom of flight into the infinite reaches of time and space and possibility, into the world of the playful gods.

If only I may hurt, he cried out to himself in silence. *If only I can drown myself in pain . . .*

The Act of Creation

And I gave my heart to know wisdom and to know madness and folly: I perceived that this also is vexation of spirit.

For in much wisdom is much grief: and he that increaseth knowledge increaseth sorrow.

Ecclesiastes I: xvii–xviii

1

When I have cast away all that is known to me by hearsay, rumour, and report, I soon discover myself confronting the proposition that all I properly and truly know is what I have apprehended through the medium of my senses. It is true that I know of instances where my senses have been deceived, so as to lead me into error; but it seems also to be true that there are many things which I see whose existence and nature I need not doubt. But when I ask myself what these things are which I cannot and need not doubt I cannot help but think of dreams, when I have seen very similar things, and thought them real, when all the while my experience was mere illusion. How can I know *now* that this is not a dream, from which I might eventually awake? How can I know that what I call wakefulness is not a condition very like a dream, in which all that I seem to see is merely a product of mind, which has only the appearance of reality?

If there is a God, who could create the world and determine all its contents and its laws, then that same God must surely have the power to shape my dream, and the deception which leads me to mistake my dream for reality. If I then argue that God is good, and would not thus deceive me, how can I counter the argument in reply which says, perhaps it is good that I should be deceived, and believe that the world is as it appears, although it is really otherwise? Is goodness necessarily served by truth? And even if it were so that the truth is necessarily good, would it follow necessarily that my *knowing* the truth would be good also?

*

If I am to serve my purpose honestly I must dare to suppose that in place of that God which is the fountain of truth there is instead a genius both powerful and deceitful, which has indeed determined that the heavens and the earth which I perceive, and all their colours, shapes, and sounds, are naught but illusions and dreams intended to entrap my credulity. If this were so, then what would I be – for I could be no longer a thing of flesh and blood and sense and thought? I would be a dreamer, for sure, but what that dreamer might in reality be, if beheld by another eye, I could not tell at all. I need not doubt my own existence, for even in this nightmare there must be a doubter whose doubts are guarantee of it – but what am I, who doubts? What is the world like, which contains this doubter?

One thing is certain, and it is this: that against the argument that this genius of deception may indeed stand in place of the honest God in which we prefer to believe, there is no defence. If his was the Act of Creation which shaped the world, and his the whim which might at any moment reshape it, then we have no way to know it. If the world is a lie, it is an impenetrable lie, and if doubt carries us to the extreme that we doubt the existence of an honest God, then we must find ourselves devoid of any anchorage within the landscapes of Creation, for we *cannot* know where or what we are, and all our discoveries are futile. And if I should ask myself, *Can I be content to live in such a world?* what answer can I give, but to say that where there is doubt, there must also be trust, and that if that trust be false, are we not lost?

I can have no faith in an honest God, *even if I am to suppose him good*, save for that which is based in hope. If that hope is misplaced which dares to assert that the world which I see must be the world which is, then the truth is something which I can never know. Even if some miraculous gift of revelation were to show me the world as it really is, if that is other than it appears to be, I could never know whether what I had seen was true or not.

If my senses deceive me – and I have no warranty but hope that they do not – then I am adrift in a wilderness of possibility where truth is indistinguishable from delusion. For that reason, if for no other, I must cling to hope, for I cannot bear to live in such a world of deceit, and I cannot bear to contemplate the God which would require it of me.

Hope and hope alone reserves Acts of Creation to a good God; for if there be others capable of such Acts the world must be their battleground, and while they contend for mastery of its form and nature there is nothing which can finally be known, and nothing which can finally be done.

René Descartes, *The Suppressed Meditations*, written c. 1640; first published in 1872

2

Of the Creation of the world even Machalalel knew nothing. No being can have a memory of the moment of its own origin; consciousness develops by degrees, and those who have the power of Creation, like those who have not, must begin life as innocents. Machalalel instructed those whom he made as carefully as he could, but he could only describe the world as he found it, for his own maker had not played the father to him, as Machalalel chose to do for his own creatures.

It appeared to Machalalel that the world in which he found himself was young, and that the Golden Age was the childhood of the universe: a time when there was an abundance of naïvety and wondrous discovery in place of wisdom and confirmed belief, when there was an infinite zest for play and an impatience with dogged toil. And yet, for all its growth and hope of becoming ever finer, there were already signs of decay.

There is an analogy to be drawn here with the life of a human being. Men begin to die before they are born and before they can know that they exist, and they continue to die while they grow and thrive – and the process of becoming by which they emerge as whole and coherent beings is always in the end interrupted by death without being properly finished. As above, so below – the macrocosm of the universe is mirrored in the microcosm of man.

When Machalalel discovered what manner of being he was there were many Creators in the world who were reckless in dispersing their power, caring not at all that in the processes of Creation they were using themselves up, becoming always less. These were the true shapers of the world, for it was their fecundity which filled it and determined its variety. But there were others who had ceased to be reckless, being afraid of how they might be affected by the processes of becoming which had been set in train.

Already, in Machalalel's time, some of those Creators who elected to hoard their power had begun to work for its increase, discovering ways to usurp the power of lesser beings. These few became not merely avoiders of change but stealers of change, predators of power.

There was conflict and strife, even in the Age of Gold – and this conflict and strife was gradually increased, throughout that later age which Machalalel did not live to see, and which I have called the Age of Heroes. When that age came to its conclusion, to be followed by the Age of Iron, the day of the fecund Creators was gone, but the conflict and strife could not end, for the predatory Creators were still enemies, each of every other, and while the warm-souled not-men dwindled in numbers, and were driven into hiding, the Creators which had been anxious to destroy them inevitably turned their covetous attentions to one another. They too were forced into hiding, but they made their places of concealment into strongholds and traps.

It might appear at first sight that human beings would be of little interest to the predatory Creators, having no warmth in their souls or creative power of their own, and thus have nothing to fear from them. This is not so, as the true history of the world demonstrates.

On the one hand, the predatory Creators have frequently taken men to be instruments of their own schemes; they have used and manipulated various tribes of men by means of petty and inexpensive exercises of their power, in order that men would help them in hunting down and delivering as sacrifices the warm-souled not-men. On the other hand, some predatory Creators have come to believe that in the nature and fortunes of man can be seen the intentional hand of the ultimate Creator, whether or not that ultimate Creator still exists – for men are the epitome of Created beings which have not themselves the power of Creation, and must therefore be regarded as some kind of end-product.

Machalalel realized this before any other, and foresaw even amid the splendours of the Age of Gold that men would ultimately become the principal inhabitants of the earth, and that the universe would change in such a way as to reflect the nature of their being. (As below; so above.) It was for this reason that Machalalel made men the special objects of his study, and attempted to simulate the Act of Creation by which they were shaped.

There can be no doubt, as we approach the climax of the Age of Iron, that Machalalel was right. Men have some crucial role to play in that fundamental process of becoming which shapes the evolution of the universe, and which will bring it in the end from the infancy of the Age of Gold to a maturity which we cannot as yet imagine.

I believe that this fourth and last chapter in the history of the world will soon begin, and that its dawn can be found in what men themselves have variously called their Age of Enlightenment or Age of Reason – which latter title I do not hesitate to borrow. This Age, it seems to me, will see the final end of that Creative power – which men now call magic and miracle, and in which they have almost ceased to believe – which was so prolific in its effects in earlier

Ages. It will see instead the triumph of a new form of power, based in knowledge and the practical arts, which we may call 'technics', and whose progress has made very rapid strides in these last hundred years. The mathematical and mechanical arts will become the means by which men may transform and perfect their own nature – and though such arts have no power to work upon the universe as a whole, my belief is that they are not on that account to be despised.

The men who surround me now, in Revolutionary France, are already full of optimism for this new era, and are determined to give it birth. The writing of this book is my own expression of faith in their ideals – or, least, of *hope* for their ideals.

I can only have hope where they have faith because I know the true history of the world as well as the deceptive history which the world's appearances have preserved. I know that the predatory Creators still exist, and that their work goes patiently on. Some are content to sleep; others are ever anxious to observe; no one knows their number. Perhaps, in spite of all that they have tried to do, they are doomed, and will discover if ever they try to exercise the power which they have so carefully conserved that all their schemes will be thwarted. I hope, fervently, that this will be the case; the world would be very well served if, when these misers finally went to their hoards, they found naught but the dry dust of impotence in place of that fecundity which they hope to save from the Age of Gold. But while I hope, I cannot help but fear, for I know these beings are still there, waiting in their strongholds, confident that when the time is right, the world will be theirs to do with as they will.

Lucian de Terre, *The True History of the World*, 1789

3

Dear Sir Edward

I was deeply distressed by your account of the invasion of your house and the seizure of David Lydyard. I quite understand that you will now be unable to accompany Gilbert Franklin to Charnley as we had previously arranged; I also understand and sympathize with your urgent desire to remove your daughter from London in the wake of such a terrible experience. My wife and I will of course be glad to receive her, and you may be sure that she shall have all the rest which she needs in order to recover from her ordeal. I quite agree that it is best that she should be shielded from the unpleasant aspects of this unhappy affair and you may be assured that Gilbert and I will not discuss the matter in her company.

No doubt we will have another opportunity to meet when all this is over, but in view of the present circumstances I have thought it best to set aside the reservations which earlier made me reluctant to commit the following information to paper. The man has, after all, been dead for some years now, and I know that I can trust you to maintain the confidentiality of the information. In a letter of this kind I can only record the barest essentials of the case, but I believe that I may still contrive to give you an adequate picture of the man who was known to me as Adam Clay, and of the paradoxical aspects of his mental condition.

I first met Adam Clay in 1859, when he was brought to me by bailiffs acting under the instructions of a magistrate. He had been arrested during a scuffle in front of Newgate Prison, which happened on the occasion of the execution of

William Barlow. Barlow had, in earlier days, been a notorious radical and prominent Chartist whose activities had more than once led to imprisonment, but he had since fallen on hard times. The murder of which Barlow had been convicted was not a political one, but his execution had nevertheless drawn a larger crowd than was usual, including many men who had know him in his prime. Apparently, the crowd became disorderly when the hangman Calcraft found it necessary to go below the gallows to 'steady Barlow's legs' – i.e. to add his own weight to his victim's, in the interests of hastening his demise. Calcraft was notorious as a 'short drop man', who rarely succeeded in bringing his charges to a swift end.

Clay told me that he and others were merely protesting at Calcraft's horrid ineptness, but that the police misconstrued their behaviour as an attempt to seize Barlow, in the hope of bearing him away. In the ensuing mêlée Clay was knocked silly by a policeman's baton, and his subsequent ravings while in police custody convinced those holding him that he was quite mad. What the police said in evidence convinced the magistrate likewise – for Clay, though evidently a much younger man than Barlow, claimed to have known him since the 1830s, and spoke extravagantly and intensely about his supposed experiences in Paris during the Terror which followed the revolution of 1789. By the time he was brought before the magistrate he was quite calm again, but refused to give his address or any further account of himself save for the name by which I knew him.

Clay was initially brought to Hanwell, where I was serving as an assistant and pursuing my research, as I still do today. He was presented to me as a puzzling and problematic case. When I first saw him he seemed far from irrational – though very listless and decidedly melancholic – and I hesitated to commit him to the wards (where conditions were then somewhat worse than they are today). Faced with my reluctance, and clearly not enamoured of the prospect of such a committal, he told me that although he was not prepared to say where he had lived he could obtain money by writing a letter to his solicitors. I invited him to do so. When the money duly arrived, I offered to bring him here to Charnley Hall, where I have sometimes accommodated patients whose cases interested me particularly.

When I questioned Clay about the statements which he had allegedly made to the police he was at first guarded, but eventually agreed that he had made them, and reiterated his claim that they were true. He was, he said, very much older than he seemed, and had indeed been in Paris during the Revolution, where he had written a book which he caused to be printed in England. He suggested that if I desired to know the full story of his life I need only consult the book, which was called *The True History of the World*, and to which he had attached the name 'Lucian de Terre'.

At first I was inclined to doubt the existence of this book, of which I had never heard, but on one of my frequent excursions to London I took the trouble to call at the Reading Room of the British Museum, where I discovered that it did exist. I read the first of its four volumes there and then, and found it to be the most fantastic tale which I had ever encountered. I never read the remainder, though my subsequent discussions with Adam Clay must have duplicated much of the information therein.

My initial impression of Clay was that his true problem was his deep melancholy, which approximated to that sinful despair which the men of the Middle Ages knew as *accidie*. He was at odds with the world, which he had come to see as a dark and hateful place, fuller of misery than it had any need or right to be. It seemed to me that Clay's delusions were a curious product of this despair, invented as though to justify it. When I discovered the nature of *The True History of the World* I was quickly convinced that he must have read the book at some time, and that his imagination had been so powerfully seized by its contents that he had cast aside his real name and all that went with it, borrowing instead a new identity from the text. He had become – in his own mind – the central character and notional author of the story: a man moulded out of clay by some quasi-Promethean creator in the very distant past.

I did not think it important to read the rest of the book because my project, as I saw it then, was to use reasoning to force my patient to see that in fact he was not and could not be the character featured in the narrative (who was, I assumed, intended by the true author to be an allegorical figure of some kind). At the same time, I sought to persuade him that the world was not by any means as dark as he imagined, and that there was cause enough for optimism. I believed that if I could only break through the wall of melancholy with which he had surrounded himself, and weaken his delusion, then he would feel free to recover his true name and his true place in the world. Alas for my optimism that I might achieve this end by my cleverness, the man proved more intransigent than I had hoped.

In the course of the three years which he spent at Charnley Adam Clay became very friendly. He seemed to like me a good deal, and I liked him. I believe that of all the delusions I have ever encountered, his was the most intriguing, the most extravagant and the most impregnable to argument. Unlike most of the unfortunates who suffer from a deranged view of the world, he quickly lost any reluctance to discuss and debate the truth of his assertions. He never became confused or stubbornly silent, even in the face of argumentative strategies which I considered clever and damning; an observer at one of our later consultations might have thought that he was studying my view of the world as ardently as I was studying his, struggling just as mightily to understand it while never for an instant being prepared to concede that it could be true. He read the books in my library, including books on madness, medicine, philosophy, and science, and would happily debate their contents with me, always interpreting them in the light of his remarkable idiosyncrasy.

In the end, I was forced to conclude that I could never break down Clay's arguments by reason, because they were wholly and very efficiently sheltered from rational criticism. He was adamant that the world is constantly changing its fundamental nature, and that the history implied by contemporary evidence is no more than an appearance. Our memories, he claimed, are so fallible as to be open to constant reconstruction, and so are our printed texts. Some of the texts which survive from the distant past, he said, bear the names of men who never existed, while many authors who wrote important texts have vanished entirely from our ken. Even those texts which were written by actual men may no longer reproduce what was originally written by them.

When I told him that I could not believe in such an ordered process of corruption and reconstruction, which would surely involve the most painstaking effort by some godlike but malicious being, he merely replied that this was a failure of my capacity for belief, and that there were indeed such beings engaged in exactly that work.

The case gave me some pain at the time, for I felt it to be a terrible injustice that such an intelligent man should so completely lose his sense of the absurdity of his claims. What kind of a Creator, I once asked myself, would mould mankind into such an image that madness could be possible at all?

I felt a certain despair myself when, after more than three years in my care, Adam Clay informed me that he had decided to die. He requested me most earnestly not to mourn him, and assured me that although he would be dead so far as I or any man could judge, still he would return to life in another time – when, he said, the Age of Iron would hopefully have come to its allotted end, and men were at last ready to give birth to the Age of Reason. He did no violence to himself, but after having made his decision his health declined very swiftly, and though I called upon Franklin for his help our attentions were to no avail. Clay's heart failed within the week.

Although I contacted the solicitors through whose offices he had obtained money for his keep, they were unable to assist me in determining what his real name had been, or in tracing any relatives. In the end I had him interred in the vault in the grounds of the Hall, to which the bones of many

Charnleys and Austens have been consigned in the course of several centuries.

During his years at Charnley Clay had but a single visitor, who gave his name as Paul Shepherd. When I first met the young man I made every effort to enlist his help in my efforts to persuade Clay of the falseness of his delusions, but Shepherd politely declined. Clay was his friend, he said, and he could not enter into any conspiracy against him. It soon became clear to me that Shepherd was, in fact, inclined to collaborate with Clay in his delusion. When I discovered this I was moved to forbid any further visits, on the grounds that it was intolerable that my efforts should be undermined in this fashion, but Clay persuaded me to relent.

Though Clay was inclined to be as discreet in regard to Shepherd as Shepherd was in regard to Clay I was eventually able to deduce that Clay believed his friend to be the person who bears in *The True History of the World* the name of Pelorus. This Pelorus is said in the book to have been made by the same Creator as the man formed out of clay, and to be one of a number of quasi-human beings fashioned from a pack of wolves.

At the time, I was inclined to believe that Shepherd was merely humouring Adam Clay in accepting this allotted role in his fabulations. I am, however, perfectly prepared to accept your judgement that I was wrong, and that your Paul Shepherd – who must, I think, be the same man in spite of his apparent youth – really does share Clay's delusion in the fullest possible measure. I am now sorry that I did not trouble to read the three remaining volumes of de Terre's *The True History of the World*; if I had, I might conceivably have discovered why it is sufficiently powerful to persuade more than one man to adopt its ideas for their own.

If there really is a group of men and women who sincerely declare themselves to be the werewolves of London I should be most interested to meet them, and to observe their metamorphoses. Even were I to be granted such a favour, though, I would be forced to remain sceptical about the true nature and extent of their powers; in the course of my career I have learned a healthy respect for the force of suggestion, whether or not it is augmented by what is nowadays called hypnotism. To accept the reality of werewolves (even mad werewolves deluded about their own nature and history) one would not necessarily be required to throw overboard the whole of our present scientific understanding of the world, but I am sure you will agree with me that belief is best amended by minimal degrees whenever we attempt to come to terms with the formerly incredible.

On the other hand, if the Creator of the world must be credited with that power and malice which allows men to go mad, and which steals away their rightful sense of the absurd, might he not equally well be credited with the power and malice to make *all* men mad, and to impose upon them a sense of the absurd whose real purpose is to make the truth unbelievable?

I do hope that these notes – vague and unresolved as they are – may be of some small use to you in pursuit of the solution of your puzzle, and I look forward to hearing a full account of your adventure when you have at last contrived to bring it to a satisfactory conclusion.

Yours very sincerely,
James Austen

PART FOUR

The Anger and Innocence of Angels

The Gateway to the city of Doom. Through me
The entrance to the Everlasting Pain.
The Gateway of the Lost. The Eternal Three
Justice impelled to build me. Here ye see
Wisdom Supreme at work, and Primal Power,
And Love Supernal in their dawnless day.
Ere from their thought creation rose in flower
Eternal first were all things fixed as they.
Of Increate Power infinite formed am I
That deathless as themselves I do not die.
Justice divine hath weighed: the doom is clear.
All hope renounce, ye lost, who enter here.

Dante Alighieri, *The Inferno*

1

Lydyard's soul was entirely possessed by the urge to escape and the desire to be safe, but safety was not to be found in any mere retreat into the world of dreams; he knew that there was no safety in the tempest of fire and fury which was Satan's Hell, nor in the cave where the gods cast their playful shadows on the firelit wall. His determination was, as it had to be, to flee much further than that, to seek the ultimate secrecy of nowhere and nowhen, to lose himself in the labyrinthine folds of time and space and potentiality.

And so, therefore he lost himself.

He sought and found confusion; he brought himself to the outside of existence, detaching himself from the warp and weft of appearance. He made of himself the merest of phantoms, and still he was forced to flee as fast as he might; to run, to fly . . .

For a long time, there was nothing to be seen but shadows, and nothing to be heard at all. While his panic lasted, he was quite disconnected from any possibility of recognizable sensation, and his panic was too powerful a thing to be easily choked. But when at last his fear did die he began again to search among the shadows for shape and semblance.

At first, his failure to discover any anchorage by which he might begin his return to sensation was by no means discomfiting, for it served to prove how completely he had succeeded in losing himself. He felt grimly glad that he was beyond the reach of sensible experience, triumphantly believing that he had thus freed himself from all possible oppressors. But it did not take long for him to realize that the ultimate escape was indistinguishable from the ultimate captivity. While he could not see and touch the actual world he could not sensibly be thought to exist at all.

The ultimate comfort of blindness, he found, was no comfort at all. It was, instead, a kind of death. In order to be, he needed to see, and in order to see, he had to place himself at the mercy of his sight, and commit himself to the care of all those Creators who vied for empery over the private and public worlds of his dreams.

Men, the Sphinx had ominously said, *should be made to face their gods, to see what cowards ignorance has made of them*.

But the Sphinx had gone on to say something far more riddlesome: that gods might be content to be what men had made of them. Was it not because of what the Creator had read in his own or Sir Edward's mind that it had accepted the form and semblance of the goddess Bast, and formed its creature as a Sphinx?

Had the gods themselves, Lydyard wondered, trod this path before him? Had they too tried, and failed, to flee the tyranny which was time and evolution, which was inside them and unreachable, as the universe itself was unreachably inside the being of that ultimate God? Was this the kind of absence which had kept them from the face of the earth since the Age of Miracles ended? And was their re-emergence now, as Spider and Sphinx, and others which were still to come, no more than the search of the defeated for reconnection – the quest which now beckoned him?

And if that were so, might not the Sphinx's riddle be inverted? Might not he ask on his own behalf: *And as for men, must we be content to be what the gods would make of us, or may we be our own Creators, commanders of our own inner sight?*

The effort of imagination failed him. Beyond the reach of fear and pain, he could feel nothing but the lostness which he had so avidly sought and the remoteness which was the only true safety.

He felt that he knew now why Adam Clay had gone to his grave as a mortal man might go to his bed, and he felt that he knew also why Mandorla Soulier and the others of her divided kind were content to bear the burden of wakefulness, in order to gamble with destiny.

But I, he thought, *am like none of these. Like Pelorus, I am the captive of an alien will whose purpose I do not know, whose ambitions I cannot trust, and for whose final victory I dare not hope.*

In spite of all his doubts, he turned away from the shadow-world beyond Creation, in order that he might begin his journey homeward. But when he tried to reach out with his mind, to see with other eyes and hear with other ears, there was at first nothing there to be grasped; it was as though the Day of Judgement had come while he had fled, and every human soul had gone to its allotted destiny in Heaven or Hell.

He recoiled inwardly from the horror of such solitude; whatever kind of ghost or angel he had now become, he only knew how to be incarnate in human form and how to answer to his human appetites. Thus was his hunger for the world made sharper; thus did he become avid for a body to contain his soul, even if it were to be a thing of dream-stuff.

And he was *not* alone. He knew it as soon as his anguish had flared into being. He found a presence of some sort, a veritable cacophony of presences. The universe was not so very far away. Hell, at least, was attainable, and also that Babel of lamenting voices which was the earth, where cold-souled men struggled to penetrate the dark mists of illusion.

For the briefest of moments he had a vision of a cellar, where he saw a man who might have been himself, asleep and peacefully dreaming. There was a misshapen candle beside his bed, and the flickering of its flame was the only movement there was. There was not a spider to be seen, nor a rat. He could hear the sound of the sleeper's even breathing. But he left the sleeper lying there, and floated away up steps of stone to a winding corridor, along which he moved until he came to a door.

The corridor was dark. The darkness was thick and deep, full of air and pregnant with unborn sound; it was the cloying darkness of the world, not the ethereal night of the shadows between the dimensions. It was a darkness which held the latent potential of light.

Fiat lux, he whispered – and waited for a golden-haired angel to come, bearing his radiant cornucopia.

No angel came, but he saw instead a hand, which appeared to glow with a dull red light of its own. The hand pushed, in a tentative and exploratory manner, met something material, and pushed harder. The hand disappeared into something that was cold, and had the texture of wood. He was taken by surprise, for the sensation was unprecedented in his experience. The hand was his, but he had never before been capable of stepping into a solid object.

He forced himself through the door and emerged on its other side, quite unharmed. Here there was light, but not the light of day, merely the dim and distant glow of gaslamps, cloaked by London fog. He could not feel the fog upon his skin, nor could his special sight penetrate its obscurity. The world from which he had been separated was all around him now, but in its own peculiar fashion it was in hiding from his eyes.

He had not the slightest idea where he was, or which direction was which, but he began to walk. He moved slowly, but patiently, and while he moved the city gradually came to life around him, as its citizens anticipated the coming dawn.

The people who passed him in the street were ghostlike. He could not hear them at all. The uncanny silence of their movement made the people seem quite unreal, although they sometimes gave evidence of their mass and solidity by brushing against him. He did not think that he was entirely without substance, but the others seemed to be hardly aware of his presence.

He was puzzled, for a while, by the fact that these ghostly others walked with more assurance than he could, but he eventually concluded that the fog must appear thicker to him than it did to them. His reconnection with the world was evidently partial.

Once, he deliberately stepped into the path of one of the looming ghosts, bracing himself against the possibility of being bowled over. Although the impact of the collision was sufficient to make the man stumble, he did not trip over Lydyard; instead he fell through him. On recovering his balance and his stride, the unlucky man looked furtively around, but went quickly on his way.

He came to a sizeable crossroads, and the streams of traffic which attempted to make their way in all four directions were here dissolved into utter chaos as the drivers of carriages, carts, vans, omnibuses, and cabs fought for space, encouraging their horses to bid for every possible advantage in the mêlée. Wherever the horses and their burdens were not there were men, women and children on foot, weaving their equally hurried way through the turmoil.

The scene seemed eerie and unreal because of its soundlessness. He knew full well what an appalling noise ought to be associated with it: the clatter of hooves and wheels; the jingling of harness; the muted thunder of footsteps; the hubbub of voices.

Lydyard shrank back from the throng, determined to stand aside from the human maelstrom, at least for a while. He felt a giddy thrill of relief at the thought that he did not belong to it, that he was of another kind. He tried to flatten himself against a brick wall, staring at the seething crowd – silent, discoloured, blurred – which was somehow the heart and soul of the world to which he had formerly belonged. He resisted the idea that he must eventually become part of it again, and he took perverse comfort from his knowledge that even if he were to throw himself into the middle of the throng he would not interrupt the movement of the crowd at all. People, horses and vehicles would simply move through him.

He shivered at the thought of it, imagining that the passing of the crowd through his ghostly body would fill him with a sensation of icy coldness, chilling his very soul. But even as he imagined it, it happened. A hurrying pedestrian who was shoving a handcart swerved to avoid another, and the cart struck him squarely from the side.

There was only the least sensation of an impact, followed

by a rush of cold wind in his soul – a sensation close enough to pain to make him wince with shock. A surge of giddiness possessed his senses, and he felt himself slipping, losing his tentative reconnection with the city to which his homing instinct had brought him.

Then, for a brief interval, he saw the face of the Sphinx imprinted upon the whirling darkness. Its great yellow eyes were luminous with love. But he saw it as though from a tremendous distance, and knew that although its incarnate self might be in London, its hot and fiery soul was somewhere else entirely.

He felt himself falling, belatedly losing his balance because of his collision with the barrow. Even as he put up his hands to save himself he realized how futile the gesture was. When his tumbling body hit the ground there was no impact at all; it was like falling into a pit of fog. He entered the bowels of the earth, and thought that he might be falling into the pit of Hell itself.

But I am not alone, he cried in anguish. *I am not alone!*

And – as if in answer to his prayer – he found that he was not.

Sir Edward Tallentyre paused for breath at the head of Shaftesbury Avenue, looking back over his shoulder at the traffic which streamed through Cambridge Circus. The very air seemed foul and alien, though the evening was cloudy and there was no trace of the fog which had spoiled the last few nights. He felt very tired, and was angry with himself for falling victim to such unreasonable exhaustion.

Lydyard, a passenger in his friend's thoughts, clung to borrowed consciousness with all the strength which he could muster, savouring the sharpness and immediacy of thought and sensation.

Tallentyre had been on the move all day, trying to find someone who had heard the name of Mandorla Soulier, and who knew where she might be found. More than once the name had struck a chord, as Tallentyre had felt sure it would if

Lydyard's description of the woman could be trusted – nothing caught the attention of the masculine sector of London Society more readily than a woman who was both exotic and enigmatic – but no one to whom he had talked knew where the woman lived, or where he might find someone who did.

His frustration was redoubled by the knowledge that he could not – dared not – be frank with those to whom he talked. Only Gilbert Franklin knew the full details of the matter in hand; with everyone else he felt compelled to be very circumspect. He could not bring himself to mention the werewolves of London, even in a sceptical fashion – not because any such statement might weaken his own reputation for sense and sanity, but because it would deter others from taking the matter seriously. He had informed the police that Lydyard had been kidnapped, and had given them Cordelia's description of the man who had seized him, but of what had happened to the man she shot – what had *appeared* to happen to the man she had shot – he had said nothing. Once a single unbelievable detail was added to the story he felt sure that the whole would become unbelievable.

He turned the corner into Greek Street, moving far more slowly than he usually did when he approached the house where Elinor Fisher was lodged. He felt an astonishing isolation, as though the world through which he moved were mysteriously different from the one which others shared. He cursed his luck and his recklessness alike, not knowing where the blame truly lay for his seduction into the magical world of second sight and shapeshifting sphinxes, of child-angels and werewolves. He felt very sharply the point which Lydyard had made; that a man who is very careful to demand exacting proofs is trapped beyond hope of recall when those proofs are given to him. Once he had been forced to admit the role which the supernatural had played in his extraordinary adventure his whole world had been turned upside down – for him anything was now possible, and he fiercely envied those who had not yet been confronted with a forceful argument to that effect.

Lydyard felt the force of Tallentyre's emotion as a perverse blast of reassurance that the world existed, and might perhaps be seized and held and made safe from those which threatened to dissolve it.

As he admitted himself to the house where Elinor lived Tallentyre glanced unthinkingly backwards, furtively checking to see whether he had been followed. As soon as he realized what he had done he cursed himself for it, and the curse was all the more forceful because his eye was briefly caught by a black-coated man who stood opposite, patiently waiting while the crowd moved around him.

There is no need for this! Lydyard heard him say to himself, sternly. *If the world is other than I thought, still I have lived in it for more than forty years, without the need to pause at every corner and jump with fear at every shadow!*

But when Elinor answered his rap upon her door, her first words were: 'Why Edward, what is the matter? I have never seen you so distraught!'

He permitted himself the luxury of having his hat and coat removed before he answered, and then was content to be curt with his explanation.

'Men broke into my house last night,' he said. 'They took David away with them by force. All day I have been trying to find a clue to his whereabouts, but I have failed.'

She was not satisfied with that, and he had to give her a fuller account – but even to her he was reluctant to mention the werewolves of London, despite that he had previously debated their existence with her in a light and unbelieving way. Lydyard was astonished to see the tenderness of Tallentyre's affection for his mistress, and how directly that affection led to concealment and deception.

'What will you do next?' she asked, when he had told her what he had said to the police, and how – after sending his daughter to Charnley to make sure that she would be safe – he had tramped around the clubs and business-houses of the city in search of anyone who might know the mysterious Mandorla Soulier.

'There is only one more thing I can do,' replied Tallentyre, 'though I hate to think of it. Charlatan or not, Jacob Harkender knows more of this affair than anyone else, and he has his own reasons for wanting to root out this gang of kidnappers. I must go to Whittenton in the morning.'

No! cried Lydyard – but while he could hear Tallentyre's internal monologue, Tallentyre was utterly deaf to his. This kind of possession did not carry with it the gift of control.

Tallentyre had already thrown himself down on the settee, and now removed his boots from his aching feet. His mistress dutifully carried them away, and returned with a bottle of whisky, and a single glass.

The baronet accepted the drink, and resisted the temptation to throw it back at a single gulp.

'Shall I have supper sent up?' asked Elinor, having divined that there was little chance of their eating out this evening.

'Not yet,' he said. 'We have time enough for that. I ought to write to Franklin, though, for I may not have the chance in the morning if I am to make an early start for Whittenton.'

'Why should anyone want to steal your friend?' she asked, pointedly. 'If they want a ransom, should they not rather have stolen your beloved daughter?'

Tallentyre was slightly surprised by the note of sarcasm in the question, though Lydyard was not. 'It appears,' he answered, drily, 'that my unlucky ward has been cursed with the gift of second sight – at least, that is what these people believe.'

'Who are *these people*?' she asked, surprised that he should speak as if he knew who had done it.

Tallentyre could see that if he continued to answer such questions, the entire story must come out, and so he hesitated. Lydyard observed that while Elinor was in some respects his trusted confidante, Tallentyre liked to keep the various aspects of his life quite separate, and well controlled. Elinor, in Tallentyre's eyes, had no part in this save to provide a temporary haven.

'In Heaven's name, Nora,' he said, 'I have had enough of it for today. Let us speak of something else, I beg you.'

He knew that she would not like that, but was nevertheless surprised by the coldness of her manner as she shrugged and turned away. He opened his mouth to say something more, but was interrupted by a knock at the door. Glad of the excuse, he cursed to illustrate his irritation.

Tallentyre felt that he did not have to instruct his mistress to get rid of the caller without delay; he assumed that she would do it as a matter of course. Lydyard was surprised – but only mildly – by the arrogance of the man. He thought, in fact, that he might have better cause to be astonished that he knew his friend so well.

Tallentyre watched Elinor go to the door, and did not take his eyes off her while she opened it. The open door prevented him from seeing the caller, and he could not hear what was said, but he frowned when he saw her stand aside to let the visitor pass.

He sat up more straightly, and set his mouth grimly – but when he saw who it was who had entered, his self-control evaporated completely, and he sprang to his feet. Lydyard did not know whether the giddiness he felt was the baronet's or his own, for he did not need the other man's thought to recognize the newcomer immediately.

'My God!' said Tallentyre. 'De Lancy!'

2

Curiously enough, even Tallentyre's amazement did not last long. Lydyard, sharing his thoughts, saw that he had crossed some threshold of the imagination which permitted no further surprise. The world had so perversely defied his hope and expectation in taking on the substance and the logic of a dream that whatever now transpired had simply to be accepted. Lydyard witnessed Tallentyre's realization that the black-coated man who had stood on the pavement opposite, watching for his arrival in Greek Street, had been the man who had vanished without a trace in the Eastern Desert, months before; he witnessed also that the realization did not seem particularly bizarre.

De Lancy made no move to disencumber himself of his hat, coat, and gloves, but simply stood still while Elinor closed the door behind him. Tallentyre found the other man's uncanny calmness puzzling, but Lydyard did not. Lydyard already knew and understood how the other was constrained.

Tallentyre took one step forward, intending to offer his hand, but suddenly thought better of it, and stood still himself.

'De Lancy?' he repeated, uncertainly.

'My name is not de Lancy,' said the other, softly. 'I am Adam Grey.'

'Adam Grey?' echoed Tallentyre, with insincere lightness. 'And why not? You are not the first man I have lately met who is the double of another. Why not, indeed? And what business have you here, Mr Grey?'

As he said this, Tallentyre glanced sideways at Elinor Fisher, who was watching him with interest, apparently determined not to intervene or to bother herself with commonplaces of courtesy which could only have seemed grotesque.

'My mistress has need of you,' answered Adam Grey, who had once been William de Lancy.

'And so has mine!' muttered Tallentyre, not quite *sotto voce*. More loudly he said: 'Who, pray, is your mistress?'

'You have met her once before,' said the other, softly. 'But she does not approach you now as she approached you then, and in sending me to do her bidding she intends to be honest with you as to what she is and of what she is capable. Lydyard is lost, and may not ever be found unless we are quick and clever. She needs to use you as she sought to use him, but she needs your willing co-operation and your fullest effort. I am here to ask you for that, Sir Edward, and to convince you of the necessity.'

Lost! thought Lydyard. *How am I lost?*

Tallentyre stared at William de Lancy, who was now Adam Grey. He felt free to be appalled by the temerity of the man, and had to suppress an impulse to laugh. But Lydyard knew that Tallentyre had taken the correct implication from de Lancy's speech. Tallentyre knew that the mistress in question was the Sphinx.

'Where is your mistress?' the baronet asked, ironically. 'Why does she send you?'

'She is near by,' answered Grey in a strange near-whisper. 'She has not our limitations, in space or in substance. She will take us away when you agree to be taken – and you will see her then, if you wish. But time is far less easy to disturb, and the net which seeks to trap us is already tightening. If you want to save Lydyard, you must give yourself willingly, and Lydyard is not the only one who may need to be saved.'

'If your mistress is a fallen angel,' said Tallentyre, 'with godlike powers at her beck and call, if she can possess you in such a way that you lose your name, and Lydyard in such a way that he can lose his mind, what can she want with me? And why, if she wants it, must she send her servant to ask my permission?'

Something is wrong, thought Lydyard. *There is something wrong in this. Is it happening at all, or is it only a hopeful invention of my dreaming soul? How am I lost, and how must I be saved?*

'We have been her eyes and ears,' said the man in the black coat, distantly. 'And we have been her intelligence, through which she sought to understand what she saw and heard. But we have not served to give her the means of understanding what is happening, and she is afraid. Those which some call angels and others gods need their subjects as much as their subjects need them, and their need extends beyond the services of slaves and cat's-paws. We need you, Sir Edward – Lydyard needs you, and others need you, and we are the only means by which you may come to their aid. I beg you, Sir Edward, to offer yourself willingly. If you do not, Lydyard and your daughter will certainly be doomed, and the rest of us may yet be doomed with them.'

I am inventing this! thought Lydyard. *I am making this happen, if it is happening at all!*

He heard Tallentyre say to himself: *Can I believe this man?* and heard him dismiss it as a futile question. He bore witness to Tallentyre's acknowledgement that he was being asked to surrender his last fragile grip upon the sanity and solidity of what he had known, to pledge himself to the arbitrary world of magic and shapeshifting and Acts of Creation. Lydyard felt that he was in some way betraying his friend in being party to it all.

Then he heard Elinor Fisher say 'Edward', interrupting at last because her anxiety for him had finally come to outweigh her satisfaction and curiosity at seeing him discomfited.

'Don't worry, Nora,' Tallentyre instructed her. 'There is nothing you can or need to do. I must go with this man, and you must close the door behind us. Do not look after us. I will come to you again, when I can, and I will tell you everything. I swear, this time, that it will be everything, for I certainly owe you that.'

I am becoming ridiculous in my invention, thought Lydyard. *Could he ever have said that?*

'Don't go,' said Elinor, in a voice whose smallness and hesitancy betrayed that it was merely a token gesture. She knew full well that he was not to be turned aside.

'Fetch my coat and boots, Nora,' he said, gently. 'Quickly now – for Mr Grey is impatient to be gone.'

She moved to do as she was bid, quickly enough. *What a poor creator I would be!* Lydyard thought. *For this is all wrong, and stupid, and I am not on earth at all, but still in darkness, still in darkness . . .*

And in his extremity, he reached out in search of another thought to share, that he might *truly* exist, and found instead of Tallentyre's very orderly thoughts a dream as wild and gaudy as any that he had ever dreamed at the behest of his poisoned soul.

*

He flew through the air, not as an angel but as some tiny selfless creature which knew naught but joy. Such an abundance of joy was his that he knew not whether he was moth or bird, but only that his iridescent wings shimmered in the sunlight, and that the air was like an ocean of light which buoyed him up, and that the gentle winds were the delicate caresses of divine love.

He floated, effortlessly, thoughtlessly free, free from memory and pain, from the inward appearance of self, from the outward appearance of . . .

All of a sudden, without any hint of warning, he was caught in the sticky strands of an invisible web. The silken threads closed about him, clinging wherever they touched, and though he thrashed his limbs with all the fervour of fear and desperation the only effect of his struggling was to bind more strands about him.

Within seconds, his wings were tight-held, and all freedom slipped away. Memory fell upon him like a predatory shadow darkening the sparkling sky, and the bewildered, frightened, uncertain self which he had put away for a while filled him up again with the burden of sensation and imagination, the horror of sentience.

He saw then what a spiderweb it was which had caught him. At first he thought that it extended over the great dark city and was anchored without its bounds, but then he saw that like a rainbow's its ends only seemed to touch the earth. In reality, it was greater than he could possibly see, huger than he could possibly imagine, and he, caught and smothered by its gentle but insistent tendrils, was so very, very tiny that the Spider which had spun the web would never notice him.

But that was hope, and futile.

The city beneath him was shrouded in grey mist, but he could see the blurred glow of a hundred thousand gaslamps. By their faint light he could see that the nearer strands of the web had trapped a dozen victims and more, each one tightly bound in spidersilk. All, he knew, had been injected by the Spider-god with an acid which would liquefy their souls and make them fit for drinking – and yet all, in some mysterious fashion, remained alive and fully aware of the hopelessness of struggling against their fate.

He knew, in his heart, that even he could not escape that fate, that no matter how fine a creature he was by comparison with these others, he was no more to the Spider-god than a tiny morsel to be savoured.

He knew that the Spider would come.

Neither hope nor ghosts from the beginning of time could save him. Neither mother-Sphinx nor mother-wolf could come to his aid, for of all the innocent angels, only the Spider knew the truth of the world and the cleverness of real power.

He cried for help, then. He cried for his mother-wolf, but her pale fur was shimmering with slime, her limbs wrapped around by unbreakable cords. He cried for his mother-Sphinx, but she was so cocooned by bandages of spider-silk that she was mummified and nearly turned to dust. And when, in desperation, he cried for the father who was not his father, his creator who was not his creator, that man could only echo his plea, begging in his turn for aid which could not come.

From an unimaginable distance, Jacob Harkender looked into his face with bright and tearful eyes, and cried: 'My son! My son! Free me! Liberate my soul!'

He believed, for an instant, that he could answer the prayer if it only pleased him to do it, that he could dissolve the spidersilk which bound him, and take wing with all the other captive souls in his charge, soaring high above the city and high above the earth to touch the very rim of Heaven; for, after all, was he not an angel?

Then he said to himself: 'I am no man's son, and it does not please me, and I have no quarrel with the Spider. I am my own master; I am not possessed; and I cannot be confined by strength or loyalty or fear.'

But this was not even hope, only mere delusion, and it was the voice of another which surged through the empty space where his own soul ought to be, mocking him with its temptations.

'I am the angel,' he said, helpless to keep the echoing words at bay. 'I am the angel of death and the angel of pain, the angel with the flaming sword and the angel which writes the book of sin. I am the spider-angel which spins its webs in the House of God, and mine is the fantasy which will write the future upon the page of space and time. Mine is the fantasy. . . .'

Gabriel Gill woke, sweating profusely. He woke to darkness because the candle beside his bed had guttered and died. In that darkness he was free to think, for a moment or two, that he was in the dormitory at Hudlestone Manor, that he was a good boy with a good conscience, unhaunted by demons or werewolves or Caleb Amalax, but it was an illusion which could not be sustained.

What is this? thought Lydyard, in utter confusion. *Is this invention too, or have I truly found the sight of the child's eyes, the angel's eyes?*

Gabriel sat up in bed, throwing off the oppressive blanket which covered him. But it was not the blanket which had made him hot; the heat which filled the room was in the air and all around.

Something was wrong – badly wrong.

It occurred to him that the house itself might be on fire, its timbers ablaze. He imagined that his little attic might be the only room which had not yet been consumed, but that it might at any moment tumble into the flames below. He reached down from where he lay, intending to touch the floor to see how hot it was.

But when Gabriel's fingers were an inch or so away from the boards, the floor disappeared. Instead of the fiery furnace which he half-expected to see, there was a great vortex of darkness, which caught him up and whirled him around like an autumn leaf, and though he grabbed for the discarded blanket, it was whipped away from him, and the bed with it, leaving him tumbling through the stormy air in his nightshirt.

Because of the whirlwind he had no sense of falling; though he felt horribly giddy he had no fear of coming to earth with a bone-breaking crash. Nothing could fly in such turbulent air, and he did not even try, but he could not doubt that he was being carried to some strange destination.

He heard someone calling his name, but the word came from a very great distance, and the last syllable extended into a long, shrill shriek before it dissolved in the whirling air. And then he heard another sound, which made no sense to him at all – a sound like distant coughing.

Lydyard recognized it as the sound of gunfire, and knew that time had folded back upon itself, that this was the moment before the spiders came . . . or the moment in which the Spider came.

Lydyard realized then how utterly lost he was.

'It is a dream,' Gabriel said to himself – speaking the words aloud, to see whether he could hear them. 'I only dreamed that I woke up, and I am not awake at all.' But he knew, when he tried with all his might to open his eyes, that it was not true, *unless the world itself had become a dream, and time itself had ceased the work which it did to reproduce the form and order of each moment with mechanical precision.*

Something had seized poor Gabriel Gill, had plucked him from Mandorla's care as easily as a man might pluck a flower from a bush, and that same something had seized David Lydyard too, and had wrapped him up in time like a mummified Egyptian, had hurled him into the afterlife without sustenance or guide, to fall . . . to fall . . .

Lydyard spread out his arms as he fell through the earth, and felt his body buoyed up by the effort of his will. Alone again now, he quickly found that the sensation of falling gave way to a sensation of floating, which was more pleasant by far.

He had never learned how to swim, but he quickly resolved that if some treachery had made a fluid of the solid world then he must perforce learn to move himself through its dark and dismal reaches. He began to move his arms in lazy arcs, as though to haul himself through the turgid earth, and found himself capable of making better headway than he had supposed.

He was quite blind in this lightless world, but his sense of touch seemed heightened, for he could feel numerous vibrations in the fluid rock, and could sense their origins. Some descended from the surface in muted confusion; others spread out sideways from the tunnels in which the underground railways and London's lost rivers ran. These told him that he was not so very far beneath the world of light and air, and he was tempted to try to swim upwards to regain that familiar world, but he put away the temptation for a while because the sensation of swimming filled him with such strange exhilaration.

Instead of going up he went further down, where all the vibrations faded into a distant chaotic susurration. Here there was a profound peace, which seemed not merely comfortable but utterly right. He felt as though this was somehow his true element, where he was infinitely more at home than he ever could be in the thin smear of organic life which was the surface of the planet and the world of men.

This is what I am, he thought. *I am not a human being at all, despite that shape in which I was made incarnate – nor am I a wolf or any other creature of the earth. I belong, instead, to solid and implacable places, to the world of rock and stone.*

But his sense of touch told him something else, as he descended further. It told him that the blissful coldness of the earth was only superficial – that there were regions below where there was great heat and much activity. Just as the world of organic life was a mere stratum, so was this world which seemed like his true home; it too had its underworld, its seething Hell.

Lydyard knew that he could swim down further – that if he wished to, he could swim to the very centre of the earth, and bathe in its vast ocean of molten iron, without any fear of hindrance or annihilation – but he shied away from the possibility. That was not where he wanted to go, nor where he wanted to be. It was not his place, as this most certainly was.

I was drawn from my cradle of rock to become a monster of flesh, and I came to think myself demon-haunted not because I was poisoned by that snake, but because I discovered at last how my soul and my intelligence so ill-befitted my form. Now, at long

*last, I know what I am and where I belong, and I may freely offer
thanks to whatever kindly god or devil has brought me here to be my
real and only self.*

He would have said as much aloud, had he thought that
there was any need. He assumed that there was not, because
he knew that something had reached out to touch and change
him, in order to bring him gradually to this realization, and he
could only presume that he was still being drawn and guided,
tempted and enlightened. If it should be the pleasure of his
guide and tempter to deliver him from this comforting womb
for further instruction, he had no doubt that it could and would
be done.

It was not a prospect that he feared in the least, because
he knew that now he had been shown the way to paradise,
he would always be able to return.

With this in mind Lydyard swam through the liquid earth,
patiently and rapturously, languishing in contentment, until
his arms grew mysteriously tired.

Eventually, he stopped, safely locked into the fabric of
the rock – and he took leave to wonder whether this was
the condition of the Creators of old. He had imagined their
fall into the shadow-world; now he imagined their fall into
the cold comfort of compacted stone. Had they made a
haven of that mantle of the world which was the flesh
beneath its fragile crust? Was he now in their own realm,
the Kingdom of Heaven which they had prepared for the
poor in spirit, to contain all those who were persecuted for
righteousness's sake, so that they might become in truth the
salt of the earth.

All too soon, however, he discovered that there was no rest
for him here, just as there had been none in the shadow-world,
and that he must seek again to be reunited with the world
of men or the world of dreams, and once again he listened
for the thoughts of another, which might bring him back
from where he was and allow him to discover what he yet
might be.

And this time, he gave forth a silent cry, a prayer of sorts, which asked not to be delivered from evil, but to feel the cleansing fire of love and need.

He cried: *Cordelia!*

And was instantly heard . . .

3

Cordelia Tallentyre was in a rebellious frame of mind. She felt, as she walked to the low wall which bounded the gardens of Charnley Hall on the south side, that she had been literally driven from the house by Mrs Austen's careful solicitude, forced to seek refuge there from the tyranny of circumstance.

It was bad enough, she thought, that her father should respond to the invasion of the house in Sturton Street by removing her from it – that he should add insult to the injury by sending her here, to what was virtually a lunatic asylum, was beyond tolerance.

This new grievance had been added to an accretion of resentments which had already become mountainous. Following their return from Egypt, neither her father nor her fiancé had consented to explain to her what kind of affair it was in which they had become entangled – though it had obviously driven poor David to the brink of distraction. In spite of their attempts to keep her out of it, she had been forced to witness David's seizure by an ugly giant, and had shot a man while he was in the process of changing into some monstrous beast – and still Sir Edward had refused to tell her what was going on. Instead of the explanation which she clearly deserved, she had been issued with summary instructions to go with Gilbert Franklin to Charnley Hall, where she would be safely out of the way. In the mean time, the baronet had gone about his secret business – but where he might have gone, and what hope there was that he might be able to find and rescue David, she had not the faintest idea.

Lydyard, abruptly precipitated into this seething cauldron of resentments, was both astonished and alarmed. He had not thought Cordelia capable of such strong and mordant feeling. To him, as to the world, she had usually presented a calm and decorous face, and though she had often teased him, he had never seen her furious. Now, for the first time, he realized what efforts went into the maintenance of her mask, and what a deep desire there was in her to break through the bounds of politeness and propriety which confined her.

She took up a careful station by the wall, from which she could look out over the meadow which separated the grounds of Austen's home from the Brent. She stared across the river at the much higher wall which hid the greater part of Hudlestone Manor, as though she were savouring the delicate touch of the breeze upon her cheeks. Inwardly, she was recalling the booming echoes of the shots which she had fired some forty hours before, feeling the recoil of the weapon, seeing the bullets strike home in the body of the metamorphic monster. Forewarned by rumour, she had known even as she fired that this was one of the fabled werewolves of London – and the thrill of seeing it hurt, knowing that she had done it, had brought a sensation of rapturous triumph which was a marvel to her.

Was that sensation, she wondered, a thing which all men learned and learned to treasure? Was that why they went so gladly to the business of war? She felt that she had begun to understand for the first time that brutish celebration of recklessness which was masculinity.

Lydyard could not share her understanding. Indeed, observing the idea through the dark window of her contemplation, he was for the first time in his life forced to call that celebration into question.

He sought within her present thoughts for evidence of that deep and irresistible current of feeling which was her love for him; but it seemed that he had mistaken either the depth, or the irresistibility, or perhaps even the nature of that emotion. He did not – could not – doubt that she really did love him, but it was nevertheless the memory of her own actions which dominated her inner perceptions, not sympathy for the plight of her kidnapped lover.

Slowly, she began to walk again, treading the paths with measured paces until she came around to the front of the house, where she turned on to the pavement which connected the door of the house to the garden gate. She looked up briefly at the ivy-clad walls and the latticed windows, half-expecting to see an anxious face studying her movements, but no one was there. Austen and Franklin were presumably deep in intense conversation, taking advantage of her absence to discuss what they would not mention in her hearing.

There was a young man coming along the path – a tradesman, she guessed, to judge by his coat and hat. He wore a curious expression of childish innocence, and instead of lowering his eyes as he approached her, as might have been expected, he looked straight at her.

She felt a tiny thrill of apprehension, but no real fear; Lydyard, by contrast, started with genuine alarm, knowing somehow that this meeting was dreadfully unfortunate.

The young man stopped on the other side of the gate, as though he intended to come into the grounds. Cordelia made no move to open it for him, but waited for him to explain his mission.

'Miss Tallentyre?' he said. His tone was very polite, but the fact that he knew her name surprised her, and made her wonder how he could possibly have identified her. She leapt to the conclusion that he must be a messenger from Sir Edward – a conclusion with which Lydyard could not by any means concur.

'Who are you?' she asked, in a neutral manner.

'My name is Capthorn, miss – Luke Capthorn. I work at the Manor, helping to look after the orphans.'

This surprised Lydyard as much as it surprised Cordelia.

'How do you know me?' she asked, a little more sharply.

'Mr Harkender told me that you were here. I dare say you know, miss, that Mr Harkender has ways of finding things out that ordinary men don't have, and what he discovers sometimes makes him anxious. He says that the werewolves of London know where you are, and that they mean you no good. He sent me to tell you that there is no safety here, that your father should not have made you come.'

Cordelia looked at Luke Capthorn much as she might have looked at a pretty snake; she was not altogether repelled by him, but he frightened her. He frightened her with his frank stare and over-careful politeness, but most of all, he frightened her with what he said.

'What on earth are you talking about?' She was trying, unsuccessfully, to be cold and contemptuous, but her heart was fluttering with confusion.

'They took Mr Lydyard, didn't they?' said Capthorn, who was clearly conscious of her distress. 'The werewolves took him, though Mr Harkender warned him to be careful. Mr Harkender asked him to come to Whittenton, but Sir Edward wouldn't let him come. Believe me, Miss Tallentyre, there's only one man in England who can defy the werewolves of London, and that's Mr Harkender. You're in great danger, miss – that's what I was sent to tell you. Only Mr Harkender can tell you why.'

Cordelia felt that the colour must have drained from her cheeks, but she was determined not to show, or even to feel, any other symptoms of distress. Lydyard wished fervently – but in vain – that he could make himself heard inside her thoughts or felt inside her heart. He could see that this web of horrid dreams was about to enfold the one person he loved, and knew that when it did, the nightmare would begin in earnest.

'What business is this of Mr Harkender's?' Cordelia asked Luke Capthorn. 'And what has it to do with you?'

'Mr Harkender can find your fiancé, if he tries. The werewolves are no friends of his – they kidnapped his young ward, too, who was placed in my care at the Lodge. Mr Harkender wants Gabriel back – and he says that he may be able to rescue Mr Lydyard too. He would like to do it, if he can, but he wants to be sure that you're safe first. You must come to Whittenton, Miss Tallentyre. It's the only way.'

Cordelia hesitated, and her hesitation was agony for Lydyard. It had been on the tip of her tongue to tell the enigmatic intruder to begone, but she dared not do it, for she had no way to know whether or not he might be telling the truth. Her perplexity must have been very obvious.

But Lydyard could see, as Cordelia could not, the spidery shadows in Luke Capthorn's eyes.

'Tell your master that I am grateful to him,' she said, finally, composing her intentions as she spoke the words. 'Please thank him for taking the trouble to send me this message, but tell him that I am safe in Dr Austen's care.' She took a step back from the gate, glancing at the house as she did so. Now she was hoping to see that someone was at a window, watching her – but there was still no sign of anyone.

'Mr Harkender will try to bring Mr Lydyard to Whittenton,' said Capthorn, blandly. 'You must come to meet him there, Miss Tallentyre, for he may be hurt and will be in dire need of a friend.'

Again Cordelia hesitated. She did not take a second step towards the house. She looked at Luke Capthorn. His eyes appeared to be frank and guileless, but she feared that the appearance was deceptive.

In God's name, cried Lydyard, desperate to be heard. *Do not go!*

'If I come,' she said, anxiously, 'I cannot come alone. Will you come in, Mr Capthorn, and explain yourself to Dr Austen and Dr Franklin?'

Capthorn did not immediately reply to this request, but it was evident that he had some objection to it. He was standing quite still, and his unblinking stare was becoming very disconcerting.

'I'm sorry, miss,' said Capthorn, in a tone which seemed

dreadfully unnatural to Lydyard, 'but there may not be time for that.'

'Then we must make time,' replied Cordelia, 'for I cannot simply step out of the gate, without a word of explanation.'

For a second or two Lydyard was ready to believe that propriety had saved her, but the ominous feeling which saturated his ghostly presence was a truer guide than hope.

'Excuse me, Miss Tallentyre,' said Capthorn, his voice suddenly transformed into something dark and menacing, 'but did you know that there is a spider on your hand?'

Cordelia gasped – much more in surprise than in alarm – and looked quickly down at her left hand. How she had known to look at the left hand rather than the right she had no idea, for she had felt nothing at all; but there, clinging to the back of her hand, was a spider of astonishing size. She had never seen such a thing in England, though her father had told her tales of meeting such monstrosities during his travels. The horror of discovery chilled her to the bone, and she froze into rigidity.

Lydyard knew that the spider was not really there – but that knowledge could not make the sight of it one whit less horrible to her.

'Be careful, miss,' said Luke Capthorn, his tone obscenely even and controlled. 'If you are frightened, it may bite you.'

But she *was* frightened, and there was no way in the world she could bid that fear begone. She opened her mouth as if to scream, and then she felt the spider bite her.

Lydyard felt it too; it was as though some predatory bird or beast had snatched up his soul like a tender morsel, to crush and crack it.

The cry was stillborn in Cordelia's throat, and she felt as if a black tide was rushing up at her from the ground, as though her spirit were falling into the maw of some great dark monster, to be consumed.

The only sound which she and the passenger in her thoughts heard, before the blackness claimed them both, was the noise of the catch on the gate, clicking as it opened.

*

Sir Edward Tallentyre dreamed that he was led into an eerie darkness which was warm and comforting, as the womb of the cosmos must have been before its first Creator first made light, and then on to a starlit strand, where the smell of the ocean was in his nostrils, and a clean breeze caressed his face, and then on to a dawnlit hillside decked by trees; but as is sometimes the way with dreams, his surroundings seemed to fade away into the background, unnoticed and unnoticeable.

It was as if the world was made of shadowstuff, as solid or as ghostly as a whim might make it. Tallentyre felt that he had been neatly separated from the ordinary and substantial world of matter, scissored from the page of reality. What surrounded him now was a mere sketch, a minimal stage-setting for the next act of the irrational drama which had caught him up in its nonsensical unfolding.

What am I doing? Lydyard demanded of himself – but he was now losing the conviction that he was the spinner of this dream. He was no mere observer, of that he was sure, but this Sir Edward was no figment of his hopeful imagination. It was the real Sir Edward after all – save that dream and reality were now so desperately entangled there was no way to be sure exactly what that signified.

The Sphinx was waiting for him. She did not wear the body of a lion or the wings of an eagle, and her hands and feet were not taloned; nevertheless, she was the Sphinx.

She was in human guise, beautiful enough by human standards, but not as exotically beautiful as Tallentyre had expected, having heard David Lydyard's description of Mandorla Soulier. Tallentyre felt that he understood well enough why these shapeshifters chose female form for their dealings with men, usurping the ready-made glamour of beauty, but he did not know why this one was so ordinary. Perhaps, he hazarded, Mandorla Soulier knew human beings far more intimately than this curious creature which had so recently been roused from an inertia lasting thousands of years.

She was simply dressed, in a costume which was little more

exotic than her face, though it would not have been regarded as fashionable in a London drawing-room. Her dress was white, long-sleeved and deep-skirted, but it had been cut to fit her body, not to force her body into any pre-determined shape. In her right hand she was holding a heavy goblet made of metal. She held it out to Tallentyre and he – knowing that there could not be any point in hesitation or suspicion – drank from it, thirstily. It was only water.

'You have cursed my friend with uncomfortable nightmares,' said Tallentyre, when it seemed to him apparent that the other would not speak first. 'And you seem to have stolen poor de Lancy's soul away. Should I be flattered that you approach me as I am? Or am I, in fact, so utterly deluded that I do not realize what you have done to me? Am I, like them, possessed by that madness which is visited by the gods on those whom they intend to destroy?'

'I needed Lydyard's powers of sight,' she replied, calmly. 'I needed his unguided dreams and his honest fears, just as I needed de Lancy's mind to shape as I might. Now I believe that I need a sharper, stronger instrument – sharper and stronger than I could create.'

And I am to deliver him, thought Lydyard. *That is what is happening here. Through me, she appoints her champion. Through me, her riddle and its answer take shape.*

'There are those who think that you might destroy or remake the world entire,' answered Tallentyre, fascinated by his own lack of emotion. 'If that is so, I cannot comprehend how a mere mortal being could be of interest or use to you.'

'Those who believe that the world might be transformed,' she reminded him, 'also believe that mortal men will attain their just and true reward, which none among the lesser angels can ever deny them. However unclearly they see, and however misguided their faith, they have glimpsed the paradox of Creation. I and others may play with appearances, but still there must be an underlying reality which *appears*, and still there must be those to whom appearances are presented. My power to change things is restricted by the potentialities of change, which I do not know and cannot properly judge, and further limited by the activity of other changers, which may cancel out or amplify my efforts in ways which I cannot always foresee. All power is based in understanding, and all understanding is limited by perception. We have our fears, our limitations, our dangers, and our enemies, just as you have.

'I am no less a prisoner of time than you are. Space I can warp to my will, within limits, but time is inexorable. In every second that passes, I can do one thing or another, but not both. No matter how many eyes I may use to see, or how many bodies I may possess, my intelligence is bound by time; one sensation must follow another, and should the stream of my consciousness be divided I am perforce confused, as you would be.'

How true, thought Lydyard.

'So much for omniscience,' murmured Tallentyre. He looked sideways at the man he had known as William de Lancy, who was perfectly still, like a statue empty of intelligence.

'I am in danger,' she said, frankly. 'Something is anxious to hurt and destroy me, and I do not know how best to meet its threat.'

'What thing?' asked Tallentyre.

'No doubt it has many names,' she answered, 'as have I. Names are no more fixed and intrinsic than appearances. Let it be a Spider, if it is pleased to present itself thus to Lydyard's sight, and let its scheme be the web in which it intends to trap me. My present concern is to resist its attack – and to reclaim that fraction of my substance which was stolen from me, if that is possible.'

Let it be a Spider! repeated Lydyard, in the privacy of his own thoughts. *All she has seen of it she has seen through the eye of my tortured dreams. All that she knows of it she knows by virtue of my inferences and what her enemies have chosen to let me know. In her own way, she is as blind as we are! Can her enemy really have any greater advantage, if its own tools are men like Jacob Harkender, and if the likes of the werewolves of London can so casually intervene in its schemes? Why, these mighty gods are fools and innocents, whose avidity to seize control of this dream that is the world is as hopeless as the quest which men like Harkender think they have, to master the world with wishes and fancied wisdom!*

'I think I begin to understand why you need me,' said Tallentyre. 'You have the power to change me, in appearance, and you have the power to destroy me, too. But there is in me, as in everything which exists, something which is essentially *prior* to change, something irreducible. You might possess my soul, as you have possessed Lydyard's and de Lancy's, but still there would be something which, in order to be possessed, must have its own existence, and force, and potency – what Francis Mallorn would call my soul. To recruit that to your cause requires persuasion, not possession. Is that why you let me alone in Egypt – not because I was the least of those you found, but because I was the best?'

'Alas,' she said, with a very human smile, 'my choices then were utterly haphazard. And yet, I think perhaps it has worked out for the best.'

Lydyard remembered that he had seen Satan, captive in Hell, struggling to raise his hand in order to redeem the world of men from suffering. He had seen *himself* in Satan, and despite the faith which he had never quite shaken off, had found himself committed to Satan's cause, raging against the injustices of God. Now Sir Edward Tallentyre found himself committed, in like fashion, to a cause far beyond the pale of his defiant rationality.

We have sold our souls to the Devil, said Lydyard to himself. *We have pledged ourselves to the cause of our adversary, in order that we might prevent the Day of Judgement. If we are deluded, how can we possibly know? And if it should prove that we will fail, and that the Spider will win after all, what hope can we have for Heaven and forgiveness?*

Tallentyre, in his turn, also knew that he was committed. There was no scope for refusal, nor for doubt. If the world was made of dreams and nightmares, still he must live in it, and doubt could not help him. If the Brothers of St Amycus were right in all that they believed, then he was both doomed and damned.

And if they were wrong . . .

Hope must be his guide now, not faith. Courage and intelligence must serve him as they might, for all that he had previously called knowledge could not serve him at all.

'Tell me your riddle,' he said to the Sphinx. 'And I will answer it as best I can.'

4

Cordelia's return to consciousness was unattended by any sensation of time having passed. She was sure that she had not been dreaming; Lydyard was surer still.

Yet time had passed. She was lying on a bed, but did not know what bed it was, or what room it was in. Nor did she recognize the two women who were looking down at her. One was middle-aged, and stern; the other was no older than herself, wearing an odd expression which somehow contrived to combine listlessness with curiosity.

Cordelia sat up immediately, and looked about her. The wallpaper and the furniture informed her that she was in a wealthy home, but one which was not as well cared for as her own. There was no sound save for the ticking of an upright clock, but the room was brightly lit by afternoon sunlight which streamed through the latticed window.

For a few seconds, she could not reconnect present and past, but then she remembered, and quickly looked down at her hand. There was no sign of any spider.

'Where am I?' she asked. 'Where is Dr Austen?'

'You are no longer at Charnley,' the older woman told her. 'This is Jacob Harkender's house, at Whittenton.'

Cordelia was surprised and alarmed by this revelation,

but she was determined not to show it. Lydyard silently commended her courage.

'How did I come here?' she demanded. 'And who are you?'

'You came by carriage, in answer to Mr Harkender's invitation. My name is Mrs Murrell – it will mean nothing to you, but your father and I have an acquaintance in common.' The woman did not take the trouble to identify her companion by name, but indicated with a flick of her hand that the girl should leave – presumably to carry the news of Cordelia's awakening to Jacob Harkender.

'So far as I know,' Cordelia said, coldly, 'my father does not keep company with kidnappers – nor does he seek the society of spiritists and Rosicrucians.'

'Neither Mr Harkender nor I belong to any of those categories,' Mrs Murrell assured her. 'You were not brought here by force, and no one means you any harm. Indeed, Mr Harkender's aim is to protect you from the danger which has pursued your father and your fiancé from the Egyptian desert. With all due respect to Dr Austen, Mr Harkender is the only person who can offer such protection.'

'Alas,' said Cordelia, 'I have not much faith in either his magic or his good intentions.' Even as she said it, though, she remembered the spider and the manner in which she had been rendered unconscious. Her father might have called it hypnotism or induced hallucination instead of magic, but the result had been the same.

'It is difficult to have faith in what you have not seen,' said Mrs Murrell, in such a carefully ambiguous way that Cordelia wondered how much faith she had in Jacob Harkender's powers. But she said no more, because the door had opened again, and Harkender had come in.

'Thank you, Mrs Murrell,' he said, and held the door open to indicate that he had no further need of her. Cordelia sensed a certain dislike in the way the woman rose to her feet, resentful and stony-faced.

Lydyard searched the shadows for signs of the Spider which

was Harkender's master, but could not see any. He did not dare to conclude that it had let the man alone.

'She is quite right, of course,' said Harkender, looking down at Cordelia without approaching too closely. 'It is difficult to have faith in what you have not seen, and Mrs Murrell has a certain blindness which makes faith very difficult of achievement. But I believe that you saw a man become a wolf on the night before last – a wolf which refused to die, though you shot him at point-blank range. Men may become stranger things than wolves, my lady, and the creature which attacked your father in Egypt is immeasurably more dangerous than the werewolves of London.'

'I believe that you tried to persuade my father of the urgency of his danger once before,' Cordelia answered, tartly. 'Whether you succeeded or not, he refused your protection. And I, alas, know nothing of this matter, and do not know what you are talking about.'

Lydyard was only too well aware of the mountain of resentments which still burdened her soul, and he knew that she regarded her host with almost as much curiosity as anxiety – but he was glad to feel the shrinking sensation which possessed her as she faced the man.

Cordelia stood up, smoothing her dress as she did so. Harkender was still tall enough to look down at her, but she did not feel at such a disadvantage while she could almost face him eye to eye. She looked into his eyes and saw nothing to add to her fears; nor could Lydyard perceive the shadowy presence of the web-spinner which had brought her here.

'Your father would not listen to me,' Harkender told her, 'and I fear that I had no alternative but to leave him at liberty to suffer the consequences of his vanity. Still, I feel compelled to do what I can to safeguard your own life, and that of David Lydyard. Lydyard's danger is the greatest of all – not because he has been taken by the werewolves, but because his soul is in thrall to something which might destroy him on a whim.'

'Some say the same of you, I think,' Cordelia replied, momentarily pleased with her skill in repartee.

'You know better than to listen to such superstitious nonsense,' said Harkender, in a curiously flattering way. 'It is true that there are those who declare that I have made pact with Satan, and am his unwitting slave – and there are those who say the same of the werewolves. The priests of St Amycus would declare your fiancé similarly possessed, and Gabriel too, but if they were right, we would all be lost to the cause of Hell.'

He was playing with her, Lydyard realized. As a cat might play with a mouse, as the Sphinx had played with the Satanists of Paris, as Mandorla Soulier had played with him; so Harkender had consented to play with Cordelia Tallentyre. *As flies to wanton boys are we to the gods . . .*

Cordelia also felt that she was being toyed with, and did not like it at all. She looked hard at her captor – for he was her captor, no matter how he cleverly elected to pose as her protector – and said: 'You have gone too far. You should not have sent your man to fetch me, and I will not help you, no matter what lies you tell me.'

While Harkender stared back, Lydyard still could not see the spider in his eyes. There was even a moment when he thought that the man seemed honestly sorry. But then the magician's expression changed, and he spoke to her in a different way.

'You are a fool,' he said. 'In your arrogance, you ladies believe that you can turn the world to your whim. You believe that it is yours to rule and command – a glorious empire in which you are enthroned, by virtue of your noble femininity. You are no better than your father. But I have seen the true world which is hidden by the appearances of this one. I have seen the macrocosm, in the light which pours from the heavens to illuminate my suffering soul, and I have seen the pit of Hell which yawns beneath the feet of all who proudly walk the earth. I would not presume to show you the face of Heaven, my lady, but I may show you the pit of Hell, if I care to do so.'

His voice was silky, full of menace. Cordelia knew that he was trying to scare her now, and she was adamant that she would not be scared – or, at least, that she would not show it.

'If you have looked into Hell,' she said, with measured scorn, 'it cannot be so very terrible, after all. Do you think that because I am a lady I am not brave enough to hear your words without shivering? I am a Tallentyre too, you will remember, and though my father will not deign to treat me as a son since David came, still I am no slave of superstition. No doubt you might hurt me in every vulgar and violent way that there is, but you cannot hurt me with your clever illusions, Mr Harkender, for I am not such a fool as that.'

Lydyard did not know whether to groan or to cheer as he felt the blood pulsing in her veins and the pounding of her heart. He did not know whether to pray that she would be quiet, or rejoice that she would not be.

'You should not taunt and tempt me thus,' said Harkender, evenly. 'For I have ever found that there is but one answer to temptation and to taunts, which is to answer them as they deserve. Will you come into the cellars with me, where the rats and spiders live, so that I may show you the pit of Hell? If you do, I promise you that you will learn the true extent of your error, and that will be a very hurtful thing indeed.'

This is what he intends! thought Lydyard. *She thinks that she is taunting him, but in fact he is tempting her. She does not know what game she plays, or what he can do!*

'I am not afraid of rats and spiders,' she replied, sturdily. 'And if you think that they will scare me away, so that I dare not look into your doorway into Hell, and thus cannot believe that it is no such thing, you have mistaken me.'

'Oh, no, my lady,' said Harkender, with a smile. 'I have not mistaken you at all.'

Then, and only then, Lydyard realized the truth which he had somehow kept from himself since the moment when he had first seen Luke Capthorn. It was not Cordelia who was the victim of this curious game; it was himself. Somehow, Harkender or the Spider knew that he was there inside his lover's soul; Luke Capthorn had not come to capture Cordelia, but through her to capture him. It was not Cordelia who was to be shown the pit of Hell, but Lydyard-in-Cordelia.

Harkender led the way from the room into a hallway, and from there to another door, which gave admittance to a stone stair. Cordelia followed, her thoughts in turmoil.

Lydyard tried to withdraw, thinking that if only he could return to the peace and silence of the rocks within the body of the earth, they might let her go. He tried with all his might to let go of her thoughts and sensations, but he could no more release himself from her body than he could have released his own soul from his own body without the help of some mischievous godling.

Down the stairs they went, the sound of their footsteps rattling hollowly. Harkender had taken up a candle which had been placed in an alcove in readiness, and with this he lit their way. The staircase turned to the left and to the right as it descended, though it did not appear to be spiralling about some central axis. There seemed, Cordelia thought, to be far more steps than anyone could possibly have expected. Though they passed several doorways which presumably gave access to cellars Harkender never paused and the descending corridor showed no sign of coming to an end.

It is an illusion, Cordelia thought. *It is a trick of some kind, and I must not be alarmed.*

Helplessly, Lydyard waited.

It seemed – though surely it could not be true? – that they had been descending for at least half an hour. Cordelia had heard the sound of animal movements more than once, though she had not seen any rats or mice in the candlelight. Nor had she seen a living spider, though the corridor was richly cobwebbed. She had lost count of the steps, and the air was very cold and still.

Go back! cried Lydyard, impotently. *In the name of God, go back!*

But he was trapped, as securely as if he had been bound into the silken threads of a spider's web, as securely as if he had been roped to the frame of a bed while a flood of spiders swept over him, consuming him with their dark avidity, as securely as if his very soul was possessed by something dark and monstrous and malevolent.

Harkender stopped at last, before an ancient wooden door decorated with iron studs and heavy bolts.

'Is that the pit of Hell?' asked Cordelia, too breathless to be scornful.

'Indeed it is, my lady,' said Jacob Harkender – whose hands, in the unsteady candlelight, seemed unusually large and darkly hairy. With one of them, he carefully drew the bolts, and then pushed the door open. It swung silently into a dark void.

There was nothing beyond the doorway – nothing at all. No walls, no floor, no stairway. It was in truth a pit.

'Will you ask me to believe that it is bottomless?' she said.

'Oh no,' replied Harkender, placing his hairy hand upon her shoulder in a gesture which was oddly comforting and reassuring, though she did not like the way his fingers spread like chitinous limbs upon her dress. 'I dare not pause to ask you anything, for I have other business to which I must attend. In any case, you would not believe it, if I could not show you.'

And with one last look at the captive soul behind Cordelia's eyes, of whose presence she had not the least suspicion, Harkender thrust her rudely through the doorway, to send her hurtling down into the infinite darkness.

Her scream did not echo, for there was nothing to turn the echoes back. The darkness snatched the sound away, and left her to fall.

For ever . . .

When the vortex let him go at last, Gabriel was grateful. There was a certain security in steadiness and solidity, and though the effect of his mad whirling through the emptiness had begun to be mildly euphoric, he had by no means abandoned himself to the pure thrill of it.

He was not in the least surprised, as he floated down to the surface of the earth again, to find that he was a long way from the point of his ascent. Nor was he surprised to find that his body, despite its comforting solidity, was capable of merging with the fabric of a house, entering into the brickwork of its walls, in order that it might be reborn and rematerialized into a place within the walls – a room where, it seemed, the whole universe was somehow gathered and focused.

Cordelia! cried Lydyard, believing in his desperation that he had lost his inamorata while she fell, and had come to share another fall instead, helplessly cheated by the confusion of sensations.

Gabriel knew precisely where he was, though he had only seen the place in his dreams. He was in the centre of the ornately decorated wheel which was inscribed on the floor of Jacob Harkender's attic room; above him was the stained-glass dome.

His arrival gave rise to two very different cries of astonishment – one, from the mouth of Jacob Harkender, loudly exultant; the other, ripped from the throat of Mrs Murrell, harshly incredulous.

'Did I not tell you?' said Harkender, whose face was white and lined with pain. 'Did I not tell you that I could summon spirits from the vasty deep?'

The kneeling magician was naked to the waist, secured to the tilted wrought-iron spiderweb. Blood was coursing from a dozen ragged wounds upon his back. Mrs Murrell was fully and warmly dressed; in her right hand she held a bundle of birch-rods, tightly tied together. These she dropped, and with a cut-throat razor she severed the cords which bound Harkender's wrists, to free him from his captivity.

Harkender opened his arms as if to welcome Gabriel into his fond embrace, but Gabriel – having only briefly met the other's eye – was looking down at the devices painted on the floor, measuring their complexity.

'Where have you come from?' asked Mrs Murrell, her voice cracking with the strain of defeated scepticism. 'How did you come?'

'I came on the wind,' said Gabriel, feeling that he was compelled to offer some explanation. 'I came . . .'

He could see that Mrs Murrell did not like the first part of his answer at all, but he could not find another to put in its place. When he looked again at Harkender, who was still struggling to his feet, he saw that the magician liked it much better, relishing its mystery and its promise.

'I knew that the werewolves could not keep you,' said Harkender exultantly, hurrying now to put on his shirt. 'Despite that they have lived for thousands of years, they are beasts at heart, and have not troubled to cultivate learning. While the Clay Man rests in his tomb, impatient for the world to become a better place, the work of discovery must be carried forward by mere mortal men – *but it can be done!*'

'Mandorla will come after me,' said Gabriel, not knowing whether it should be a warning or a threat. 'And Morwenna too, and Perris, and Siri. They will come as wolves, if they can.' He remembered, as he said it, the terror of the man who had watched Mandorla change, that strange terror which had held so little of surprise and amazement, so much of the sense of guilt repaid by the wrath of Hell.

Morwenna cannot come, thought Lydyard, *and I am by no means sure of Mandorla*.

'The werewolves cannot harm me,' said Harkender, boldly. 'I am more powerful than they ever imagined. With your help, I can do and discover anything.'

But that, thought Lydyard, *is hope and not conviction*.

Something inside Gabriel knew it too, and the child felt again that there was something strange and alien in his soul, which told him things he should not know, which had made him a thing he should not be.

Harkender took him in his arms for the first time, as a father might take a long-lost son.

'Gabriel!' he said, in a voice hardly above a whisper.

Gabriel could not tell what thoughts and feelings were in the magician's mind. He could not enter that mind with his own inner eye, and could not know what possessiveness was in that whispered name. But he struggled, not wanting to be held, and Harkender let him go.

Harkender stepped back, uneasily, leaving Gabriel to stand alone at the centre of his map of all experience, his wheel of all wisdom, his painted microcosm. Mrs Murrell stepped back too – and looked as if she would gladly step into the wall if she only could.

Gabriel looked down at the bloodstained mandala where Jacob Harkender had followed the way of pain into the further reaches of extra-sensory experience, and touched the rim of it gingerly, as though expecting it to be sticky. Then he looked up, at the coloured dome lit from within, and he remembered the mirror which Mandorla had given him for a plaything.

It was night now, but he could imagine how much more gorgeous that panoply must be in the full glare of daylight, and as he wondered, he could not help but reach out with the power of his whim, as he had learned to do with the mirror, and draw a trickle of light from without the dome – from without the universe itself – to bathe the room in colour.

He said nothing, for he needed no charm or incantation to achieve his end, but he did reach up with his right hand, as though to catch a single ray of the magical light in his open hand, quite innocently.

The trickle became a flood.

The riot of colour which erupted at his command took Gabriel's breath away. The light which he had summoned was brighter and whiter than the fiercest sunlight, and as it poured through the tinted glass it seemed to dissolve the material of which the dome was made, so that instead of arching above him like a great curved window the dome vanished utterly, and where the light fell upon the painted, polished floor the boards were dissolved with equal ease, so that only their surface remained, only the tree of knowledge and meaning.

Gabriel and Lydyard heard Jacob Harkender cry out, not in anger but in sheer delight, as though the miracle had drowned his darkling soul with ecstasy.

And Gabriel knew that he was himself transformed by the cascade of light, that he had ceased to be a small child in a ragged nightshirt, but had become instead a tall angel, like those he had seen in Sister Clare's pictures, with great dove-white wings and a dazzling halo, and eyes of the purest imaginable blue.

Gabriel! cried Lydyard – and for once, at last, was certain that he had been heard.

And Gabriel said, with a voice which was entirely his own, and more his own than any voice he had ever used before: 'I am the angel of joy and the angel of deliverance, I am the angel of the Lord!'

As Lydyard's presence within him was shattered and banished, there was such an explosion of power in Gabriel's being that it seemed the very walls of the world must be blasted apart. Lydyard, knowing that he had time for one last blast of thought before he was returned from Heaven to the pit of Hell, cried out as instinct led him to:

Sed libera nos a malo! Sed libera nos a malo!

Deliver us from evil.

Harkender cried out again, no longer in delight but in anger and anguish; but Gabriel heard – and in the triumph of his self-discovery, he looked down at the world beneath his feet, bathed by the glorious light of Heaven, and discovered that he was still, after all, what the Sisters of St Syncletica had made of him.

He was not the Devil's toy at all, but was *good*. And so he stretched out his hand to answer prayers with miracles, to redeem the wretched earth itself . . .

5

Mercy Murrell had never said a prayer in her life, and had never set foot inside a church. She believed in God, but did not love him. She believed in the Devil, and found his imps incarnate in all the death-cap parasites which hung from the bellies of hairy men, swelling and shrinking to the drunken rhythms of passion and cruelty.

The Devil, in the eye of Mrs Murrell's imagination, was black and bat-like. His wings were vast, his body furred, his face pig-like; he had a great wet snout and huge soft ears. He had no arms save for the ridges of his wings and his legs were short and stout, hugely taloned so that he might comfortably hang from his roost in the high belfry of Pandemonium, huddled like a rotting fruit or a shrivelled, sated prick.

Mercy Murrell's Devil had many guises, all of them archetypally male. At one extreme he might appear as a subtle flatterer and sly offerer of bribes and favours; in this lubricious vein he had earned the title of Father of Lies by his incessant babbling of love, his casual mastery of the soft caress and the false promise, his Judas kisses and his mock-maternal hugs. At the opposite extreme he might appear as a callous rapist, and wrathfully resentful of those who stirred his feelings and made unwarranted claims on his compassion; in this hateful vein he was the Prince of Darkness, imperious and adamantine, for whom the only certainty was that he could cause pain, and who welcomed the pain which he caused as the only proper affirmation of his effect within the world, his presence of mind and his absence of responsibility.

Mercy Murrell had met the Devil on countless occasions, in both these guises and all the subtle combinations in between, and she knew full well that in spite of these transformations he was always and fundamentally the same: brutal, bestial, despicable, damned.

Mercy Murrell did not believe in angels of virtue at all. She knew that women, by and large, had not so much of the Devil in them as men had, but she was not convinced that there were any whose souls were entirely innocent. In her cynical view, none of the myriad encounters of Beauty and Beast was truly to be counted as spoliation; she knew only too well that women were the users and exploiters, not

the helpless vicctims, of their prettiness. She could believe –
just barely – in sirens and lorelei who cunningly employed
their glamour as a lure to turn the demonic hunger of men
into a careless rush to destruction; but she could not believe
that the saintly protestations of comely virgins were aught but
vile hypocrisy. In her eyes, only the ugly and the grotesque
could possibly begin to be good, and she knew enough of the
perversity of demonkind to be sure that even the ugly and the
grotesque had some capacity to awaken lust, and the chance
to put a market value on their souls.

The only angels in which Mercy Murrell could believe were
dark and fallen angels. She could accept an angel of death,
clad in the shadows of the grave, with features permanently
twisted with contempt for the follies and vanities of mankind;
she could accept an angel of pain, all clothed in blood with
polished claws, with eyes as cold as marble; but she could not
accept a guardian angel, or an angel of mercy, for in her eyes
all guardians were prison-masters and all acts of mercy were
usurer's loans to be repaid with blood and sweat and tears.

And because of this, when Mercy Murrell saw the son of
Jenny Gill transformed, she did not see an angel at all, but
only an ominous thing of fire and light, false in appearance
and false in intent. There was something inside her which
wanted to scream, and something which wanted to laugh,
but nothing which wanted to pray or plead or beg, nothing
which believed that he was anything more than a comedy of
appearances, a mockery of faith, a folly of hope.

When he turned those eyes of wondrous blue towards her,
to look at her with pity as Jesus might have looked at Mary
Magdalene, her instant response was to meet his stare, and
call him a liar and a lie. His eyes were the eyes of a child,
but even so she would not credit them with freedom from
lust and greed and cruelty, and though their blueness was
the blue of a perfect sky, she would not accept it as the blue
of Heaven.

And for this reason, he did not see her. He looked her in
the eyes, but could not see her at all.

When he was gone – dissolved into the riot of coloured light – she did not cry out, as Jacob Harkender did, in anger and anguish at an unexpected loss, but with a kind of triumph. What she cried was 'Begone!' and though she did not really believe that she had caused him to vanish, she felt that she and she alone was in tune with the unfolding pattern of events, in harmony with the real rhythm of life and change, in concert with the true way of the world. All her life she had been a whore and mistress of whores, selling souls to the Devil and his vampire host, and there was no other life which she could imagine, let alone desire.

When she saw the flames which remained, and her nostrils filled with acrid smoke, tears came to her eyes at last – but they were tears of pain, not tears of joy or shame, and the heat which reached out to her was not the torture of Hell but the radiance of a very ordinary fire.

Jacob Harkender had once believed in God devoutly, but had ceased to believe when he discovered himself alone in a violent world, surrounded by hate and helpless to appease it. When first he had been severely abused – when he had been no older than Gabriel Gill was now – he had prayed for deliverance and taken comfort in his prayers; but those prayers had brought him neither answer nor release, and their failure had made such a mockery of his hopes that all comfort fled, and was turned instead to bitterness.

For a little while he might have hated God, but he quickly came to see that God was not deserving even of his hatred.

In time, Jacob Harkender came to believe in God again, but in a God of a very different kind. He came to believe, in fact, that atheism was an impossible creed – an illusion based in confusion as to the meanings which words could bear and the rational interpretations which the perceived world could sustain. That there was a world of which his senses had experience he could have no doubt, that its matter was in motion and that its motions followed laws of a kind was likewise indubitable. Given this, he thought, it clearly mattered not whether all might be illusion and the world a mere show, or whether the laws which appeared eternal and unchangeable were mere temporary whims; whatever the case, there was something outside himself which was vast and partly knowable, which had order if not purpose, and authority if not will, which could honestly be called God. Like many before him, he had deserted the God of the Testaments only to discover the God of the philosophers, and found the latter infinitely grander and more congenial to his taste.

This God of the philosophers could have no adversary, for there was no conceivable anti-God within this system of thought, and so Jacob Harkender could not believe in the Devil. But he saw and understood, even before he came once more to believe in God, that the world was a great arena of conflicts and cruelties, of collisions and destructions and warring impulses. Hate and violence could not be alienated from *his* God to some dark and vicious Other, but neither could their awesome force be denied. And so, for Harkender, Christianity's great legions of angels and demons had at least a metaphorical meaning, as contending ideas within the great mind-universe whose dream – or nightmare – was phenomenal reality.

In Jacob Harkender's eyes, these legions did not array themselves under the opposed banners of Good and Evil, for those were human ideas based in the experience of pleasure and pain, which must appear in the God-mind as mere differences. In taking command of his own life and his own experiences, even before he became a philosopher and man of wisdom, he had acquired the gift of transforming pain into a kind of ecstasy, into a difference of state instead of a condition of Hell. Hell held no terrors for him, for he felt himself the master of pain and not its slave.

In becoming the master of pain Jacob Harkender had done his utmost to go beyond the herd-made limits of good and evil, to overcome the mereness of man in search of superhumanity. He had shed by calculation and sheer effort of will the most miserable and loathsome aspects of his own human nature;

he had escaped the twin traps of conscience and duty, and had tried with all his might to be fit company for those angels and demons whose ways he yearned to discover and whose power he yearned to acquire.

When Jacob Harkender saw the transformation of Gabriel Gill, he fought astonishment with all his might, but could not fight regret. He knew that what he saw was mere appearance – a reflection of what had been taught to the boy at Hudlestone – and was not confused by it; but his heart was torn by the conviction that it was all such a dreadful waste, that the power which he had sought to harvest for his own was exploding long before it could be brought to ripeness.

Not for the first time Harkender found himself lamenting the folly of his decision to give the boy to the Sisters, for the anxieties which had made him do it seemed so utterly inadequate now. If only the whore who bore the child had not died; if only he had mustered courage enough to let her death be known and to face the whispers of accusation openly. But a death was a public affair to be investigated, and there were those who had helped him who might have been panicked into saying what they knew of his magical rites, in which case he would have lost the child entirely, and might even have been brought to court himself. It had seemed so much easier then to cover up the death, and hide the child, and so very cunning to hide the child in a convent, but he had not expected that the child would begin to come into his inheritance so soon, or that others would find him and seek to steal him away.

He had not reckoned with the werewolves of London, who had contrived to spoil everything.

So Jacob Harkender cried out in anguish for what he had lost and for what he had unwittingly made: for the loss of the angel which might have guided him to the wisdom and power which he coveted, and for the making of this vain vessel of mercy and light, which had no Olympian Heaven to which it might fly, no kindly Father-God to protect it, no mission to fulfil. Even as he cried out, though, he had a prayer of sorts to utter, a plea to make.

Look into my heart! he begged. *Look into my heart and see the truth of what you really are, and what the world is really like. Feel the glory of my pain and the triumph of my enlightenment, and see what you were made to be! I am your father and your mother and your one true friend. I have suffered more than any to redeem my world from desolation. I am the one and only, the man above man, your brother in blood and pain. If only you could see what I have borne and what I have done; if only you could know what I have found and what I have glimpsed; if only you could be what I have been and feel what I have felt you would surely consent to all that I have hoped and planned for you. Only share my soul, which is not cold like the souls of other men, but warmed by the fires of violence endured and humiliation overcome! Only share my soul . . . my soul . . .*

But even as Jacob Harkender prayed, even as he laid his claim before the court of destiny, the angel Gabriel was gone – fled into the world of light and symbol, knowing not where he went or how or why, but refusing and denying the man who had been his creator, as thankless as any natural child.

And when Jacob Harkender turned again to face his white-faced accomplice, he felt that his eyes were burning like coals, and that darkness had possessed him, turning his every atom into hot black ash. Hell was in him now, he knew; a demonic fury sufficient to set the world itself afire, if he would only consent to be the wayward spark which triggered that destruction.

David Lydyard's eyes flew open, as they sometimes had before when he had dreamed of falling, and he saw Caleb Amalax looming over him. Amalax had no spiders swarming over him, but he still had the long-bladed knife in his hand, and his eyes were like huge globules of grey and dusty cobweb. It was as though the spiders had gone into his body, and had filled him up, so that his very soul was made of spiders now – spiders which had devoured his heart and his liver and his eyes, and which looked out from his skull with their own horrid powers of sight.

Lydyard could not look away from those eyes of dust, but from the corners of his eyes he saw that Pelorus no longer stood at the head of the stair, nor did Mandorla still crouch at its foot. Instead, there were two great wolves which whirled madly around, snapping and snarling as they struggled in the grip of some mysterious grappling force. It was as though they were fighting the empty air, and losing the battle.

Lydyard could not tell how much time had passed since he had used the leverage of the cords which bound him to agonize his arms and hurl himself into the world-as-dream. Perhaps, he thought, no time had passed at all; perhaps he had returned to a moment before the cataract of spiders, which was still to come, still to be faced, still to be lived through.

But if that were so, he realized, then he would never reach that moment for a second time, for Amalax had the knife in his hand and a darkness in his eyes which said that he meant to use it murderously.

Lydyard had escaped the impossible tide of spiders by the simple expedient of hurting himself, but he dared not do the same again, for he knew now that while his soul might flee his body must remain, and that if Amalax intended to cut his throat he could do it whether or not body and soul were united. There was no escape in dreams, and the dark angel of pain could not rescue him from this fate.

From the corners of his eyes he saw the wolves become mere blurs of shadow, drawn into the substance of the walls as he himself had once been drawn into the bosom of the earth. By that token he knew that magic and miracle were still here and all about him, there to be commanded, if he only knew how.

Lydyard held his arms as still as he could, and he looked Caleb Amalax in those unearthly eyes. He opened his mouth to speak to the man, trying with all his might to muster some kind of voice, not caring whether it might be the voice of command or the voice of reason.

No words came, because he knew – knew because he could see, as plainly as he could see the slimy walls and the yellow candle-flame – that Caleb Amalax was beyond the reach of any command which he might utter, and beyond the reach of reason too. Amalax was not Mandorla Soulier's man now, and certainly not his own, for there was a demon in his clouded eyes, whose filthy stare was more malevolent than any merely human stare could ever be.

Lydyard found that he could now remember how Amalax had screamed and screamed and screamed while the spiders had burrowed deep into his body, devouring his flesh until there was nothing left inside him but a host of spiders, and nothing left of his soul but filthy clinging cobwebs. Caleb Amalax was human no longer, and his intended butchery of David Lydyard would be a sacrifice to a blacker god by far than had lately appeared to the luckless Satanists of Paris.

Lydyard tried again to speak, to find the spell which would save him – and something came to him.

It was neither the voice of command nor voice of reason which welled up in him, but a very different voice, which had no need of his dried-up tongue and bloodied lips. It cried inside him, and its cry was pure prayer, addressed not to the God in which the Jesuits had so assiduously taught him to believe, but to any god at all who might come to save him from the demon with the spidery soul.

It was a prayer so forceful that it did not need a word to bear it, or a scream to give it sound. And yet, Lydyard had still to watch as the dagger drew back, had to feel the horny hand gripping his hair and forcing his head back to expose his wounded throat, had to choke with the effort of breathing, while the prayer went unanswered.

He saw the blade come forward to deliver its fatal stroke, striking like a snake, glistening with a momentary flicker of reflected firelight. He felt the blade touch his windpipe, and felt too – in a shock of precognition – the slicing effect of the blade as it sheared his sinews and tissues, severing the delicate thread of his life.

That same shock of precognition told him what death would be like . . . how the thoughts in his brain would slowly decay as language and imagination died, becoming plaintive nonsense long before the light of consciousness was utterly extinguished. After death came, he realized, he would still be able to say *cogito, ergo sum*, for there *would* be a thought, and because of that thought he would exist . . . but the thought would slowly dwindle like a dead leaf on fire, eventually disappearing and becoming nothing but the dust and ash of a thought, while he became nothing but the dust and ash of a being . . .

Then the miracle intervened.

The blade never completed its deadly arc. No sooner had it touched him than it was wrenched aside by an incredible power, and it was the knife which flared up briefly like a silver flame, and then shivered into a cloud of pale white ash. Amalax's stare, which had been fixed with awful feculent glee upon his victim, was also wrenched aside – and as those horrid eyes were dragged about to face that which had denied them, Lydyard heard the man's neck break like a rotten twig, and saw him fall like a discarded rag doll.

That was when he saw the other face – the face of the angel with eyes like the sky.

The angel reached down with a slender hand, and the cords which bound Lydyard to the bed burned away, and the fire with which they burned cleansed and healed his wounded wrists, his lacerated ear, and his charred feet.

And the angel took him up, and said: 'This is mercy; this is truth; this is right. *Sed libera nos a malo. Sed libera nos a malo.*'

And Lydyard answered, in the only way he could, with another prayer.

'Cordelia!' he said. 'For the love of God, let me go to Cordelia!'

Through the grey shades of evening the wolf-pack ran, through Osterley Park and over Lampton Hill, leaping over Hatton Brook and the railway line at Langley Grove, racing across Stoke Place and Burnham Common, past Hedsor Wharf and Cook Marsh, heading all the while for Ridgeley Wood and a certain house on its southern edge.

While they ran the wolves were free and full of joy; they felt their sense of destination not as command or constraint but as pure, unquestionable purpose, perfectly alloyed with instinct and inner nature. As wolves they were in harmony with one another and the world; as wolves they owned no fragile hope or bitter apprehension; as wolves they were energy and movement, pursuit and predatory potency; as wolves *they were not burdened with humanity*.

As wolves, they ran together, a pack united for the first time in centuries. TThe enmities which they had made in other guises were for the moment set aside, dissolved by the fire of joy. As wolves they did not belong to London or to any other place which men had built and named; as wolves, they were free.

They did not run unseen, for civilization had crept upon the wooded land like a scouring blight, clearing fields for crops and grazing cattle, making roads for horses and carriages, digging cuttings and canals for those riotous leviathans of steam and steel which were the newly born children of Man and Mammon. The world of men lay about them like a great web, from whose coiling strands there was no possible avenue of escape, and where once the wolves had made their own ways as migrants and masters, now they cut across the myriad paths and trails of another kind, and could not go unnoticed. But far the greater number of those who saw them did not know them at all as they glided by like shadows beneath the hedgerows, and called them lolloping dogs or illusory ghosts as wayward rationality persuaded them.

Only a handful of children, widely separated one from another by the rivers and the roads, the railways and the canals, dared to cry out that they had seen the werewolves of London going to the hunt, and all that those cries brought forth from older and more foolish mouths was laughter buoyant with the vanity of unbelief.

But they *were* the werewolves of London, going to the hunt. They were the werewolves of London, who had put aside their adopted names and their desperate hopes and their wild ambitions for the brief while which was given to them twice or thrice in every year; and while they ran, as brothers and sisters in blood, they were not pitiful but pitiless, not doltish but deadly, not glamorous but truly beautiful, not cocksure but proud.

They were going to the hunt and going to the Devil, but they went as wolves – as creatures of the wild; as air and fire and earth and blood instead of common clay. Though the darkness waited for them like a pool of noisome smoke, though Hell itself had opened wide its greedy maw, though the fever of their beating hearts was but a whisper in the vast silence of the tomb of time, still they ran.

For every one of them, to be a wolf was simply to be, and never to be denied.

The wolves ran, and the angel looked down upon them with a loving eye, protesting the dire justice of Machalalel, which had struck iciness into their very souls in the service of the hope that Machalalel might thus understand how another god had shaped the wretchedness of man.

'Run on,' whispered the angel. 'Run on.'

The angel knew, even before the darkness came to claim him, that he could no more do what the werewolves of London had asked of him than he could turn aside the tide of time, or hold back the growth of infinite space.

But the wolves ran on, until the darkness which had already claimed them gave them back their names.

Sister Teresa had once been a mere orphan, more wretched than all the rest by virtue of having been born in the asylum at Hanwell. Now she was so very nearly a saint, and in pursuit of that end she lay with her arms outstretched on the bare stone floor of her cell, savouring its cold unyielding solidity. She was light-headed and light-bodied, and was sure that it was only the force of her determined effort, and not the claim of gravity, which held her down.

The scratches made by the crown of thorns which she had placed upon her head, and the running sores on the palms of her hands, had ceased to hurt her – but there was a grinding pain in her abdomen which was readily transformed by her imagination into the ravages of a spear-head thrust into her side. That pain rumbled inside her like the muttered curses of an angry demon, moving her to the ecstatic delirium of infinitely repeated prayers.

She had no rosary near to hand by which to count and measure her *Ave Marias*, but she had the shadow of a standing cross before her inner eye, lit from behind by an eerie light which was divinely scattered by the clouds into all the colours of the rainbow.

It seemed to her that a very long interval had passed since she had last heard the voices of the saints. She had tried as best she could to cast herself adrift on the ocean of eternity, paying little or no heed to the cycle of day and night, relying entirely upon her sisters to keep track of the hours and the weeks – and yet she could not quite transcend the ties which bound her to the earth and the leaden sequences of time: her young and obstinate heart beat on at the core of her frail form, measuring her separation from the Kingdom of Heaven. She did not dare to be disappointed that her locutions and visions had ceased – how could one such as she deserve the intimate attentions of Christ's emissaries? – and yet the knowledge of her loneliness could not be other than a dull weight upon her weary earthbound soul.

Her outer eyes were closed, as they usually were; the sight of the inner eye, no matter how uncertain or imprecise, was infinitely preferable. The shadow of the cross meant more to her than whited walls or smiling faces, the greenery of spring or the blue of a cloudless sky.

Had a spider fallen from above to land upon her head, and walked in its flowing fashion to the very soles of her feet, she would hardly have felt its passage at all, and would not have been afraid. No such spider fell, but there was a different and more substantial touch, as though a hand had been laid upon her shoulder. For a moment or two, she paid no heed, but when it would not leave her, she consented to prop herself up on her right hand, and turn her head, and open her eyes.

When she saw the angel standing over her, she thought for a moment that she had not opened her eyes at all, and saw him only with her inner eye – but when the warmth of his radiance flooded her thin body, driving away the cold and the pain which savaged her lights, she knew that it was indeed her outer eyes which beheld him.

She stood up then, to face him more openly, more honestly and more generously than she had ever welcomed any merely human being.

And when he took her in his arms to hold her tight against him, she did not resist. And when the sores in her hands and feet were healed, she was glad to accept that it must be done. And when he lifted the crown of thorns from her head and crushed it underfoot, she made no complaint.

And when the glare of his golden halo dispelled the shadow of the cross which had been her constant companion for half a lifetime, she felt no sense of loss.

And when he carried her through the wall of her cell, and through the earth itself, then up into the bright and beautiful sky, she wept tears of pure happiness, that she was saved and free at last from the vile cage of flesh which had hurt her so much with its insults and its accusations.

But she never saw the shining gates of Heaven, or felt the beating of the Heart Divine, for even as her angel flew above that pitiful earth which suffered so horribly for want of a redeemer's touch there erupted from its Hellish core a demon more monstrous than any she had ever faced in the labyrinth of temptation: a malodorous thing of darkness and nausea and choking fumes which swept about her deliverer with all the ragesome force of a tornado, crushing his great white wings and striking terror into his bright blue eyes.

She realized then that even angels could be hurt, and

that the innocence which forbade them fear was no mercy after all.

And such was the horror of that revelation that she screamed in undiminishable anguish, and screamed and screamed and screamed, until the demonic darkness closed her mouth with its stinking stickiness, and carried her off with her broken angel to the uttermost depths of Hell.

6

Cordelia soon lost all sense of falling. In the illimitable darkness there was nothing to be seen, or heard, or touched and because there was no wind about her it seemed to her that she was quite still, and floating free. She did not know whether she had come to the centre of the earth, or whether she was nowhere at all, but there was an interval when she seemed to have no weight, and hence no substance or situation. She could not feel the beating of her heart or the pulse of the blood in her head, nor could she clench her fingers to feel the flesh of her own palms. If she were still clothed, her garments were frictionless upon her skin; if there had been pain within her body, it had died – and with it had died every vestige of hunger, every twinge and tautness of bodily awareness.

Absurdly, she was moved to wonder whether this was how God had felt before some passionless whim had moved Him to His first and greatest Act of Creation, but she had sufficient piety to refrain from any blasphemous whisper of command which might summon light to mitigate her sightlessness. Nor did she pray for release, for she found a certain strange comfort in her utter loneliness which banished terror from her soul.

She waited, as though she were waiting to be born.

And when sensation returned – when she felt again the clutch of her corsetry, and the tiny stirrings which mapped out the weighted form of her body – she felt that she was indeed newly called to existence from the well of souls. Although she was still falling, she drifted as lightly as thistledown, and could not believe that she would hurt herself when she came again to earth. Anxiety returned, but only as a mild unease, not stark terror. She felt curiously insulated from the callous cruelties of eventfulness, as though she were only a dream-self after all, or a mere phantom conserving only the illusion of the body which had been hers in life.

When she eventually came to rest she was confirmed in the opinion that she must be a dreamer or a phantom, for she found herself in a strange and cryptic Underworld which, she thought at first, could only be the Land of Death.

It was a world which had soil but no sky; whose coiling mists shone with an eerie radiance which surely did not come from any sun or starry firmament; whose trees were all broken-boughed and bare of leaves, white and skeletal; whose paths were strewn with pearly shells and bleached bones and jawless skulls; where nothing moved but languorous grave-worms and decrepit toads; where the faintest of wayward breezes stirred nothing but the mist and yet drew forth from the landscape a faint and heartfelt sighing sound, like the soft lamentations of ghosts which were denied the joys of Heaven and the tortures of Hell.

It was a noxious and sinister world, but the fright which she felt when she first discovered it was soon ameliorated, for its every appearance spoke to her of falsity and deception. Once, when she was a child, her father had taken her to the Egyptian Hall in Piccadilly to see Albert Smith's diorama describing the ascent of Mont Blanc; though she had never confessed it to her father she had been disappointed, for the images of light, though vast and strange, had seemed to her so obviously transparent, so evidently superimposed upon the vulgar reality of the theatre and its stage, as to be silly. Her father – who had once seen Koenig's Diaphanorama in Leipzig – had been far more entranced than she, and she had always thought it odd that a man like him should have so readily surrendered the power of disbelief which he cherished so ardently, merely for the sake of a picture-show. This Underworld, she felt, was like Smith's Mont Blanc: a captured semblance failing dismally in its attempt to be wholly real.

If this is Hell, she thought, *then Jacob Harkender must truly be the Devil – and if that be so, then the world has far less to fear from his machinations than pious men have urged us to believe.*

She set out to walk through the forest, which was so lifeless that it seemed petrified, yet had not the hardness of stone. The trees were soft and brittle, as though they were formed of pale ash, and had contrived to hold an echo of the shapes which had long ago been burnt only because no careless touch or casual tremor had ever come to crumble them to dust.

She felt that she was closely observed as she walked through the derelict landscape. The whited eyes of the toads were blind and unseeing, and the worms had no eyes at all, yet something watched her: something curious, something predatory, something strangely afraid. She knew that she was completely in its power, body and soul, and was so utterly the victim of its godly whim that she saw only that which it offered her to see, felt only that which it offered her to feel, could be only that which it offered her to be – and yet it hid itself, desperate to be unseen, a fugitive spinner of world-illusions which knew not what it could or ought to catch.

She knew that she was supposed to be terrified, but she was not. What fear she had could not drown out her power of intelligent thought, which saw that this was not a part of the world she knew, but only a stage whose scenery was crude and luridly imagined.

If Hell be real, she thought, *and a man once dead should find himself there, what should he do but live in it, and make what life he could? When damned souls come to the Gate of Doom, and see the message written there which commands them to abandon hope, what else can they possibly do but refuse?*

She felt that her father might be proud of her for that, if only her father had the capacity to be proud of her at all.

When she first became aware that there were other wanderers in the Underworld she thought that they were less substantial than herself – mere ghosts and shadows which were unaware of her presence, and which could not move of their own accord but had to be drawn, unresisting, through the silver mists by some arbitrary magnetism. It was with a sudden burst of uncomfortable enlightenment that she realized that these frail drifting forms of shadow-and-light were exactly like herself, and that her perceptions of her own substantiality were echoes of life. She discovered with a small shock of alarm that she was only dreaming that she was walking by her own efforts; in fact she was floating, helpless in the grip of the force which drew her gently and inexorably to her destiny.

Why, she thought, *perhaps I am dead after all. Who could have thought that this drear place was the actual Seat of Judgement? How absurd it would be if the disappointments of life and the shabbiness of cities were only a rehearsal for the disappointments of eternity and the desolation of infinity!*

But she did not despair. Even then, she did not despair.

Long before she saw the cross, and a human figure hanging there, she had been convinced that she was most certainly dead, and had been called to account for her sins. Sight of the cross itself was only one more tiny shock to be added to the register. She felt no particular shame at the thought that she might stand accused in the sight of one who had suffered and died for her and all her kind – and for all the petty failures of her pity and her honour. She felt a certain shaft of terror, to be sure, but she answered it very hastily.

I have loved, she said, defiantly. *Not as honestly and wholeheartedly as I should – but with all the strength and hope which I could bring to it, I have loved. And whatever harm I have done in the world, I have done the greater part of it passively, because I was given no other choice by circumstance.*

The person on the cross was not the Christ she had expected to see. It was a male child, no more than nine years old, with the face of an angel. Nor did he seem to be suffering, in spite of the nails which were driven through his wrists and feet, for his eyes were closed as though in sleep, and the softness of his face forbade her to believe that he was lost in a nightmare.

At the foot of the cross, staring up at the boy, were two phantom figures. One, who had fallen to her knees as though she were too sad and tired to sustain herself, was a young girl, thin to the point of starvation. The other was a man so faintly limned that he seemed to be made out of shadows.

Cordelia knew what an effort it must have been for the girl to lift up her head and look at the crucified child, but saw that she could not tear her unbelieving eyes away. The man, by contrast, stood in a curiously arrogant fashion, despite that he was very uncertain and perplexed. Cordelia did not know the girl, but she recognized Jacob Harkender.

Harkender did not turn to look at Cordelia, and gave no immediate indication of being aware that someone else was near by.

Cordelia stopped, further away from the cross than the other two. She did not know how frightened she was supposed to be, or what should happen now, but simply stood there, content to wait. She waited until someone touched her shoulder, and then she turned around to look into David Lydyard's face.

Somehow, phantoms though they were, they embraced one another with a greater fervour than they had ever allowed themselves to do while they were awkwardly alive and forced to bide in the world above.

'David!' she said, as though the name were a strangled sob. 'Oh, David, we are dead, and lost in the great graveyard of souls.'

'No,' he replied, in a voice less steady than he was dutifully trying to contrive. 'We are not dead – though whether we will ever find the land of the living again I must take leave to doubt. We are the victims of a very tiny Act of Creation, wrought by a dark angel which has long lived in the very substance of England's rocks. This is the heart of its web, in which it has trapped us, and many more besides – but what it means to do with us here I cannot tell. Do not be afraid of what you see here, for this place has been spun from the fabric of our own nightmares. That cross on which the poor boy hangs was forged in the human imagination, and if the angel which has dominion here is the Devil incarnate, it has taken that name and nature from our own anxious expectations. Dare to hope, if you can, that we might save ourselves, if only we can find the magic of deliverance.'

Harkender turned then, and looked towards them, but could not see them at all. Cordelia was not surprised by that, for the magician's eye-sockets seemed quite empty; his eyes were gone and there was nothing within his skull but the darkness of the void.

A brief flicker of puzzlement passed across blind Harkender's brow, but vanished in the shadows which were his eyes. He turned back to the cross – which, by some mysterious means, he could see – and addressed the child.

'Gabriel!' he said, in plaintive entreaty. 'You need not consent to this! You have power of your own, which is not yet extinguished. Come down from the cross, Gabriel, and lead me from this dungeon. Only lead me to the light, Gabriel, and I will make you wiser than all the men on earth. *I will make you wise.*'

There was no response from the sleeper on the cross, but the mists around them seemed suddenly busy with swirling eddies. Cordelia thought for a moment that a host of lost souls had come from the lifeless forest in a hopeful crowd, but quickly saw that these were not the ghosts of men. They were instead the spectral forms of sinister beasts; a pack of wolves had surrounded the clearing where the cross stood, and now converged upon the human shades which waited there.

Two of the ghost-wolves, and two only, reared up on their hind legs, and with deceptive flourishes of whirling mist became human. One became a pale-haired woman clad in a black dress, with eyes like mirrors; the other became a blond young man, with eyes like opals. They stood apart, one to the right of Lydyard and Cordelia, the other to the left. The woman smiled. To Cordelia it seemed a bold temerity that any creature should smile in a place such as this, but the wolfwoman smiled nevertheless.

'Why, David,' she said, in a soft, purring voice, 'was it you who brought us here? Or was it Gabriel who summoned us, from loyalty to his own unhuman kind?'

'This is Mandorla Soulier,' Lydyard whispered in Cordelia's ear. 'She does not fear that she is dead, for she is the mother-queen of the werewolves of London, who lost such fears a very long time ago. She believes that she is immortal, but does not care, for she is of the *vargr* – the restless, reckless ones who would laugh in the face of God or the Devil, and would not shame to tease either with entreaties or demands.'

'And who is the other?' asked Cordelia.

'My name is Pelorus,' answered the young man. 'I have worn others, but my name is Pelorus.'

'I see that it was not you, or Gabriel either,' Mandorla said, answering her own questions with a sigh. 'It was only that inquisitive angel which stole Harkender's soul. No doubt it is eager to see what might be made of us all. What a luckless thing it was that its sleep should be stirred by a man like Harkender, whose soul is dark and shocked with grief! The thing which found you was surely more fortunate by far!'

'What does she mean?' whispered Cordelia, clinging more tightly to Lydyard's comforting spectre.

'Harkender's pain-driven magic broke through the barrier of the material world,' Lydyard answered. 'I do not know when or how, but his cold soul found warmth enough to strike a spark in the slumbrous substance of some dark thing which should have been left to its rest. He woke this angel into a world from which it had been long banished, and after its fashion it possessed him, to use his eyes and pollute his dreams. But it can only understand the world as he understands it – it has inherited all his pain, all his anguish, all his hatred. He willingly made a Devil of himself, long ago, and now he has made a Devil of this creature which he awakened in the earth. When it used him to re-enact the little miracle by which its consciousness was renewed and reshaped, it acted as a Devil might, with fearful and cunning malevolence lest its new companion and adversary might be more powerful and wiser than itself. Its intention was to pervert and destroy, cleverly and deceptively – but Mandorla is right; the pity is that it might have found a better servant by far than such a hateful man as this.

'The other Creator, once awakened, found its own instruments – it stole de Lancy's soul and made a prisoner of mine, and where Harkender made a creature to reflect his weaknesses, de Lancy and I have made a creature which reflects our own. Harkender began his dark dream in the pit of his private hell, but I began mine in Plato's cave. Harkender saw Satan in the world around him, but I saw Satan in myself. His possessor became a monstrous predatory Spider; mine became a dubious Sphinx, which did not know the answer to its own riddle. And now we are here, all captives of that nightmare which grew from the seed of Harkender's bitterness.

'I believe that Harkender has already begun to learn the folly and futility of his past bitterness, and his possessor, in drawing others into its web, may also have discovered doubt – but what the consequence of that doubt may be, I cannot tell.'

'That is very clever,' said Mandorla, who had drawn much closer to Lydyard's right side. 'Did I not tell you, David, that I could help you to enlightenment? You had not the courage to hurt yourself, but you only needed the loving pitilessness of one who understood. You must put your little sister aside now, though, for we will have to face your wrathful Spider very soon, and only you and I are fitted for that task.' To Cordelia she said: 'Fear not that I want him for myself, my child, for I love only as a wolf and I like him too much to make him meat for the devouring. Let him go now, I beg you.'

Cordelia understood what was said to her, and though she was bewildered she had begun to see the nature of the case – but she could not let go as she was asked to do. She could not abandon that embrace, which was all that she and her lover had left to them in the midst of this curious wilderness of desolation.

'David,' she whispered. 'Don't leave me. Don't ever leave me.'

He did not relax his grip at all, but he looked at Mandorla Soulier and not at Cordelia.

'You mistake this enemy if you think that it will take heed of the likes of us,' he said. 'Do you think that the child is nailed to the cross for *our* amusement or annoyance? This net was drawn to catch a Sphinx, and we are merely the dross which circumstance has gathered about it. Immortal though you are, and far above the human beings which you despise, you are nothing to this Spider-Devil, nothing at all. I think it has brought you here only because Harkender was roused with wrath against you – only because it intends to punish you.'

'No!' said Mandorla. 'We are worth more than that!'

'Alas,' said Pelorus, 'I am sure that he is right. And whatever chance I may have had to invoke the power of Machalalel is lost, for the Spider has us in the very heart of its lair.'

For the first time, Cordelia saw the smile disappear from Mandorla's face, and knew that the truth had hurt her. But her mirror-bright eyes were not darkened, and her gaze merely returned to the child who slept so incongruously upon the frame of his torture.

'She still believes that Gabriel is hers to flatter and cajole,' whispered Lydyard, 'and that with his aid she may yet find a voice in this affair.'

Cordelia read a certain admiration in his tone – but she looked away from the wolfwoman at the silent figure of the girl, who stared up at the sleeping child with an unfathomable kind of agony in her eyes. Cordelia wondered then whether any one of those who had been summoned here had any right to think that he or she had a greater part to play than any other.

Jacob Harkender still had not shown by any word or sign that he was aware of the werewolves' presence, or Lydyard's and

Cordelia's, or the girl's. Suddenly, though, he turned sharply to stare out into the misty gloom, as though he had heard the sound of someone approaching. His shadowy features became strangely bright with hateful anticipation, as though he knew that an enemy was coming near.

'It is the Sphinx!' said Lydyard, his lips still very near to Cordelia's ear.

They turned to look – every one of them rapt with anticipation.

But when the expected figure had emerged from the dancing mists to stand between two whitely gnarled and leafless trees, Cordelia saw that it was not a Sphinx at all, but only a man as ghostly as any other here.

Even so, she could not help but gasp with alarmed astonishment, for the man was her father.

7

Tallentyre was almost the last person that David Lydyard had expected to see in this nightmare arena, and it was with mixed feelings that he saw his friend walk confidently forward. On the one hand, he was glad to see another ally; but on the other hand he was anxious that it might be he who was somehow responsible for Tallentyre's presence, and must bear the guilt of it if things went awry.

For the moment, it was direly difficult to see how things might go other than awry.

But there was nothing uncertain in Tallentyre's stride, and there was no doubt in Lydyard's mind that the newcomer intended to try to take control of this situation as casually and assertively as he took charge of all others.

Tallentyre did not look at Lydyard as he passed by, nor at Cordelia who was still tight-held in Lydyard's arms. Lydyard did not know whether that was because Tallentyre did not see them, or could not recognize them, or only because his attention was so firmly fixed on the dark thing which wore the outward appearance of Jacob Harkender.

Harkender, who had earlier been a fragile ghost made of uncertain shadows, seemed suddenly to have put on mass and solidity. He wore a thick black cloak, which concealed the contours of his body but made him bulk very large. Tallentyre, though he was a little taller, seemed much lighter, partly because of his ghostliness, and partly because he was dressed in the frail khaki suit which he had worn in the desert on the fateful night when he had first met the Sphinx.

Not until the two old enemies stood face to face did Lydyard realize that he had been right after all. In some sense, the Sphinx was here, with Tallentyre – just as the Spider was present in Harkender. He thought that at any moment the two of them might change their forms as mercurially as Mandorla Soulier had, to show themselves as they had really been before silly fate had given them the minds and dreams of men.

'So you are here at last,' said the figure in the cloak, in a new and very ominous voice. 'In the end, you had to come to me, as I always knew that you would.' It spoke as Jacob Harkender speaking to Sir Edward Tallentyre, but also as the Spider drawing yet another victim into its web of woe.

'I am here,' agreed the other. 'We are, after all, more alike than I once believed, and we need not be enemies.'

'Do you concede, then, that I have the right of it? Do you admit that the world as it exists is the world in which I have believed: a thing of mere appearances and creative magic, ripe for control by those who have true wisdom?'

'By no means,' replied the baronet, serenely. 'I come to show you that in spite of this nightmare which you have spun to catch us, you are mistaken.'

Lydyard heard Mandorla Soulier laugh lightly, and could not help but feel the force of apparent absurdity. Here they stood, all drawn into the very depths of the earth by some vast supernatural creature of heavy rock and quiet fire, brought to stand in this sullen and shabby Underworld, in the shadow of a crucified angel. The speaker himself was no more than a phantom echo of a fleshy man, but still he was content to say that the world was not what it presently appeared to be.

Lydyard reminded himself, though, that this was not merely the rationalist Sir Edward Tallentyre addressing the charlatan Jacob Harkender, but the riddlesome Sphinx prepared to face at last the Spider which had beckoned it from rest by stealing an atom of its soul to make a wonder-child.

Harkender, at any rate, did not see fit to laugh. Nor did he scowl. There was, instead, a fugitive gleam of hope in his 'hooded eyes as he stared unblinkingly at his adversary, and said: 'I can crush you where you stand. I have such power here that I can consume you with fire upon the instant, and scatter your dust upon this dismal soil.'

'No doubt,' answered Tallentyre. 'But it would not prove that you were right. And you, who face the unknown future like the rest of us, need proof as well as power to sustain you – for until you have that proof, you cannot know what the exercise of power will cost you.'

There was something breathtaking about his arrogance, but even while Lydyard paused to admire it Tallentyre flinched as though struck by a whip, and clutched at his right arm, looking down at the palm of his hand, which had been pierced by a foot-long dart. Blood flowed sluggishly down the shaft towards the point of it, and Tallentyre could not hold back the rictus of pain which convulsed his face and body.

'Draw me a cross, then,' hissed the baronet. 'Make crosses for us all, or stakes at which to burn us. Waste yourself in the creation of this foolish little Hell, if this is all that your feeble mind is able to conceive. No one can save you from the Devil, if that is what you are avid to be. None can spare you from petty hate and malevolent fury, if you will not see, *but I tell you now that those for whom the world itself is but a dream cannot truly dream at all!* I was not sent here to play the painful fool, but to answer your need – a need which remains, despite what this cruel and crippled man has done to pervert it. I have that answer, if you can only bear to hear it.'

Harkender's empty-eyed face was contorted into a perfect apparition of wrath. 'Liar!' he cried. 'You are blind, and cannot see. You have never penetrated the veil of appearance, but I have trod the way of pain and I have *seen*. You are but a man, but I am more than man, and there is no other answer to be given than the one which I have found!'

'You have seen,' answered Tallentyre, 'but you have stood alone, and what you have read inscribed upon the walls of eternity is the reflection of your own fevered dreams. You have stood alone, unbefriended and untested, but even in this – your private Hell – there are others who stand with me, and will testify that my vision is not mine alone but a truth which all may share.'

'A thousand blind men still cannot see,' said Harkender, with a sneer. 'And are you so sure that Lydyard sees as you see? Are you so sure that he is still your acolyte, now that the Sphinx has shown him the riddles of Creation in their true light?'

Lydyard could feel the fevered beating of Cordelia Tallentyre's phantom heart, and knew that she had bit her lip to save herself from crying out in anguish at her father's plight.

But Tallentyre had straightened up again. The dart had gone and his hand was whole again. He too could work miracles, here.

'I need not even ask him,' answered the baronet. 'I know him – his mind, his heart, his courage. If he does not see as I see, then what I see has failed its best test.'

A second dart sprang through the air, this time aimed at Tallentyre's heart. It struck hard and true, and Tallentyre looked down at it, but did not fall. Lydyard heard Mandorla laugh, but could not tell which of them she was laughing at.

'I do not deny that you can hurt me,' whispered the baronet – though the words were distinct enough to all who could hear. 'I only deny that it matters. If you will condescend to share my dream, and forsake your own, then I will show you what a sad and stupid fantasy you have been sold, and though I cannot swear to soothe away that poisonous anger which torments you, I will medicate it as best I can.'

Lydyard was certain in his own mind that Harkender would have refused, if he had only been Harkender and nothing more; but he was equally sure that Tallentyre would not have offered so much, if he had only been Tallentyre and nothing more.

'What does he mean to do?' asked Cordelia, very faintly.

It was on the tip of Lydyard's tongue to say that he did not know – but then he realized that he did know, and that in his own perverse way he had helped the Sphinx to see it. While he had struggled so desperately to solve the riddle of his own salvation, the creature which possessed him had struggled with equal urgency to solve the riddle which he presented to it . . . and between the two of them, they had reached an understanding. He saw why the Sphinx had chosen Sir Edward Tallentyre as its advocate, and why he too must put his final trust in what the baronet had taught him.

'He means to show this self-appointed demon what truly lies beyond the surface of the earth,' whispered Lydyard. 'He means to show us all what we have been too slow and small of mind to comprehend: how very different the world now is from what it was before!'

In a louder voice, intended for all of them to hear, he said: 'You must see what it is that this man has to show you, for you little realize how much you need to know it.'

'They are blind!' wailed Harkender, reaching up to his face with clawlike hands, as though he wished that he might tear out his dark and empty eyes. 'They are blind, and only two. I am one, but *I can see!*'

'We are not two,' said Cordelia Tallentyre, bravely. 'We are three, and though we have seen the pit of your dismal Hell, still we have a better dream which is our own!'

'Nor are we so few as three,' said Pelorus the manwolf. 'We are four, in truth, and one of us has lived ten thousand years. Hear this man, or though you be the Devil incarnate you will be a sorry fool, and damned because of it.'

Jacob Harkender clutched at his own face, and raked it with his nails. There was only one there to whom he could possibly appeal for aid, and that was Mandorla Soulier – but Mandorla was laughing louder now, with a helpless delight which had abandoned calculation. And the web which had trapped and confined them all was blown apart by a stormy wind.

The Underworld dissolved, with the consent of its Creator, and they saw that where they stood instead was the painted floor of Jacob Harkender's attic at Whittenton, which was ablaze with hungry flames. For a few brief moments they were bathed by the coloured light which spilled through the ornamented dome, but that dome which stood in place of the sky and aspired to represent the arch of Heaven was soon obscured by the stinging smoke, which swallowed them up and carried them away.

When the smoke had gone, so had the earth; the night sky and the pale light of the scattered stars were naked to their gaze.

'I have seen the sky before,' said Jacob Harkender spitefully. 'While the surface of the earth has been so markedly transformed by the work of man, the sky has altered not at all.'

'You have hidden the sky behind its effigy,' answered Tallentyre, speaking not merely to the Spider, but to all of them. 'You have said to yourselves, the sky does not change and the stars are eternal, but that is not true at all, for whatever the hand of man has wrought upon the surface of the earth is next to nothing compared to what the eye of man has seen in the farther reaches of infinity. It has been said to us constantly that comfort blinds us, because it will not show us the world as its Creators might remake it – but I say now that the comfort of Created dreams breeds a blindness of its own, and that the greatest blindness of all is the blindness of those who can only see with eyes of faith and fantasy. It is the dismal world of anger and fear and pain and nightmares which is truly blind, and I can show you a grander world by far, if only you will condescend to see.'

They saw the stars.

They saw that the faintness of the stars was mere appearance, because the stars were really suns far huger than the earth: great spheres of radiance fulsomely pouring the gift of their power upon tiny worlds like the earth.

They saw that the number of the stars was mere appearance, because for every star which they could see with naked eyes there were thousands upon thousands more revealed by the telescope; and even this was but the beginning, because they saw that for every star which the telescope revealed there were thousands upon thousands more, hidden even from augmented eyes by the gaseous envelope which shrouded the earth, and by the dark clouds which lay among the stars themselves.

They saw that the uniformity of the stars was mere appearance, and that there was more variety among them than could be imagined in colour and size and quality of substance; and they saw that the pale nebulae which shared the sky with the stars were in reality great clouds of stars, which filled the dark vast distances beyond the particular cloud of stars which was home to the sun that gave its radiance to the tiny, lonely earth.

Lydyard, who had always known what Tallentyre knew of this, now saw for the first time what Tallentyre saw with that cold inner eye which was blind to the brightness of dreams.

He saw the stars, and the distances between the stars, and the distances between the island universes which were teeming hives of stars, and the huge dark nebulae and the blazing nurseries of stars unborn.

He saw the macrocosm for the first time, and saw what a vaulting ambition there really was in the hopeful litany of 'as above, so below'.

He saw a man made all of stars, a man who was the universe, a man whose heart was the stuff of stars, who had stars for eyes and great wings of stars, and semen streaming with starlight and the energy of life. He saw a man whose tears were stars and whose blood was stars, and understood how vast that man must truly be, and what an unbearable cage of darkness there was about every one of the stars which were his atoms, and every one of the island universes which were his cells.

And Lydyard saw, as he had once seen before, that paradoxical boundary which was the edge of infinity and the body of God the Ultimate Creator.

He saw that the man who was the universe was the inverted image of the mould which was God.

He saw that the God who was the Ultimate Creator, who was as impotent to put his meddling hand into his own Creation as a man would be to reach into the chambers of his own heart, had a face which neither wept nor smiled but turned to His Creation eyes which were utterly and hopelessly blind.

Nor was it simply Lydyard who saw these things. They all saw them, and knew that whatever they were seeing, it was no mere dream.

They saw in that Eden of stars the second tree, of whose fruit neither Adam or Eve had eaten, which was the true Tree of Knowledge and the true Tree of Life.

They saw that where light flooded the surfaces of worlds by the billion – many like the earth and many not – there stirred among the atoms of those worlds the molecules of life, the molecules which turned that light to the purpose of building and rebuilding and building anew, which tried and erred and tried and erred a billion times more, until they had made tiny things like rods and globes and worms, and bigger things of convoluted shape, and bigger and yet bigger things. And they saw that the trying and erring went on, and that the cells which were the atoms of life tried and erred a billion times more, and a billion times more, and more and more, until they changed and changed and changed, so that wherever there had been one kind there became many, and wherever the light of life fell, there grew an Eden in microcosm.

They saw that some of these myriad Edens gave birth to Adams and Eves, in many different guises, while some did not, but still they tried and erred, tried and erred, and tried.

Lydyard, who had known what Tallentyre had known, saw now what Tallentyre could see with the eyes of his cold and clinical soul, and what the rhythm and music of life and Creation really meant to that sharp and sceptical mind.

He saw the march of evolution embodied in the tiny pinpricks of matter which whirled around the glorious stars which floated in their cages of vast and empty darkness.

He saw the legions of cold-souled beings in all their myriad forms, struggling to see and to build by the efforts of their hands and minds, without the magical heat of Sight and Creation to guide them.

He saw the transience and the permanence of what they made, eroded by time and yet sustained by hope and reproduction and improvement.

And Lydyard saw, as he had not quite seen before, what a deceptive glamour there was in the kind of Golden Age which Pelorus and Mandorla remembered; how easy were its transformations, how hollow its achievements. He understood how tragically mixed were the desires which Mandorla had – and Pelorus too, despite the alien will which worked within him – that the Golden Age might come again, and that the werewolves of London might have joy, infinite and unalloyed, and blind.

Nor was he alone in seeing this, though there were some there who could not like what they saw.

'This is the dream which you might have dreamed,' said Tallentyre to Jacob Harkender, and the Devil which Jacob Harkender had raised. 'This is the dream which can still be dreamed, by those who will not sell their souls to nightmares. There are millions of men too sick at heart to dream it, and millions more who prefer the comfort of their blindness. Perhaps those angels which have fallen to earth are far more like them than they could ever consent to believe! But I say only this: an angel may make a Hell within the earth, and draw a thousand or a million men to torment and destruction, but such is the infinity of All that its efforts are as nothing. If ever there was a Golden Age, it is dead and gone, and forgotten by the universe itself, which has found a better beginning and a finer future. Only learn to see, and you will understand.'

'Is there comfort in this?' whispered Mandorla Soulier in David Lydyard's ear. 'Is there joy? If you could only know what it is to live as a wolf, and to be free.'

'I can destroy the earth,' said Jacob Harkender, with a voice as deep as the Devil's own. 'Doubt me not! I can do such work with hatred as to turn your dreams to direst nightmare!'

'I do not doubt you at all,' answered Tallentyre. 'You may walk the earth as a nightmare of destruction, but when you are gone and all your kind are no more than the dust which now contains them – the dust which they now are – it will all be the same, and it will all have been for nothing. No matter how many men you kill, there will be more; no matter how many suns you extinguish, there will be more.

'I offer you something better than this vengeful vision which was stitched from misery and confusion and regret – I offer you a future made by the men of a million worlds, more rich and strange than anything you can imagine. I cannot live to see it, but you have lived ten thousand remembered years, which have become millions while you slept – and you might live ten thousand more, or millions, if you will only condescend to try. Go to your rest, and come again, and one day there will be dreams enough to make the waking more worthwhile. *Better by far the Heaven which you cannot know than the Hell which you know too well.*'

Lydyard was certain, in his own mind, that if Harkender had been only Harkender and nothing else, he would have refused. But he was only a shadow caught in a web, which was not entirely of his own spinning nor entirely of his own design.

Harkender would have refused, but the Spider which looked out from the darkness of his empty eyes did not.

Gabriel Gill opened his own eyes, which were as blue as the sky, and he stepped down from the cross, to embrace Teresa and look Mandorla frankly in the face.

'Gabriel . . .' said the wolfwoman; but there was no seductiveness in her voice.

It seemed that Jacob Harkender was trying to pronounce
the name too, but his lips, which were bleeding where he
had raked them with his fingernails, could not even form
the word.

Gabriel smiled – and then, like a star exploding in the
remoteness of the desert void, his body blazed with the quiet
fire of light and hope, and was consumed.

8

Long afterwards, David Lydyard could remember every
instant of that last strange dream. What faded into vagueness
was its aftermath, when they came to earth again. It was then
that confusion took command and memory failed in its work.

He knew that he and Cordelia Tallentyre had stood together,
arm-in-arm, and watched Jacob Harkender's house burn. He
remembered that half a dozen servants, reinforced by men
from the village, had tried ineffectually to fight the flames
with water borne in buckets from the stream. They might as
well have tried to turn back the tide of time. The only useful
task which had been left for them to perform was to keep the
fire from the stables, at least until the horses had been led to
safety.

He was less sure of other things which he might have
seen. Had the strange dome above the attics been lit for
several minutes from within like some great bauble – a
Hallowe'en lantern or a child's toy? Or had it already been
blackened by smoke, the darkened panes shattering in the
heat? Had there really been a woman who came to stand
before them, her face stained by smoke-induced tears and
eyes strangely baleful? Had she really demanded, in a voice

hysterical with anxiety, to know what they had done with Jacob Harkender?

Perhaps the last, at least, was true, for Lydyard had a memory of saying to someone: 'No, we have not seen him – here.'

He did remember that Cordelia had asked him what must have become of the magician, but that might have been at some other time, though he could remember well enough what he had replied. 'I suspect that he is dead,' he had said, 'but I cannot say for certain. I believe he found it hard to discover that he was not the master of his own power, but only the instrument of another. I do not know whether it hurt him more to know that he had helped to shape that other's consciousness in the image of his own distress, or to know that the image was ultimately rejected upon the persuasion of a man he hated and despised. In either case, I think that he might have been too proud to flee the flames, for he had long since given up his fear of Hell.'

None of the others had died – except, of course, for Gabriel. But had Gabriel ever truly lived, except as a phantom which had never properly belonged to the real and actual earth? As to the fate of the Spider he could only guess, but his guess was that it had returned into the earth, content to wait for the unfolding of the world's strange destiny – no longer a spinner of labyrinthine webs, but only one more impotent Creator, comforted by blindness.

When enough time had gone by, Lydyard could not even be certain how he and his future wife had contrived to return from Whittenton to London, though he knew they had not walked, or flown, or ridden upon a magic carpet. They must have come by road, or rail, or river, by the power of horses or engines, borne along by wheeled carriages or wooden hulls, made and decorated with all the artistry and artifice of which modern men were capable. In a way, it was all the same . . . it did not matter.

He could not even remember what he said to Sir Edward

Tallentyre when they had faced one another again, though he remembered that it had been a very joyous meeting.

He felt sure that he would have remembered the words better had it not been for the joy, and that he would have remembered the joy better, had it not been overshadowed by a more extraordinary elation, which was to do with Cordelia, whom he had brought from the pit of Hell itself.

He forgave himself for all these lapses of memory, and told himself that no one could possibly blame him for being so blindingly elated, when he had done what even Orpheus had failed to do for the woman whom he loved.

Elinor Fisher also found, after a time, that her memories of that particularly vexing day had become confused. There had somehow arrived a moment when she could not help but stare at her lover while he lowered himself once again to the sofa which he had so recently quit – though she could not figure out quite where he had gone or why. She was certain, though, that his face had been unprecedentedly leaden with shock, and yet his eyes were illuminated by an odd excitement, a kind of pleasure which she had never seen in him before.

She had given him whisky in a glass, which he drank in a curiously greedy manner.

She could not believe, afterwards, that he had really said much of what she thought he had said. He could not really have murmured, 'I went with de Lancy, to see the Sphinx,' because she knew that he had seen the Sphinx in Egypt, with William de Lancy and David Lydyard, several months before. Nor could she have said what she thought she had said, which was: 'You swore to tell me everything.' She could not have said it, because he could not have sworn it.

She thought that she remembered well enough something else which he had said, but that seemed equally puzzling in its way. She was almost sure that she had heard him say it, but perhaps it was wishful thinking that made her so confident. 'If I cannot honour one pledge,' he had almost certainly said, 'I will offer you another. I swear to you that you need never fear to lose what you have. I swear to you that I will take care of you, until my dying day, and then will not leave you unprovided. It is a promise I will find much easier to keep than the one I could not, and one whose keeping will comfort you far more than had I kept the other.'

He had added, though it seemed ludicrously out of character even at the time: 'Will you forgive me, now?'

It all seemed improbable – and yet she was sure that she remembered the reply which she had made, and remembered it with pride. 'I must,' she had said, perversely determined to say it more lightly than he would like. 'A mistress must always forgive, must she not? What else is there which makes her different from a wife?'

Had he replied to that, she sometimes wondered? Had he managed a riposte? She thought that he had, but was not at all confident that she was right. 'Nora,' he had said, 'there was a time when I might have compared you to an angel, and laughed at your refusal to be pleased. But I know now what it is to be an angel, and I am glad that you are only what you are. I mean it as a compliment, I do assure you.'

She could only suppose that she had believed him. She had sat down beside him, and accepted the compliment as gracefully as she possibly could. At least, that was what she had done if it had ever happened at all.

There were, however, those who remembered more clearly what had happened, even after many years. One of them, at least, could relive the memories as though the events had happened only the day before. One of them was perfectly certain that she would never forget.

In her cell at Hudlestone Manor, Sister Teresa had sat for several hours, shivering. She felt the cold very keenly, and she was very hungry, but she knew that there could be no possibility of release from her distress until morning came.

When morning had come . . .

She had known, even then, that the path from sainthood to humanity would not be easy for one who had gone so far in search of Heaven, but she had never asked for ease. Though the cold and the hunger had begun to hurt her, in a way that they had long since ceased to do in the ordinary course of her extraordinary life, she knew that she could bear the pain. Certain other pains had gone, by way of compensation. Her stigmata were healed; where she had proudly worn her oft-renewed crown of thorns, there was not the slightest trace of a scar.

Reverend Mother and Sister Clare would not accept that as a miracle, but she knew better.

She knew, too, that the greatest miracle of all, which had given her the will to turn away from Heaven, would never be understood by anyone except herself, and about the manner of its working she would never, as long as she lived, say a single word.

Gabriel was gone for ever; she knew that for certain. She knew, too, that he had not been the kind of Heavenly messenger she had always expected and believed in; but neither was he an instrument of Satan, as she had once thought. He had been, in truth, as innocent as any other child. And somehow, in the manner of his passing into fire and into glory, he had soothed the other fire which had almost consumed her own soul. She was cool now, and that which had so nearly burned to ashes was magically restored. She had life.

Life was not easy, but it could be lived. She had proved that, by living it as best she could, and she continued to prove it for many long years.

Meanwhile, the wolves ran as they had always run, restlessly and hopelessly, ever unredeemed. They were the *vargr*, the unquiet ones, unquiet still and unquiet for ever.

They ran possessed by anger and by joy, free from the knowledge which would return with consciousness and thought, with memory and fear. Wherever they were seen, those who loved the world as it was would look away, and scoff at the deceptions of the shadows – but the children who had not yet learned to care whether the world was really magical or not would mouth the phrases of ancient rhymes, and shudder with delicious terror.

The children it was who had the right of it. The werewolves of London were fierce and real, and the enemies of all mankind, but fear of them need only be a thrill, fugitive and sweet, for they were not after all to be dreaded in the way that men had once dreaded all their kind.

They were, in a way, to be pitied, for their impotence and for their fate. And they knew it; in their hearts, they all knew it.

One day, not long after his descent into Hell, Pelorus watched a carriage draw to a halt on Vauxhall Bridge. He waited for a few minutes, while the stream of traffic flowed past, before he stepped out on to the bridge and walked slowly towards the vehicle. The coachman saw him immediately, and watched him approach, neither welcoming nor hostile.

'Hello, Perris,' said Pelorus, when he drew level. He paused for a moment to look up at his brother, who nodded to him in a polite fashion and then looked round to stare unrepentantly at a passing wagon-driver who had cursed him loudly for blocking the way.

Pelorus climbed into the carriage and sat down opposite Mandorla, bracing himself against the inevitable lurch which came when Perris stirred the horses to action.

'You have your gun, I suppose?' said Mandorla, with contrived amusement.

'I do,' answered Pelorus. 'Unlike poor Lydyard, I shall not be tempted to release it if I find myself under attack.'

She laughed softly. 'It is over,' she said. 'We need not be enemies, at least for a while. You have won again, though I scarcely know how. And as for poor Lydyard . . . I did but help him to see what had become of him, and I would not have hurt him too badly. It was only when the other came to claim him, and drove Amalax to madness, that he came to be in real danger. I could not like the boy, but I never meant him any harm.'

'I have heard you say the same of other men,' Pelorus observed, 'but it often did not save them from coming to grief. You have an unhappy knack of causing more harm when you do not intend it than when you do.'

'You should not try to wound me,' she told him, chidingly, 'for I know as well as you do that whenever you succeed in thwarting me it hurts you as much as it injures me.'

'You must not try to play with me like this,' he answered, 'for I know as well as you do that it does not really make you happy. You have nothing to blame me for, this time – I did nothing at all.'

'You underestimate your luck,' she said. 'I have heard the rumour of what happened in Egypt, and I know that you could not have been hurt for nothing. If the will of Machalalel put you at risk, it can only have been because the Sphinx, in its angry confusion, came close to killing Tallentyre. If you had only let it . . .

'And then again, you could not help but offer warnings to Lydyard, could you? You were compelled to keep him from my tender care just a little too long, and to help him understand. In the end, it was through Lydyard as much as through Tallentyre that the Sphinx found a way to answer the Spider without conflict. You do not know how near the world was to destruction by the wrath of angels, and without you, I swear, I might have tipped the balance.'

'Preserve that illusion, if it pleases you,' said Pelorus, indifferently. 'But if that is what you believe, why come to me now? Do you think I am human, to be beguiled by your seductive flatteries? I cannot help but love you, Mandorla, for that is the way a wolf is made, and I am wolf enough inside my skin, but I will never trust you, while I have the power of human sight and human thought.'

'It is only the will of Machalalel which makes you say so,' she said, reproachfully. 'I am your mother, your sister and your lover, for neither you nor I can have any true life outside the pack. I love you as you love me, and not unwillingly. For human men I am all glamour and all deception, and if they are hurt by their affection for me even when I do not intend it, it is only the treason of their own stupid lusts that hurts them, and they deserve it fully. But you do not see the mimicry of human beauty which Machalalel forced upon me, you see only the wolf which is within, and that is what binds you to me. It is yourself that you cannot trust, dear Pelorus, for you have that wretched will upon you, forever turning you away from what you are and what you truly need. If you could only surrender yourself to me . . .'

She left the sentence dangling, smiling the most seductive of her human smiles.

'You mistake me,' Pelorus replied. 'And it is you who should strive to be different. You cannot do it, I know, because you are presently too much the wolf and too much the woman, and not philosopher enough; but you are immortal, Mandorla, and cannot tell what you might be able to achieve, with effort and sincerity. Whether or not you are right to believe so passionately that your only salvation is to be a wolf again and nothing else, I cannot tell – but I believe that you never can and never will be a mere wolf now that you have been a woman, and should accept it even if you cannot train yourself to like it. There are worse things by far than being human, and though I will not try to tell you that it would be better for a true wolf to be a man, I insist that a werewolf must accept the human part of himself – or herself – as well as the wolfish part. Men are not your enemies, Mandorla, and it is wrong and foolish of you to desire that destruction might fall upon their world and all that they have made.'

She looked at him with every appearance of pity and concern, but he would not believe that there was any honesty in it. 'Poor Pelorus!' she said. 'Not wolf, not man, but *philosopher*! But what else can you love but sophistry, when you will not cleave to your own kind, and cannot make love as a man? Even that kind of playful love which I can make with human men is worth a little pleasure, but for you there is nothing, nothing at all but the tortured logic of the celibate . . .'

She leaned forward as she allowed the words to die away again, and showed her pearly teeth in a mock-grimace, which would have been a playful temptation had she been in wolf form, but upon her human face could be nothing else but mocking parody.

'What did you see?' asked Pelorus abruptly. 'What did you see when the Spider consented to dream Tallentyre's dream instead of Harkender's nightmare?'

Her eyes narrowed, and she sat back. 'You were there,' she said. 'And I know that you have seen Lydyard, and that he told you what he saw. Do you think that I hid my eyes?'

'No,' he said, softly. 'But there is more than one kind of blindness, and I wonder whether you truly saw what there was to be seen. The Spider saw, did it not? But Harkender, though he was dreamer and part of the dream, saw only an end and a desertion, only the frustration of his hatred and his enmity. I wonder if you saw any more than that.'

'Harkender is dead,' she answered, shortly.

'And you can never die, but that does not answer the question.'

'I saw nothing to obliterate my enmity and contempt for humankind,' she said, sullenly. 'I saw a battle lost in a long hard war, but there will be other battles, and I do not know that Tallentyre's hope for the universe is any more to be trusted – or any less Hellish – than Harkender's morbid fears. What does he tell us, after all, but that we are each and every one of us mere motes of dust, of no consequence at all? It might please you to dream such a dream as that, but you are a philosopher, while I am a wolf. I know joy, and Sir Edward Tallentyre never will, nor will the Sphinx, who might have played the wolf, but chose instead to play the man.'

'If it has returned to its Creator, to sleep in the timeless sands,' said Pelorus, 'it will at least have peace and patience.'

'It has not,' Mandorla told him. 'It wears human form,

almost as bewitching and beguiling as my own, and every bit as false. It sails with its puppet Adam on the evening tide, bound for America. It has conceived some strange ambition to know the world more intimately, and because it has consented to let go of your frail and fickle friend, it must find other instruments to serve its purpose. I have by no means given up hope for its future, because I know already what its present guise will ultimately teach it about the ugliness and nastiness of men. One day, dear Pelorus, its thoughts will surely turn again to the making of Hell, and then, perhaps, there will be time to treat with it.'

'I have more faith in its judgement than that,' said Pelorus. 'Because I know what it saw, and what it came to understand, far better than you do.'

Mandorla shook her head. 'One day,' she said, lightly, 'I may seek out David Lydyard again. It might be interesting to pit myself against his pretty human, to see how resolute his love for the pretty Cordelia really is. I would not hurt him for the world, but if I tried as hard as I might, perhaps I could give him the merest glimpse of joy.'

'And in the mean time,' said Pelorus, 'you will no doubt find yourself a richer man, with a comfortable home, and tell yourself that although you despise what humans find in luxury, still you must draw breath and see to the safety of the pack, and make ready for the next mad plàn which seizes hold of you.

'And from time to time you will write to me, and invite me to come to you, and join you in your entertainments, and once in a while, I will come, to see my brothers and my sisters, and bandy words with you as we are doing now. But in my pocket I will have my gun, and though my sight may be softened by affection, I will never, never give myself into your power. To sleep for ever would undoubtedly be peaceful, but in that sleep there are no dreams, and even you – who could not hear or heed the will of Machalalel – are ever avid to return to hopeful wakefulness, and all the strife and stress of the world. We are not angels, after all.'

456

'We are not angels,' Mandorla answered, 'because we are wolves.'

'Alas,' said Pelorus, 'we are wolves no more. We are only the werewolves of London, who have no proper place in existence or belief, and cannot make one, no matter how we may try.'

'But we will live to see the end,' Mandorla said, maliciously, 'whenever and however it comes. We will live to see the end, and Tallentyre will not.'

'Now I know that you did not truly see what Tallentyre saw,' retorted Pelorus. 'For if you had you would know; you would understand that Tallentyre's triumph and Tallentyre's joy is that he does not need to see the end any more than he needs to remember the beginning. For in the world which he sees, there can be no vestige of any sensible beginning, and no prospect of any meaningful end. And that is the better way of seeing, Mandorla, that is the better way.'

She could not believe him, of course. In her heart, she was a wolf, and her dreams were of the Golden Age, when the world had been bright and the dark between the stars had not been infinite at all.

EPILOGUE

The Solace of Pleasant Dreams

Every thing possible to be believed is an image of truth.

William Blake, *Proverbs of Hell*

1

Today, a man named David Lydyard came to us to bring us the news that the world will not end very soon. He believes with all his heart that this news, if true, is good. He came to suggest to us that we have been wrong in our beliefs, but he came gently and kindly, not swollen up with triumph and contempt as some have come in other times. He believes, in all sincerity, that he has seen a truer vision of God than the one which we have taken for our guide, and that he has taken arms against fallen angels.

I said to him, as duty bade me do: 'Beware the sin of intellectual pride, which tempts you from the path of faith. It may be that the end is not yet, but still it will come – and in that destined end, and the return of Jesus Christ, who is God made man, is the only true hope which mankind has.'

He replied that he could not believe it, and his answer was not without honest regret.

I tried, as is my duty, to soothe his doubts and lead him from his heresy to the safety of the faith. I told him that the macrocosm which is the universe and the microcosm which is man are one and the same, that the beating of the Heart Divine is the beating of the human heart. I said to him that Jesus Christ, our one and only saviour, is God-in-man, and hope made flesh.

'When I came here before,' he said, 'you reminded me that seeing is an active process, and that our sight is no mere mirror in which the world is passively reflected. It is the mind which sees, and the eye is only its instrument. Clear sight requires clear intelligence, and no matter what reverence we have for the authority of tradition, we must recognize that men see more clearly now what the world is really like than they have ever seen before. In future, they will see it more clearly still. When next these blind and dull Creators are shocked from their sleep they will not come as echoes of forgotten idols or monstrous beasts of nightmare, because the imagination of future generations will have put away such childishness. The day of Spiders and Sphinxes is very nearly done, and I am certain in my heart that you have waited too long for your apocalypse and for the magical making of Heaven. There will be no end to the world now, Father, and Heaven will be made on earth in the human fashion, by the effort of hand and brain.'

There are others in today's world who say such things; this man speaks for many, and many who would reckon themselves wise. But the truly wise put their faith in prophecy and not in progress. David Lydyard and his kind would declare this house an anachronism, anchored in a past which is already dead, looking forward to a future which is obsolete, but we have our own ways of seeing, and our own clear intelligence. We know what kind of a world it is which lies beyond our gates. We know its squalor and its misery, its dirt and desolation, its madness and its wars. David Lydyard and his kind believe that the world is getting better, but their belief is founded in the comforts which are enjoyed by a tiny minority of the world's people – and those comforts, like all comforts, serve to blind that minority to the anguish of the mass of men.

Those who have truly seen know well enough that the world is getting worse, not better, at least for the great majority of those who live in it, and that it has yet to experience its extremes of war, famine, plague and death. The visions which the way of pain has yielded up to our Order are not to be doubted; we have seen the battlefields where vast armies will clash and die amid the mud and the barbed wire; we have seen the legions of destruction which soar upon the winds like iron eagles, pouring fire and death upon cities; we have seen the poisoning of the rivers and the seas; we have seen the holocaust.

All this we know, and are commanded to hold secret from those who know only hope and faith. The carnival of destruction is yet to come, and may not be set aside by the paltry efforts of mankind.

David Lydyard says that the apocalypse can never happen; we know that it has already begun. He says that the world will not be destroyed, but will instead be rebuilt as Heaven by the effort of the human hand and its machines; we know that the work of the hand and the machine *are* destruction, and that when men see at last how their efforts have brought an end to the world that they loved, then they will turn to the only possible redeemer, who is the God-made-man.

This is our hope, and the only hope which the world truly has.

> Zephyrinus, *Journal of the English House of the Order of St Amycus*

2

If we seek to understand history as it should and must be understood, it is by no means sufficient to know what events occurred, and when. We cannot claim to understand the Crusades if we only know the names of the crusaders, and where they fought their battles, and how many died. We can only claim to understand the Crusades when we know how it came about that these men called themselves crusaders, and why they felt it desirable and necessary that they should go where they went, and why they thought it right and dutiful to fight their battles and risk their deaths.

For this reason, history should not be called a science – or, if it is to be so called, it must be considered a kind of science very different from the study of the chemical elements, or the mechanics of motion. The events which are studied by physical scientists can and must be seen only from the outside; what we need to know of them are the laws and conditions which determine them, their frequency and regularity, and the forces which shape and compel them. This is what we mean by 'understanding' in natural philosophy. The events which are studied by historians, by contrast, can be understood only from the inside, in terms of the beliefs and desires and fears of the men who were their makers.

Alas, we have no certain way of knowing the beliefs and desires and fears even of the men we know, among whom we live. We may know what they say, and what they write, and may judge from the pattern of their actions something of what manner of men they are, but one thing that we know of men is that all of them are liars and deceivers, who never truly bare their hearts and thoughts even to those who know them best.

If we are honest with ourselves, we must admit that we lie most frequently, most earnestly and most persuasively to those we are most determined not to hurt, and that we shore up those lies with our loudest protestations that we would never lie to those we love so much. If we are honest with ourselves, we will further admit that we do not entirely know ourselves, and often act without knowing what the true reasons for our actions are, subsequently making up excuses for our own consciences just as we make them up for the soothing of other men, in order to appear more virtuous and more rational than we really are. And if all this be admitted, we will see that the task of the historian – which is to understand the unwritten beliefs and unspoken desires and unadmitted fears which must have crowded every thought which dead men ever had, and every decision that dead men ever made – is one which can lead only to speculation, and never to certainty.

We cannot conclude from this that the work of the historian

is so nearly impossible that we should abandon it, for the work of the historian is a very necessary thing. Unless we can have a measure of understanding – of true understanding – of what other men have believed and thought and felt, then social life itself would be impossible. We must have history in order to have progress; we must have understanding of the minds of men in order to be men ourselves. History is therefore possible, even in the absence of certainty; understanding is possible, despite the ever-presence of deception. But the achievement of the historian is an achievement of imagination and not of scientific method; it is an act of creation as well as an act of discovery.

All history, including the truest and the best, is a kind of fantasy. All understanding of the past is based in our understanding of the present, and the understood past is something which we invent, with the aid of relics – be they stones or potsherds or printed texts – not something which we find engraved upon the world, waiting to be read. In the multitudinous deceptions and misunderstandings of the present there is an infinity of pasts that might have been, pasts fantastic and arcane, pasts lost, and pasts that never were. The past in which we agree to believe is not necessarily the best of them, nor is it necessarily the past which our descendants will claim to know.

All history is a kind of fantasy; this we must admit. Admitting it should not lessen history in our eyes, for history remains as vitally important as it ever was; nevertheless, our view of what history is and can be must be altered by this perception.

By the same token that all history is a kind of fantasy, though, all fantasy is in its own fashion a kind of history. Whatever we invent we must build from the foundations of what we know of the hopes and fears, desires and ambitions of men. All fantasy reflects that knowledge, just as all knowledge partakes of fantastic speculation. For this reason, we should by no means despise histories of pasts which never were, for they may help us nevertheless to understand what we are and may become. Perchance they may even help us to a better understanding of ourselves than that history in which we have consented to believe.

Sir Edward Tallentyre, 'New Reflections on Buckle's *History of Civilization in England*', *The Quarterly Review*, September 1873

3

Dearest Cordelia,

I had a dream last night, before I had to rise and come away.

In my dream I returned once more to that Hell where Satan is confined. I looked again into his handsome face and his tearful eye. I felt again the pain of the huge nails which pinned him to the fiery floor, and the indignity of that rain of blood which fell upon his golden body.

I thought, for a moment, that nothing at all had changed, and was instantly consumed by a terrible bitterness which said that nothing ever could change and that nothing ever would, and that the future could be nothing but more of the past, with the eagles of vengeful fury forever diving from the sky to tear and devour the flesh and heart of every living man.

I looked at the Earth which hung from the vault of heaven, half-hidden by the great grey cloud of strife and desolation, and I wept for that redemption which could never come.

But then I saw you, and saw you reach down with your own right hand, which took hold of Satan's unpinned limb, and lifted it up; and in your left hand, you seized the devilled Earth, and held it where it was; and then you brought your two hands together, so that Satan's healing touch was allowed to reach the Earth at last, and when I looked up again, the rain of blood had begun to abate, and the sky was empty of eagles.

And when I awoke, I found that I was with you, and that you were smiling as you slept.

I do not need Austen to help me unriddle this dream. It says very clearly – as all true dreams say to those who are capable of hearing – that we may deliver ourselves from evil, if only we have the heart and mind to try.

I will return as soon as I can.

I love you.
David

All Pan books are available at your local bookshop or newsagent, or can be ordered direct from the publisher. Indicate the number of copies required and fill in the form below.

Send to: **CS Department, Pan Books Ltd., P.O. Box 40, Basingstoke, Hants.   RG21 2YT.**

or phone: 0256 469551 (Ansaphone), quoting title, author and Credit Card number.

Please enclose a remittance* to the value of the cover price plus: 60p for the first book plus 30p per copy for each additional book ordered to a maximum charge of £2.40 to cover postage and packing.

*Payment may be made in sterling by UK personal cheque, postal order, sterling draft or international money order, made payable to Pan Books Ltd.

Alternatively by Barclaycard/Access:

Card No. | | | | | | | | | | | | | | | |

Signature:

Applicable only in the UK and Republic of Ireland.

While every effort is made to keep prices low, it is sometimes necessary to increase prices at short notice. Pan Books reserve the right to show on covers and charge new retail prices which may differ from those advertised in the text or elsewhere.

NAME AND ADDRESS IN BLOCK LETTERS PLEASE:

....

Name ————————————————————————

Address ————————————————————————

————————————————————————————

————————————————————————————

————————————————————————————

3/87